Land of Hope

Book Three

'Journey to the West'
Trilogy

By Junying Kirk

Land of Hope - "Journey to the West" Trilogy

Published by Junying Kirk
Copyright 2012 by Junying Kirk

All Rights Reserved

Acknowledgement

Many friends, family, and fans have encouraged me towards the publication of my 3rd and final book in my Journey to the West trilogy, and no other more than my husband, John Kirk. He is instrumental in building my characters and devising plots in this rich mix of stories in an international setting. Not only has he helped me with developing the main male protagonists – Jack Gordon and Andrew Church – but also he has spent many hours writing parts and polishing my not-so-perfect drafts with his tremendous insights and sharp critique. Most of all, he put up with my obsession with writing and other challenging behaviour associated with being an Indie author.

Katy Sozaeva (USA), as with my previous two books, has allowed me flexibility within her busy schedule, and dedicated herself to making my book as error-free as possible. I salute her attention to detail; her help has been invaluable and is much appreciated.

Like my previous titles, the original paintings for this book cover are from artist and great friend Yongqun Guo (USA), who gave generously both her talent and support. The author is eternally grateful for the assistance of Eri Nelson, for her time and efforts on the cover design, expertly turning the beautiful paintings into an amazing book cover, with which I am delighted.

Special thanks to fellow authors Denise DeSio, Eri Nelson, and Madeline Sloane for their beta-reading and proofreading. They have spent many hours of their precious time and offered generous comments and critique.

I extend my heartfelt thanks to my worldwide readers and fans who have bought and read my first two books, and encouraged my writing pursuits. Special mention here: Eve ZHAO, Zoe Cooper, A Tran, Florence Chan, Julie and Matt

Posner, Mira Kolar Brown, Bin YUAN and Maria Gonzalez Munoz.

After the publication of my e-books, a number of friends have helped me from organizing book tours, hosting guest blogs, doing reviews etc. Among them, Sandra Valente, Eden Baylee, Lisa M Stull, Vanessa Wu, Jim Thompson, Mariam Kobras, Rob Pruneda and Andy Wood - the list goes on.

J J Collins not only read and reviewed my book during my book tour, he kindly wrote a fabulous Forward for this edition. His staunch support goes above and beyond, to whom I'll always be grateful.

A number of people from China deserve unreserved appreciation: Mr HUANG Xiao Dong, XU You De and ZHENG You Peng, who provided much needed and invaluable assistance during my research trip to Fujian in the spring of 2011.

Last but not least, thank you to Deb Hanrahan of Philyra Publishing for the formatting of this book.

Hope you will enjoy Land of Hope, no matter where you are.

About the Author

Junying Kirk came to Britain from China in 1988. She was born and grew up in the turbulent times of the Chinese Cultural Revolution. A British Council scholarship led her to study English Language Teaching at Warwick University, followed by further postgraduate degrees at Glasgow and Leeds. She has worked as an academic, administrator, researcher, teacher, and cultural consultant. For the past decade, she has been working as a professional interpreter and translator, while spending her free time writing books, traveling far and wide, and blogging/bragging about the wonders of the world. Her Journey to the West trilogy has seen the publications of *The Same Moon* and *Trials of Life* on Amazon Kindle. *Land of Hope* is the third and final book, to conclude this contemporary fiction series. She lives in Birmingham, England with her husband.

Author's Notes for Reading

This book contains a lot of Chinese names, which may cause difficulty to readers who are not used to foreign names. Here are a few guidance notes to help you.

1) All Chinese names used in this book are based on Pin Yin in Mandarin, the official Chinese dialect, used all over China, Taiwan, Singapore, and the Chinese diaspora worldwide.

2) The Chinese surname comes first, followed by first name: for example, Wang Ming. His surname is Wang and his first name is Ming. In the UK, however, he may call himself Ming WANG, to make life easier for a British person.

3) In Southern China, people often use nicknames by adding 'Ah' in front of their first names. So in Wang Ming's case, he would introduce himself as '**Ah** Ming', or his friends would call him 'Ah Ming'. Please note that I have several characters whose name starts with 'Ah', for exactly this reason.

4) Another customary Chinese use is adding 'Lao' (Old, Senior) or 'Xiao' (Small, Young, Junior) in front of their surnames, such as Lao Li, meaning Old Li, or Xiao Li, as Young Li.

5) The Chinese people are generally vague when talking about dates and time, or their age, in comparison to Westerners. This is further complicated by the Chinese calendar (according to the moon) and Western calendar (according to the sun). So when a Chinese person says that he is 21 years old, it is likely that his actual age is twenty. In Chinese, he/she would normally prefix it by telling you that it is his/her 'fake/false age', adding one year to their real age by counting the nine months he/she has spent inside his/her mother's womb.

6) Pearl Zhang is also known as Pearl Church or Zhengzhu, her Chinese first name.

To John – My One True

Inspiration

Forward

They are shuttled, in mini-vans, the length and breadth of continents, often sleeping in the vehicles between working shifts of up to 17 hours on farms, in brothels or back alley factories. Much of this type of work happens at night, a few hours here and a back-to-back double shift there. Beatings, rapes, sometimes even torture if they object, death a very real possibility if they try and escape. What is this modern insanity? This is the very real world of human trafficking and exploitation, the forgotten people shoved into cramped, dirty and degrading living conditions in the pursuit of "The Land of Hope."

These vulnerable people, usually poor, are deceived or forced into working abroad with promises of a better life. When they get there their passports are taken off them, they are forced to work behind locked doors and beaten or starved if they refuse. Sometimes they are killed and the threat of murder is always there. Their "masters" or "owners" make money by forcing them to work in sweatshops, dangerous jobs or as prostitutes.

These intolerable circumstances are experienced by workers trafficked and deprived of their liberty and the very basic freedoms we take for granted the world over. If the victim manages to get to the police, she is often not helped because she has no documents or the crime is not taken seriously. Because she is likely to be deported to her own country where she will probably be murdered, she doesn't usually try to contact the authorities and so human trafficking continues to grow.

I first read this book in October 2012, and found it one of the most powerful, captivating and emotionally stirring fictional books I have read in a very long time. Junying Kirk manages with great persuasion and artful writing, to bring this modern moral dilemma right into our hearts and minds, through the fantastically created main character of Pearl Zhang.

The story sucks you in immediately and with perfect imagery, Kirk most effectively uses Pearl's character to narrate the story, and introduce the reader to the dark and painful world of human trafficking, where individual stories are sometimes heartbreaking and often frustrating in their outcomes, as public and private agencies fight, often valiantly, but often with little or no useful result, to help men, women, and children who have been kidnapped, tricked, or forced by violence; into a world they never wanted or can handle.

It is a book of extremes with characters of ultra confidence and manipulative brilliance, through to the petrified characters often deeply emotionally troubled, due to the nature of their experiences and life's reflections. The book contains many frightening, unfortunate, and true messages, told with imaginative twists and turns.

We often read fictional thrillers in the pursuit and desire for escapism for ourselves however; by the time the reader is introduced to each character and personal story, you will find yourself egging on the vulnerable to succeed in their desire to escape and seek a better life.

Every country is affected by human trafficking, whether it's an origin country where people are trafficked from; a transit country where people are trafficked through; or a destination country where people are trafficked to. Men, women and children are trafficked. Due to the hidden and illegal nature of human trafficking, gathering statistics on the scale of the problem is difficult. Look beyond the surface of the fight against trafficking, and you will find misleading statistics and decades of debate over laws and protocols.

Each personal story in this book is enthralling and testimony to the author's knowledge of the subject matter and intelligent writing. Each person, like all immigrants believe "The Land of Hope" in Europe, Japan or the USA will be the answer to their problems. Too often immigrants only realise that the life they left behind, was in many ways, better then the life they now find themselves exposed to. They can only think pleasant things in their dreams and hold onto the happiness of home in their hearts, not their day to day reality.

Human trafficking is a global phenomenon that each year forces millions into lives as prostitutes, labourers, child soldiers, and domestic servants. This modern form of slavery impacts every continent and type of economy, while the industry continues to grow with global profits reaching nearly $32 billion annually.

This book is absorbing, cleverly written, and fast-paced style throughout with an informative and educational element driven by great characters. The book is powerful in its culmination with an action packed yet, heart tugging ending. It leaves the reader considering this very real world issue and yet, the characters are so credible, you are left wondering if there is an Ah Fang, Madam Lin or even a Dragon in your locality.

Remember, this modern day form of slavery could be happening on your street, in your town and most definitely within all major cities. If you want to help tackle this issue and don't know how the answer is simple. Read this exceptional book by Junying Kirk and tell someone else the story. By giving these faceless and oft forgotten victims a voice, we can turn the tide on this outrageous crime.

As for the real issue itself, the lack of agreement on how to define "trafficking" hasn't slowed campaigners' fight. Rather, defining trafficking has become their fight. Most of all, what is lost is any understanding or appreciation of the challenges faced by the millions of people working, struggling and surviving in abusive conditions, whose experiences will never appear anywhere except as a statistic. It is for all these reasons that makes this book - "The Land of Hope," by Junying Kirk a book of immense and incomparable modern importance.

A truly compelling and potent read.

J.J. Collins, Author of American Presidents: Life, Career and Legacy

Content

Prologue

HE WAS SO damn tired. He desperately needed a fag and a break.

Lao Li felt the strain first on his legs, then his back, his arms, and shoulders, distracting him from what was in front of him: the never-ending mountains of strawberries. After days of continuous sorting – retaining good, juicy ones and discarding rotten and imperfect-looking ones – his attention was drifting, and his vision started to blur. He no longer saw ripe, tempting strawberries in his bloodshot eyes; all his senses were overwhelmed by streams of bright, bloody things flowing through his cream-white, gloved hands. They moved automatically and mechanically, just like the many pairs next to his and opposite him, resembling the Charlie Chaplin film *Modern Times*. The robotic movement had a momentum of its own. All these fingers, hands moving back and forth – pick, pass, or throw – picking out unwanted fruit and putting them in the white, plastic container on the metal workstation. The ones good enough to pass the rhythmical picking of human sorting machines flowed into a big, blue bin bag, to be taken to the next workstation, ready for packaging.

At long last, at the clap of the supervisor's hands, all hands stopped moving instantly. The women, and a few men, filed across the factory floor and made their way to the side room, where they took their short convenience breaks.

No smoking was allowed anywhere in the factory premises, a rule strictly observed: especially during the day shift. Lao Li had signed up for a night shift, secretly hoping that he could sneak out for a few much-needed puffs. Even when he was not working or feeling so damn tired, he craved nicotine, a lifelong, acquired habit, not unlike eating or sleeping. "Smoking Kills", the package always reminded him; but why should he care? Everyone died one way or another. At his age, and with his miserable life so far, he had stared at death's pale, ugly face more than once, and this night and at this moment, death could not have been further from his mind.

Nobody paid the slightest attention as he headed for the exit. He eagerly pulled out one of the two Panda cigarettes he had squashed into his left trouser pocket and rummaged through the other pocket for the lighter. He lit up – a long, deep, and satisfying inhalation – and sucked in the addictive nicotine.

Instantly his spirits lifted, his tiredness lessened, and his head became a little clearer. He looked out of the large window at the end of the corridor but could see nothing, just an enveloping darkness; even the moon did not bother to show her face.

It was, after all, midnight, and even in June the British dawn was still four hours away.

The door behind him cracked open, shedding a thin, long, shadowy beam across the darkness around him. His pulses raced, his heart nearly leaping out of his chest like a scared rabbit. Guilt seized him like an iron claw as he quickly tossed his half-finished cigarette. The smoldering butt rolled under a grease-stained box.

"I thought you must be out here, Lao Li. I don't want you to be sacked by the *guilao* boss," a gentle, female voice soothed.

He turned around, ashamed as if caught in a dirty, unspeakable act, his ruddy face a darker shade of red. From the light streaming through, he saw the smiling face of Ah Lan, a girl from his home village, a petite, young woman he had taken a fancy to in this isolated, lonely place, where his heart was lost, yet his desire was given free rein.

It was Ah Lan who had introduced him to this job after he was released from prison, convicted of assisting the management of a brothel. After serving half of his eighteen-month sentence, he was let out. The prisons and detention centres in the UK were pretty full, and the authorities could not deport him, since he did not give them his real identity, hence no country of origin could be confirmed.

Despite it being a job designated mostly for fit, female workers, the fruit-sorting manager took him on. During the high season of summer fruit packing, an employer could not afford to be too picky. Apart from illegals like Ah Lan and Lao Li, and Eastern European seasonal workers looking for handy cash, who else would want to waste their precious reality-TV-watching time or shift off their benefit-scrounging backsides to slave in such a godforsaken place at these ungodly hours?

The average English chavs would most definitely prefer to sit their lazy asses on the couch, eat their greasy chips, smoke their joints, or go out to rob innocent neighbours of their iPhones and laptops.

******

The bleeping sound of the digital alarm next to his bed gave DI Jack Gordon a start, dragging him from his stream of unconsciousness.

It took him only a second or so to register where the sound came from. He reached to the bed stand to switch it off, muttering a curse towards someone's mother at the same time. He had been so dog tired in the last few days, without a blink of sleep for nearly 48 hours. Despite his years of training, and the demanding routine in first the Army, then SAS, and then as a police officer, he was beginning to feel its toll on his body. *I must be getting old*, he mused as he scrambled for his clothes on the floor.

He found the zapper and switched on the small TV in the corner of his hotel bedroom, as he made his way to the bathroom. At six feet tall, with a muscular build – his 40th birthday a fairly recent affair – he was the picture of a perfect Scot: one more like Sean Connery than Rab C. Nesbitt.

After he brushed his teeth, he heard the news reporter's serious tone as she made the grave announcement. At the bottom of the screen were highlights of *Breaking News* on BBC.

"Dozens of workers jumped to their deaths and hundreds were injured when a fire swept through a factory at an industrial estate outside Ledbury, Herefordshire, UK. The factory had tons of lard and hundreds of thousands of pounds of food grease stored in its buildings. Apart from meat packing, there were several vegetable and fruit-packing facilities there. As one of the largest food-packing factories in the country, it supplied to all the major supermarkets, including Tesco and Sainsbury's.

Six crews of firefighters battled to put out a giant blaze from Saturday night through to Sunday morning. Firefighters had to don breathing apparatuses to enter the buildings with their hoses and tackle the widespread, raging flames. As well as six fire engines, a control unit and an aerial ladder from Hereford were dispatched. Their job was made extremely difficult by the fact that the area was supplied with high-voltage electricity and steam power.

Witnesses told our reporter that the blaze engulfed the multi-storey building, forcing some of those trapped inside to leap from the windows. Authorities have confirmed that the fire initially broke out on the building's third floor, where fruit and vegetables were sorted, and then spread up to the floors above and below. The exact death toll of the blaze is yet unclear, but one witness confirmed that he saw people jumping from the windows to escape the raging fire.

Fire crews remained at the scene for hours to ensure that the fire would not reignite. The cause of the fire is believed to have been accidental, but the investigators have not ruled out arson. The exact cause is still under investigation, which will take some time due to its large scale and severe damage, estimated to be in the millions of pounds by insurance experts."

Jack returned to the room with a clean, shaved face and turned the TV off. He knew what was to follow. A local reporter would speak from the ruins of the factory and relay whatever information they had extracted from the police, the firefighters, and the eyewitnesses they managed to get hold of at or near the scene.

For Detective Inspector Gordon, this was not just news from the media, but an investigation he was leading. Tough days ahead.

He took the stairs and went down to the breakfast room. *I'd better get some food down me before the shit hits the fan in the days ahead.*

In his head, he'd already visualized a to-do list, long and expanding by the minute. Never one to back down from a challenging job, he was mentally and physically prepared. Approaching the coffee machine, he filled his cup to temper his craving for the first strong coffee of the day.

About eight o'clock Monday morning, more than 30 hours into the rescue effort, Jack made his way to the disaster zone again.

Six hours after the local police were alerted to the fire Jack had been on the scene, and spent the best part of his Sunday getting his team together. He had managed to snatch a few hours' sleep at his hotel, and now he was back on duty.

Jack was suffering because the West Mercia Chief Constable was a mate of his boss, and had called for help more or less straightaway. Following his successful investigation of some very large arson attacks on the rural edge of London his name was on the police grapevine.

Working with the rural officers is not going to be easy. On the drive up from London, his mind was full of memories of the Herefordshire countryside, familiar from his days in the SAS regiment based in the county town of Hereford.

"It will take us at least another 24 hours to extinguish the flames on all six floors." The firefighter section chief, a man in his early 40s, approached and briefed DI Gordon.

"Our initial investigation indicates that the fire may have started in an area fueled by cardboard and plastic packaging materials in a storage space. Whoever or whatever started it, the fire got into a couple of roof and wall voids, travelled quickly, and was helped by the strong wind coming from the southwest. There are parts of the structure which are too unsafe to enter, and may never be so. We might have to pull it down and sift through the debris, unless we can be sure of the structural integrity. A lot of the steel frame is twisted all over the place. Frankly, I don't really know what's holding it up right now."

"Have you any knowledge of who alerted the Fire Brigade?" DI Gordon enquired.

"Yes, workers on the 4th floor smelled smoke and their supervisor dialed 999 about 0015 Saturday morning."

"How long did it take for the firefighters to arrive on the scene?"

"The first twelve firefighters arrived on the scene after 40 minutes, but they quickly grasped the sheer size of the fire and immediately radioed for help. Four other crews were sent to assist."

By then, the fire had taken such a grip of the building that it took them many more hours to bring it under control. After pouring thousands of gallons of water and foam on the burning buildings, the fire eventually subsided. They had drained a nearby canal basin, and the narrow boats that had been happily parked there were now resting on the mud. Owners were going to and fro in their rubber boots, getting stuck and looking stoic about it.

In the meantime, local residents living within one mile of the factory had been ordered to evacuate their homes, primarily because of the threat posed by leaking anhydrous ammonia stored in the plant, which was used to chill the products packed there. They were all in the school gymnasium.

"Any idea how many workers were working on the night shift?" enquired Jack, his voice grave and his steely eyes sharp, despite being a little bloodshot.

"Let me see," the firefight chief paused, perhaps adding up the figures from different floors. "From what we've learnt so far, I'd say around six hundred, or thereabout."

In Jack's mind, he was already dispatching his team to talk to the survivors. They needed to establish the possible causes and events surrounding this disastrous incident. They needed to know quickly.

It would be a very long day, leading with grinding certainty to many long and painstaking weeks of investigation ahead.

Part One: Summer Heat

Chapter 1: A New Chapter for Pearl

IN HER CITY-CENTRE apartment, a stone's throw from China Town, Pearl Church was unpacking.

Only a couple of years ago, she had bought the two-bedroom pad, using up all the savings from her interpreting job. "As a freelancer without a steady employer or a pension fund, having a property in your name would be a wise investment," Andrew had suggested, always on hand to offer sound advice.

Her husband was a man with vision, always planning ahead, forever expecting bad things to happen to good people. Their decision to 'buy to let' also coincided with the economic downturn, when the banks' overlending messed up the economy big time; properties were being repossessed and mortgages hard to obtain. With his well-paid job, however, the Churches were able to secure the lending and hence something solid in Pearl's name. One day the rent from property would provide for her welfare when her body was too frail and bones were too old; however, from her optimistic outlook, she hoped that her mind would remain agile for a little longer on this earth.

Oh Andrew, Pearl's heart quickened at the thought of her husband. She stopped what she was doing momentarily to regain her calm, waiting for the slowing of her heartbeat.

Classic FM was playing one of her favourite lyrical pieces, Albinoni's "Adagio", sad and deeply moving, a piece she had fallen in love with on first hearing. Tears stung her eyes, as it subsided towards its final movement.

Was it music or thoughts of Andrew tearing at her very core, tugging the tender parts inside? Probably both. Nowadays she found herself ever more ready to shed tears, her hormones all over the place. Was it because she was racing towards her big Five Zero, hence the imminent threat of menopause? It was one of Andrew's attempts to explain her increasingly unpredictable behaviour.

The music came to a melancholy end, without an immediate announcement following; perhaps even the DJ was too mesmerized to speak. In the moment of dead silence, Pearl's mobile burst into song.

Stretching to reach the top of a cardboard box where she had left her iPhone, she hoped that it was Andrew. *Perhaps he is feeling lonely in Colorado and regretting his move? Perhaps he misses me just as I miss him? Maybe he is simply ringing to ask about the sale of our house in Edgefield?*

Over time she had developed the habit of always keeping her mobile close by, either hanging it in a small phone pouch around her neck when out and about, or placing it close by when at home. Her job demanded it.

"Hi, it's DI Jack Gordon here, am I speaking to Dr Pearl Church?" spoke an unfamiliar, deep, and gravelly male voice. Pearl detected a small trace of accent, yet was not quite able to register its origin.

During her interpreting career over a decade, she had received numerous calls like this, rushing across many parts of the United Kingdom at all hours of the day and night, helping police officers with their various duties.

In recent months, however, as the Western economy began to fall apart, Pearl's contact with law enforcement had been reduced significantly. Cuts in public spending were biting all over. Self-employed services like hers were the first on the firing line.

"Yes, it's Pearl here. How can I help you, officer?" she answered, quickly disguising her sadness, and resuming her professional and cheery voice.

******

On booking his Mandarin interpreter, DI Gordon decided that he had a bit of time before her arrival. She had promised to leave straightaway, but it was at least an hour and half's drive from her home.

"Please come to Ledbury Police station," he had instructed her.

"I shall brief you first before taking you to the hospital for interviews. It could take quite some time," he had remembered to warn her just before he ended the call.

He drove to the nearest station and took a shower. His normal office base was in Barking, North London, where he led a team of 80 officers whose responsibility covered a wide range of serious crimes, from murder, drug dealing, kidnapping, and human trafficking to pedophilia and other sexual offenses. A few months ago, his remit increased significantly with his promotion to Detective Inspector.

After the disastrous fire, he had set up a temporary base in Ledbury, which quickly attracted unwanted media attention. This usually quiet town between the border of England and

Wales was, all of a sudden, the centre of a story that had gone national and then international within a matter of hours.

DI Gordon had been brought in from London to lead the enquiry because the local force couldn't cope, and then the story had really hit the headlines. As far as reporters were concerned, he was assisting the West Mercia force; but in reality he was in the driving seat. The TV vans and satellite dishes dotted the site with reporters doing their best to keep out of each other's shots.

Jack made several calls to officers placed under him, getting up to speed on their actions. The investigation had already begun, from getting forensic evidence at the scene, to liaising with the coroner's office for body identifications, as well as interviewing those who escaped the fire and were now receiving treatment in Hereford County Hospital. Health and Safety inspectors were also getting under his feet.

Normally, Jack would leave his officers to carry out the interviews while he oversaw the operation. Due to its seriousness and the scale of this incident, on top of its prominent, newsworthy significance, lack of staff, and pressure to get to the bottom of it as soon as possible, he decided to cover some groundwork himself. It would help him gain some much-needed credibility with the local officers, who he knew were already asking, "Why is he here?"

Preliminary findings indicated that the workers in the factory were largely ethnic Chinese immigrants, with a few from Poland, Romania and the former Yugoslavia splitting into smaller countries, whose long names were quite challenging to unsophisticated English tongues. The Chinese names were even more complicated, despite their short, apparently 'simple' forms. From their strange sounding syllables, they were close to impossible to pronounce, or to determine the gender of each name. To make matters worse, the majority of the survivors could not understand any English at all, let alone speak it.

11

On top of the language barriers between those still alive — and some hanging on for dear life to a thin thread — the dead bodies posed extra, unprecedented difficulties. Since the fire victims were mostly illegal entrants to the country, there were no identities to trace or official data to rely on. The Chinese Embassy had been notorious in not collaborating with the British when it came to this political, highly sensitive issue, like treading on thin ice; or more like playing with fire, in this case.

Earlier, when he was handed the list of Mandarin interpreters with police clearance, it had over a dozen or so names. Although Pearl's name was somewhere in the middle, he picked her out due to her surname Church, as well as her title of doctor. *Is she a real doctor practising medicine, or a doctor of another kind?* A query ran across his inquisitive mind. Another question filed away, waiting for the right moment to be clarified.

As if right on cue, Jack heard the station tannoy announcing the arrival of Dr Church. The mystery of her title was soon to be revealed.

He took a quick look at his face in the mirror in the gents, and smoothed some stray, graying hair.

He was ready to meet his interpreter for the coming weeks.

Chapter 2: Ah Ming: "My Life is Shit"

I DON'T LIKE my life. In fact, I hate it. I hate it so much that I have tried to remove it from this world, not once, not twice, but several times.

Not a bloody clue what the hospital patients' record says; I am quite sure that attempting suicide *is* the reason I am now in a psychiatric hospital in Derby, a small town somewhere in the middle of the UK. My geographical knowledge has always been limited. Before I left China, I had never been out of my home province.

If I had a choice, or any say in my destiny, I would have wanted a different life, to be a different person, or to live in a different era, or to belong to a different race. If I had a choice, I definitely wouldn't want to be born Chinese. What good has being a Chinese done for me? It is all suffering, sacrifice, and surviving. It is not much of a life, worse than being an animal sometimes. Even animals have better welfare than people like me, an ordinary peasant.

What have I done in my previous life to deserve this? I've asked myself this question a thousand times, but there is never a good-enough answer. No one will ever tell me. Even though I wear a cross around my neck and pray to Jesus – or whoever above supposedly watches over us mortal souls – asking Him in my despair, I get no reply, nor any kind of a sign that He has heard me. I don't know if it's because He cannot hear, or worse, does not care, about a poor sinner like me. Still, I wear my cross, and I persist in asking Him. One day, maybe He will hear me, and change my life forever.

Is my life some kind of a sick joke? I sometimes wonder.

I was born in a rural village in Fujian Province, with beautiful coastlines and bountiful produce. Yet memories of my childhood were of nothing more than starvation and deprivation. I came out of my poor mother's womb sometime in the Chinese year of the Dog, aka 1970. Neither my mother nor father could tell me when exactly according to the sun calendar, except that it was on the fifth day of the spring, following the movement of the moon.

My father was too occupied toiling on the worn-out land that his ancestors had worked for generations, while my mother was busy giving birth to one child after another, until she had me, the son she had craved more than anything in life. I was to give her social status as a deserving wife and daughter-in-law. None of my sisters counted, of course, because they were to be married off, sooner or later, to someone else's sons. Only *my* birth validated my mother's place in the family and on this Earth, a proud producer of an heir to carry on the Wang family line, and a son to look after them when they could no longer work the fields and were too feeble to take care of themselves. My duties were decreed the day I entered this world, and they would only cease the day I chose to depart for the next.

One of my earliest memories was my parents' arguing about whether or not I should be sent to school. My father, the eldest of 10 children, never had a chance for literacy. He had to help out in the family from a tender age. My mother, a girl and from an even poorer family: her education had not been deemed worth mentioning in her household. What was the good for a girl to be educated? All the learning she needed in life was to know how to marry a decent man and to produce sons for her in-laws. She had watched her lucky peers go off to the school in town, admiring the gaiety in their walk and the colourful books in their school bags. Her longing to walk in their shoes had been secret, yet undeniably strong. I could sense it even at my young age, and see it in her eyes, although she never voiced it or hinted at it to anyone. The way she argued with my father took everyone by surprise. Before that, she hardly ever raised her voice, and then out of the blue she became a fierce, protective creature who would not back down until she got what she wanted.

"My son is going to school, no matter what it takes," she declared in a determined tone, which nobody in my family knew existed until then.

"No," my father had persisted, his tone already less firm.

My father was a quiet man of few words. Too much responsibility too young must have killed any joy and fire in his belly. He seemed an old man before his time, and all I ever remembered of him was his slightly hunched back, squatting outside our small mud house, smoking nasty, cheap tobacco. When he saw me and my siblings running around half naked in the courtyard, he showed no interest in joining in. It was our mother who would be there to pick me up, when she happened to be watching, taking a quick break from her busy household chores.

"Yes, he must." My mother had the last word.

The school was 15 kilometres away from my village, at the nearest town called Wu Zhen (Black Town). It was deemed not revolutionary enough during the Cultural Revolution, so was temporarily renamed as Hong Qi (Red Flag) Town. But old people like my grandma still referred it as Black Town.

At seven years old, it seemed an awful long walk from my house to school. I rose before dawn, arriving at school just before the morning exercise. All the teachers and pupils gathered at the small courtyard in front of the one and only school building. We followed the instructions on the radio, spoken in perfect Mandarin, quite different from the local dialect we used both in class and at home.

It took me a while to do these physical exercises properly. I usually stood at the back row and went through the motions. I did not see any point in stretching my arms or turning my small body around. I had enough physical exercise when fighting with my sisters and other boys in the fields and running family errands.

I did not mind school. It was neither fun nor interesting, but it gave me a chance to learn the basic Chinese writing and to perform simple calculations. I remembered my first Maths teacher, whom I really liked. She was the youngest teacher in our school, probably twenty years old, though quite old in my young eyes. She came to our school after graduating from a college in Fuzhou, the capital city of my province. She wore nice clothes and spoke our dialect in a Fuzhou accent, which was different from how we locals talked. Some pupils laughed at her accent, but never in front of her. Even naughty boys showed respect to their teachers. I was never naughty, never missed a day in school, no matter rain or shine.

Now when I reflect upon my life, as people do when they are on the verge of ending it, I think that my school days were perhaps the best times of my life: certainly the easiest part when I had the least worries. Five years of continuous studying, playing with other children, and repetitious rote-learning of Chinese characters and Mathematics was to last me a lifetime. From then onwards everything seemed to go "pear-shaped", a path beyond my control, a spiral going downhill.

What have I done in my previous life?

Chapter 3: Jack Gordon Meets Pearl Church

JACK POPPED HIS head through the security door and saw the side profile of a woman who was signing in at the front desk. She was wearing a smart, white jacket, and a dark-pink skirt was just above her knee, showing off a shapely pair of legs. There was no one else around. *She must be the one I am after.*

"Doctor Church?"

He saw her turning her face towards him and greeted her with a warm smile, the one he usually reserved for good-looking members of the fairer sex, and hardly ever used with his male colleagues and underlings. He'd learned from experience that to show authority, it was important to keep your face straight and keep your distance. This general approach had served him well.

He reached out his hand and gripped the one she offered, nice touch.

"I'm Jack Gordon. We spoke on the phone earlier." The corners of his mouth still had an upward curve.

"Of course, sir. Lovely to meet you. Call me Pearl," she replied, in perfectly pitched, educated English, returning his smile, her hands still in his grip.

"Sure, Pearl. Likewise, Jack will be fine by me."

On closer inspection, he saw a rather pretty face, with shining, black eyes and a naturally full, sensual mouth, which was turning upwards generously, showing her even, white teeth. A broad smile was always a good sign, he noted.

It was hard to gauge her age, because her face was completely free of wrinkles and her hand was soft and firm at the same time. She had a matching pink- and white-striped T-shirt under her summer-linen jacket. Without high heels – wearing instead a pair of smart flats – he towered over her, his muscular build in sharp contrast to her slim frame. She couldn't possibly be a day older than 35, he decided, and let go of her hand at last.

Recently, his wife of the last 20 years, Moira, had been acting more distant than ever. It was probably more to do with him, as well as the fact that their eldest daughter had just left home to go to university. Moira worked as a nurse, which didn't always go well with his night duties and regular absences away from home. Slowly, and over time, she stopped complaining, and they no longer bothered to argue, simply letting the quiet space between them stretch further and further. When they did speak, it was mostly to do with either Heather, their 18-year-old daughter, or Jimmy, who just turned 15 and seemed to be going through some kind of typical teenage angst.

Jack, despite his reluctance to articulate his feelings and a sustained habit of displaying little emotion if he could help it, missed the close proximity of a woman, a loving embrace or a deep kiss. Mostly, these days, he was either away on business in hotel suites, or had only a brief stay in the spare room when at home.

He led Pearl down the corridor and into a small interview room, where he gave her a brief outline of what they needed to do in the hospital.

"Gosh, it's a hot day today." Pearl took off her jacket before sitting down on the chair he pulled out for her, her face blushing, matching her outfit.

He watched her; his scrutinising eyes could not help noticing a fine pair of breasts under a tight, summery top that accentuated their perfect shape.

******

Her first impression of Jack Gordon was good.

After she had come off the phone, she made a quick change of clothing and eased herself into her car, recalling her short conversation with the Inspector. *Oh yes,* her brain clicked. *He sounded Scottish: in fact, Glaswegian.*

It was a very dear accent for Pearl, but it had been quite a while since she had last heard anyone speaking it. Jack's accent was not strong enough to be identified in an instant, unless you had a particular ear for it. Typical Glaswegian had a rough, musical colour to it. It always brought back memories of her time spent in that cold, wet country – memories that were, nonetheless, filled with warmth and nostalgia. So much history and fond memories.

Watching DI Gordon and listening to his briefing, she saw a passionate man, a confident man, a man who had seen a great deal of action and knew what he was doing.

She felt his eyes on her: intense, even a wee bit intimidating, a deep, hazel brown, sharp, intelligent, and piecing. He was at least a head taller than she was, with broad shoulders and a muscular build, exuding an unmistakable maleness. For so long, since she had been married to Andrew, this kind of sexual attraction had eluded her.

Now that Andrew was gone, with no one to hold her at night and kiss her good morning, her natural sense of the opposite sex began to resume. For the first time in a very long time, she felt keenly the attention this handsome Scot was paying her. She involuntarily blushed at the realisation. Trying to hide her embarrassment, she asked a question which she regretted immediately.

"Are you from Glasgow?" The question had been playing in her mind, so it burst out without her considering whether it was an appropriate moment. *I have not been summoned for a casual chat.* She could have kicked herself as the thought hit her.

"How did you guess?" Jack's eyes widened slightly.

Over the years in the Army, with tours in Iraq and Afghanistan, he had managed to erase many of the traces of accent those early years had embedded in him. It seemed that, despite his leaving home at the age of 17, with only occasional visits back there, Jack had maintained some of his working-class roots from his humble beginnings in the Gorbals of Glasgow.

"I'm an expert on accents." Her embarrassment was quickly replaced with a pleasure that she had surprised him.

Her blush deepened, together with the happy knowledge that the conversation was now on more familiar ground.

"I lived there for a few years and went to university there," she explained. Another wee smile.

"Oh, I see." Jack smiled back, nodding. "I take it that you have a PhD rather than being a medical doctor, right?"

This was more a statement than a question, displaying his knack of putting people at ease with a little extra touch.

"How did you guess?" she replied, suppressing a laugh, but a wide grin was spreading from her ears across her whole face.

I am going to enjoy working with this man, she was certain, and for the first time in days, her spirits truly lifted.

Chapter 4: Ah Fang: "My Young and Foolish Ways"

SHOULD I CRY, or should I remain calm, as if nothing has happened?

Different thoughts are playing in my head, as I sit in my cold cell, so far away from my home, so foreign, so alone, and so unfair. All I did was try to make a living, and here I am, detained in a guilao police station whose name and location elude me, except for the knowledge that it is not London, but somewhere in the UK: the land of hope for people like me.

I am 20 years old, but really I just turned 19 a month ago according to the calculation of the Western calendar. When I left home in Changle, Southern China, I was barely 16.

I was not good at school, not because I was stupid, but because I didn't like most of the subjects or the way they were taught. The teachers were boring, authoritative, and strict: even harsh sometimes. I was not keen on discipline, the never-ending homework, and the competition to stay ahead in class. What for? To go to university, which would mean more hard work and even more fierce competition? No way: thank you very much, but not for me.

To be honest, the boys and girls I hung out with in my school did not care about a higher education either. In Changle, the prevailing ambition for us all was to go overseas. Most people had relatives in America, Japan, or Europe, and most of the young people ended up migrating sooner or later.

My family was different, perhaps because my father was a Northerner – from Sichuan actually – and he kept saying that it was in the Southwest; my mates did not understand that. Fujian people considered everyone outside Fujian and Guangzhou a 'Northerner'. So my blood is slightly mixed, in wrong proportions perhaps.

As far as I know, my father gave up his meagre, salaried job as a teacher in a school in a county in Sichuan that I had never visited, or wanted to. After his parents died in a freak accident, he relocated to Changle to work, and eventually started his own business in exporting seafood from Fujian to the rest of China. He met my mother, a local Changle girl, and then they had me.

My mother worshipped my father and supported him in every way, including his dissatisfaction with me. Row after row with my parents did not result in my giving in to their demands. Like the Chinese saying goes: "You can lead a horse to the river, but you can't make it drink water." I know many of my contemporaries bowed under relentless parental pressure, in the name of family, filial duties, or whatever they glorify to make us surrender our will to theirs. I was born to have a mind of my own.

"I don't care what you do to me, and you can throw me out of your bloody house if you like, or you can beat me to death; I am not going back to that stupid school." An ultimatum? No kidding: certainly not an empty threat, because I really meant it.

Neither my father's angry fists, nor my mother's chiding and pleading tears made me relent.

"Such a disloyal and spoilt girl. What have I done to deserve this?" My mother moaned constantly and pitifully, but neither her Buddha nor her Guanyin seemed to hear, or care to answer her prayers.

They tried everything, involving relatives, teachers, and trusted friends to 'talk sense' into me. They came with small treats and promises of more, bigger treats, all to no avail. They could not make me 'see sense', or instil any ambition into my young mind. They called me stubborn, ungrateful, and many other unsavoury descriptions, but I prided myself on my determination – to get away.

"You have no qualifications; you're never going to find a job; you're too young to marry; we can't support you forever…"

My mother's nagging went on and on, in front of me, and in front of anyone who was prepared to listen to her. She drove me nuts. All I could do was to get out of her sight as much as I could, hanging out in shopping malls, wandering the streets, and creeping back home when everyone was asleep. Some days I stayed out all night.

You see, there were others like me: young girls and boys who rebelled against their parents, and society in general. We just didn't fit in anymore. We did not want what everyone else wanted: in my mother's words, 'a normal life'. A life that looked like a chart, clearly programmed, with progression step by step from birth till death. I did not want a life like that; in truth, I did not know what I wanted at all. All I knew was that I wanted something different from the life my parents expected me to lead.

I found kindred spirits on the streets, other kids who hung out in public places because they were bored, or thrown out by their furious parents, or their lives were too desperate back home to stay, or they had no home at all. Together we ate when we had money, or stole from the street vendors when we were skint. Sometimes we just did it for fun – a bit of thrill-seeking – to see if the adults would give chase, or if the authorities – those severe-looking officers in uniforms – would catch us.

We did get into trouble, of course, when we became wilder and more adventurous with our endeavours. My parents had to bail me out with bribe money a couple of times from temporary police detentions. This made them more furious and more anxious to solve my 'attitude' problem. They had locked me in the room, refused to give me food, threatened to send me away to a boarding school, and so on, until they ran out of devices to crack me. Their desperate measures only served to push me further.

One evening, one of the boys in our gang suggested that we rob a jewellery store.

"You girls can go in there first and pretend to be interested in buying his stuff. We boys will distract him, and there you go: grab as much as you can and run as fast as you can. He can't run after you, because if he does, he'll lose more than he'll ever know." He sounded so confident, as if he'd done it a million times without fail.

One or two other boys were eager to chip in – to show that they were streetwise too – by making alternative schemes. One girl looked worried and hesitated before being persuaded to participate. In the end, we were bored stiff and listless, and after all, nobody wanted to appear cowardly and gutless, especially on the streets.

It was a busy summer night, hot and humid with no breeze, and full of sweaty people who, instead of staying at home watching tedious TV programmes, sauntered along the bustling streets, haggling enthusiastically with different vendors who sold everything from edible goodies to fashionable cheap copies of famous foreign brands: Gucci scarves, Pierre Cardin shirts, Luis Vuitton bags, and Rolex watches. Whatever took your fancy, you could find it in the buzzing market stalls.

With teenage bravado, I marched towards the little jewellery store at the corner of Renming Street, a junction with a narrow side street – less well-lit and with fewer stores and shoppers – which was to be our escape route. Two other girls were side by side with me, quickening their steps so as not to be left behind.

"Hello, girls." A middle-aged, short, stout man – the store owner – was all smiles, a practised expression which meant that he wanted money from us.

He trained his small eyes on me. "Look at these pretty charms. They'll suit you perfectly, pretty girl. They are bargains. You can't get a better price anywhere else, I guarantee."

Bloody lies, of course. I ignored him, focusing on the task at hand. A little nervous, my mind raced furiously towards what was to come.

The cheap stuff was all laid out in the front counter; I touched some plastic beads with distaste as I scrutinised other items in the store. One of the girls became quite excited, trying on a ghastly metal necklace with strange symbols, pretending to be Tibetan but maybe nothing of the sort, while the other girl made complimentary remarks.

"Hey, boss." I called for the attention of the owner and pointed at a locked, glass display cabinet full of expensive items: shiny, golden rings with semiprecious stones, sparkly crystals and silvery bangles, brooches and necklaces.

My eyes followed him intently, my heart beating so loud that I could almost hear it thumping against my chest as the man opened the small sliding door in front of him. In my peripheral vision, the lads strode towards us, announcing their arrival with their cheery whistles.

What followed seemed to have taken place in a dream, a dream from which I was yet to wake up. It was like an out-of-body experience, my spirit hovering above, witnessing my real, physical self grabbing the items that the man had cautiously laid out in front of me, and hearing echoes of screaming voices: "Run. Run fast!"

"You little, thieving bastards!" "Chase them." "Call the Police!"

The shouting and thunderous footsteps overwhelmed me. My feet became lead-heavy, unable to keep up with my brain. With adults, men and women, chasing from all sides, I failed to make headway.

The next thing I knew, I was sitting at a deserted, derelict house, with my hands bound and my mouth gagged with a dirty cloth. My mates were nowhere to be seen.

A few men stood by, one of them in uniform with a truncheon in his hand. *Am I in police detention? Damn, my parents would be furious. They will have to spend more of their hardworking cash to bail me out again.*

I did not realise it fully, but it was then that my true nightmare began. Not straightaway, but soon enough.

My former life, the life I had known yet fought against vivaciously, was gone, irretrievably. I would then discover the many horrors of human cruelty against fellow human beings. I would experience first-hand unspeakable, inhuman treatment from bad, nasty, evil people.

If God existed, these people should not be allowed to breathe the same air as we do. They did not qualify as human beings. They were scum of the earth.

Chapter 5: The Inspector and His Interpreter

IT WAS USUALLY hot, almost a scorcher, compared with a standard British summer day, which was usually cool, even if not overcast, or pouring with rain. There was a reason why so many Brits crowded the beaches on Greek and Spanish islands, or simply uprooted themselves one day, emigrating to sunny Florida or further ashore to places like Australia's Gold Coast.

Pearl had not been able to enjoy the sun, having been confined to the hospital wards for what seemed a never-ending shift. She had been working nonstop, visiting different wards, interviewing fire survivors, and taking statements if they were fit enough.

With nightfall the temperature had cooled, but the air was filled with an unknown heaviness that added to her mental stress and physical exhaustion. It was well after midnight when she was eventually released from her duty, and all she wanted was her head on the pillow and her overstretched brain put to rest.

She had just returned from another of her hospital visits. It had been two weeks since she was first called upon by DI Gordon, and her schedule had once again become busy and erratic.

On getting into her flat, she kicked off her shoes, which had been hurting her soles, and slipped into a pair of soft, pink slippers by the door. Dragging her tired body to the bathroom, she decided she needed a shower to wash away the lingering, horrendous smell of the hospital, full of people wounded and dying – the sensation was more to do with her mental state than her nose.

The scenes from the hospital had been both distressing and heartbreaking. Not a squeamish type, she had never shied away from gritty movies or the violent endings of crime series on TV. In fact, she favoured the British and Scandinavian crime thrillers for her usual bedtime reading or holiday treats. Still, she had not been comfortable when face to face with bloody limbs and disfigured, burnt victims. She had seen one too many that day.

By the end of her interview with Ah Lan, the young woman whose face was scarred so badly by third-degree burns that she looked nothing like the pretty girl on her passport photo, Pearl had enough. She felt nauseous.

No doubt a series of nightmares would stalk her at night, even if she managed to temporarily forget the ugliness of the day. Dreamless, deep sleep had never been her friend.

In recent days, apart from assisting DI Gordon with his difficult job in taking statements from survivors of the fire, she had familiarised herself with interesting terminology from the medical staff. By no means an expert on burn injuries, she had at least learned to tell the difference between minor, first-degree burns and the more serious second- and third-degree burn sufferers.

First-degree burns were superficial, similar to that of sunburn: even though painful for the victims, they could heal quickly without scarring for life. Second-degree burns, however, could be either superficial or deep, and they needed specialist assessment and treatment, taking a longer time to heal.

In Ah Lan's case, her burns extended through the dermis and into the hypodermis, damaging bones, tendon, and ligaments below her skin. The extent of her burns was disfiguring and would need skin grafting. According to Dr Singh, it could very well have been her youth and resistance to pain that had kept her alive, for now, while quite a few other victims in her condition were already dead or dying.

The long list of surviving victims had proved labour-intensive to work through. Pearl was only one of several interpreters working on the case.

On the plus side, over recent days, DI Gordon had come to regard her as not simply an interpreter, elevating her status to more of a 'consultant'. Whenever he needed clarification or advice on how to deal with the Chinese victims, he referred to her and trusted her judgement. *Is it because of my academic title, or that he has taken a fancy to me? Or perhaps both?*

The thought of his handsome face made Pearl's pulse race a little faster every time, especially when she remembered his handshake a couple of hours ago. It lingered, as if he was reluctant to let her go. His grip was warm, almost a clench, with his eyes watching her intently; it sent minor electric shocks through her hand, coursing through her body. A thrilling feeling and a welcome change to her bogged-down routine.

Since Andrew flew to America three months ago, she had been struggling to get used to sleeping on her own again. As independent and unwilling to bow to defeat as she had always been, she had begun to feel the emptiness and coldness of her bed more and more acutely.

Andrew? Where exactly are you and what are you up to?

******

Sunday came, his day off at long last.

Jack felt that he needed it more than ever. The investigation into the massive fire had been keeping his body and mind on

29

full alert for weeks. The endless interest from the media and the constant press conferences had him on his toes during all his waking hours, not to mention the interviews he had been conducting with victims and witnesses, and the medical staff who now had 24-hour care for those tragedy survivors.

His team worked day and night, tirelessly, keeping Jack fully up-to-date with any developments, big or small. The online file was now broken down into scores of directories, with summaries at the head of each. The key facts were established, but it was the connection between them and the big picture beyond that had yet to be drawn. The last thing he needed was to get his facts wrong and land himself in hot water with the press or his superior officers. On the plus side, he really enjoyed working with his attractive, female interpreter.

The mere thought of Pearl brought him a smile, slowly spreading from his brain to his face as Jack stretched himself in his bed, trying to conjure up her face.

There was something about the woman, tugging at his heartstrings, making him feel more alive. He did not know exactly what, but it was a feeling both new and exciting. It was not simply the attraction between a male and a female; rather, it was both subtle and strong, pulling him towards her like a magnet. Behind Pearl's obvious exotic looks and lithe body, there was a mystery, an unknown quantity, which Jack found most alluring. He wanted to know what it was that made Pearl unique, different from all the other females he had worked with. She was not the first interpreter he had called upon, nor the last.

From the chest of drawers next to the bed, Jack fished out a fresh polo shirt and a pair of black CK underpants. As he pulled up his trousers, a plan formed in his head.

Moira was working, nothing new there. Even when she wasn't on duty and they were both free, they no longer did things together. It had been too long to pinpoint exactly when they started sleeping in different rooms, using the convenient excuse that they both needed their sleep and Jack a bad snorer.

The last time they had a verbal bust-up Moira had not even raised her voice, using an accusatory tone nonetheless. "Look at yourself, Jack; you're married to your job, not me. Oh no, definitely not me."

"Is that what you think?" Jack had replied; counterattack was a necessary weapon to defend himself. "How about you, Moira? Do you feel married at all? I certainly don't feel that way. When did we last have sex? Donkey years ago, if I remember correctly."

"Is that what you are concerned about? Sex?" Her temper was rising; so was her voice.

"No, it's not just sex. It's what this relationship is based on. You probably think that being a mother to our children is good enough. No, it's not. Simply being a housemate to your husband is not good enough." Jack's disappointment and anger were just beneath his accusing statement.

"At least I still perform my duties as a mother, while you bugger off to work and are never around when we need you!"

Ouch! She had him.

As for his two children, Jack maintained a relatively easygoing, hands-off approach to Heather, who occasionally texted him, or dropped him an e-mail when she was in the mood to communicate or in need of some cash. With the freedom of university and discovering a new life outside home, her contact was minimal and she appeared to prefer it that way.

With Jimmy, despite efforts on Jack's side, the teenager remained distant and uncooperative, avoiding his dad whenever he could and hiding in his room. Doing what? Probably playing his computer games, like most other lads his age. The perfect nuclear family. Not so much 2+2, more like 0+0.

31

After a quick breakfast with Bran Flakes and a Cox's apple, Jack headed out to his car. A fine day; he had nearly 10 hours to spare, a luxury which he had no intention of wasting. He pulled out his mobile and dialled a number that he had now stored on his favourite list.

"Hi Pearl, it's Jack here. Have I woken you up?" He smiled without even realising it when she greeted him back, in her slightly groggy voice: music to his ears.

"Yes, you did, actually. But no worries." She sounded fully alert, even cheerful.

"You need me to come to work?" She proceeded with a question, fully expecting a positive answer.

"Oh no." His smile deepened. A diligent soul, that woman. "You've earned your break."

He may have served as an unwelcome alarm clock, taking her away from her sweet dreams, but he was not going to back up from his well-thought-out scheme.

"I am thinking that if you have nothing planned, I can come around and see you. I'm actually not far from you. I'll be at yours in about an hour."

Yes, I did it! Jack had blurted it out. He had already rehearsed his little speech in his head before placing the call. He did not want Pearl to have a chance to say no.

"Okay," was what she said.

Time to give his beloved BMW 530i a bit of extra gas. He sped onto the M40, heading towards a nonworking day and the chance of who'd know what?

Chapter 6: Ah Ming: "My Other Life in China"

I AM NEITHER politically astute, nor do I give a damn about what politicians say or do, but as a Chinese person, we are generally aware of how our country is faring economically, largely down to the tireless propaganda pumped out by the mass media.

The papers and radio announcements inform us that China has experienced a gigantic economic boom, with a growth rate higher than any other country on Earth. True or not, every Chinese person seemed to have been empowered by the rallying cry that 'Getting Rich is Glorious', a famous Deng Xiao Ping quote from the 1980s.

Even a poor-educated, ignorant peasant like me; I get the picture. The Communists are still the power on the throne, but the once-dreadful capitalist approach has become China's new, ambitious economic drive. No more slogans like 'Down with the Stinking Capitalist Roaders'; instead, smell the wondrous fragrance of materialism and consumerism. Forget your ideals and ideologies, embrace modern China: where money could buy anything, and money is everything.

After five years of schooling – enough to read simplified characters, write straightforward letters, and become better at calculating than my parents were ever able to – my formal education was over. This time even my mother could not argue on my behalf. No money was available to pay for school fees, which had been increasing dramatically year after year, so poor families like mine would either get into heavy debt or were forced to abandon school. The only secondary school was much further away from my village. My parents could not afford to put me into boarding school, and walking there each day was simply not viable.

In China, enlightened parents regard education as the key to their children's bright future, and so they are willing to sacrifice everything to achieve that end. My father had no such vision, and he was right: anyone with average intelligence could see that I would never be a scholar. My father was a simple soul and a practical being, and he was content that his son would follow in the footsteps of his forefathers and labour on our small piece of land, as generations of the Wang family had always done. Grand ambitions were a luxury reserved for the rich, the powerful, and the intellectuals, never for the poverty-stricken, the underprivileged, and the deprived peasants like us.

From then on, I began full time on what we Chinese label, 'face towards the yellow earth, and back towards the sky'.

There were no weekdays and weekends; each day was identical and only the seasons changed. We counted the days according to the farmer's calendar: when to dig the earth, when to sow the seeds, when to harvest, and when to repeat that very cycle. There was never a day of rest, even when I was sick. I didn't get sick easily, because I was toughened up. I got up before dawn, and when bedtime came, it was well after dark, especially in the winter.

Days ran into months, stretching into years, and time just passed me by, without anything special worth remembering. Then came the day I found I had turned from a boy into a man.

Despite my ever-degrading memory, I can recall when I first became attracted to girls. For a couple of years before that, I felt the growing urge in my body and I had no idea who to do it with, so I soothed myself in the middle of the night when everyone was deep in their sleep.

Life on the land was too harsh and mundane to even think of courting a girl. Marriage, yes; I heard my parents talking about it, with my father saying that it was time to find a wife for me, while my mother objected that I was too young. In the end, the fact that they had no financial backing to attract a decent girl for me won the argument.

It was one summer, in the middle of the 1980s, when I met a local girl who would became my wife.

It was in the farmers' market where I spotted her when I took various produce from our land to sell, from sweet potatoes to cucumbers. She often wore a bright-coloured, flowery top, with a feisty personality to match, which seemed to have attracted attention from a lot of coarse peasants. They swarmed around her like flies over the leftover food from nearby restaurants.

The townies came and bargained their way through various vegetable and fruit stalls, selecting fresh produce for their fancy dinners at home. The country bumpkins like me, we did our due to haggle a reasonable price to take home, small dirty notes and coins, so we could buy seeds for the next year or simple farming equipment.

Ah Yan was older than me. Of course, I didn't know her name or her age when I first set eyes on her in the market stalls. She was loud and flirty, confident in her dealings with the men around her. She had to be, surrounded by unschooled and uncouth peasants. It was not a good place for a young woman, but she probably had no choice. I later found out that she was the eldest girl of four, so she had to behave like a responsible 'big brother' in her household.

"A tough cookie, that one, I tell ya. Not good wife material, not for me, anyway," I heard the short, ugly man next to me mutter. He must have caught me stealing glances at her sometimes, yet too shy to openly flirt with her, as one or two older and bolder fellows did to earn her disdain.

After the third or fourth time seeing Ah Yan without speaking to her, I noticed her returning my glances, and once a smile. She was well built and as tall as me, but appeared taller. She had thick, dark eyebrows, small, slanting eyes, and a big, flat nose. She was not what people would call 'easy on the eye', but when she smiled at me it softened her otherwise stern, sharp face. I blushed at the thought that she might like me just a little.

I found myself fantasising about her, especially without her clothes on, but I had no imagination, because I had never seen a naked woman in my life. When I thought about Ah Yan, I felt an erection and had to do something to release the urge. For the first time I had a specific object to think about after long hours of hard toil in the fields. I reminded myself that the next time I saw her; I would pluck up my courage to speak to her.

To my own disgust, all my bravado disappeared when it was needed. I found myself not even able to look at her properly, when once or twice she walked right in front of me.

"Hey, Ah Yan, fancy a bit of action with me?" I heard one of my neighbours, a man of fifty, shouting at her, with a dirty leer to match, followed by jeers from a few other men within earshot. I felt blood rushing to my head and it made me hot with embarrassment.

"Shag yourself, you dirty old fool," Ah Yan shouted back without a flutter.

"Look at your ugly self in the mirror first." She spat. As she spoke, she shot a look at me. Did she think that I was just like them, or did she blame me for not standing up for her honour? I was not sure, and it bothered me.

It took another couple of weeks before she came to my stall. It was a quiet time when most shoppers were having their snooze after lunch. She bought two packets of noodles from the street vendor nearby, walked towards me, and held out one of them in front of my face.

"Hey, you hungry? Have this?"

"No," I declined nervously, not knowing how to respond to her unexpected hospitality. "I'm not hungry. You eat it." I pushed it back to her. After a few pushes back and forth, I eventually accepted it and slurped the still-steaming noodles without a word.

Once she started chatting, it got easy; all I had to do was to nod here and there, or simply listen to what she had to say. She told me where she lived, how many in her family, and what they were like. She did not question me, for which I was grateful.

To my surprise, she offered, as a matter of fact: "You can walk me home later, when the market closes for today."

Before I could think of something to say, she was gone, back to her stall, which sold herbs and spices.

I tried to rearrange the cucumbers, spring onions, and tomatoes in front of me, various future scenarios playing in my head. Six hours to go before the market sellers would disperse into darkness.

It was the most confusing time I had ever felt, not sure whether I was looking forward to it or dreading it. It was probably both.

Chapter 7: The First Date

THE SUDDEN SOUND of the buzzer startled Pearl, despite her anticipating it.

Filled with unwanted, foolish thoughts, and feeling a nervous energy in the air, she had been surfing the net randomly, as if a hare had taken temporary residence inside her. Or was it butterflies? Nothing registered. Her mood would fit in quite well with Confused.com. Ever since that unexpected call from Jack, during the hour or so when he was racing towards her, her heart had been thumping in her chest, giving her neither peace nor concentration.

What was happening? Would it turn out to be a casual social visit from someone she had only met professionally, or would it be more? From the commanding tone in Jack's voice, and a subtle but undeniable eagerness, Pearl's sixth sense pointed at one possibility: Jack wanted something else beside her interpreting skills.

Her speculations came to a sudden halt with his intercom announcement: "Hi, Jack here."

Who else? She smiled nervously, resting one hand on her chest trying to compose herself, her other hand pulling open the door after the first ring of the bell. She had already identified the face of the handsome officer through the intercom when he buzzed outside the apartment buildings.

From behind his back, Jack produced a bunch of red roses.

"These are for you." He grinned broadly as he handed the flowers to Pearl, who was wearing casual attire for the day: blue jeans and a dark-pink T-shirt.

Fast worker. The amusing thought warmed her heart as she took the flowers, her hand brushing against his briefly, unsure if she should offer her cheek, which competed with the pinkness of the roses.

"Thank you so much." She managed a typical, English response.

To cover her embarrassment, she added, "I love roses, they smell wonderful."

She bowed her head close to the soft petals, hoping to calm her nerves, gratefully taking in the subtle, sweet fragrance. *I'm so lost in this dating game, out of practice.*

"Please make yourself comfortable." She remembered her role of hostess and quickly led the way into her living-room.

With a quick glance at Jack, she asked, "Tea or coffee?" An escape to another room, even just for a short while, would help ease the awkwardness.

"A cup of strong coffee would be nice," he replied, his eyes taking in her apartment; a few cardboard boxes appeared yet to be opened.

"Oh yes, black with two sugars, if my memory serves me right." She smiled at her recollection of how he took his coffee and wondered if he was pleased she remembered.

"You got it, clever lass." His smile and comment confirmed that he was.

"Thanks. Won't take long," she said, her voice still tinged with nervousness.

Moving towards her small kitchen, she felt the urge to get away from his strong, male presence, which she found just a little disturbing, although not in a bad way. Just before reaching her temporary hideaway, she saw Jack taking a seat on the single sofa chair facing the kitchen door.

She wondered what he thought of her home, but that was the least of her worries right then.

In her apartment, at the far corner by the large windows overlooking the city, a black sofa was strategically placed opposite the matching, black TV stand on the other side of the wall. On it stood a big Sony plasma TV, a DVD player, and a hi-fi system, through which the classical music channel was playing Mozart with the volume just loud enough to be audible.

Most of the furniture was in contrast to the pale wall colours, including black-and-white photo prints on the magnolia walls, giving her flat a modern feel. Any visitor could tell that she loved colours, as several soft, red cushions were scattered on the settee and a little, red coffee table adorned the middle of the room, not to mention the bright-coloured vases with decorative, dried flowers on top of her bookshelves. The shelves were filled with printed books of all kinds: mostly fiction and travel books.

The paperbacks and hard-back copies were her treasures, collected over a long period of reading history. She had fought hard to keep most of her stock when Andrew gave away the majority of his books to the charity shops.

"You're unlikely to read them again," had been his argument.

"Maybe not, but I love having them and being surrounded by my books," she had defended her corner.

A sudden, cracking sound from the kitchen interrupted her train of thought and made her mutter. "Shit," came out under her breath. As if by magic, Jack appeared at the door in a flash.

"You all right?" His voice was filled with concern.

He is awfully quick on his feet, she noted, as she knelt down on the now-wet floor, sweeping up broken pieces of glass.

"I broke the vase, but it's no big deal." She stood up and glanced at Jack quickly before diverting her eyes, her face burning scarlet, reflections of the red roses.

Before she opened the cupboard to locate another container for the flowers, she heard Jack's tender yet commanding whisper behind her. "Come here, Pearl."

An electrical current shook through her as his strong arms reached out and drew her close.

Her back touched his first, before he turned her around to face him. She smelt a faint aftershave, assaulting her super-sensitive senses. His touch was so charged with an electrifying passion that her body responded with an unmistakably earthy desire. Involuntarily, and fatally, she allowed herself to fall into Jack's inviting, enamoured embrace.

What happened next was beyond her control, as his ardent kisses showered first on her face and neck, then moved on to her mouth, which was already on fire. As soon as his lips touched hers, Pearl's body started to tremble.

She let out a soft moan under his hot kisses and found herself responding to his fervent touch. Instinctively she pressed her body against his, willing herself to melt. The feeling of being wanted was so powerful that it overwhelmed all her other senses. In one quick movement, he picked her up and carried her towards the bedroom next door.

"Oh Jack," was all she managed to utter.

Chapter 8: Ah Fang's First Encounter with Immigration

ON THIS GREY day, I am sitting in a waiting room at Heathrow Airport, outside London.

It seems like a hundred years ago when indulging in the cheap thrill of stealing jewellery provoked a chain reaction that eventually transported me to this foreign place, without saying good-bye to my parents. In my wildest dreams I had never expected that, at the age of 16, I would be forced to leave my family, my hometown, and – indeed – my country.

In the first days after my kidnap, following my 'misadventure' in Changle centre, I raged against my captors, demanding to know where I was and why they had taken me against my will. I cursed them, cursed the eight generations before them, bit and kicked them whenever they came near me. I refused food for two days, hoping against hope that they would relent and let me go. In the end, all to no avail.

By the third day when the 'Big Brother' came to me, and ripped open my clothes and bruised my young flesh, I had no energy left to fight him off.

The pain he inflicted on me was excruciating, unlike any pain I had ever known before. Other men followed, and in my delirious state, I lost count how many dirty dicks had invaded my temple and destroyed my purity. All I knew was that my body was no longer mine, filled with filth; my mind, although still my own, could no longer distinguish these evil faces. They had the same loathsome look, stank with the same cigarette smell, and had the same disgusting yet satisfied look after they got off my ravaged body.

I wanted to die, there and then! I wished that a black, endless hole would open up under my feet and swallow me whole. *Let me die, God*, I had prayed fervently. And God did not answer to my prayers.

Strangely, in time, I started to come round and my sanity returned, bit by bit, piece by piece. No more wishful thinking; I chose to accept my fate with calm and resignation. I learnt quickly that my captors had no wish to release me from their clutches until they had used me up completely. When arrangements had been made for me to travel overseas, I didn't even bother asking where they were taking me. It made no difference. I had been condemned.

Not only had I lost count of the men who had raped me along the way, I had also lost track of the time. I had no idea how long it took to get to the end of that long and hazardous journey.

Now here I sit in an uncomfortable, airport chair, watching a high-nosed, cat-eyed, female official walk toward me.

"What is your family name?" she asks, through a Mandarin Chinese-speaking interpreter.

Mr Li has a strong accent, which I can't identify, but I am sure of the fact that he is not from my region, where Changle dialect is spoken. My Mandarin is not perfect, so it is quite difficult to understand him fully. Still, his presence makes life easier for me. At least I understand him better than the pale, unhealthy-looking guilao, the foreign ghost who is, according to Mr Li, an Immigration officer working for the UK Border Agency. Everything sounds so strange and means little to me, but I'm smart enough and, over time, I will become more familiar with the system.

"My surname is Zhang," I lie, turning my attention to the interpreter, not the official.

Given my limited contact with officials back home, where the police rough handled me for getting into trouble, I do not trust any authoritative figures, whatever their ranks or titles are.

"What are your other names? What other names have you used? Your maiden name or alias?"

I watch Mr Li's mouth move, yet I cannot understand what is being asked. What maiden name? Ain't I still a maiden, a girl of 16? Does it matter what nicknames my folks had called me back home? Why do they care so much about my name? It's just a label given to me at birth, or something I have acquired on the street. There is no significance attached to my name.

"Everyone calls me Ah Fang," I murmur in the end, letting my real name be known. What's the worst that can happen to someone like me?

I hear the interpreter explaining to the officer that my first name is Fang, but back where I come from, everyone adds "Ah" in front of our first names, like a nickname, more intimate and friendly that way. I do not understand either of their English, but I get the gist.

Momentarily I am lost in my train of thoughts, as more questions come pouring out from the painted mouth of the official.

"Do you understand the Home Office interpreter?"

I nod. Even if I don't fully comprehend what is said, I don't want to come across as stupid or thick. Besides, all I want is for them to let me go. There are people out there waiting to take me to places. I am not a free agent, whatever they may have assumed I am.

Through Mr Li, official statements are read out to me, the majority of which fail to register.

"I have never applied for a National Insurance Number, and I am not waiting for the outcome of the application." Not too fluently, Mr Li repeats this to me.

"What is National Insurance number?" I ask, genuinely puzzled.

"It is something you have to have if your asylum application is granted, or if you were to work to pay tax, and to receive benefit," the official explains in a flat tone, expressionless.

Is she kidding me? Paying tax? I am not even legal here and how the hell do I go about paying tax by selling my body? Would they ask the snakehead for his profit share, from bringing young girls to this country for sex?

As for 'benefit', I would learn from other fellow illegals in time. Apparently, had I applied for asylum to the British government, they would have assigned me free accommodation and even given me money to feed myself.

Is the British government generous to a fault, or is it just being stupid? Nothing is ever free in China and I was born Chinese! Here we are in a foreign country, being smuggled in illegally, yet instead of throwing us out by putting us on the next aeroplane home, they offer us food and bed, and ask us about our life story. How incredible! No wonder people say that they have 'human rights' here and the snakehead would charge so much per head to get people over here. What are 'human rights'? I don't fully comprehend its implications, but if it means money for nothing, then I'd have it.

I suffer another hour or so with more confusing questions, when the officer queries me about my journey to the UK. I am asked to sign at the bottom of each page.

"Are you still fit and well?"

"Yes."

"Have you understood the Home Office interpreter?"

"Yes."

"This is the end of your screening interview. I'm going to photocopy these records and give you a copy. We'll write to you to come in for a full asylum interview in due course," she concludes, and I am free to go.

Once outside, I take out the piece of paper I was given before landing. There is a mobile number on it.

"You call this as soon as you're out of the airport, do you understand? If you think of doing anything clever or bold, we'll find you, and we'll kill your parents."

Even in England, it is not the land of the free for people like me.

Chapter 9: A Heady Affair

JACK PROPPED UP his elbow and looked at Pearl lying next to him.

Hours had ticked by since he got to Pearl's apartment early that day; now it was late afternoon. He could not get enough of her. Her body was so soft and silky to his touch, yet firm and welcoming, unlike Moira's, who had been steadily refusing intimacies between them. He forced the thought of his wife away and leaned over to kiss Pearl, his hand brushing away a few strands of hair that had covered part of her face.

"Hey, beautiful," he teased her, and momentarily stopped his sensual assault on her delicious lips.

They had made love three times, each time slower than the time before.

He was full of life and supercharged with a passionate energy, a wonderful 'chi' that vibrated with his every move. With Moira, after the kids came along, their lovemaking had been reduced to once a week, which eventually became once a blue moon, usually at his initiation and her obliging cooperation. Even when he was away in the Army, with limited time on leave at home, Moira did not show a great deal of passion. Eventually he had lost interest in initiating sex. It must have been at least three months since he had last made love to his wife before he made the guest room his semipermanent residence.

Pearl stirred from a sweet slumber at his sensual touch, as his mouth claimed hers more firmly than before. It was electric.

"Did you sleep?" he asked her, after waking her with a lingering, loving kiss.

"Yes, sort of," she replied, smiling up at him, his face inches away from her.

Her fingers touched his chin, which, despite the shave earlier, was already a little prickly and rough, with stubble fighting to burst out of his skin.

He lowered his head next to hers, burying his face into her hair, tangled from the sweat, and he licked her earlobes. His mouth found hers, which were soft and sweet, like an exotic fruit he had never had before but got hooked on upon first tasting. He felt himself harden against the softness of her thigh. She started giggling and her body arched up to meet his, muscular and strong. One of his large hands reached under the bedcover and found her right breast, still swollen and supple from earlier stimulation, instantly responsive to his teasing and squeezing. With his fingers wrapping around her nipple and giving it a gentle roll, it hardened, begging for more attention. Her desire transmitted through her quivering body and he applied more pressure with his expert finger movement.

Softly moaning with pleasure, he sensed that she wanted more of him: his mouth, his touch, his whole being. His body was urging him to comply, letting go.

As if on cue, he responded to her escalating tension and fuelled her desire, which was seeping from her every pore, her body heat relentlessly transferring and fusing with his own. He released her lips and shifted down her writhing body. He wanted to be where she wanted him to be. Their longings were in synch, and their movement in rhythm.

With each move, she groaned with a delicate, sensual sigh, which drove him wild with urges of his own, pent up and eager to be released. Slowly and painstakingly he travelled down, soothing her flushed, highly sensitised skin with hot, wet kisses that sent shivers down her spine and scorched her soul. She was warm and wet, her body on fire.

With a powerful push, he drove into her. He wanted to please her and excite her, take her to places she never knew existed. Even with her eyes closed, he wanted her to see starbursts, like fireworks against the dark sky.

This woman he barely knew had taken his breath away. He seemed to know instinctively which part of her was sensitive to his touch, and he was more than happy to satisfy her needs.

******

"So what's your story? How come you're living here all on your own?" he asked.

In the short breaks between their long sessions of lovemaking, he had already revealed his status, exactly like one of Pearl's favourite TV series: married with children. Nothing wrong with that, except that there were no more sparks between him and his wife. He was not wearing a wedding band, never did.

During their previously limited chitchat at work, Pearl had mentioned the existence of a husband, from whom she had obviously acquired her surname Church. She did not seem keen to go into her private, unresolved domestic affairs. Now here she was, stark naked with another man, someone with whom she had a professional relationship.

Jack was good in bed: great in fact, although Pearl was not about to tell him that just now. *I need to let myself go sometimes, allowing myself to swim freely in the sea of sensual delights. Despite Andrew leaving, I still have needs and there is no harm satisfying them with a gorgeous man who wants me,* she reasoned with her inner voice.

"My husband and I are separated." She paused, as if to let it sink in, for herself and for him. "He's got himself a job in Colorado and went there a few months ago."

No, don't tell him that we are on the verge of the big D, because it's not what I want.

In the depth of her heart, she still loved Andrew dearly, so much that it ached for him at most unlikely moments.

When she married him nearly 13 years ago, it was for keeps. She never dreamt that he would one day leave her and spread his wings across the ocean to another continent. It was not like he was 25 and eager to explore the world. Between the pair of them, Pearl was the more restless soul, while Andrew had been far more content with his life in England. In the dead calm of sleepless nights, Pearl had expected that he would suddenly appear in front of her and take her back, as if he had never been away.

Despite the red light flashing in her mind, her body had responded to Jack's passion before her mind sent signals to stop it. She had so missed Andrew, and wished that he had not gone to America, leaving their marriage hung on a very thin line, threatening to break at any point. Her face went a shade darker, her earlier bliss replaced by a shadow of sorrow.

"Oh, I'm sorry," Jack said.

"Actually, that's a lie." He paused, a teasing wink. "I am not sorry. What kind of fool would leave someone like you and bugger off to America, eh? Come here."

He leaned closer and planted another kiss on her sensual lips. She welcomed his kiss with an appreciative smile, her spirits lifting a little. She wanted to brush away thoughts of the heated rows she had traded with her husband, which eventually drove him away from her side.

"Thank you, Jack." She meant it.

Feeling the weight of their conversation, she began to fumble for her scattered underwear on the floor. Talking about her estranged husband in her naked state did not feel right: exposed, vulnerable and almost immoral, as if being caught in a sinful act of betrayal.

"Now, it's probably time for that cup of coffee you wanted earlier, don't you think?"

Pearl pulled her T-shirt over her head and got out of bed, without her jeans, heading towards the kitchen. She felt his cool eyes following her, caressing her bare skin.

I need a strong one myself. A headache was looming.

Jack had to leave soon.

Chapter 10: Ah Ming: "I Wanna Change My Life"

THE FIRST TIME I walked Ah Yan home, I felt nervous, unable to look at her, terrified of our physical proximity. I could not speak either, as if tongue-tied. Fortunately, the chatterbox Ah Yan was, she did not seem to have noticed nor cared about my lack of response. It was good enough for her that I followed her one step behind and listened to whatever she felt like nattering about.

On the next market day, at the end of a long day's hard selling, I saw Ah Yan packing up what was left of her stock. I quickly finished what I had to do, and walked over to her. We seemed to have formed an unwritten pact that I would accompany her home again.

At the peak of a steaming summer, even at dusk the temperature remained high and humid. My bare upper body was unbearably sweaty and sticky. It felt strange to walk so close to a girl, and I could smell her body odour mixed with sweat, which made my heart beat faster than usual. As we passed through the fields, stacked with hay, a strange but undeniable urge rose from that secret, private part, quickly shooting up through my veins to reach my brain.

No time to reason or to think it through, I was suddenly overcome by the impulse to get hold of her and release the tension inside me. I had let my fantasy run wild the night before and it was her fault that I was feeling like a caged animal. In any case, she had to be the one to liberate me from that torturous need, to free me from the prison.

In a swift movement, I had her pinned down against the hay with my full weight on top of her. I was breathing so heavily that if I didn't do anything to her quickly, I'd pass out.

Thankfully, she seemed to be aware of the effect she had on me, or perhaps she had liked me enough to let me rip down her shorts and thrust myself into her, down there in her dark hole. She didn't cry, nor moan. She just closed her eyes and let me come fast and furious inside her.

After I was spent, I rolled off her. We never exchanged a word, but continued to walk the rest of the way towards her home.

For a month or so afterwards, because we had run out of vegetables to sell, as well as having to plant more seasonal crops for the future, I did not return to the market stalls. The hay incident had made me feel more than a little ashamed to face Ah Yan.

Then Sunday came, and a strange impulse led me back to the town market. She did not notice me for a while, as I stood at a corner, shaded by a large, ancient pipal tree, observing her.

She appeared subdued somehow. Even when she talked to her customers, she sounded less loud, as if she was troubled. Sure enough, I discovered what was troubling her very quickly.

'I'm pregnant,' was all she had to say to me.

What the hell; or was it luck? After a rushed, hushed encounter with a near stranger in the hay on a hot summer day, I was to become a father. I did not know whether to laugh or to cry, but I knew damn well what I had to do.

To be a man, an honourable man, it was my duty to marry her and support our future child.

As simple as that, with an official nod from my village chief – who sanctioned the marriage certificate – I extended my family and my filial duties towards that of my in-laws, Ah Yan's whole family, on top of my own parents and siblings. My one-time, premarital shag propelled me into a marriage of no return.

That was my former life back in China, and now I was stuck in a mental hospital in the UK, and for some weird reason, I was confiding in a virtual stranger, my interpreter. No denying that she had a kind face, the kind which won people's trust quickly. That's what I thought anyway with my limited dealings with clever people, those smart intellectuals far above us poor peasants in the social order.

"The government told us that we should grow fish, and it would make us rich." I told my story, not looking at her, afraid to identify what's there in her eyes. I stared at my feet instead. I heard my own words, bouncing in the space between us, as if they came from someone else; in my mind's eye I saw a life that used to be mine. A bit like an old Chinese watercolour painting, its ink disappearing over time, faded, the thin rice paper crumpled with dog ears, but the main brush strokes still visible, identifiable, reminding people what it was or what it could have been.

"For two months, it rained, rained, and rained and the river overflowed into our fish ponds. Then all the fish were gone, disappeared. We lost everything."

To fund the fish-farm venture, my family borrowed large sums from a local bank, as well as from other available sources: loan sharks, people with power and influence in our small pond. In no time, I ended up with a hefty debt of 200,000 RMB, an astronomical amount for an ordinary family like mine.

Had the farm survived and the fish business prospered, my life would have turned out differently. That would have been wishful thinking.

With my debtors breathing down my neck, and no other business or job prospects except our small piece of land, which the government was in the process of taking away from us little people. "To build motorway," we were told. The development of our motherland demanded it. "It's good for you," they assured us.

Nothing left but despair. Only one way out of that mess – the snakeheads, gang masters, agents, or whatever name people used to label them. They were the only ones who could 'help' me and my family, and seemingly saving my debt-ridden arse.

"Go to Europe, go to the UK. We guarantee that you'll make a fortune."

The word had been out for years. Local snakeheads had grand and imposing mansions and posh cars to demonstrate what they preached. Sensible people knew that their riches came from heartless exploitation of those poor souls desperate to get work and get rich overseas; yet who, in their right mind, could resist the allure of fortune in the land of hope and glory, a promised land, with streets paved with gold, waiting for us?

The situation at home was so dire and hopeless that poor sods like me would do anything for a glimpse of hope, no matter how slim and distant.

Although I could not articulate it, I knew about hope, and it was everything when you had nothing else worthwhile. Hope sold; it did not matter where and how – just look at those of us stupid bastards who gambled at casinos or bought lotteries using up our last pound coin. It was hope that had kept us going, and ultimately was keeping us alive, no matter how miserable that life had turned out to be.

No guarantee of safe journey or human loss was ever offered or needed. Smuggling humans was a risky adventure, and everyone knew the score: if you were leaving your country of your own free will, illegally, you should be prepared to pay whatever price that would cost you and your family. Human loss was part of this chess game, and in this world, only the fittest survive. Who could argue with that timeless, indisputable theory? Certainly not a half-witted, semi-illiterate idiot like me.

The going rate for smuggling had been astronomical for many, and the more costly the option, the easier the passage. Even the cheapest option was huge, as it was only reasonable for the snakeheads to charge an arrangement fee, which would include paying bribery to government officials, forging passports and visas, and paying for the international networking and facilitation among the gang masters, not to mention the profits necessary to build and maintain their massive mansions and associated luxuries.

My family, like thousands of families in my village and other villages, believed in the Promised Land. So many people pinned their hope for a better future on distant shores. Europe, Japan, USA, Australia: take your pick. They have been the hottest destinations for Chinese economic migrants, with great prospects and greater returns.

Like the modern-day gold rush, you heard stories that your neighbour went and made good, so what do you do? I followed suit.

Soon enough, though, the 'wonder drugs' wore off and you woke up, feeling the after effect.

It did not take long for me to discover that the promised 'grand prospects' were in stark contrast with the grim reality. My 'safe passage' from China to the UK lasted six months, with numerous stops en route, many of which had remained unknown or meaningless to me and my fellow travellers.

We were packed in boats, trains, coaches, and in the back of container lorries; even walked long distances at night, for days on end, climbing mountains, which were exhausting. I had seen people passing out and being abandoned en route: left to die, sometimes. I still have hardened blisters and scars to remind me of that horrendous journey.

"Was it true that you were in Russia for three months before you went to Holland?" the Home Office Presenting Officer had asked me during my appeal hearing for asylum in the beginning of 2001.

"I don't know which country I was in. Nobody told us, and I didn't speak any local languages," I had answered, truthfully.

The moment I decided to use a snakehead, I became a puppet, my life and death in their hands. I was instructed never to ask questions. I remembered once when I was in the back of a lorry for 'God-only-knows-how-long'; I nearly passed out before I was eventually allowed out. For my ever-shrinking belly, I was given inedible, dried bread and no water to wash it down with. I was so thirsty that I thought that my lips would dry out completely, or I would bleed to death from the split lips.

Nor could I complain. How dare I? To whom?

"You can make your own way back to your fucking village," could hardly be construed as an empty threat. Few things were worse than that. I would have no face to show and nowhere to hide if I went back home empty-handed, and never, ever be able to pay the debts. The outcome would have been too horrible to even contemplate.

Truth be told, I was considered lucky. At least I did not drown in the river, or freeze or choke to death in stinking containers on the back of a lorry, as some poor sods did. I even knew one of the families whose son died on that ill-fated crossing to Dover. My mother spoke to his mother after the tragedy made news in the West, eventually making it through word of mouth to local attention. As a result of the son's death and the ever-mounting debt, the family had to borrow more money to send his younger sister overseas. God knows what she would have to do to pay back both her own debts and that of her brother's.

Despite incredible hardships during my journey to the West, I made it to my destination. I was definitely lucky – I was not packed off to a secret location to pick fruits in the fields, or collect cockles in the freezing, unpredictable sea: another tragic story which would be etched in the memory of many Fujianese for years to come.

Lucky me, I was dumped by the agent in China Town.

"Go and find yourself a job. When you get caught, apply for asylum. They can't throw you out." Standard advice they gave to nameless 'ghosts' like me.

I did, and sure enough I soon got lost in the masses of thousands of illegal immigrants scattered around this wonderful country they call the United Kingdom.

Chapter 11: Pearl VS Andrew

JUNE CAME AND went, and time flashed by.

The frenzy of police work had been exhausting, but it was a welcome change from Pearl's routine, as well as providing a satisfying bolster to her bank account. Now that she had to depend solely on her own income, she needed regular work more than ever.

There was a time when she was bombarded with police calls day and night, weekdays and weekends. She remembered Andrew's displeasure at the 2 o'clock duty call in the dead calm of the night.

"From now on, we unplug all home phones at 11:00 p.m." He had issued an order and that was it. Nonnegotiable. When she left her mobile on, he stormed off to the guest room.

As much as Pearl hated being aroused at ungodly hours, she understood the nature of her work, and the pitfalls of working for law enforcement.

Through her extensive service to the Criminal Justice System, she had come across many fellow interpreters and became friends with quite a few. Mrs Candy Wong was one of them. Originally from Hong Kong, Candy had worked with the police and Immigration for over 30 years, a legendary figure in interpreting circles. Everyone knew Candy Wong, or had heard tales about her.

"She is such a lovely person, so dedicated and helpful towards others." "Last time I saw her at Stanton Police station, she told me that she had been there for two days, only managed a couple of hours' catnap in her car." "Mrs Wong does five Chinese dialects. No wonder she is in such demand. An amazing woman."

In her relatively short time working as a professional interpreter, Pearl had experienced many of its challenges: a stressful and demanding job, although immensely rewarding too when her help was acknowledged and appreciated.

Mostly an isolating profession, Pearl enjoyed the occasions to work with colleagues like Candy, who had many pieces of insider advice to pass on, and once in a while an assignment here and there when the 'most sought-after interpreter' was snowed under. Humble and modest by nature, Pearl held her senior colleague in high regard. However, when she relayed 'legends' of Mrs Wong, Andrew was not impressed: sarcastically nicknamed her "The Iron Lady".

"If ever you became her, I'd be gone," he had joked then.

She never expected that to happen, either she becoming Candy or Andrew being gone. Then all of a sudden, she looked around; she was on her own.

A week or so passed since Jack's first visit to her flat. He called her a few times in between his busy schedule, and they had a few text exchanges.

Work came and went, and again she was left in a limbo, waiting for her mobile to ring. She had time to think: perhaps too much time. Shadows of Andrew often followed her, and everything she did reminded her of him: his purposeful walk, his witty comments, and the colourful cycling clothing he used to wear. Everywhere she turned, she saw her husband's fine-featured face and his smiles. He did not smile much, but when he did, it lit up his cool, blue eyes and made them sparkle, like stars in the night sky. When she lay down on her double bed, her heart ached with love and longing: for his sweet kisses, his loving touch. At times of loneliness and despondency, even his occasional 'telling off' seemed to have become endearments that she sorely missed.

He used to text her all the time, enquiring how she was doing, sending her updates of train times if she didn't have her car with her, or simply texting her a photo, and once in a while surprising her with a short video clip of himself, doing a silly walk just to make her laugh. She felt a tightening of her throat, her eyes welling up, a pinch in her chest recalling those moments to mind.

Andrew had been gone only a few months, but it felt like light-years ago, another lifetime. At other times, his images were so vivid and lifelike it was as if it was only yesterday when she still had him.

Ever since becoming a freelance interpreter, her timetable had become unpredictable. The interviews of fire survivors were completed, and the police had moved on to other aspects of their investigation. Her services had, for now, been sidelined. She was, after all, just a pawn – if that – in a big chess game, which the police play with their opponents.

"I'm really sorry that we have no more bookings for you." Jack was apologetic on the phone, acutely aware of her need for work.

"You don't need to apologise," she assured him. "It's not your fault. That is the nature of freelance work, and it's my choice. Nobody is to blame.

"As a matter of fact, it gives me the flexibility to do other things." She went on and reeled off a number of benefits of interpreting. Typical of her. What's the point in wanting for things she could not have and forgetting what she was blessed with, work, or otherwise?

On Monday morning, Pearl woke up early; well, earlier in her standards. She was a 'night creature', an 'Owl' in Andrew's words, one of his favourite animals due to his lifelong support of Sheffield Wednesday. She loved staying in bed in the mornings, and especially on the weekends, when she would be served breakfast in bed. Such a treat, that was.

She reached out to her iPhone on her bedside table, the screen lit up, and on the screen saver a familiar face smiled back at her. It had become a habit to have her phone charged at night and placed within easy reach, to allow her quick and easy access. Even when the work calls had diminished, the habit was hard to break. When going out, she still carried it around in a special phone pouch, hanging around her neck. She hated missing calls from a caller with a "withheld number", or "blocked" – she certainly did not try to block any calls – but she had come to regard that as fate intervening.

Like many of her peers, she had adapted well in the era of modern technology, especially when Andrew was around. "We have the fastest internet connection there is, and all the gadgets required for our work and leisure." He had been proud of that very fact. With the new generation of iPhone, she enjoyed the luxury to reach out to the rest of the globe at her fingertips. The big wide world in a three-inch screen.

Time to begin the day with her virtual world of Facebook, Twitter, YouTube, Hotmail, and – if she felt really motivated, with nothing else to do – she may even write a new blog and make a new video with her many holiday snaps. Within the screen and the beyond, she had met online friends far and wide, and in no time at all she became hooked.

Everyone nowadays had a website, or blog site, or both. Pearl was no exception. Not exactly a trendsetter, but an early adopter nevertheless, she signed up with Wordpress and started blogging intermittently a few months before, on the books she had read and enjoyed, travel logs and, once in a while, reminiscences of her childhood and turbulent times when she was growing up in China.

Following the general economic depression in the UK, and public services in particular, the prospects of professional interpreters were subject to a major threat, and most jobs had been taken away by agencies who regarded interpreters as just people that could speak two languages, without adequate training, relevant qualifications, or experience. Agencies run by greedy businessmen or women who had no understanding of what interpreting was all about decided that this was another industry they could exploit and benefit from. Consequently, qualified interpreters were forced to work for peanuts or sat at home waiting for calls which never came, work going to students or non-interpreters instead.

Perhaps I'll start a blog on the problems faced by interpreters and educate the public what it is like to work as a professional interpreter and translator. With that ingenious thought, she went to her iMac and started typing.

Half an hour later, her post was completed and ready to reach out to readers on the World Wide Web. Simple; she pressed "publish" and out it went.

Still ample time before lunch, she went back to her other social media platforms.

Let's have a look at what Andrew is up to. She smiled as she clicked open her Facebook page.

That was a great thing about social media and its various forms: they allow ordinary folks to 'stalk' their friends and family; virtual strangers to check on their status updates, and follow them, either openly or discreetly, on Twitter. Good or bad, it was here to stay.

He has not responded to my invitation to join the newest trend of G+, but surely he did not think that it was another way of me keeping tabs on him?!

******

Life on the other side of the pond had not been too bad so far. As much as I loved dear, old England, I did not miss its constant rain and dark clouds.

The sun was already soaring over the mountain ridge and steaming the dew from the buckskin cover of the tepee. I ought to get up, but for the first time in weeks I really couldn't be bothered. It was only 5:00 a.m. and my legs could not face another three hours grinding in a low gear up that mountain pass. The bike sat there – willing me to get on it and ride some more. The lactic acid from the day before told me that was not a good idea.

Maybe time to go back to Boulder for a rest? At 52, my body took longer and longer to recover. I had work to do in the library before the start of my first semester at University of Colorado. I had heard that these US students needed even more spoon-feeding than their UK peers, and lucky me, I was blessed with first years who had not been long out of nappies – or was that diapers?

The language differences were small but intensely irritating. I once heard an English colleague who had commented that only 8 percent of those that speak English were English, and that the language no longer belonged to us. "Get over it," she said, doing her best "Valley Girl" accent.

Elevator not lift. Trunk not boot. Pants not trousers. People had even asked me to "say something in English" because they were "wild about the accent."

When asked where I was from I would say "England", thinking they might know where that was. Some did but one guy said, "Oh, yeah… Let me see now …England, yeah that's in London."

But why should they be bothered? England was vanishingly small, fitting twice into one state like Colorado. A historic curiosity of decreasing relevance. Should I have expected anything different? Probably not.

Why was I here? Chasing a teenage dream of the great outdoors, formed during a six-week stay back in the early 1980s. It had all seemed so magical back then. The blonde girls with their tanned legs, the Budweiser beer, the Häagen-Daz ice cream, the smooth roads. It wasn't so bad now, but not quite as good as I told myself back in Birmingham, England, not Birmingham, Alabama.

I reconnected with my friends Aaron and Mandy, whom I met years ago in my youth, once I was sure of my move to this side of the pond. However, they have split up so I have to see them separately, and they spend 90 percent of the time complaining about the other. It was nothing like when I shared their small flat and flirted with Mandy. It had never gone anywhere and it won't now – she's a bit of a basket case after all the drugs.

The longer I stayed in Boulder, the more I realised I was probably making a big mistake.

"What am I chasing here?" I spoke the words out loud, to no-one in particular.

"Not me, that's for sure!" It's the voice of Geraldine, a massive hippy from Brighton who was renting me the tepee. I got a discount because living in a tepee in Estes Park was going out of fashion. People preferred RVs these days – better TV reception and a proper "bathroom". Bathroom not toilet.

Better get up and face the world. Wonder what Pearl was doing right now? It was lunchtime in the UK, so she was probably having her noodles with spicy sauce. Was she thinking about me right now? Probably not. Wasn't that the problem: that she was spending less and less time thinking about me?

Working all the hours God sends, loving the money but hating the boredom and stress.

Over the years we had grown apart, reverting to patterns of behaviour from before we met, like we merged for a few years and then de-merged. This 4,000 mile gap seemed like a full de-merger. She had not called me for two weeks.

We used to talk to each other all the time. Then it seemed she just could not be bothered anymore. Now, with me thousands of miles away, what could we talk about anyway? It was not like she could imagine what it was like over here. She had only visited the US once, a very brief, flying visit to see her friends on the West Coast. She knew nothing about Colorado.

I felt free, but also trapped by memories of how it was before. We did have some good years, great years in fact. We were so close, but slowly we formed reasons to be apart. Little niggles became open sores and we stopped talking.

"You getting your arse out on that bike today, Andrew?" enquired the Brighton hippy.

"I don't think so; I'm knackered," I responded, without much enthusiasm. "Think I'll head back down to Boulder and spend some time working on the head muscles instead of my glutes."

The sun was really cooking the tepee skin now, and it was getting too hot to stay in the down cocoon of the sleeping bag. Even though I wanted to go back to sleep, I'd have to get up. The bladder wouldn't wait much longer.

Wonder if Pearl would call today? Probably not.

Chapter 12: Ah Fang's First Day in London

THERE ARE DAYS in our lives which are so significant that memories of them stay with us no matter how much time has passed.

The day when I arrived in the UK was one of those days. I have forgotten what Heathrow Airport was like; after all, most airports look the same, don't they? But I do remember what happened upon leaving the airport, so vividly that it was like yesterday. Once in a while, like a film, it has played out in my mind and made me wonder: if I hadn't followed the orders to call the number the snakehead gave me, instead choosing to disappear in this foreign country, what would have happened? Would my life have turned out differently?

Stop it, I tell myself. What's the bloody point? I am a Chinese girl, and my fate had more or less been sealed the day I entered this world. Everyone's life path has been predetermined: not only in this life, but in previous lives and the next one. I am no exception. No, I'm not a cat and I know people say that cats have nine lives. I hate cats. They are cunning, lazy, dirty, and their claws are sharp and spiteful. That's not the point either. I do not have to be a cat to have many lives.

Being Chinese and sort of a Buddhist believer, I am blessed with the knowledge that if I do good in this life, my next time around will improve. So hopefully nine or so life cycles down the line, my life will be so different from this one that I no longer have to go through any of the pain, hurt, and suffering that I have been subjected to in my still young, "current" life.

After I was picked up by a car with blacked-out windows outside the airport, I was taken to a place, which I learnt later to be China Town in London's Leicester Square.

At the time, I was utterly and completely disorientated. The 'long march' across all those borders between China and Europe had seemed a never-ending, torturous marathon. Only after talking with other girls who shared my experiences did I discover the names of some of the locations I had been smuggled through.

For the men who ravaged my body and soul, I was not the only victim of their heinous crimes. They did the same to many other innocent girls.

I doubted if any of these nasty bastards would ever be brought to justice by the laws of the countries we had travelled through. How would anyone find out what they did to us, or would they even care? Even if they did get caught, would any of their victims be brave enough and strong enough to go to court and give evidence against them? No way! These bastards remain nameless and faceless even to us, the young girls and women they have abused and assaulted, ravaged and ruined, against our will. Even if some of us were willing to speak out, who in the real world would represent us, the weak, the poor, the underprivileged, the downtrodden, and worst of all, the invisible and illegal?

Over time, I have learnt to see the world I live in. For the majority of the people in Western, democratic countries, we are illegal immigrants; although not exactly untouchable, we drift along under the surface and remain most of the time hidden in places like takeaway kitchens or fruit-packing in remote areas.

We are like shadows in the dark, ghosts who have no physical form in the real world, hence are insignificant. Once in a while, we cause a bit of stir in their news and media, when their politicians want votes from new immigration laws, or when illegals or underworld gangs or drug dealers committed a terrible crime, too horrendous to be swept quietly under the carpet.

As hidden as I have been, I was not totally blind to what was happening around me. I did not have to read the newspapers to discover how the invisibles were suddenly made visible in the UK: once by the dead bodies in the back of a packed lorry, and another time more bodies washed away by the unforgiving sea at Morecombe Bay.

Within the Chinese community – even the hidden, secret one – we communicate: good or bad, news spread, perhaps even more effectively than the mass media. How did people communicate before the invention of modern media? Word of mouth.

We may be insignificant and invisible, but whether the indigenous people want us or not, we are an integral part of the modern society. Inevitable events led to unwanted revelations about our existence, when the tiny, tiny bits of our lives became exposed to the ordinary, decent folks in the West.

There are more sympathetic and liberal-minded ones; they do not fear us, nor blame us for the problems in their society, because their intellect and vision allow them to see the truth behind negative portrayal in the media. It is us, the nameless/homeless/rootless beings who do their fruit-picking/meat-packing/dirty-dishwashing and other minion jobs which their own folks don't want to dirty their hands on. We are the cheap labour that allows these peace-loving, charitable people to enjoy a good living standard, so when they are hungry, they can go to a good-priced Chinese takeaway, or when they are mentally stressed and physically depressed, they visit an

Oriental massage parlour or try some herbal medicine. All at a good price – for them.

Oh yes, the massage parlours. They are 'fond' memories for me, personally. It was my very first paid job in this world, a masseuse.

It sounds pretty cool, even somewhat noble, doesn't it? In your description, that is, if you're really a professional masseuse, you relieve your customers' mental stress and physical discomfort. It sounds almost as good as being a nurse or doctor.

But no, my 'job' as a masseuse did not strictly adhere to the above job description. It was a totally different kind of service altogether, not noble at all, nor cool. It was damn bloody disgusting and degrading. Why do they choose such grand and misleading titles for us poor sex slaves? Yes, that's right, we are simply slaves. We serve the needs of dirty men, whatever their needs might be. They use us to their satisfaction, and they exploit us to the bone.

That day when I was taken to China Town, I braced myself with positive thoughts: *This is a new beginning for me. I am going to forget what has happened on the journey here and start afresh. This is England, a democratic country where everyone is supposed to have human rights and ordinary people are respected and protected by the law. I shall learn to speak English properly and work hard. I shall pay back whatever is owed to the snakeheads for bringing me into this country, and I shall live an honest life.*

How naïve and unrealistic I was. In no time at all, my big dream of starting afresh was shattered to tiny pieces, bits so small that I was never able to pick them up again and make it whole.

En route through the rainy, misty streets of London, the driver didn't say a word.

Another man, who simply introduced himself as 'Ah Tai'. I called him Uncle Tai. He looked so much older than me, almost as old as my father. Even after my respectful address to him, he didn't smile or acknowledge my presence as anything of note. Never mind.

Perhaps I was just an errand he had to run for his boss, whoever that might be. On planting himself firmly next to me at the back seats, he instructed the driver to move, in Cantonese. Not a dialect I could speak fluently, I picked up enough vocabulary to get by, thanks to the Canto-pop I practised in KTV bars back home.

As the car sped off, Ah Tai took out his mobile and dialled a number. I tried my best to make out what he was saying, but only managed to piece together a fraction. In his loud and bad-tempered shouting down the line, he spat out that he had collected the goods (could that be me?), and he asked the person to deliver the message to Ah Long, "The Dragon", whom I would eventually learn to be the boss to lesser gangsters like Ah Tai.

An hour or so later, I was dropped off in front of a rather fancy building, colourfully decorated outside anyway. Ah Tai led me through what appeared to be a restaurant, busy and noisy with people's chattering and sounds of metal cutlery. We squeezed along a narrow, dimly lit corridor and then through an iron door with strong locks to a passageway leading upstairs. The carpeted stairs were so well-trodden and threadbare that I could see and almost feel the wood underneath.

"You are here now," Ah Tai led me to the top floor and left without another word. There was no tour.

He said something to an older woman, which I didn't catch.

Taking in my new accommodation, I saw six girls including me. I was glad to see two other Chinese faces. One young girl — no more than 15, who looked like a scared rabbit — was probably a new arrival like me. No use talking to her, because she didn't appear to know anything, or had lost her will to speak somehow. Unless asked directly, she didn't utter a word or volunteer any information on her part.

Three others girls, aged between 16 to 25, were speaking English to one another. They looked like people from Southeast Asia, perhaps from Thailand, Philippines, Vietnam, or Indonesia. I could not distinguish either their appearances or their accents, nor could I communicate with them at all.

"Where are you from?" I directed my question to the older Chinese woman, who seemed to know Ah Tai, and was more at home there than the rest of us.

"Fuqing. How about you?" She looked at me up and down with a small grin on her wrinkly face, the first I had seen since landing on the foreign soil. My spirits lifted instantly.

"How nice. I'm from Changle. We are *laoxiang*." My cheery voice shrilled with delight, meeting an elder from my native province. *Laoxiang*, persons sharing the same hometown: an instant draw of closeness in us Chinese anywhere in the world.

Fuqing was only about 30 kilometres from where I used to live. Both Fuqing and Changle were close to Fuzhou, our capital city in Fujian. Although Fuqing dialect was difficult for me to understand, just as mine to a Fuqing native, we compensated by communicating through our heavily accented and rusty Mandarin.

In reply, she said to me, "I have relatives from Changle." It drew me even closer to her.

Ah Hua, whom I respectfully called 'Auntie Hua', seemed to welcome a newcomer like me: keen to help, answering all my enquiries without hesitation.

"This is China Town in London. Most Fujianese come here before they go elsewhere."

"How long have you been here?"

"Let me see, four, nearly five years." She made some calculations and went on to tell me the month and year she left and how she came over.

An old hand, from whom I could learn a great deal. I smiled. Words and sentences poured out of me, like from a broken dam. So many unanswered questions had been preying on my mind during the journey, and there was so much more I wanted to know. Ah Hua seemed a perfect lamp to shed light on them.

Thankfully, she peeled away some of the mysteries surrounding my circumstances, like where I was. When I asked her what she did for a living, she became a bit vague and evasive. I did not press her.

What was to come? My mind wandered aimlessly, lying on my bunk bed that night, eyes wide open. Would I have a future that is painted in rainbows and bright colours, or would it be bleak, grim and utterly miserable? I stared into the darkness enveloping me, seeking answers to the unknown, only spotting a huge question mark, written in stark white against the huge black void above my head.

I felt a chill, and pulled the thin cover tighter around my body. It was still summertime.

Chapter 13: Passion in a Pub

ONE SECOND, JACK was drinking tea at Camp Bastion, flirting with a pretty Eastern European barmaid. The next, he was sitting on a military van on a bumpy, dirty track, churning up clouds of dust as they rumbled their way forward. Jack peered out with one hand above his eyes, which was to shield his sight from the sun and dust, trying to see where he was through the dust cloud. It looked familiar, and came then a sudden realisation: he was crossing the desert of Sangin, the cockpit of Taliban insurgent activity in Helmand, Afghanistan.

As he adjusted his body to a less uncomfortable position, he heard helicopters above him, the noise so piercing that it seemed to deafen him. He tried covering his ears, and could almost feel their powerful downdraft on his face.

He had played rugby there on the landing zone, but now they were heading towards the 'Fob Rob', a NATO base. Not far away there was heavy artillery – from the Americans and Canadian forces – pounding Taliban positions. Then a thundering explosion sounded right next to Jack's vehicle. His body shook, he was jolted by a powerful force: wide awake.

For a brief, microsecond, Jack forgot that he was at home: a safe haven that he had craved while he was with the SAS in Afghanistan.

He checked the digital clock next to his bed and it blinked 5:00 a.m. back at him: two hours before his day officially kicked off. The nightmares that haunted him had been a regular occurrence following a familiar theme. With only 4 hours' sleep, they haunted him even after he awoke.

With conscious effort, he tried dispelling the unpleasant afterthoughts by diverting his mind to something more tangible: Pearl and her smooth body.

His senses were aroused, remembering what it felt like when he first touched her. He could vaguely recall her scent, different from anyone he had ever shared intimacies with before. Not that he had that many women in his life, despite his 40 years of life on earth and having been sexually active for nearly two-thirds of that time.

Moira was his school sweetheart, the first girl he had slept with. She lost her virginity to him on a hot summer day after school when they were both 16. As far as he knew, he has been the only man in her life, and in all the years while he was in the Army, away from home, she worked hard bringing up his two children. Towards his wife, even if lust and passion has gone, he took his responsibility seriously. It would be so wrong to abandon her, now that he was back from the war zone in one piece and had secured a stable job as well as a respectable position.

Blessed with at least an hour to spare, with no sleep imminent, Jack indulged himself in his reminiscences of his romantic adventures. Someone at his age was bound to reflect on life from time to time.

During all his years away from home, he had cheated on Moira only twice, once with a journalist who had come to Afghanistan to cover the war and took photos of him as he desperately tried to save a mate who was dying in his arms. He was so distraught by what had happened that day that when she came to his tent that night, he had used her body to escape, and fucked her and himself to sleep. All he had wanted to do was to hold another warm body and forget the cold, stiff body of

Johnny, the 19-year-old fellow Scot he had taken under his wing.

Johnny's death was one of several escalating reasons that eventually led to Jack abandoning his Army career.

There was a slightly more sustained affair with another police officer: a trainee officer actually. Jack was asked to give a talk at a National Police Conference where he had met Joanna. Jo, as she had preferred being called, was a determined 23 year old, who had graduated from a university in Birmingham and was a sports fanatic. Their liaison lasted just over three months, when her training ended and she was assigned to North Yorkshire Police force, near her home in Hull.

Now here he was, a middle-aged man who had come to a crossroad in his life. He was the one who initiated the affair with an interpreter. A married Chinese woman with a husband somewhere in America! Was this the kind of middle-life crisis psychologists and women's magazines went on and on about? Or was it the 'empty-nester' syndrome, which pushed his wife further away from him, and he pursuing an exotic and exciting adventure of his own?

Jack stopped his musings, got out of bed, and put on his T-shirt and trousers in quick succession. He was suddenly consumed with the desire to see Pearl. He located his mobile and scrolled down to her number, labelled as MIP-Mandarin Interpreter Pearl.

MISS U - CAN U COME TO PUB FIGHTING COCK IN LUTON AT 3PM? LOVE TO SEE YOU THERE.

Before he could change his mind, he pressed SEND.

******

Naked and satisfied, Pearl had one of Jack's tattooed arms draped around her neck, which showed off his muscular torso and biceps. It felt so good having her soft curves nestled against his taut muscles, exuding strength and unmistakable maleness. He smelt damn good too.

She traced the shape of the Scottish flag on one of his arms, and dragons on the other. She let out a soft giggle. "What a funny name for a pub! What were they thinking when they came up with names like that?"

"They probably predicted that someone like me, with a fighting cock, would come here and spend a sticky afternoon with his lovely hot lass?" He also chuckled at his own joke.

Laughing, she leaned over and her pouting lips brushed against his nose, a feather-like kiss, just to tantalise him.

"Seriously, how did you know that they had rooms upstairs and we could, you know...?" She paused, still embarrassed that she had driven 80 miles at his beck and call, so she could get much-needed attention to her body and soul, from this man she had only met over a month ago.

"Have you brought other women here?" She did not meet his eyes, turning her head away, aware that she sounded like a jealous wife. The urge to probe simply emerged and burst out. She knew she had no claim on him, nor him on her. Still, a question hovered in her head and she was not the type to torture herself with questions she had no answers for, so better out with it.

"Oh no." He raised his hands and turned her face towards him, looking her straight in her eyes, deep, dark-brown pools, drawing him in. "What do you take me for? I have been to this place before when I was still a sergeant, and investigated an arson here a couple of years ago. I was a bit surprised that this pub had a B&B upstairs, but no, I've never stayed here: until today, that is. Besides, I just invited you for a late lunch here, and it was you..."

Before he could continue, their mouths had found each other and their limbs were reaching for the other's sensitive parts, probing and claiming. Their bodies became blissfully entwined, giving and receiving. Time was precious and it was silly to waste it on unnecessary chitchat.

She wanted him, badly, and he matched her in her every move, satisfying her every whim.

An hour or so later, when she had consumed his yang and he had greedily taken her yin for the second time that afternoon, Jack reluctantly disentangled himself. He went to the bathroom to remove his condom, and his sweat. Instead of feeling spent, he was energised.

"Sorry, Pearl, but I've got to go. I can only manage a few hours today. Double duty day."

"Of course." She nodded, a little disappointment in her eyes.

He returned to her side of the bed and knelt down, as if about to propose.

"I promise to make time next time. The past few weeks have been just crazy. We are really short staffed, not to mention further cuts on the way..."

She put her fingers on his mouth and stopped him from further explanation.

"I understand, Jack. I really do. I know you want to see me, and I love seeing you, but time is against us, and you've got work to do."

In her moments of sanity, she was still incredulous that she had acquired a Sean Connery look-alike who wanted her and filled her with unbridled passion. In her wildest dreams, she had never expected to be conducting an extramarital affair with a police officer.

It was obvious that Jack had become besotted with her, or with her body at least, which was in wonderful shape for her age. *For him, I am exotic and from a different world, hence more alluring, adding spice to his usual, bland English diet.* Pearl smiled: food for thought.

For her, Jack filled a hole in her life, left empty by her husband.

But Andrew. Oh Andrew, how would he react if he finds out that I have a new man in my life? Or has he also found someone?

Chapter 14: "The Dragon"

SUMMER DAYS IN Fuzhou are bloody awful, unbearable.

Ah Long hates Fuzhou and he hates China. Unlike many of his fellow countrymen and women, his memories of Fuqing, where he was born, have always filled him with disgust and distaste, as if he were being force-fed rotten oysters.

Ironically, he just came out of a banquet where he was indeed served oysters, the freshest kind, the kind that even money can't buy back in England, where he owns several restaurants on whose menu seafood features prominently. In his mind, the best thing, the only thing that is positive about China has been the food: its variety, the way food is prepared and served. He has been picky about chefs for his UK branches of Dragon's Seafood Gourmet restaurants, named after himself and Bruce Lee. After all, Long, aka dragon, is a lucky symbol, signifying power and might.

In London's China Town – as well as many other China Towns in British cities – Ah Long's name is like thunder; anyone who runs a business in the Chinese community has to kowtow to him, the powerful and authoritative 'Big Boss', not unlike the Godfather in Coppola's trilogy.

Apart from his highly profitable chain of restaurants, Ah Long also runs several casinos, both the legal and the underground kind. All his restaurants have KTV bars where the rich, the corrupt, and fun-loving Chinese visitors can belt out Hong Kong, Taiwan, and Mainland pop songs when in the mood. There too they can choose to retire to more private quarters for a sensual massage by hand-picked, pretty, young girls. If they are really in for an all-out indulgence to their body and minds, these girls can perform miracles to satisfy their wildest fantasies. Thai foot treatment, full body massage, full intercourse and anal sex, S & M, a *ménage à trois*: whatever takes a client's fancy.

All Ah Long's girls have been through stringent selection and 'trained' well by his underlings, and none of them dare to defy their boss.

Ah Long has designed an almost-perfect system, or so he believes. As God exemplifies, by providing those girls with certain level of free will, he actually exerts more control. If any of them somehow gets excited by strange ideas and does something stupid, Ah Long's power will be shown in its full glory and might. If he has learnt anything in his criminal career, which spans 30 years across different continents, he knows how to make a grim example of those who fail to observe his rules.

What's the point of being a big boss if your subordinates do not follow the path you have laid out for them?

Like just now: Ah Long is called out of the sumptuous feast he is throwing to entertain his business associates in Fuzhou, because some girl in England was stupid and daring enough to defy him. She pulled a stunt and did a disappearing act. How dare she?!

Consequently, he has to excuse himself in the middle of important business negotiations and be distracted by this crisis, which though minor in scale, is still a nuisance which needs to be dealt with swiftly. He finds a quiet corner at the back of the car park, where rows of top-of-the-range Mercs, Rolls Royces, Aston Martins, Ferraris, and his own ride – a high-spec, shiny, black Lamborghini – stand proudly. He presses the speed dial to his nephew, his right-hand man back in London.

"Now tell me exactly what has happened, and make it quick." He more or less hisses down the phone, totally pissed off at having been disturbed and dragged away to such an unsavoury moment.

None of the usual calm and cool, only anger and frustration. If he had time to analyse its cause, it could all be explained: Fuzhou's unrelenting heat, the peace-shattering noise, the bloody pollution, the ever-more-complicated *guanxi* structures, and the ever-more-extravagant business dealings.

One hand pressing the mobile to his ear, the other fishes out a specially rolled 'grass', as they call it in his slang: known for calming nerves and combatting stress. He listens attentively for a few minutes to the rambling report, before he spits out his burning question. "What did you say was her name again?"

"Ah Fang, you've never met her."

"Find the bitch, dead or alive."

With that, he touches the 'End', and heads back to his VIP Banquet Hall in the fanciest restaurant in Fuzhou.

******

Of those who knew Ah Long as a young boy, and his humble upbringings, few dared to mention his past to anyone else: ultra careful even when talking to their family and friends. Fuzhou walls have ears, and who could predict what punishment and retribution would come from Ah Long if such 'rumours' ever found their way back to him? Better to be safe than sorry.

Ah Long was actually born in the year of Snake, the year when the Great Cultural Revolution began and brought the Chinese economy to its crumbing knees.

His mother died giving birth to him. He was later told that his mother – a simple, illiterate peasant woman from Fuqing, on the edge of Fuzhou – was taken to the hospital in the city centre after a twenty kilometre ride on his father's home-made, three-wheeled cart.

The doctors were wearing heavy placards to be "struggled against", while all the nurses and other staff were busy shouting revolutionary slogans and punching the air with their angry fists, showing their undying love for their great Leader Chairman Mao.

Nobody took any interest in the pregnant peasant woman who was already bleeding. Her husband's incoherent pleading to save his wife and baby fell on deaf ears, or was simply drowned out by their passionate, frantic shouting. Only an elderly cleaner woman took pity on the crying man and ushered them to the store-room, where she helped deliver the baby.

Ah Long survived, but his mother bled to death, never even opening her eyes to see her son.

Growing up without a mother, and with a father who hardly ever spoke, was no joy. When his father did speak, it was more with his fists than his mouth. The quiet man had become increasingly bitter, twisted, and nasty after the loss of his wife, and was too poor to afford another bride.

His father named him Xiao Long (Small Dragon, also Bruce Lee's Chinese name), as dragon has always been more auspicious than Snake, so many people born in the Year of Snake were called Small Dragon. When Xiao Long was old enough, he would claim that that he was born a dragon and put his birth year forward to 1965. He lost the Xiao (Small) and Ah Long had stuck ever since.

Despite his lack of motherly care, and poor nutrition, he was bigger than his peers – maybe because he always got into fights with others – and these early signs of physical violence helped him develop his muscles, skinny though he may have been.

Ah Long was wild; news of his naughtiness and his crazy antics spread far and wide, making him a notorious bully in the

Fuqing area. Younger kids were either too scared of him and followed their parent's advice to avoid him at all cost, or they looked up to him for protection and became his minions to carry out his orders.

By the time he was old enough to go to school, he had already acquired quite a following, and school became an extension of his playground, where he was a disruptive and ruthless bully, preying on the good and the weak.

He did not finish school. In fact, even when he was in school, he did not pay attention. If Fuqing were like the rest of China – where parents pushed their children hard and teachers pushed them even harder for academic excellence – Ah Long would have not progressed at all from Grade One.

But Fuqing was different. In Fuqing, most parents could not care less if their children failed their exams and didn't progress academically. Some children were never even sent to school: for what? How would that hinder their prospects in life? The only driving force and prevailing grand ambition for parents in Fuqing was making money, lots and lots of it, even in days when there was little money to be made in China and everyone was busy with their revolutionary class struggle.

In Fujian Province, perhaps Fuqing even more so, there was only two classes in the residents' eyes: those who had gone overseas, and those who didn't or couldn't.

Ah Long dropped out of school at age 10, after only three years of primary education. He didn't consult anyone. He simply got up one morning and decided that he could no longer be bothered.

He went out as usual though, as there was no way that he wanted to end up like his old man, whom he despised. His father knew nothing except toiling on his small piece of land, growing sweet potatoes and seasonal vegetables that brought him a meagre income, on top of a few chickens in their backyard.

There was a brief time when his father depended on his fists to control Ah Long, forcing him to work when he was younger and physically vulnerable. As soon as Ah Long was old enough and could outrun his father, he kept his distance and fought with defiance. After his threat to cut his father's balls off if he dared to lay his dirty hands on him ever again, the old man took heed, and more or less left wayward Ah Long to his own devices.

Ah Long may have been born a snake, but he would not crawl like one. He would fly like an almighty dragon and he would kill like an eagle.

Chapter 15: A Day at a Magistrates' Court

PEARL PICKED HER way through her favourite shop, TK Maxx – which in America, interestingly, was TJ Maxx – trying to sift through rows and rows of tightly packed outfits, and searching for bargains.

Her wardrobe was already overflowing and there was no room. Yet she could not help it. If a stranger approached her and asked if she had any vice, she would probably come clean, admitting shame-faced: "I am addicted to shopping."

Her well-trained eyes spotted a cotton-linen mix dress with black background and pink flowers on green leaves, a lovely combination. She checked the label and then held it up in front of her, looking at herself in the mirror.

Erm, not bad. She smiled at her reflection. She had turned 49 a few months ago and, according to the Chinese calendar, she would have celebrated that 'half century' already. She thought of her mother at this age and her dowdy clothes, looking ancient with her wrinkles without makeup. She took another glance at her mirror image and was pleased with what she saw, at that young-looking face smiling back at her. *Let's try it on.*

Just then, her mobile rang and vibrated at the same time. She fished it out from the side pocket of her trendy D&G white and purple handbag, another good buy from the same shop only weeks ago.

"Hello, it's Pearl Church here, who is calling please?"

"Dr Church, it's Central Magistrates here. Can you come to court today? We need a Mandarin Chinese interpreter." A woman's voice, a listings officer from her local court.

"Sure. What time do you want me to be there?"

Checking her wristwatch, which read 11:00 a.m., she continued her phone conversation and made her way towards the cashier.

"We'd like you to be here as soon as you can. When can you get here?"

"I'll be there in 30 to 40 minutes, depending on traffic."

She ended the call and handed her dress to the woman at the till. Fortunately, for once, there was no queue. *I hope it will fit. Only a size 10, but I've lost a bit of weight recently so it should be okay.*

Half an hour later, she had found a space in the parking lot, paid the silly parking fee, and walked briskly towards the court house. It was pouring down with a late-summer rain: typical.

Central Magistrates Court stood magnificently on John Street, a landmark building in the city centre of the second-biggest English city after London. Built in 1891, it was one of the great architectural and sculptural achievements, in Pearl's view. Her Majesty Queen Victoria was seated above the main entrance, and under her throne the keystone position is a small St George and Dragon.

Being an interpreter, and fairly local, Pearl had been a frequent visitor to the Magistrates Court. She passed through the security check and surrendered her dripping umbrella, as well as her handy, pink iPod, a constant companion that had helped reduce her boredom in many assignments over the years: a present from Andrew.

Approaching the Reception to collect her claim form, her heart sank. *Oh no, not her again*, she moaned inside as soon as she laid her eyes on the receptionist. *That wretched woman!*

During her visits too numerous to count, this woman never smiled: not once! Every time, without exception, the receptionist either kept her waiting unnecessarily, or pretended that she had no idea who Pearl was. Her face was hard and her tone even harder.

Maybe she hates her job, Pearl assumed, always looking for an explanation for other people's actions.

Once or twice, perhaps that time of the month when her hormones were all over the place, Pearl had become so frustrated with the woman's mannerisms that she felt like screaming: *Why is it so damn hard for you to give a friendly smile, or even an acknowledging nod? Why are you such a miserable bitch?*

Still, being in a country where one has to be polite and behave with good manners at all times, Pearl did her best to smile, at the same time harboring an increasing contempt towards this miserable woman.

"Thanks," she muttered an obligatory response and, picking up her form, rushed out of the reception.

Letting out a sigh of relief, shaking off the grey spell cast by the grumpy receptionist, Pearl checked her green form. It clearly indicated two cases, at two different courts. She made herself known to each usher, then planted herself outside Court 8.

Perhaps the number 8 would improve my luck from now onwards.

Case one was straightforward, and lasted no more than ten minutes in front of three magistrates. A student used his daddy's cash to purchase a Toyota sports car, yet he didn't bother to get insurance or a valid UK driver's license. Unfortunately for him, he was stopped by the police on a one-way street in the early hours, shouting in a language that the officers could not understand, and had later identified as a dialect of Chinese. A Mandarin interpreter was called to assist communication.

Pearl looked at her client and remembered a discussion she'd had with Andrew some time ago, about Chinese people in the UK.

"They fall mostly in two distinctive types," Andrew had commented. "On the glossed surface, devoted parents and grandparents pour all their life's savings into their one child to further their education in privileged Western schools and universities. Their arrival in the UK is legal and their contributions stop many university departments from falling apart or closing down."

Andrew would know. He worked in one of the universities, and his faculty boasted one of the largest numbers of Chinese students. She nodded her agreement before she put in her two pence.

"Below that shining surface of international students, in near invisibility, there are the less fortunate ones like Ah Ming. They saved, scrimped and borrowed, from whatever sources available, and paid the ever-increasingly greedy snakeheads for a journey full of hardship and danger, often taking months or even years to accomplish, and eventually landed in the UK with no legal status, an eagerness to work, and a hope to 'make it' one day."

Her wandering thoughts were called back by the prosecutor, who was addressing the magistrates on the bench at the front of the courtroom.

"Mr Chen was taken to a police station and was breathalysed. His sample was 68 milligrammes per litre, higher than the legal limit."

The prosecutor went on to explain the circumstances under which the defendant was arrested, and later charged with 'drink driving', 'driving without a valid license', and 'driving without insurance'.

"Do you plead guilty, Mr Chen?" The question was asked and interpreted to the defendant.

"Yes."

He pleaded guilty to all charges, following advice from his solicitor at the police station. Due to his lack of income and dependence on family support, he was given a nominal fine and let go.

Would he go and buy insurance on leaving court? Pearl wondered. She doubted it.

The Chinese believed in luck. Getting caught was bad luck, while getting away was one's good fortune. Legal or illegal, they were simply terminologies for the lawyers, not the concern of poor students from overseas.

Her other case was slightly more complicated. The defendant was an illegal immigrant, and was charged with selling counterfeit DVDs, an offense she had often come across in court.

His solicitor must have been very familiar with his speech – probably repeated numerous times – giving mitigation in his client's defense: "This man has no legal status and is not allowed to work in this country. So he was taken advantage of by organized gangs, forced to work to pay back the huge debts he owed to the snakehead who had arranged his passage to the United Kingdom."

Similarly, he could not be fined due to his lack of legitimate income, and was unable to do community service due to his lack of English. In the end, he was given a conditional discharge, and a hollow warning not to repeat the same offense again in the future.

How likely could that be? Where would this man get money to pay off his debts and support him and his family back home? Since he was not allowed to work legally, and not entitled to any State benefit, how could be make money without breaking the law further? Even the dumbest ass could see that.

On coming out of the red-tiled court, the sun had made an appearance and was shining brightly high above. Typically, the rain had stopped.

A quick glance at her watch showed her it was only minutes after one o'clock. Her stomach was making familiar, funny noises, reminding her of its need for food. Without further ado, she headed into the Chinese Buffet restaurant just a few doors away.

Equipped with a plain, white plate on her hand, Pearl piled it up with various dishes on display, not prepared by the best chefs, but tasting good enough, and certainly fast enough to satisfy her hunger.

Five minutes later, everything on her plate had been consumed, washed down with a bottle of J2O, the orange and passion-fruit variety.

After putting on her jacket and stepping outside, she saw that the sky had changed its mood yet again and was pouring down, its big mouth wide open. She remembered then that she had forgotten to ask for her umbrella and iPod back on leaving the court earlier.

Not her day after all.

Chapter 16: Madam Lin's Origins

IN HER BEDROOM upstairs, Madam Lin was putting on her makeup, applying her black eyeliner and a red lipstick. Although still early on a Saturday morning, there was no rest for the wicked. Many years of hard work had not just become a habit, but part of her very being.

Rain or shine, she had her routines on Saturdays. Weekends were the busiest for her, when she had to make her rounds to the few herbal shops she ran in the Midlands area, covering a 60-mile radius. Usually the buzz and the excitement of swapping girls, and having new girls on the scene, gave her mood a boost, but something was amiss today. *What the fuck is fat Malcolm doing now? Must be binging on my tea and biscuit, no doubt.*

Walking downstairs, she saw her boyfriend sitting by the dining table in the middle of the kitchen, which he had recently refurbished. No surprise there for Madam – he was sipping his beloved English shit, probably his second tea or third cup in the morning.

Madam was constantly disgusted by the traits shown by her English boyfriend – that man enjoyed his daily tea rituals, dipping his Rich Tea biscuits in his sweet, milky tea. That was one of the most annoying, unsavoury sights to Madam. *He must be doing it just to get on my nerves.* It must have been that time of the month when she found fault with everyone around her. Some people were born to upset her balance, which was fragile at the best of times.

Today especially.

"What the hell are you doing, you stupid twat? Can't you see I'm waiting?" She shouted at him, her voice high pitched, standing at the bottom of the stairs, with both hands resting on her slim hips, looking at him in utter scorn and distaste.

Her accent was heavily tinged with Fujian influence, despite spending nearly 10 years in the various parts of the UK, and therefore using more English than her mother tongue.

Part and parcel of her job, really, was to communicate mostly in English, of which she had no special love but had become a competent user, excelling especially in swearing slang. It showcased her authority and control over her fellow beings. By God, how she loved being in total control.

Despite the obvious sting in her yelling, Malcolm seemed not to have noticed, or perhaps he knew her too well to acknowledge her outburst, especially since her tantrums and rage had been his weekly diet, sometimes more frequent than others. *This man has no backbone, weak and useless.* Madam felt the contempt rising with each second.

Once in a while, Madam would change tactics and speak to him in an unnaturally soft voice, and sometimes even indulge him with a rare smile; he would become so overwhelmed with gratitude and all the more keen to please her. "You're my queen," he had told her, with that pitiful, devoted look in his eyes, reminding Madam what a dog looked like when they were being treated after a day of starvation. Despite her uncontrollable contempt towards him, she had become reliant on him. After all, a mistress needed lapdogs to run errands for her. Who better than an Englishman when her wish was his command and her pleasure his ultimate reward?

Besides, Madam Lin pitied him. It had been precisely his devotion to her that had alienated him from all his family and friends alike.

"What the hell did you see in that tiny, brown creature, a Chink for God's sake?" his father had hissed at him. "What's so goddamn desirable in this skinny, dark-skinned, East Asian bitch?"

"What do you know? You're just a fucking drunk who has never left your front yard without taking the piss of everyone," Malcolm had shouted back, defending Madam's honour.

Madam knew that she could hardly be viewed as an exotic beauty even in Englishmen's usually stupid and untrained eyes. Yet, she prided herself in her petite build, which many Oriental girls were born with, and which gave her an ageless feel and aroused a kind of protectiveness among a proportion of large, Western men like Malcolm. However, if anyone were to take a closer inspection of her face, it was not difficult to see that she was not your average China doll, even if you were not exactly intelligent and sorely lacking in analytical brain cells. Madam meant business and nobody should ever make the mistake of messing with her. They would be sorry if they did.

"If you are smart and sensible, son, you should get as far away as possible, and stop your association with that China woman." Malcolm's father had waved his hands, unsteady on his feet, before he banished his son from their house in Kingstanding, one of the roughest areas in Birmingham, England.

Towards his useless, unemployed, shit-faced father, Malcolm gave as good as he got by shoving his way past the drunk, old fool. "You're just a bloody, racist pig, and you have no fucking idea what you're talking about, do ya?! I'm leaving this stinking hole anyway!"

That scene, however, played out in Madam's mind today, not making her relent in the way she was treating Malcolm now, but making her more certain than ever that Malcolm was a piece of useless shit that even his alcoholic father could not care less about. *It is a terrible shame that I now have to put up with this wanker instead.*

With obvious irritation all over her face, she watched Malcolm shifting his overweight body into the driver's seat and twisted his new TomTom onto the screen in front of him.

"Where do you want to go first today?" He turned to her, still fuming at his seemingly slow response to her command. If he had to wait for her, it was fair and square, but not the other way round: never!

Men in this world should be punished, in her view. Being a lady and being waited on was her right, for which she had fought ferociously, and had been hard to come by. This privilege was to be defended at all costs.

******

She was not always the high and mighty Madame Lin. When she arrived in this world in the middle of the 1970s, she was a tiny, helpless baby to her parents, who were too poor to keep her.

Her birth name, if she actually had one, was unknown to her; nor had she any knowledge of her birth parents. All she had ever learnt about her background was limited to a few black and white, mental sketches, fading fast due to her confined imagination and staunch resolve not to look back.

Before she could walk and talk, she was sold by a man – an uncle of sorts – who put her in a bundle of rough clothes and passed her to a local gang that specialised in child trafficking. They made it their business to either steal healthy babies from unsuspecting parents, or take abandoned, baby girls to be trafficked to coastal areas where people were generally better off, or to parents who were desperate to have children but infertile.

Her life had so little value that she was exchanged for a 20 kilogram bag of rice. In a remote village in Henan Province that was all her birth parents had asked for in exchange, in order to feed her older siblings. Rice was still in short supply at that time and was rationed for city folks. For the poor peasants, there was no ration at all if they could not produce any for themselves.

The Lin family in Fuqing, where she was eventually sold, called her Ah Mi: 'Mi' meaning uncooked rice. That was how she found out what she was worth when she turned five, having been subjected to battery by her 'Second Brother', who tried to shame her further by revealing her 'true worth'.

"You're just a worthless piece of meat, a girl even your own family did not want." He had spat on her face, which was dirty, her tears mixed with snot.

"No, you're lying," she had cried out, trying desperately to defend her honour.

"No, it's 100 percent truth, you stupid, ugly girl." He had continued his vicious, verbal assault. "Who the fuck do you think you are? Stinking dog shit. If you were so precious, why would your parents sell you for a bag of rice?"

To emphasise his point, he kicked at her chest and her thighs, and smacked her face again and again until it turned purple. The girl they bought had refused to please him by touching his dick. How dare she?

She was too young to understand why Second Brother wanted her to do that thing: putting her small hand inside his pants, touching the 'little brother' he used to pee. But she was clever enough to feel the insult to her worthiness. Like a permanent tattoo, it was imbedded in her young mind, something she was unable to get rid of even if she tried.

If she had to pinpoint a time when her hatred towards the male species began, that moment could have been the starting point: when the seed was sown but quickly buried, hidden from view. Slowly but surely it grew and thrived, given time and nurturing in the sun.

Her new family had not bought her as a daughter to love and treasure; they needed a servant and Ah Mi was it. They were not rich at that time; just enough to feed an extra mouth. Old Lin was already in his fifties when she came along. His wife had given him three sons. The eldest had gone to Japan and was working there illegally. The money he was sending back made sure that the family did not fully depend on the old man's small salary as a mechanic in a local factory. The factory was not making any profit and was additionally in the middle of reform due to the new government policy.

When Ah Mi started school at seven, Old Lin was laid off. She became the natural punching bag, a release for his frustration and ever-worsening ill temper. After all, hitting his own wife for over 25 years had become just a tad too boring. It took the old woman longer and longer to recover from her bruises. With the young, tender flesh of Ah Mi, it brought him more gratification, especially after getting wasted with his cheap rice wine.

Ah Mi grew up fast in her new environment. Who wouldn't? Only in school did she find a temporary haven, away from her violent home life. Her natural ability to learn and to adapt served her so well that she won affection from one of her female teachers: Miss Sun.

From an early age, Ah Mi was able to pick up on people's moods quickly, and she learnt instinctively how to make the best of her intuition. She was happy when Miss Sun took her under her wing. Without her protection, the small, skinny Ah Mi would have suffered far worse bullying from other local boys. It was common knowledge that she had been purchased, hence had no status: no significance of any kind.

Her haven would be taken away, and her fortune was to change, when she turned 12.

"Your father said that it's no use for a girl to have any qualifications." Her 'mother' made the announcement on the last day of her summer holiday.

"We have already informed the school that you're not going back," she stated with finality; it was not a consultation.

"We need you at home now that your Second and Third Brothers are going to Japan to join your Big Brother. Your father and I are getting older. You should do what you are here to do, looking after us, especially after we've been feeding and educating you all these years."

Ah Mi didn't cry or make a scene. She knew it was no use, no matter how many good grades she had achieved or how much she wanted to carry on with her education.

It was only much later that she learnt that Miss Sun had fought for her and tried to persuade her parents into letting her stay on. No use either. Nobody could help her. Ah Mi had known that all along, for as long as she could remember. In this cruel world, she was totally on her own. Whether she stood or fell, it was all up to her; she reminded herself of this time and again.

I'd be a damn fool if I ever forget that.

Part Two: Autumn Leaves

Chapter 17: Pearl's New Calling

IT WAS A long story: how Dr Pearl Church, formerly known as Zhenzhu Zhang – her proper Chinese name prior to her marriage to Andrew Church – became a professional interpreter.

How did it all begin?

If her career could define her as a person, she had shed another layer of skin in her middle age. Not by design: certainly not what she had conscientiously strived for. *Such is the reality of life; we end up not doing exactly what we really want to do, but what we have to do.*

When she was 16, a bright-eyed, innocent-looking girl growing up in Southwestern China, had anyone enquired about her future then, she would have been caught off guard, lost for words, unable to articulate herself except perhaps by repeating empty slogans such as, 'I would follow Chairman Mao's call and go to the countryside to be reeducated.'

Just imagine that scene: a frail, slim Chinese girl as the poor peasant toiling in muddy rice fields. Whatever that really entailed never dawned on her, being young, naïve, and full of grand idealism.

The simple truth was: nobody asked her of her dreams, her ambitions, or her plans, and nobody cared.

Then, at 17, everything changed, almost overnight. There she was, going to university.

From that moment on, her professional life was carved out, precise and clear, in straight lines, step by step. In the 1980s, in post-Mao China, a university qualification invariably led to a permanent job, her career path an upward staircase, climbing steadily from junior teaching assistant to an eventual professorship. Aside from the usual stress to win favours from the authorities and to try to get promoted more quickly than some of her colleagues, she would never, ever had to worry about losing her job. Her highly prestigious academic background, after all, guaranteed a job for life: aptly named 'iron rice bowl'.

What happened? one might ask.

The short answer: she got a break.

The other answer was long and complicated. Fate could not explain everything in life, as much as some fatalists would want the mere mortals to believe.

She was picked for a scholarship by the British Council, among the hundreds and thousands of hopefuls. Was it luck or destiny? At 26, leaving behind an unhappy marriage and a young daughter, she found herself in another country, so vastly different from her own that she battled and struggled to adjust to it, and make it her own.

That was only one of the many challenges in her long journey. Adapting to a Western culture and settling down in a foreign land had its downsides too – readjustment, if she decided to go back to her motherland, would be a future full of unimaginable obstacles, maybe obstacles too great to overcome. Who could tell? As future history books would confirm, huge economic transformation took place in China before and after the new Millennium, and that trend was set to continue.

There was a time Pearl had considered returning to her 'Motherland'. She still had family and friends there, and she missed the familiar culture without a language barrier.

Then memories of her unhappy childhood came rushing back, haunting her. Her doomed first romance and subsequent failed marriage. There was no going back. Life is forever in forward motion. Like snow melting from the Himalayas: it flows down in the spring, across the massive land of China and beyond, all the way to the sea. Diversion, maybe, but no stopping.

Her former familiarity with China was gone, replaced by feelings of alienation and mixed reminiscences. Through ups and downs, ultimately she had found her true "HOME", in the once-alien land called United Kingdom, and with a husband in the form of Andrew Church.

Feeling at home in a foreign country was no easy fare, even for the most adaptable. As a student, life had been fairly straightforward, except the occasional financial hardship and unwanted but inevitable hassle from the Home Office. As an immigrant, even a legal one, it was far more complicated and challenging. When it came to job hunting, the law stated that a 'foreigner' could not be employed for anything that a British person could do, which was virtually everything, or almost.

Does the Chinese law state the same? No foreigners wanted in the Middle Kingdom? She did not know. They never needed any 'foreign devils' before, when China was shut off from the rest of the world for decades in the 20th century, and for centuries before that. Why would China need the West now, a sleeping dragon long woken up, fully alert and moving forward in bounds and leaps, a superpower ready to take on the world by her economic power and huge potential?

After the Employment Tribunal where Pearl sued her former employer – more specifically a nasty piece of work in the fat, big lump of Dick Appleton – for bullying and sexual harassment, she chose to leave. It seemed a good option at the time: turn over that unhappy chapter of her life and leave it where it belonged: in the past.

The consequence? Her fragile academic career in ruins: fact of life. A new calling as a professional interpreter? So be it. After all, an average British person changes his/her career three times in his/her lifetime.

One fine autumn day, sitting comfortably in their well-lit kitchen, reading and relaxing, Andrew pushed the paper over in front of Pearl, who was sitting opposite him reading her glossy magazine.

"You can do that, can't you?" he stated, full of confidence in his wife. It was a small advertisement in the *Times*: Asylum and Immigration Tribunals (AIT) recruiting professional interpreters.

"Not many English people can speak Chinese, and your English is certainly good enough: better than many British people, I'd say." Flattering, yes, accurate assessment too. She had written Master's and PhD theses – how many British people did that? How many British people speak better Mandarin than a highly educated native speaker like his Chinese-born wife?

Yet, despite her dogged determination and unrelenting drive, she had been rewarded with nothing but constant knock-backs and occasional despair.

"Let's face it, Pearl: you're a female, from an ethnic-minority background, and not exactly 21 years old; the British system, as we know it, is inherently racist and sexist."

Again, Andrew nailed it to the head, and even Pearl, forever the optimist, had to involuntarily accept his reasoning. Great

Britain may boast a long and democratic history and freedom of speech, but she remained, regrettably, largely sexist, sometimes racist, and definitely ageist. The painful memory of her one year of hellish battle against her former employer, and racist bully, Dick Appleton was still fresh in her mind, casting a lasting and damaging shadow on her professional pursuit.

No dole, of that much she was certain. With freelance interpreting, Pearl did, at last, find a niche market to deploy her skills: or rather, it had found her.

Following a few rounds of applications and interviews, and months of patient waiting, having passed all assessment and training, she got her name on the panel, working for the Asylum and Immigration Tribunal courts.

Her new job took her to different AIT centres all over, from across the border in Scotland to the north, Belfast on the other side of the Irish Sea, farther down in South Wales, and everywhere else in between on the British Isles. The interpreters' rooms she frequented were like a mini UN. On any given day, Pearl would meet people from dozens of countries, speaking different languages and dialects, many of which she had never heard of nor was ever able to understand. They enchanted her.

Soon, she had made friends from Kosovo to Kurdistan, from Senegal to Zimbabwe.

I have the whole world within my reach.

******

The music from her mobile increased its volume and vibrated slightly on the bed stand at the same time, disturbing the sheer peace and quiet, and her habitual lie-in on a weekend. It was a crispy Saturday morning. Pearl was still in the thrall of her dreamworld.

"This is the Social Services from Derbyshire. Is it possible for you come to the King's Hospital this morning? We have a Chinese patient here, and we need a Mandarin interpreter to communicate with him." The booming voice at the other end of the line belonged to a stranger.

After clarifications on whether Pearl would be able to go and how much she would charge, brief directions were given.

Damn, I should have asked where he had obtained my contact details. Perhaps my membership fee to a professional body has begun to pay dividends at last, or maybe someone has recommended my service?

Until then, her work was solely limited to the Asylum & Immigration courts. Little did she know that it was the beginning of snowballing, and soon her client base would extend to the police, courts, and other public-service providers as well as private companies.

Fully awake due to the unexpected call, she pressed 1 for internal call to reach the ground floor where Andrew was pottering around.

"Guess what?" Before she got a response, she added quickly, "I've got a job."

"Really? Where?"

Andrew sounded both surprised and pleased: surprised that she was awake, two hours before his supply of customary coffee, a brioche, and banana in bed, a treat in which she indulged blissfully at weekends. He was pleased because Pearl was, at last, climbing out of the dark shadow following that damned Tribunal case against her former employer. In a battle between big, powerful sharks and a tiny fish in the raging sea, who was the ultimate loser?

The Churches had to pay a hefty price for their fight, justified though it may have been. They were made to suffer, not just financially. Two years had passed before Pearl finally got a break. Had that been an unfair punishment for standing up and fighting against injustice? Or simply the trials of life? Whatever that may have been, she had faced it with grace and dignity.

"I admire your strength; never say die and keep your head high, even at the rock bottom," Andrew had commented once, pride spilling over from his voice, which Pearl loved. "You are one feisty Sichuan Spice Girl, no doubt about that."

Ten minutes later, Pearl was downstairs and dressed in her smart work outfit, a black, linen jacket and a matching, knee-high, black skirt. It was a cool October day so she had a red, woolen, V-neck sweater under her jacket.

Always important to leave a good professional first impression. She smiled at her husband's subtle approval of her choice. He leaned towards her for a kiss before making an offer she could not refuse.

"Here is your chauffeur for the day, at your service, me lady." He bowed slightly, making her burst out with a cheery laugh.

Outside their town house, on the drive, he opened the passenger door for her. His and hers were parked side by side: his a blue, diesel VW Jetta, and hers a red Polo automatic. The lucky, blue Jetta was to get a spin in the country.

"It's such a blessing to drive on a day like this, hardly any traffic." Andrew had a rare look of glee on his clean-shaven face.

"Guess what, at this time of the morning, most people are still dreaming, and getting over their hangovers after their binge drinking on a Friday night." He maintained a condemning attitude towards chav behaviour and drinking culture among some of his fellow beings.

Pearl simply nodded.

They were sailing along the A38, which made a nice change from the usual jam getting in and out of this metropolitan city in the Midlands. Three quarters of an hour later, they arrived at their destination.

"Don't worry about how I'll spend my time. Just give me a call after you've finished your job," Andrew assured his wife, having anticipated what she would say next before she actually did it. There were certain advantages of being married to someone you knew so well.

"Off you go," he reached over for a quick kiss before dropping her off right in front of the building, and went on to find a parking space.

At the reception area, Pearl was given directions to Psychiatric Ward 34. Minutes later, she was greeted by half a dozen new faces upon entering the said ward.

Introductions were made; most of their names failed to register straightaway. The South Asian man appeared to be the most senior, and he was a psychiatric doctor. There were three or four nurses of different ranks, a student trainee, and a middle-aged woman from the Social Services. They were all gathered to conduct an assessment on Wang Ming, a failed asylum seeker who had been with them for the past two months.

Peter – whose name Pearl did manage to catch during the session – the staff nurse, gave a brief introduction to the circumstances.

"Mr Wang was transferred to our ward in the summer," he began. "Apparently he had stabbed himself on a London street and was taken into a private hospital. The 1000-pound daily cost proved too expensive, so he was transferred to Derbyshire. Apparently he was dispatched to us by the Home Office when he first arrived in the UK back in 1999, so here he was again."

A couple of people present nodded in agreement; nobody said anything and they all waited for Peter to continue.

"He was given medication and seemed fine in the beginning. But in the last couple of days, he was seen going out of the ward and asking to buy sleeping pills from other patients. Once or twice a security guard had to be sent to locate him. We have now sectioned him, under the Mental Health Act."

End of his summary.

Following a brief silence, the South Asian doctor, Dr Raja, turned to Pearl, his eyes imploring.

"I understand that it's probably not your job to make any judgement about the patient, but I'd really appreciate it if you can help us on that front. As someone from his culture and who understands his language, you are in a better position to make a valid assessment of him. Can you help us, please?"

Slightly thrown by the unusual request, Pearl did not know what to say in response.

I am here to offer interpreting, not psychiatric assessment, she wanted to say, but the doc's imploring, sincere expression stopped her. She saw his point of view: yes, she was no doubt in a unique position to understand the patient. At least she and Ming shared more than the same language.

Another woman – probably the senior nurse – spoke, although to no one in particular.

"Mr Wang claims that he speaks no English at all, despite being in the UK for six, long years. He has so far refused to communicate with the staff, although he was heard talking to other patients in English, as well as being a keen watcher of soaps on TV every day."

Pearl nodded knowingly. Her intuition told her that it might have been born out of Wang's instinctive distrust of authorities, often the case with many ordinary Chinese folks. The one Party rule and their corrupt officials have made sure of that.

Looking into the doc's earnest eyes, and everyone else's silent expectations, Pearl felt its weight. Duty and obligation, for someone born Chinese, was in her genetic makeup.

Perhaps I should make use of what I have learnt from my psychology module at university, and the in-depth research I have conducted into cultural differences between different countries after all. Now that my expertise is sought after, it would seem silly – and definitely ungracious – to disappoint these people, she concluded, making up her mind.

"Of course, I'd do my best to help." She smiled to Dr Raja, and at others present.

Chapter 18: Madam Lin's 'Education'

SEASONS CHANGED, AND time flew by. For the helpless, young girl Ah Mi, some memories were best left behind.

After being 'forced' to leave school, she helped her 'parents' full time, both at home and outside.

With the Yen her 'brothers' sent back from Japan, her mother started a small business in Fuqing, a massage parlour in the busy town centre, one of the first of its kind. The Chinese coast towns and cities were full of girls from inner provinces who were eager to make cash to support their folks back home. Working in massage parlours may not bring in a lot of income, nor an easy earning, but it was at least not as hard as slaving away in sweat factories, which were mushrooming throughout China, manufacturing all kinds of products and supplying them to meet the insatiable demands of Western consumers.

The old Madame Lin – small in build but massive in her ego and greed – was not an easy-going boss. Many years of physical and mental suffering in the hands of her old man had not made her weak; it had made her stern, bitter, and foul tempered. Payback time at long last.

Intriguingly, it was not Old Man Lin who had to pay for her past sufferings: it was the whole world who owed her and now was at her mercy. Under her iron-fisted management, there were no idle moments from anyone, least of all Ah Mi, the serving 'slave girl' who was bought. Anyone who dared to defy her would incur severe mental and physical punishments, and financial fines.

Old Lin – laid off by his factory and with no other work available – fancied himself the boss of the boss of the parlour. He could now legitimately lash out at girls for his pleasure, either for his sexual gratification or in exerting power over and fear in the poor and the helpless. Oh my, how he loved the touch of the young, tender flesh! At the slightest displeasure from his wife towards anyone, including their 'adopted' daughter, he took it as his duty to 'discipline' naughty individuals: 'put their minds right', so to speak.

The 'Lin' surname did not automatically grant any special treatment for Ah Mi, but, once in a while, she was allowed brief spells of favourable 'time-out' on condition; usually after she had done favours to Old Lin of a personal nature, like massaging his private parts or a quick blow job when his wife was not around. A boss's privilege.

Despite her knowledge that he had a thing for their 'daughter' – and had been 'sampling the goods' with other young girls behind her back – the madam could not care less what Old Lin did with his coarse, little hands or his disgusting, shrinking dick, as long as he stopped forcing himself on her.

The madam had never developed any interest in having sex with her husband. His antics of jumping on her when he wanted it, and rolling off her as soon as he was done, had never given her an ounce of pleasure: only pain and disgust.

When one never tasted sexual and sensual bliss, one didn't miss it. In old Madame Lin's book, women did not enjoy sex. They were born to serve men in the different stages of their pitiful lives, the way life had prescribed for women from ancient times. Outside their work – no matter what that may be – men were generally useless, not capable of doing anything for themselves. They needed their mothers, their wives, and their daughters to do everything.

In her view, men had been endowed with different roles in the world, and it was only natural that men should pay for everything, especially if they sought pleasure from others rather than from their own wives. There was no free lunch in this world.

It was no secret that the massage parlour was in fact a brothel, a business that provided vital services for their customers. Given the choice of a body massage or the more satisfactory sexual intercourse with a strange, young girl, what would a regular man choose? As soothing and relaxing as a massage could be, if modern men no longer had to dig the fields or sweat in the factories, and instead they have acquired cars, drivers, and hundreds and thousands of RMBs in their banks and pockets, how they chose to spend their ready cash would be anyone's guess.

Old Madame Lin had no disagreement with money, and she certainly wasn't going to argue for the stupid sake of old-fashioned morals, thereby refusing steady income from someone else's hard labour. In truth, she had the foresight of getting in there first, addressing the needs of China's *nouveau riche*, while reaping the benefits of the rampant return of once-banned prostitution and the exploitation of sex workers.

Ah Mi's sex education started early, despite it being a rather complicated and unconventional one.

In the small hours of a dark night, her Second Brother, 15 years older than her, came into her room. Stinking of beer and cigarettes, he forced a piece of cloth in her mouth to stop her from waking up others in the house, jumped on her young body, pinned her hands back, put his prick in her vagina, and released himself in quick succession. He had ripped open her pants with one hand as he rubbed himself with the other hand before he drove his dick in. Seconds later, he pulled himself out and was done, leaving her bleeding and in pain for days afterwards.

She was barely 10 years old when her virginity was taken away: by force, not choice.

Third Brother followed suit not long after. Unlike Second Brother, who didn't give her a second look when she was around, Third Brother had at least performed some form of 'courtship' or 'foreplay', if it could be called that.

He had pinched her bottom, often with a glee and a whistle. Whenever he had the chance, his dirty hands would grab her chest, where her breasts were starting to develop from a very small mound to a more alluring combination of soft and firm pertness.

One summer afternoon, when it was hot and sweaty, Ah Mi was having her siesta alone in the house, her pose innocent, her sleep shallow but without dreams. Third Brother sneaked into her little room and crept up to her small, wooden bed. Lying on her back, with only a thin, summer vest and a pair of cotton underpants on, she was utterly oblivious to the danger approaching.

Her body gave a sudden jerk and she opened her eyes. To her horror, her white, cotton vest top had been rolled up to her neck. Third Brother was staring at her bare breasts, which were rising and falling in rhythm with her heartbeat. His eyes was shining with lust, and his mouth hung half-open, saliva drooling.

"Third Brother, what...?" Shock stopped her at mid-sentence.

She made an attempt to cover herself, but he was quicker: one of his hands pushed her head down as the other grabbed one of her breasts, squeezing it so hard that his nails cut into her tender flesh, sending a piercing pain through her young body like a knife. She let out a squeal.

"Shut the fuck up, or I'll kill you," he muttered.

Then just as quickly, he changed the harshness of his threat to a crooked smile and a softer tone.

"If you are a good girl and do what I ask, then I'll buy you a pretty dress."

With that, he rolled her over on her side and pulled down her underpants in one quick act. Like his brother, he forced his erection inside her tight hole and released himself in a two quick, hard thrusts, accompanied with, 'I'm fucking you, motherfucking bitch,' and ended with a loud grunt and more foul swearing.

Despite Ah Mi's resistance to the Lin brothers' sexual abuses, it proved futile.

By the age of 13, her body had ripened so much that she could no longer hide her feminine features with the baggy clothes her mother had instructed her to wear.

Third Brother did keep his word and bought her cheap, nylon, skimpy clothes, in exchange for regular sexual favours. Again and again, by force, not choice.

"Put them on tonight before I fuck the daylights out of you," he had whispered to her ear as he handed her a black, lacy bra and a see-through pair of nylon undies.

In the end, it was the son's wish that won over his mother's.

******

The eldest of the Lin brothers left for Japan just before Ah Mi's arrival. After working in various restaurants in Tokyo, Kyoto, and a few other cities in Japan, he soon realised that there were quicker ways of getting rich.

His distant cousin Ah Long had been in Japan a bit longer than him and had already established himself as a gang leader; Big Brother Lin started to run errands for Ah Long, harassing various Chinese business premises demanding protection money, or hanging out in casinos, even once in a while robbing innocent, unsuspecting pedestrians, exercising his muscles rather than his brain. As Ah Long's business interests expanded and the gangs got bigger and stronger, Big Brother Lin sent more and more Yen home.

One of the new businesses Ah Long branched into was trafficking, its huge financial returns far outweighing its risks. Japan was in need of cheap Chinese labour, and for many people in Fujian the small, yet highly developed island was a man's wet dream, a status symbol, full of honey and cherry blossoms, and wads of foreign currency that could stretch hundreds of sea miles: all the way back home.

Bringing in people through borders was not easy or cheap, but with the grand promise of betterment in life, families were dying to invest in their joint future. Literally dying to, not figuratively.

For a while, Second Brother was one of many internal contacts for Ah Long's gang in Japan. A network quickly spread, like a spider, and was vigorously reinforced, reaching many levels of government agencies as well as spilling over onto the streets, both urban and rural.

Far too many people in Fujian looked up to Japan, a way out of their 'little muddy huts'. Second Brother worked his way through the ranks and prided himself as the guardian angel of those who desperately wanted to cross the East China Sea to the other side: Isle of Japan.

Brothers Lin did their 'basic training' for a few years, running the operation in their home province, with duties ranging from corrupting police officers to networking with a large chain of underground gangsters known as the Snakeheads, who specialised in organised crimes of all sorts, especially human trafficking. On 'graduation', Second Brother decided that it was time to join his Big Brother and Ah Long in the Land of the Rising Sun.

Once Second Brother was gone, it was only a matter of time before Third Brother would follow suit. That was what brothers did. They helped each other out, and they stuck together to 'help' others. In the meantime, the cash just rolled in, seemingly no end to it. And it was with their blessing that Old Madame Lin bought a rundown place in town and renovated it into a fancy massage parlour; Lin's Paradise was born, and in no time at all, flourished.

Ah Mi was not stupid. She may not have been blessed with many years of schooling or as many privileges as some of her peers, but she had a comprehensive education in hard knocks: the School of Life.

She hated what her brothers had done to her, and she hated what Old Lin did to her, and she hated what Madame Lin was doing to her. In one word: Hate. A strong, unrelenting, all-consuming feeling: sharpened by time and suspended in time. It was felt so keenly that it had become the most prevailing emotion she had harboured within her, nourished and grown stronger the longer she had lived with the Lin family.

Ah Mi was clever: more so than she was given credit for, or she was prepared to show. Nobody in the Lin family ever knew how much she really hated them or to what extent she would go, if ever she had the chance. All they cared about was to fuck her ruthlessly, without a second thought.

When Madame Lin was in her notoriously foul mood, Ah Mi was the one subjected to the cruelty and hurt the old woman distributed randomly. Young Ah Mi may not have elaborated how she felt to anyone; but deep down, she had swore repeatedly: *One day, I'll show you! Why? Because I have what it takes, both mentally and physically, and more importantly, because I am going to outlive you all.*

What does not break you only makes you stronger; she would prove that true, when her time came.

Chapter 19: Ah Ming: "Why Couldn't I Even Kill Myself?"

"NOW WANG MING, we've got another interpreter for you." Dr Raja smiles at me and extends his hand. "This is Miss Church."

Of course I notice her as soon as I am ushered into the room by the fat nurse. In a place full of guilao – foreign devils – another Chinese face is not easy to miss.

Even so, I can't be bothered acknowledging her presence, despite her friendly smile and warm greetings in my mother tongue. Well, not quite my mother tongue, but my Mandarin is competent enough to speak with other Chinese people: Northerners.

I have met quite a few Northerners, in recent years. They all have this superiority complex. Just because they speak the guilao language and dress in fashionable and smart outfits, they think they can talk down to me and dismiss me as subhuman. I know their type. They are everywhere in China.

Those living in big cities and speaking with posh accents always look down upon us peasants, the shitty bottom of the society. Only in the 1960s and 1970s was our status raised a peg or two. Chairman Mao sent those city intellectuals to be reeducated, *by us*. Can anyone imagine that? We – the uneducated, poor peasants – were to educate those who spent years practising their calligraphy and reciting Tang poems. It was beyond my comprehension, but that was indeed the case, as my father had proudly confirmed. Those days are long gone.

"How are you?" Dr Raja asks me, his usual opening.

Having understood him perfectly, I am tempted to answer, "I'm fine and thank you very much," in my not-so-perfect, spoken English, but I restrain myself and my tongue. What's the point?

I have no intention ever to communicate with him, or the nurses: why should I? My life is in their hands, and they have the authority to do whatever they like with me, without really giving a shit about me. Why should I trust them? Who in their right minds would trust a figure of authority? Not back home in China, and certainly not here in a foreign country.

I shoot a brief look at Dr Raja, the Indian man not much older than myself. Then I turn my attention towards the new interpreter. I notice that she is wearing a photo badge, which probably has her name on it, with some kind of balance symbols. The print is too small to be intelligible, not that I am really interested in who or what she is. She is here for a purpose, and I'll be damned if I'll waste this opportunity.

"Dr Raja is asking you how you are." She speaks in a very crispy and soothing voice, her Mandarin sounding like a presenter on TV, clear and without accent. Even if she does, I cannot detect it anyway. She does not look like someone from my home region, or Hong Kong: far too fair to be a Southerner. But I have no interest in her origin.

"I want sleeping pills." Words pour out of me. I cannot stop their flow now. "I can't sleep at night, and I haven't been able to sleep for a very long time, and it's killing me."

Yes, sleeping pills, that's all I want from these doctors. Every time I see the doctor, I ask him for more pills, and every time he refuses. I try with nurses too, but they always say the same to me: "You have to ask the doctor."

So I keep asking: doctor, nurses, other patients, their visitors or whoever they are. If you don't ask, you don't get anything: that much I have always known.

Maybe if I persist long enough, they will eventually relent, and give me what I ask for. As my father has said to me, passing on a little Chinese philosophy: Constant water drips can wear the stones.

******

For several months, Pearl made regular visits to Ward 34.

Not long ago, she had watched *One Flew over Cuckoo's Nest* on the Sky Classics Channel, and wondered if it had anything to do with the numbering of the ward. While there was nothing else in common between Jack Nicholson's character and 'the lunatic' asylum seeker, she recalled vividly her very first encounter with Wang Ming.

Mad, he was not. Desperate, no doubt he was. That was the essence of her first impressions of Wang Ming.

He was the same height as her – about 5 feet 4 inches – so for a male he was quite short, perhaps fitting perfectly in with the Western perceptions of a Chinese man. He was wearing an old, grey T-shirt, dark-blue, nylon tracksuit trousers, and a pair of worn-out trainers. It was the same outfit every time she saw him in. A question flashed across her mind: *Does he ever wash them?*

During one of their meetings, while waiting for the others, they chatted and she discovered that he owned no other items of clothing.

"These were given to me by a nurse," Wang Ming informed her, and followed this with a request.

"Can you buy me a pair of trainers? This pair is leaking now."

He lifted his feet in front of her, right under her nose, to prove that what he had said was true. The stinking smell of unwashed socks and worn-out trainers made her nearly sneeze; she grimaced.

Before she could reply, he pulled out a dirty, crumpled five-pound note from his pocket, trying to press it into her hand.

"I'll pay for it. Here is five pounds."

It was possible that he took Pearl's lack of immediate response as a sign of unwillingness to help.

"No." Pearl shook her head, refusing the money, pushing the note back into his hand. His request came as an unexpected surprise during a routine job, but there was no way that she would take his cash and became his 'shopping assistant'.

Instead, she smiled at him and said, "I'll get you something, I promise. You don't need to give me any money. I'll bring clothes and shoes next time."

On returning home that evening, Pearl raided Andrew's wardrobe.

Unlike her, whose clothes' racks were jammed with outfits for all seasons – many of which she never managed to wear – Andrew kept his self-assembled, IKEA units with significantly fewer items, hence making it easier to locate what she was looking for. Having been blessed with a decently paid job, and a big heart, he never hesitated in giving away unwanted clothes, and regularly updated his wardrobe with a clearing-out.

No difficulty in 'persuading' him to part with a couple of his shirts, T-shirts, and a few pair of trousers and jeans, complete with two pairs of last season's trainers; these items duly found their way to Ward 34 and Wang Ming at the following assessment meeting.

To her slight dismay, and then resignation, when she visited again Wang was still in his grey and dark-blue combination.

Perhaps he feels safe in these familiar clothes, when everything else seems strange and alien, she surmised.

Wang looked to be in his 40s, perhaps the same age as her. Pearl soon found out that he was actually ten years younger. Apart from his full head of youthful, black hair, his face was wrinkled, pale, and puffy, making his small eyes even smaller. During her first few visits, he was always showing off the nasty scar on his potbelly. It was a dark-coloured cross, healed from a dried, bloody, messy cut, against his pale skin, prominent and quite unnerving for those with a weak nerve.

Is he showing it to disgust people or to win sympathy? She was not sure, but his eagerness to display it to anyone and everyone shocked her.

Asked by Doctor Raja how he was, Wang complained: "I cannot sleep at all. I want more sleeping pills."

There he went again. This scenario was almost like a faulty CD, playing the same parts repeatedly, with Wang requesting more sleeping tablets, and the doc refusing to budge.

"You've already been given the maximum dose, and I cannot give you any more. That's it: end of story."

Dutifully, Pearl interpreted it word for word every time, adding emphasis to her tone and facial expression, all to no avail. Wang made the same demand every single time. It had occurred to her that perhaps she could make a tape-recording of what Wang would say so the doctor could just play it back the next time. It would save her time to travel, and the NHS interpreting bills. The thought did amuse her, in a strange way.

To monitor his situation, regular blood tests were required, only to be consistently declined by him.

When he was discovered as having diabetes, he was asked to inject insulin, which was expensive but absolutely necessary for his condition. However, whatever his reasons, Wang maintained a staunchly uncooperative attitude towards the staff.

"He is so difficult," Peter complained to Pearl.

"If he wants something, he wants it right now. Then he would refuse to have blood tests, and nobody could get him to do it." There was more than a hint of resignation in Peter's report, as he shrug his shoulders slightly.

Stubborn and incomprehensible, the staff maintained. For someone who was eager to take his own life and cut himself up in public, he was unwilling to give up tiny drops of his blood for tests for his own good.

So a new task for the day: going for Wang's blood.

"You will have your blood back soon enough," Pearl reassured him.

"Believe me. It's true." She tried convincing him the best she could. "My husband is a regular blood donor."

His look said that he was still suspicious, but he nodded eventually.

It was during these visits that Pearl began to win a little trust, picking up a few strands of his life story: not a life he had desired, yet he was unable to escape from it. Full of sympathy, and from the scattered bits and pieces of anecdotes that he had shared with her, she pieced together the motivations behind his various attempts to relieve himself from his life: or rather, the misery and suffering of it.

"What's the point for me to live like this? I tried to kill myself time and again. I couldn't even kill myself. What's my use?"

His said it, spelt it out, his face bland and expressionless, his voice flat, underlining traces of despair.

His words and his face remained in Pearl's mind long after she returned home, making her despondent and sad: her heart heavy with sorrow. Determined to get distracted and dispel unwanted images of Wang Ming and his woes, she went online and searched on foreign holidays.

When Andrew got home and asked how she was, she did not reply.

Chapter 20: From Gorbals to an SAS Man

GROWING UP IN Glasgow was tough, especially if you came from the wrong side of town, as it was for Jack Gordon.

Situated on the South Bank of River Clyde, Gorbals had long had a reputation for being gritty and rough. Efforts were made by the Strathclyde Regional Council to clear slum tenements, but with heavy job losses after the shipping industry collapsed, and other industrial restructuring and shifting, many old factories and buildings fell into disrepair and ruin. New, high-rise towers built to replace the old, outdated, and crowded housing in the 1960s did little to improve the general living conditions of the area. Ask anyone who has lived in, or has any knowledge about, Glasgow: Gorbals would be a place to avoid, for their own good. What would they find when there was concentrated poverty and lack of employment? The short answer: high rates of crime. Only those who had managed to advance in education and thus improved their economic status were able leave it behind and seek better prospects elsewhere.

Jack was the youngest of seven, and the only boy, born to his Irish-immigrant father and Scottish mother,. By the time he was born, in October of 1970, his eldest sister was old enough to get married. Being Catholic, Irish, and poor, contraception was an alien concept back then in Scotland, as it was the case in many other parts of the world. Partly due to his father's love for alcohol, his mother was regularly subjected to varying degrees of violence, depending on the old man's state of sobriety.

With the collapse of the shipping industry in 1969, Jack's father lost his living and was unable to hold on to another steady job. With the simultaneous decline in the other heavy industries, and coal mines, steelworks, and engine factories all going out of business one after another in quick succession, it was a small miracle when he found work at all, so the little benefit money had to stretch a very long way in the Gordon household.

Although Jack wasn't aware of it at the time, the 1970s and early 1980s were the darkest periods in modern history for the City of Glasgow, when the mass unemployment and urban decay resulted in streets full of violence and paved with danger. Gangs thrived and crimes were prevalent. With no escape from the cruel reality of the time, young Jack had his own share of street fights during his school days. His saving grace had been an obsession with playing sports. He was a fast runner and a first-class swimmer, but he especially loved football. He harboured a dream of playing for his beloved team Celtic, not far from where he lived with his large family.

By the age of 16, when he was about to finish secondary school and had failed to be picked by the professional football scouts, he had come to accept that he was not going to play professionally. He left school and spent a year working at different temping jobs, before finally, being physically fit and fuelled by his desire to get away from his home and family, he signed up for the Army. He knew that if he didn't, he would end up bashing his old man to death one day, or getting sucked into the bad crowds that his good sense had warned him to avoid. Despite its gradual recovery from its economic pit in the middle of the 1980s, Glasgow did not have much to offer to ambitious young lads like Jack.

Jack set his sights high and focused on the Special Air Service, which had earned a widely recognized reputation after its mission of assaulting the Iranian Embassy in London, rescuing the hostages in 1980. Equipped with an underlying determination to better himself, Jack wanted a piece of the action; it was burning in his Irish/Scottish veins like fire. The Army – especially the SAS – became his new dream, shining on the top spot like a silver star.

Luckily for Jack, he found his calling this time. His application to the Army proved a better shot after he passed each of their stages of selection: from paper application, the initial interview with Army Careers Adviser, and through the subsequent medical report and potential soldier tests. He was on his way, up and out.

With his career prospect bright and shining, Jack decided to settle down, sorting out his affairs of the heart at the same time. In the summer of 1988, two months before Jack turned 18, he married his school sweetheart Moira in a small church wedding in the Gorbals. Independent Scottish law allowed persons of 17 and over to marry legally. Had he lived across the border, he would have had to wait a little longer to tie the knot.

Many soldiers did the same, tying the knot with their honey birds at home before joining in. It was not uncommon to get married young; after all, his mam and dad did the same at more or less that age. Jack, however, had no idea back then that the day he got hitched was the day when Pearl Zhang landed in the United Kingdom, or that some twenty-odd years later he would meet this stranger from afar and begin a passionate affair.

During his one-week honeymoon, he went trekking with his new bride in his beloved Scottish highlands. They climbed Munros during the day and made camp at night. They didn't have much money, so Moira would continue to live with her family. She trained to be a nurse as Jack made his way to Pirbright.

Jack's military career kick-started following a vigorous, 14-week training, that would serve him well in the years to come. Apart from the basic competence – how to operate in the field – he was taught the core values of the British Army: courage, discipline, integrity, loyalty, commitment, and respect for others.

The second phase of training was more specialised and challenging and, at the same time, more enjoyable and satisfying. He went to the School of Army Aviation in Middle Wallop, once base for the Royal Air Force during the Second World War and famed for aiding the Allies' landing in 1944. It was there that Jack Gordon learned to fly.

When Jack joined his regiment, stationed in Germany, it was the height of the so-called "Troubles" in Northern Ireland. The IRA was targeting British army personnel in Germany. During the car-bomb attack in 1989, many West Germans and British were hurt. Other attacks had resulted in the deaths and injuries of both soldiers and civilians. During one bomb attack on his base, several of his mates were injured, including himself. The force of the blast from the explosives was so great that extensive damage was caused to the cars and nearby buildings. He was treated for shock and minor cuts from flying glass.

After a three-year stint in Germany, Jack's dream of joining the SAS seemed attainable. After all, all members within the British Army were eligible, as long as they could pass the vigorous selection. Jack had an advantage – the majority of SAS came from airborne forces.

Jack enrolled and participated in the SAS summer selection in 1992, since his application was too late for the annual winter selection at the end of 1991. The selection lasted five weeks and took place in Sennybridge in Mid Wales, where the Ministry of Defence owned a large area of land for training purposes.

Among the 200 or so candidates, Jack excelled in the first round, where they were required to march across the country against the clock. Being a keen runner, and having kept up with his running regime while in Germany, had no doubt served him well. A 14-mile run, carrying full equipment, while scaling and descending Pen Y Fan – the highest peak in South Wales – was no easy feat; certainly it was not for wimps, especially in the summer heat. Jack accomplished it in just under four hours. After that, all he and others had to do was to run another four miles and swim for two miles within 90 minutes. No wonder only 15 percent or so of the candidates made it through each time.

On successful completion of his endurance test in the Hill phase, Jack was flown to Malaysia for the follow up. Jungle time!

Jack didn't like the humidity but welcomed its cooling showers, which came pouring down like cats and dogs, then stopped just as suddenly, leaving a clear, blue sky and refreshed air. He fell in love with the amazing variety of yummy food Malaysia had to offer. Well, not the extensive gourmet food available from KL to Penang, but what he was fed at the Army training base and during occasional outings in between his training. He longed to be a tourist in the tropical, Southeast Asian country, so he could more fully explore its intriguing culture, the rich mix of ethnicity and different religions, but as a trainee he was exposed to the full, unforgiving nature of the jungle. Jack learnt how to navigate through the forests, and how to survive in harsh conditions. After all, our ancestors had found themselves faced with all kinds of perils in the wild: hunted and being hunted. The human race had not simply survived, but had thrived.

Time moved forward relentlessly. As a modern, urban-living creature, Jack had to go back in time and pick up the skills his ancestors had possessed and perfected: skills that became insignificant and underused through centuries of civilisation and progress. Again, Jack's speed on his feet and his natural, quick response gave him an edge in successfully completing the test, where both agile movement and patrol formation were vital.

After returning to England, Jack was put through more vigorous training, some of which he had never seen before. He was taught to develop battle plans and to participate in various combat exercises, with a primary focus on survival, such as how to escape and evade recapture.

Years later, Jack would still vividly picture his young self: just under 22 years old, dressed in an old WWII uniform and carrying a small tin of survival equipment, setting off at dawn and arriving at his destination starved and thirsty, exhausted inside and out, but alive with a mighty sense of relief, like a cool dip in the water after a long day of toil in the sun and heat, a physical and mental test to the extreme: something he had never known.

Most SAS candidates, if they made it that far, found the final part of the assessment the hardest: RTI, Resistance to Interrogation lasted 36 long hours. Jack was no exception. It was sheer hell, no other word for it. On coming out of that gruelling ordeal, he said a prayer, even though he had not been to church for years. *Dear God, please protect me from ever being subjected to that kind of torture.*

His persistence and endurance during the gruelling assessment and training paid off. Jack got his wish – only 28 from his group succeeded, and he became one of the true, special ones.

A new SAS man in the British Army; and also, in that year, Jack became a father for the first time.

Chapter 21: A Rude Wakening for Ah Fang

THE NIGHT AFTER I arrived in England, I was in too much of a shock to sleep. The knowledge that nobody could save me was hovering above my head, gripping my heart tightly and refusing to let go. The fact that I was in a foreign land where I had no friends and family was one thing. More importantly, the people who had me smuggled through the borders: what did they want from me? What's going to happen to me?

My mind was in so much turmoil that it hurt to think what was to come: *Is there any way to run away from what's in store for me? Can I defy the "gang" who brought me here, or am I just another unknown quantity who should accept my fate and do as I am told? If I run away, where can I go? In a country like UK, is there a safe haven for an illegal entrant like me?*

For the briefest moment, the unknown scared me: a deeply unsettling feeling I had never known till then. Only one thing I knew for sure: I had no one to depend upon from then on, and I had to do everything for myself. Think carefully. Act wisely. Perhaps more so than my years of experience had taught me. I told myself that I couldn't stay scared and I must do something to protect myself. But what?

I did not know much English, except a few words I picked up at school, but no matter. I was young and full of life, so I kicked my fear out of me that night, determined to put up a fight. I had harboured hopes and dreams, and I certainly did not expect to spend my precious youth being exploited by dirty men. Oh, *no*, that was definitely not the life I had in mind; not in a million years.

Despite what had happened since my kidnap, I was unprepared for what lay ahead of me. I had no idea what steps to take to save my skin or find a safe space. I had no money, no one I could call for help. Even if I could get away from the clutches of my kidnappers, I could not get very far. I knew that.

Lying quietly on the top bunk, my head was spinning, as if on a roller coaster. Aunty Hua was sleeping below me, any tiny movement from her piercing through the mattress between us, and the girls were on the bunk beds next to mine or on the other side of our room; I could hear one of them snoring loudly enough to wake up the dead. I heard another girl turning and tossing, her bed making creaking noises.

Outside, there were chattering and flushing water from the toilet every half an hour or so. Sometimes I heard footsteps coming up or going down the stairs, and occasional shouting in dialects and languages foreign to my ears. How anyone could sleep in such an environment was beyond me, but somewhere in the back of my mind I knew that, given time, I would have to. Human beings are adaptable: especially us Chinese people. When we realise that there is nothing we can do to change the circumstances, we change ourselves.

Darkness enveloped me like blanket as I lay awake for what seemed ages, my thinking disturbed by the happenings in the mad household. I did not have a watch, so I had no idea how long I had been lying there wide eyed, staring at the ceiling; a small window let through a sliver of natural light from the night sky and I wished I could go out and watch the stars, as I had done so many times before while still in China. I started to really miss my home, even the times when my father scolded me severely and my mother's constant nagging and pleading for me to behave. Why did I not listen to them? Had I been a good and dutiful girl, I would still be there, going to school and returning home to hot meals every day.

Before my thoughts went any further, allowing bitter regrets and shame to tear my heart to pieces, I stopped myself. *There is absolutely no point savouring those days gone by,* I reminded myself. *It is too late!* Still, the next minute my thoughts returned, and images of my mates back home came to haunt me. God that seemed so long ago, when I roamed the streets of Changle, hanging out with Lily, Ah Qing, Ah Hua, and Ah Gang. We had so much fun, playing truancy, and sharing food we stole from unsuspecting street vendors. I wondered where they were now. Were they also kidnapped by snakeheads and taken overseas as they did to me? Perhaps not. I hoped not anyway.

After what seemed forever, I eventually drifted into a shallow sleep, troubled by jumbled dreams where my parents and my gang mates from back home came and went, like flashing images. I didn't understand why they didn't speak to me – as if I didn't exist – even after I tried talking to them. Were they upset that I left without saying good-bye?

Noises in both my room and outside woke me up. It took me only a second to realise where I was and that I had been dreaming.

"Get up, Little Sister, time for breakfast." I heard Auntie Hua's voice and knew she was addressing me. Other girls in the room were already up and I heard water flushing, voices shouting, and footsteps up and down the squeaking stairs, just like the night before but even noisier. But in the morning light, it seemed almost a cheery atmosphere. I quickly sat up and climbed down.

I had slept in exactly the same clothes I had on the day before. There was nothing to change into either.

I made a mental note that I needed to make money soon, and all of a sudden memories of my wardrobe back home flooded back. When my mother used to buy me nice dresses, I threw them at her. "What kind of clothes are they? Are you fashion-blind? They are too ugly and untrendy; even dogs won't wear them. Take them back to the shops."

Why did I do that to her? I was fully aware that no Chinese shops would accept returns. Even if I did not like her dressing me like a good girl with pretty girlie dresses, why didn't I just tell her to buy me ripped jeans and tight T-shirts? Instead I just shouted at her with pathetic accusations and used it as excuse to throw tantrums.

How I wish that I could turn back time and take back all the hurtful words I spat at my parents from my foul mouth. How I would love to be able to wear some of these bright-coloured, cheerful summer dresses my mother had picked for me. I never even thanked her, not once.

A step behind, I followed Auntie Hua downstairs to the first floor, passing two girls who were coming up. They'd had their fill and were now getting ready for whatever they were supposed to do. I considered my own situation and decided to watch and see if there was a chance of getting out without being noticed.

In the kitchen-plus-dining room there were four others, three of them sitting around the table, which would have served many meals and was covered with a worn, plastic table cover. I saw grease everywhere: on the walls, on the cookers, and even on the door and windowpanes. I followed Auntie Hua and waited for the girl, who was standing by a big pot of thin, plain, rice porridge. Auntie Hua passed me a plastic bowl; I helped myself to fill it up and carried it to the table.

Two of the girls sitting opposite me were conducting a conversation in an unknown language, so I turned my attention to the girl who looked Chinese, and who had taken a seat at the far corner with her bowl and was now slurping down her breakfast, helping herself to pickles and what looked like leftovers from the night before on the table.

She noticed my curiosity towards her and gave me a crooked smile. Before I could say anything, I heard Auntie Hua. "Pinko, have you got your ticket for today?"

"Yes." Pinko's face turned slightly pink, reflecting the pink T-shirt she was wearing. It had some English writing on it, which I didn't understand fully at the time. Only later, after my English got better and I got to know Pinko, did I recognise what was printed on her chest: Night Is Calling, Join Me Baby.

"Where are you off to?" Auntie Hua queried again.

"Leicester, somewhere near there anyway. So my train ticket says," replied Pinko, casting curious glances at me, probably wondering if I knew what they were talking about. Then she addressed me: "Are you new? You look new to me."

Before I could speak, Auntie Hua replied on my behalf: "She just arrived last night. But she is part of us now, aren't you?" She turned her face towards me.

My nodding in response to Pinko's question halted; all of a sudden I didn't know if I should continue the nod or shake my head instead. *What does she mean by 'part of us'?*

Auntie Hua didn't elaborate, nor did she use the word 'prostitute' – the Chinese colloquial 'chickens', as we call them back home in China – yet I was smart enough to work out what they did for a living. I had no idea why a petite, pretty girl like Pinko was here.

Auntie Hua was different. She had been chatty and shared her life story with me the night before.

"I have two children in China, one attending university and the other still in high school," she had confided, even though I did not probe. She had found a willing listener and was in the mood to talk.

"My husband disappeared a few years ago after he went overseas. I don't even know which country he ended up in; that bastard just vanished without trace. We had to borrow more money to pay for my passage to Europe.I have been working nonstop since my arrival in the UK, scraping and doing different casual jobs in different parts of the country. If I carry on for another year or so, I'd be able to pay off all my debts and even save a bit for my kids to finish their education."

Oh God. Thankfully I am not as desperate as her.

I banished the thought quickly enough. My fate was no different from hers after all.

I lowered my head to my bowl of tasteless congee, which had cooled down, and quickly finished it off in a few big gulps before getting up from my seat.

"I think I should go out for a walk and see what's out there," I said to no one in particular, simply making a statement of my intention.

"No, no, no," Auntie Hua repeated quickly, more sternly than she had spoken to me until then and shaking her head vehemently at the same time.

"Why not?" I challenged her loudly, fear suddenly registering in my brain and transmitting to my croaky voice.

"You can't go anywhere, unless you're told to do so. Ah Tai will come soon, and then he'll tell you what you should and shouldn't do. I'm with you at all times until he arrives."

I stared at her, my eyes widening with disbelief. My caretaker had all of a sudden morphed into my jailor. *Can this really be happening to me?*

Chapter 22: The Interpreter and The Immigrant

IN THE CHURCH household, Pearl was the designated chef most of the time. Food, to a Chinese stomach, seemed far more important than to an average English man.

"For me, food is just fuel," Andrew had repeatedly said to his wife. "Unlike you; you dream about food," he had teased her, in good humour.

"Well, at least I don't raid the cupboard as soon as I arrive at home." She felt the need to defend her healthy obsession with her diet. "I eat proper food, not junk."

"Course you do, my dear," Andrew conceded. "To be honest, I never had much fruit till I met you."

That much was true. Apart from an apple once in a while, and perhaps bananas, Andrew's fruit intake was limited. Now their large fruit bowl was filled with grapes, mangos, pineapples, peaches, kiwis, and many other seasonal varieties like cherries and sharon fruit.

"The only fruit I shall absolutely not eat is durian. I was force-fed one once in Malaysia and it smelt like shit. Stinking. No kidding." His facial expression emphasised his distaste for that tropical fruit, much loved by the local people in the Southeast Asia.

"I believe you." Pearl smiled. She had seen durians being sold in Chinese supermarkets; as adventurous as she was where food was concerned, she had not ventured so far as to consume that particular fruit. Everyone had a limit to how far they would go. If Andrew said that durians were a no-go area, she trusted his judgement. After all, she would not want her kitchen to be filled with an unwelcome smell. Spices in the air were what she really, really wanted.

Earlier that afternoon, Pearl had made a special trip to Wing Yip, her usual Chinese supermarket, which was a short three miles away from her home. She picked her way through rows and rows of Asian offerings: from fresh, exotic fruit flown in from Malaysia, to the local fishermen's corner selling fresh seafood – formerly residents of the North Sea – soon to be seafood lovers' potential yummy dinner. The colourful displays included various Indian spices and sweet Chinese snacks.

Her monthly outing to this Oriental special hangout was fun and purposeful. She was there for a simple mission: getting the essential ingredients for dinner that night. In that case, it was a Chinese green vegetable called jiucai – a cross between leeks and chives – and wrapping cases for dumplings.

Jiucai Pork Dumplings, combined with her signature spicy sauce, had become a regular diet in the Church household and a finest treat in Andrew's staunch point of view. Northern Dumplings, more often labelled as Beijing dumplings, were popular among the Chinese people everywhere. It was quite possible that they had once tickled Marco Polo's taste buds and that as a result, after he had returned to Italy, he had instructed his chef to create ravioli for him especially. At least, that was what Pearl and her husband agreed upon while sampling the Italian version during one of their trips to Tuscany.

Pearl's special dumplings had all the usual ingredients: lean pork mince mixed with fresh jiucai, creating a delicious, delightful filling. The sharp, fragrant smell and strong taste of the green vegetable went perfectly well with red meat: a rich but healthy combination. To make them stick together, Pearl added an egg, a few drops of sesame oil, and then her unique, secret touch: her Sichuan pepper powder, fresh ginger and chilli, finely chopped into the mix.

Over time, the husband and wife team had developed another trick to make this special meal a successful joint venture and smooth production line.

To start with, Pearl made her special meat-vegetable fillings, wrapping them in pastry cases formed into beautiful shapes and lining them up in the tray. Andrew took over from then onwards, bringing the water to a boil in a big pot and then adding dumplings to the pot to cook until they surfaced to the top of the boiling water, just right for his wife to consume.

Andrew liked it slightly differently. He fished out a dozen or so boiled dumplings and transferred them to the pan on the cooker next to the pot. With a drop of sunflower oil, Andrew shallow-fried the dumplings. The end result: a divine dish, with a soft, tasty mixture inside and crispy, golden-brown pastry outside, accompanied by the spicy sauce Pearl had prepared, with soy sauce, vinegar, spring onions, corianders, more chilli, and Sichuan pepper. Heavenly!

"Great effort, Zhenzhu. 8 out of 10." Andrew reached out his hand and shook that of his wife across the dinner table, displaying a satisfied smile after having had a delicious fill of one of his favourite Chinese foods, the pot sticker – as the Chinese called the fried dumpling.

In acknowledging his appreciation – or rather, his gastronomic satisfaction – he had developed a rating system used after consuming it to his heart's content. 8 out of 10, coming from a harsh critic like him, was a huge compliment. He almost never rated anything food-related higher than that.

"Now, time to work off some of those calories." Andrew patted his belly and went to the back garden.

Pearl – after finishing washing up and putting everything away – moved on to the kitchen table to read her paper.

"I'd like to go and watch *The Interpreter*. It's coming out this Friday," she called out, even louder than usual, from inside the French window. *I need something fun to distract me from the not-so-pleasant part of my job.*

Andrew, always the keen gardener, was at the far end of their back garden. It was not big enough for his taste, but was sufficient to grow his beloved flowers and plants, among them a selection of roses, of different colours and shapes (his favourite type was called China Town, a scented, yellow variety), hydrangeas, clematis, azalea, and even a cherry tree, which he had planted at the far corner when they first moved into this townhouse a few years before.

The grass had steadily grown following the constant mix of sunshine, rain showers, and downpours in recent weeks, and it demanded immediate attention. Andrew was in his element, trimming branches, watering plants, and cutting grass.

Despite the booming noise from the lawn mower, Andrew sensed that he was being spoken to. He switched off the machine and looked up across the garden. He wiped the tiny beads of sweat from his forehead, and raised his voice. "What did you say, Pearl? I didn't hear you."

There she was, scanning through the *Times* newspaper, which Andrew purchased on a daily basis. Over the years they had lived together, he had converted her from an occasional *Daily Mail* reader to a habitual *Times* devotee. "You were obviously not used to reading papers when growing up in China," had been one of his many insightful comments. Andrew had a habit of analysing everything, and could not help but draw conclusions from whatever he had seen, read, or observed. To give him his due, his comments were usually spot-on, more accurate than Pearl was prepared to admit.

"If you'd known the kind of papers we were allowed to read, you wouldn't have wanted to read them either," Pearl had retorted, feigning offence, and dispelling unwanted memories of the times gone by when she had to copy large chunks of literature from the Chinese official newspapers to demonstrate loyalty to Chairman Mao and the Communist Party, or to denounce whichever Rightist or Leftist was being 'struggled against' in the nonstop political upheavals, especially during the Cultural Revolution.

"Yes," Pearl looked up, a wee smile spreading across her face. "I was just suggesting that we go to cinema this weekend, to watch *The Interpreter.*"

"Who's in it?"

"Nicole Kidman and Sean Penn. She's an interpreter for the UN, and he's a …"

"Stop right there." Andrew raised his hand. "Don't tell me anymore."

So typical of him, not interested in learning what would happen at the end of the story, be it a film or a book. "What's the bloody point?" Andrew, always the one to turn off the TV before the preview of the next episode was shown, complained bitterly. "Why do they assume that we'd want to know what happens next *now* and spoil it for us?"

"Some people do." Pearl offered an alternative. She did not take to heart such petty matters as easily as her husband. Presented with a different view, Pearl would take it on board and give it a thought before making up her mind about it. With years of practice and tireless academic research training, she prided herself as being relatively understanding and open-minded. It was not in her nature to criticise without reason. She had come to see that regular and constant critique was perhaps a typical British habit, nurtured by their education from a young age; or perhaps it was more simply Andrew's family's trait? As a foreigner – and hence categorically an outsider – she was prone to notice such characteristics, but she knew better than to point it out to Andrew every single time. *Men can be such sensitive creatures.* She smiled. Andrew did not like to be contradicted too often.

"Guess that's a date then. After all, I live with an interpreter, and let's see what Hollywood makes of this career of yours." With that, Andrew turned his lawn mower back on to full power.

******

"Tell him to give me sleeping pills," Ah Ming said to Pearl, who was standing between Dr Raja and him. She had just arrived minutes ago for another one of her regular visits to Ward 34.

"Doctor." Pearl turned to the man in charge of Wang Ming's medication and care. "He's requesting more sleeping pills from you."

"No," The doc replied, his voice firm. "Mr Wang, We have talked about this before, and I've told you the same thing. You're already on the maximum dosage, and I can't possibly give you any more."

Pearl translated what was said between the patient and the doctor, the same conversation, with little variation, one demanding, the other refusing.

During their very first meeting with Dr Raja and the nurses, even before Wang Ming was introduced, Pearl had understood why Wang Ming wanted more sleeping pills. Among the Chinese – especially among the more ignorant and uneducated – swallowing those white tablets was one of the most popular ways of killing themselves: an overdose. There must be dozens of more effective – or even foolproof – methods of suicide, but hell no; obtaining sleeping pills was seen as an easy option, not as messy as some, combined with perhaps the unwarranted reputation of less suffering in the dying process.

She was right on as Wang Ming later confirmed it. "The first time I tried to commit suicide in China, I took many sleeping pills. No good."

Why? The automatic question was on the tip of her tongue and nearly burst out there and then. She suppressed the temptation to probe.

"How many times has he attempted suicide?" The nurses on the ward had been curious, and one of them had directed the question to their interpreter. "We could not ask him directly. We only know what's recorded when he was transferred to our ward."

"Do you want me to ask him?" Pearl enquired.

"Yes, if you can. I don't think that he will tell us, but maybe he'll talk to you. You are in a better position to ask questions and receive answers."

"I guess so. Perhaps once I get to know him a bit better, I'll ask him."

"Thank you. We think he likes you. We had a couple of interpreters before, and he simply refused to talk to them. We don't know why. It's quite a relief for us all that he seems to respond to you."

"That's good. I'll try and talk to him, and see if I can find out a bit more for you."

Pearl had no idea why Wang Ming did not establish any rapport with the previous interpreters before her, but she did have an inkling why he had refused to communicate with the staff there. Most Chinese people bore an instinctive mistrust of foreigners yet, ridiculous or irrational as it may sound, they place their trust on their fellow countrymen or women for no other reason than the fact that they share the same culture.

She was proved right again in her assumptions.

"My parents are dead. My wife had divorced me, and she had custody of our daughter. How can I ever go back? I'd rather be dead than going back," he had said to her as a matter of fact. Without Pearl pressing him, Ah Ming somehow decided to open up to her, shedding a sliver of light on his life and what led him from the South of China to the middle of nowhere in the United Kingdom.

It was the thought of having to go back to China that had driven him into attempting suicide again, twice, before he was admitted into the psychiatric hospital.

Even though she did not have the heart to probe as to why he had to take such drastic measures, common sense told her that too much unbearable misery and suffering could prey on vulnerable people and their minds. While many of us would face their challenges, others struggled to cope and ended up cracking. Who was she to judge?

After his first attempt came inevitably the second and third, none successful. Wang had climbed to the second floor and jumped. It must have hurt; Pearl grimaced at the thought. Well, he lived to tell the tale, and he wasn't even limping.

What made you want to kill yourself after arriving in the UK? After all the unimaginable hardships on the way, having paid a fortune to the gang masters, surely you would want a new life, and to build a future here?

"A restaurant took me on as a kitchen assistant; I was paid £200 a week, working six days and a minimum of twelve hours each day. It was damn hard and a drag. Despite having my food and rent free, I did not earn enough.

"The letters from my family kept pouring through the door, asking for more money. The debts were mounting, snowballing by the day: especially the high-interest loans from loan sharks. They harassed my family, giving them no peace until the debt was cleared. I was their only hope."

Pearl rarely spoke when Wang Ming talked. Being a good listener was a blessing for her. It served her well over the years, making her trusted friends and winning confidantes. As Wang Ming rambled on, Pearl painted a series of pictures in her head, one frame after another, imagining a life that was not just Ah Ming's but that of many Chinese immigrants.

At two o'clock in the morning, after the restaurant was cleaned and shut, where could those poor bachelor chefs and kitchen helpers go? Few interesting places were open at that ungodly hour: except casinos. Like many in his shoes, Wang allowed himself to be sucked in by the get-rich-quick scheme. Where else would he find the amount of money he was expected to send home? How wonderful would it be if he could double, triple, or multiply by ten what he had made? How wonderful indeed!

It did not take long; he lost all his earnings, and more. He borrowed; soon it was all gone and, faster than ever, he found himself penniless and friendless. He was then fired and subsequently found himself chased by debtors who used to be his gambling soul mates. In his paranoia, he suspected that the Chinese mafia was chasing after him everywhere he turned to look. He woke up at night, caught in his unrelenting nightmares, and could no longer go back to sleep. Peace of mind became evasive and out of reach; sleepless nights and nightmares were his constant companions.

Without speaking English, he could not even go to the chemists to buy sleeping pills for himself. To complicate matters, most serious medication needed prescriptions from doctors and, as an illegal, he did not have a GP – General Practitioner – nearby like all normal UK residents would have. After one too many sleepless nights, Wang Ming wandered to the streets. *If I had to die a nasty death, so be it.* He was desperate.

Those in despair could not think straight and did the most stupid things. Wang was no exception.

On a busy London road, during broad daylight, he threw himself in front of a moving car. The driver was sober and alert, and his brakes worked. The sudden noise of the car tyres squealing, and his car nearly being swirled around, irritated the driver no end.

"You fucking, stupid Chink. Are you fucking blind, or you want to fucking kill yourself? You stupid, fucking idiot." The man was furious, tooted his horn and swore at the top of his voice.

Wang Ming stared back at the driver, his eyes vacant, his face expressionless. The driver was fuming that a bloody foreigner had nearly involved him in a fatal accident. It most definitely had spoilt his mood for the rest of that miserable day. He continued his swearing – winding down his window and raising his two middle fingers – as he watched the Chinese man being pulled back to the pavement, like a robot, by another pedestrian behind him.

Witnesses at the scene started speaking to Wang Ming, and an old lady patted his shoulder: "Young man, you should really take more care. Those people drive like maniacs." She shook her head as the driver pressed his gas hard, further testing his horn, just to make a point. Nobody realised that Wang Ming did it intentionally; he wanted it all to end, there and then. Was it a good omen or bad luck? His death wish was denied, yet again.

Maybe somewhere in his subconsciousness, he did not really want to bid farewell to this world just yet; Pearl could not help pondering. If people truly wanted to kill themselves, they would have succeeded. Wang could have jumped from the twentieth floor, not the second, for instance. Or perhaps he could throw himself into a raging river, or from a steep sea cliff, rather than in front of a car with an alert driver in broad daylight. Even when he cut himself open with a knife, he could have aimed better at his heart or stabbed a bit harder and deeper. Maybe it was his survival instinct that had kept him alive. Maybe all his attempts were cries for help. But who could help him?

She knew she couldn't. Her help would not be significant enough nor by any means sufficient. All she could do was to help him to communicate a little better, and at that not even to the point of fully understanding what was really going on, because comprehension did not come from accurate translation or interpretation alone; it came from the mind and the heart, an ability to reason and a willingness to accept whatever differences our cultures and languages have created. Wang was beyond that. He could not understand his fate: "Why couldn't I even kill myself?"

Pearl was lost for words. What possible reply could she give to that question?

Neither was Wang Ming expecting an answer from her, or anyone else. It was more a question directed at himself, his inability to get rid of his misery, which had possessed him, not letting him go, making him suffer without a way out. If he was blaming anyone at all, it was his fate, all his own fault.

The consultation session that day with Doctor Raja and the nurses lasted ten minutes. When Wang Ming repeatedly demanded for sleeping pills, he was turned down an umpteenth time. "I told you so," obviously made no impact on Wang.

"Dr Raja," Pearl addressed the doctor as he got up to leave, no doubt seeing other mental patients who were in his care. "I'd like to let you know that I am taking my annual holiday in a week's time. I'll be gone for three weeks."

"Lucky you." The kind doctor smiled. "Where are you jetting off to?"

"Nothing exotic, just China. I'm visiting family there." She smiled back. "I can give the nurse the contact detail of a colleague. If you need anyone during my absence, you can contact her."

"Wonderful, Dr Church. Thank you. You've been a great help. I think we'll probably wait for you to come back." He offered his hand and shook hers firmly, a sure sign of his appreciation.

It was a good time to travel to China, when the weather was mild: neither too cold, nor too hot. She had been visiting Chengdu and Chongqing regularly for the past few years, especially since her father's health had been increasingly deteriorating. Every time she returned to Sichuan, she thought that it might be the last time she would see him alive.

Before she left, she gave the nurse the contact details of Mrs Wong, one of her trusted colleagues. "Just in case that you need an interpreter, in an emergency or something."

When she had a moment earlier with Wang, she had mentioned her imminent absence. She sensed that even though he never said anything, he seemed to look forward to their meeting every time. After all, it was the only time he had someone who could speak his language, even though she was a far cry from his world.

Poor man, he has lost contact with all his family and relatives in China. Although my parents are elderly and faraway, at least, I can still see them from time to time. Life is not fair, and I should definitely count my blessings.

Chapter 23: Jack in Belfast

IT WAS DARK and wet, with that typical, cool, Irish drizzle, misty, windy, and chilly.

Jack knew that it was going to be a long night. Despite the fact it was only early October, the air was filled with a chill and the rain on his face was cold and slippery, further diminishing visibility. He looked around and could just about make out one of his teammates – Jimmy – some distance away, keeping his watch to the right and back. Jack was crouched down, his hands checking again that the weapons he carried were still in place even though the weight had not lessened: growing heavier instead as time ticked by. He waited, holding his breath as he focused his watchful eyes on the farmhouse only several hundred metres from him. He was equipped with night-vision binoculars, which he had pointed towards the narrow entrance at the front. His duty was to keep his surveillance on the front and left side.

After finishing his SAS training in the summer of 1992, he was granted a short leave to visit his growing family. The moment he saw his new daughter, Heather, she had him - he fell in love with that sweet bundle instantly and permanently. She took after him, with her auburn, curly hair and hazel eyes. He had no idea what it would be like to be a father but, as soon as he locked his eyes on his wee girl, he knew that he would guard her, protect her from any harm, and love her always as only a father could.

Duty called; his first assignment was to cross the Irish Sea and go south of the border. Two nights before, Jack and his squad of five were flown in from Loch Lomond just outside Glasgow. Their orders were clear: to be dropped into a secure zone and mount a deadly attack on a location where the IRA was suspected of keeping the arms they had recently secured from the Libyans and their dictator Gaddafi.

Before the mission, Jack and his teammates were briefed at one of their bases in England, and given an introduction to SAS's involvement in Northern Ireland and the kind of losses they had subjected the IRA to in recent years. Back in 1987, when the IRA members attacked and tried to destroy Loughgall police station, SAS men were sent in to ambush the enemy. IRA ended up losing eight of their fierce fighters. Since then, SAS had added more victories to its glorious history and killed more IRA members in subsequent attacks.

For two nights and two days, Jack and his mates had been hiding in the grown hedge, battling the wind and constant rain, using up their survival rations, and waiting for an opportunity to attack. It reminded him of his jungle days in tropical Malaysia only weeks before, but this time it was real, with some full-blooded enemies nearby and a mission to kill.

With a slight jolt, Jack was alerted and brought back from his drifting thoughts. He heard a short, buzzing sound from his radio and instinctively tightened his grip on his binoculars. As a new SAS recruit, his task was to watch the farmhouse near Armagh – on the border between Southern and Northern Ireland – while his squad leader, Sgt Graham, led the attack, aimed at destroying whatever weapons they could locate, and killing the guards and any IRA terrorists on sight.

The operation was underway at dawn. Jack put away his eyepiece and readied his sniper rifle, aiming at the entrance of the farmhouse. He heard an explosion after the grenades were thrown, and the target was set on fire, shattered pieces of stones flying all over, and debris creating a massive, dark cloud in front of him. Three members of his team closed in and started shooting amidst shouting and scrambling. From their intel, as well as the surveillance they had kept on the location, they knew that there were eight men inside. One was killed in the explosion, five were shot by his teammates, and two were trying to escape.

An Irish guard, who looked no older than 18 years of age, ran out of the burning farmhouse and across the muddy field in his underpants. Jack raised his powerful weapon, the L96 PM rifle, took aim, and pressed the trigger. The escapee jerked and fell backward, crying out in pain, as blood seeped from his, skinny white leg. Jack hesitated only a microsecond before he dashed closer to where the wounded man lay. Jack's mind was giving him an order: finish him off now. The soldier in him obeyed – as he watched the dying man writhing in the mud, gasping for breath, holding up both his hands to cover his face, as if that would save him – and hit the young lad with a double tap to the head and heart. It made Jack's job a little easier. He did not want to remember what his enemy looked like.

The firing continued, and the sound of bullets echoed in the dark night, not unlike fireworks on New Year's Eve. One of his teammates, a lad known as Johnny from Newcastle, retreated from the target. He had been hit, a gunshot wound on his left shoulder. Jack moved closer and quickly took out his first-aid kit. He put a cloth under Johnny's wound and tightened it up to avoid further bleeding. "Fuckin' hell!" he heard Johnny curse under his breath, and saw him grimace with a shooting pain. Jack helped him up.

"C'mon, lads, let's get out of here." It was Sgt Graham's voice, heavily tinted with a Geordy accent.

Jack took one last look at the farmhouse, which was now burning brightly against the still, dark sky. He did not linger. He broke into a run – making sure that Johnny was right next to him – towards the RV point where they were to be extracted by a helicopter. It was three miles away, and they did not have much time. They were in the hotbed of the IRA, not exactly in the relatively safe haven of the English countryside.

What Jack did not know then was that, due to the casualties caused by the SAS involvement, the IRA would launch a reactive assassination campaign against the British police, the loyalists, and leading members of UDA (Ulster Defence Association) and UVF (Ulster Volunteer Force). Each side would acquire more casualties as the killings and reprisals escalated. It was not called The Troubles without good reason.

As for Jack, like his time in Germany, it was another memory chip he stored, filed, and buried. He never told anyone about his stint in Ireland, least of all his family, who had their cherished roots in that part of the country. As for his Catholic background, only his inborn sense of guilt remained.

Even that, he managed to keep it at bay, quite successfully, most of the time.

Chapter 24: The Asylum Seeker and The Solicitor

PEARL'S VISIT TO China came and went.

Back in the late 1990s when she went back to visit, she got excited for months before the trip, savouring its memories fondly months after her return, already dreaming about her next trip. Then came a time when she met her second husband Andrew, acquired her UK citizenship, and had her daughter Liyuan join her in her adopted country. China and her pull started to fade, although the Chinese blood still ran deep in her bloodstream, keeping her heart beating.

There was a popular song she used to sing. It was called "My Chinese Heart", loved by her countrymen and women. Now after two decades in a Western country, having been through years of western education, she could not help but wonder: *Do I still have a Chinese Heart? Or has it now been through a heart transplant?*

In the twentieth century, her motherland had gone through transformations so great that Pearl sometimes found it hard to adjust when she went back, brief though those visits had been. Nowadays, excitement over going 'home' eluded her. Perhaps, at long last, China had ceased to be 'home' to her. After all, even her brothers treated her as a 'foreigner' – "You're too Westernised," they had said to her, with more than a hint of accusation, as if she had betrayed her origin, her roots.

Time marched on, and Pearl had fought to reach a balance – keeping her Chinese upbringing intact, her language skills in use, while integrating herself as best as she could in the new, now real home to her being. In Andrew, and in her own way, she had truly found a place called home.

Two days after she returned from her visit to see her family in Chengdu, she had a call from Derby.

"Hello, Dr Church," The caller was a woman – not the usual nurse from Ward 34. "My name is Jane and I am a social worker. We'd like you to come with us to a solicitor's," she requested.

"Of course, Jane." Pearl had met Jane once, but didn't place her voice until she mentioned her job title. "When would you like me to come?"

"This Thursday, if that's okay with you. I have already made an appointment with a local immigration solicitor. How about two o'clock?"

"Sure. Shall I come to the ward or meet you at the solicitor's?"

"Come to the ward. I'll drive us to the solicitor's address. I assume that I know the city better than you." End of the call.

Thursday arrived, grey and damp with showers since the early hours. Time to visit 'the Lunatic Wang'; a nickname Andrew had chosen for Ah Ming, not in a sinister or sarcastic way, just a private joke between them. After all, Andrew was the king of labelling people, something he excelled in, often to the glee, and sometimes exasperation, of his wife.

From the row of hangers by the door, Pearl picked her dark-blue, windproof raincoat and put it over her work outfit. Out of the door and into the driver's seat. First things first; she switched on the radio. Advert for Kidderminster carpet: how boring could it get? She changed from Heart channel to the

Classical channel: the same, more adverts, trying to sell stuff she would never buy!

She pressed the CD player, and Chris Rea's "Road to Hell" came booming out! Catchy tune and great song. She smiled, wondering if it was appropriate or unlucky to play such a song while driving to see a mental case.

Ten minutes later, she had turned onto the familiar A38 heading north, a smooth drive all the way to the ward, where she was expected.

With Jane and Wang Ming, they arrived at the solicitors' firm in the town centre in time for their scheduled appointment. They were shown into the waiting area, where Jane briefed her interpreter. "We saw the solicitor last week, and Wang refused to speak with him. I don't know why, but I guess it's his lack of English."

"I see." It was probably more than that, but Pearl nodded her agreement. She waited for Jane to continue.

"Our requests for funding from the Home Office have been rejected. Basically they don't want to know. They wanted to deport him, actually." Jane's facial expression was grave. She paused, glancing at Wang Ming, probably wondering if he understood what was going on.

"We've consulted the immigration solicitors, and were informed that Mr Wang might have another chance to appeal. Because he came in 1999, before the Human Rights Act, he might be able to apply again under the new legislation. I don't know anything about immigration rules, and that's why we're here." Jane concluded her brief.

It was obvious that Social Services was at a loss about what to do next. The hospital had decided that there was no need to keep Wang in their ward any longer, and the Home Office simply wanted to get rid of him. The doctors were left with a dilemma – they could not just dismiss their patient without him having some place to be released to. Social Services seemed the only viable option, but how would they deal with him? What was his legal status in this country? A failed asylum seeker, sure, but what did that say about him exactly? Wang had made it absolutely clear that he would rather kill himself than be returned to China.

Half an hour later, Pearl, Wang Ming, and Jane were ushered into an immigration advisor's office. A young, South Asian male greeted them with a fleeting smile and introduction. Before Jane could speak, he held up his hands and came clean. "I'd better tell you now. We are actually extremely busy and we are not taking on any more new clients at this moment in time. But if you tell me what it is, I can give you some advice."

Jane looked at Pearl, and Pearl at her, and then at Wang Ming. She translated what Mr Singh had just said, and saw Wang's face tightening up. Of all the times she had visited him, she had never seen him smile, not once. Nor had he shown any other emotions, like anger, or sadness. It was as if his expressions were frozen in time – no feeling whatsoever underneath – or all those feelings were well-hidden. His eyes were vacant too, as if nothing in this world was of interest to him.

When did that happen? He couldn't have always been like that, Pearl thought, filled with sadness. Despite coming from a backwater town in southern China, he must have had hopes and dreams. He must have had some fire in him, some Chi or energy. Whatever he might have once had inside him, it was not there to see: not anymore.

Slowly and clearly, through Pearl's brain and her voice – the channel of communication – Mr Singh asked Wang Ming questions. "When did you arrive in this country?" "What was the reason that you had applied for asylum?" "When was it rejected?" "Did you appeal?" "What did the Home Office say in their refusal letter?"

Instead of answering the questions, Wang responded by repeating one statement: "I want to work."

"But you're not allowed to work in this country," the solicitor told him, matter-of-fact.

Wang's voice raised a notch. "The Home Office gave me a refugee card, allowing me to work. I lost that card. The Home Office can give me another one so I can work."

Mr Singh tried again. "That may be the case. If so, the card only allowed you to work while you were waiting for your asylum claims. When your appeal was rejected, you became ineligible to work."

Ignoring Mr Singh's efforts, and Pearl's, Wang repeated that he had lost his card, and the Home Office should issue a new card so he could work.

Simple logic, right? Except that the English law did not state so, nor did the lawyer. Wang did not budge, and refused to accept any reasoning other than his own firm belief.

"I want to work, that's it. Why can't I work?"

"Because you are illegal here. You are not supposed to work. That's the law."

"But I had a card. I lost it, and I should get another one from the Home Office. Why not?"

The explanation, and Wang's continuing refusal to accept reason, carried on through Pearl. It was like a tennis game: back and forth, again and again. This fruitless dialogue stretched out, with Pearl trying different ways of clarification while becoming more and more exasperated. She could see that Mr Singh's patience was wearing thin too. As for Wang Ming, he was visibly getting more and more agitated, to the extent that his left fist lashed out at her arm, right next to him.

156

Jane was on the other side, with poor Pearl squeezed in the middle, unable to move away from her assailant. Stuck, she had no shield, so she sped up her interpreting. She wanted to get out of there.

Finally, Mr Singh called time-out. He shrugged his shoulder, shook his head, and told Wang Ming one last time, "There is absolutely nothing I or any other lawyers can do for you. I'm sorry.

"Nobody would represent him, to be honest with you." He addressed Jane and Pearl. "He does not listen, and he does not understand that he has to. He has no reasons for claiming asylum: not for political opinions, not religion, not even belonging to a particular social group. And he can't even communicate reasonably with a legal representative. There is no way that any solicitors would take him on."

As Pearl interpreted what was said, Wang's clenched fist hit her arm a few more times, repeating a new demand: "Let's go to another lawyer. Let's go somewhere else."

Pearl looked at Jane and Jane back at her with resignation.

Chapter 25: Andrew: An Interpreter's Husband

"THAT'S PRETTY GOOD. I really enjoyed it." Andrew was the first to comment – after coming out of their nearest Showcase cinema – while heading towards the car park outside.

"Yeah, Nicole did a fabulous job, as usual," Pearl agreed. She looked a bit dreamy, probably with the images of the film still occupying her overactive mind.

"Sean Penn did better, though. I thought his performance was very strong," Andrew added, stressing to make a point. "He did well after Madonna."

He opened the passenger's door, a true gentleman, while she continued her commentary on how the situation in the film mirrored what was happening in the real world. Paul came to mind, her colleague from Zimbabwe, whom she had introduced to her husband and they had chatted about the political situation in that African country. Corruption seemed to be the name of the game everywhere, with the mindless slaughter of innocent people occurring with frightening regularity, and dictators getting away with it all.

"My job is hardly as exciting," Pearl spoke in a voice that was unnecessarily loud for just addressing the man next to her. Whenever she got excited, the volume of her otherwise-sweet voice raised a few notches. Sometimes, when she was talking to her Chinese friends, Andrew thought they were having an argument. Apparently it was a Chinese trait. They all had to shout until their lungs were ready to burst to make their voices heard or their points count. Guess it was understandable; with a population of 1.3 billion it was pretty hard to be heard.

"It's not as dangerous, either, thank goodness," she concluded, smiling, still looking a little sad, the aftereffect of the movie.

Deep down, Andrew understood his wife: she minded neither excitement nor danger. She possessed quite a fearless nature, and thrived on challenges. In the years he had known her, and even before they met, her life had been anything but clear sailing, with perhaps more than her fair share of ups and downs, tears and heartaches. Despite it all, she had maintained an amazingly upbeat personality. In her relatively new line of work, she encountered people from different walks of life, and heard many horrid stories.

There was no doubt some immigrants would make claims that were embellished and untrue, while once in a while there would be a truly appalling case where a genuine asylum seeker had been tortured and persecuted, for no reason other than human cruelty and power-crazed obsessions. It was unfortunate that, in parts of this world, countries were war-torn or governed by ruthless dictators.

Reading her mind and sensing her rising emotions, Andrew tried to lighten up the heaviness in the air. "So, what's the story this morning? Falun Gong member or 'One Child Policy'?"

Talking about her work may not be the best distraction, but it did get her to divert her attention elsewhere for the moment. Even to her husband she did not divulge specific information on the cases with which she had been involved; neither was it in her nature to indulge in unnecessary moaning and useless complaining, which was one of her attractive traits. Nonetheless, endowed with an analytical and inquisitive mind, and having worked in both public and private sectors – as well as a brief stint in barristers' chambers – Andrew was well-versed in company law, as well as a bit of criminal and immigration too. He was also widely read and a keen observer of current affairs, which provided him an insider's knowledge on Pearl's profession.

Not strictly by choice: Andrew was the nerd in the household. In recent months, he had downloaded relevant information on Falun Gong – a banned religious practice in China – when Pearl had trouble with the PDF file. That was not the first time Andrew had come to her rescue when dealing with modern technology. Her short temper simply did not go well with the frustrating process of WWW and some of its complications, although her competence has been steadily improving over time. Who could tell; in a short few years down the line, she might catch up and surpass the capacity of her 'technician' husband, but that would be later.

"Well, I had two cases today," she began, as the driver did a left turn at a junction. She turned to look at her husband, with a short, quick laugh, another of her endearing traits.

"Guess what? Nobody showed up for the first case: surprise, surprise! The other appellant was there, and she had a baby, so we were in court first, and it finished quickly."

She sounded disappointed. Freelance interpreters were paid by the hour, so longer hours meant better financial returns. On her part, chatting to fellow interpreters or reading papers in the waiting room was more preferable than staying at home wondering what to do. Nobody was paid to do housework, after all. She had it all worked out in that smart head of hers.

"I had a good adjudicator this morning." She was in her chatty mood, while Andrew just wanted to concentrate on the task at hand: driving.

"I don't think some immigration judges realise just how much they can make our job easier by telling the appellant what would happen and explaining the court procedure first. So it was nice to have a helpful and understanding judge for a change, who actually made it very clear to the appellant that I was not there to help her with any answers."

Andrew nodded his agreement, fully aware of Pearl's frustration. With her Chinese clients, it was especially useful to make the rules clear at the outset. Otherwise, when they failed to understand a question, or when they were struggling with a convincing story, they would turn to their fellow countryman or woman to help them out. Doing anything more than straight interpreting was not her job, and against her work ethic and principles.

"I'm not sure how significant my job is in the grand scheme of things," she continued, while Andrew's attention remained on the road ahead.

"I mean it's obviously very important to have an interpreter, when the appellant speaks no English. Otherwise there will be a complete communication breakdown. I have no say in what actually goes on in court. I cannot pass any judgment. Even if I know that the appellant is lying, I cannot say or show."

As Pearl continued her 'rant', they turned into their cul-de-sac. Andrew reversed in order to park on the drive, facing the street. It would be easier to get out next time; the man liked to plan ahead.

"Yes, it must be very frustrating for you, my dear," Andrew spoke eventually, moving to her side and opening the door for her. "You don't like to hear people lie or talk nonsense, do you? And you can't tell them to shut up either."

"No, I can't, unfortunately." She shook her head, looking serious.

"But sometimes they are so bad at making up stories. I mean, if I was to tell the judge that I was a Christian, the least I could do was to find out what Christianity was about. For God's sake, reading up on the Bible, or do some research."

Her face flushed a little as she became fired up. What irritated Pearl more than most was not stupidity, which could not be helped other than inheriting smarter genes, but ignorance. Ignorance by choice and persistent lack of knowledge could only be excused in the short term. Andrew and Pearl had discussed this before, and agreed that no one should plead ignorance and use that as an excuse.

"I cannot believe that, in this day and age when opportunities are abundant and learning tools endless, some people would choose ignorance. No excuse is good enough in my book," she stated firmly.

"Maybe you can start a special service, offering coaching to the immigrants as to what they should say to the authorities," Andrew said, more as a joke rather than being serious. It pleased him to see her smile spreading. It softened her face and she looked so cute that he could not help himself from leaning over to give her a kiss on her full mouth – the most kissable kind in his view: her very best feature.

"Okay. *Wo Men Hui Jia.* Forget about your work for now." He put an arm around her waist and gave her a loving squeeze. His other hand reached the door with the keys.

"You love using that phrase, don't you?" She smiled.

"Of course. Haven't you heard the saying that 'home is an Englishman's castle'?"

Indeed, *'Wo Men Hui Jia'* was Mandarin Chinese for 'we're home': one of Andrew's favourite Chinese words that he practiced on a regular basis.

Chapter 26: Madam Lin's Paradise

MY 'HOME' WAS hell. I could not wait to be free from the clutches of dirty, old man Papa Lin, and that ugly, old bitch Mama Lin.

During the two years when I was working under the nasty pair, I kept my hatred hidden well under wraps, secretly nursing my burning desire for escape and revenge one day. I knew I needed a plan if I was to get away successfully, and to that end, I was prepared to do anything.

The Plan did not form in one day, but came together gradually.

I didn't have to try too hard to become a hit among our regular customers; and it was not because of my 'hiding the moon and shaming the flowers' good looks, oh no. Natural beauty is important in this world: especially for a nobody in China. For a girl from an ordinary family, who wants to marry well and make headway in society, physical beauty is her ticket to prosperity, more prized than any other inner qualities she might possess.

In my case, I had learnt very early on – and very quickly – that in the grotty underworld and seedy hangouts for the immoral, the greedy, the corrupt, and the evil, something else proved far more useful and effective. An uncanny knack for understanding men and giving them what they wanted: a wonderful skill not every working girl could master. On top of that is required a bit of scheming combined with a portion of pretence and eagerness to please, fake or genuine.

It does not take psychological mumbo-jumbo to know that human nature is basically weak and fundamentally flawed, especially in men whose heads are in their pants, with their brains governed by their dicks. It did not take me long to learn the ropes in this flesh-market business. I knew when and how to behave like a 'good girl', thanks to the harsh 'training' by my brothers. If you live with evils, you either become them, or let them destroy you. I am far too smart to allow them to make a victim of me.

"Oh, Chairman Wang, long time no see." The instant the pockmarked, pot-bellied official came into view, I was back in my real life, leaving my musings for another day. "I've missed you so much," I cooed, using my little-girl, super-sweet voice.

"How can your heart be so hardened as to forget me for so long?" I purred, in my softest and most seductive tone. Chinese men love feeling important and in control.

I threw myself to his side, using a silk handkerchief to brush against his shoulder, giving him a slight nudge, filling my eyes with a fake 'blaming' look that I quickly replaced with a coy smile: enough to melt a stony heart. My painted nails reached for his fat, fleshy hand.

His eyes did not stop at my face, but greedily fixated on something more prominent and sexy: my best asset, a proud pair of fine breasts barely covered by the low neckline of my tight, black top, chosen to show my curves to their maximum effect. Wang drooled over my twin peaks, calling them "fountains of joy" and squeezing and sucking them like a baby needing a mother's milk.

Occasionally, if the clients were half-decent with passable appearances, I allowed myself to enjoy what they did to my ripe, feminine body. To my shame and delight, my breasts were sensitive to male touch and responded eagerly whether I wanted it or not. They seemed to have a life of their own, begging for attention and release.

Unfortunately, most men I entertained were rough and only came to me for their own pleasure. They groped, they bit, and they shovelled their dicks into my vagina as quickly as they could get them hard enough.

Most of the time, it suited me. After all, it was their pockets I was after, not their bodies. If they treated me like a whore, so be it. They paid for the fuck and then off they went; I could not wait to see the back of them.

Pockmarked Wang was the nickname we used behind him. In front of him, all the girls cooed and respectfully called him Chairman Wang.

He was married, with a wife and child tucked away somewhere in a big house, who probably had no idea what he was up to during his frequent 'business dealings' with his clients and after-dinner entertainment. He came to us a year ago, but recently had his eyes only on me, and I knew why. He liked to be nursed by a good 'Mommy', and I was more than happy to satisfy his needs.

On entering the little, dimly lit room, which was the best in the premises, I wasted no time shedding my clothes. It felt more natural to be naked than scantily dressed. Wang loved nothing better than seeing naked flesh, and he was obsessed with my fine pair of tits. "I want to suck you dry," he had said more than once.

He had never offered any compliments on what I wore, and had only one thing in mind: exploiting my young flesh and satisfying his fantasies. He was an easy man to please and, in a strange way, he gave me pleasure too.

Sitting down by the side of the bed, he kept his eyes glued to my wonderfully creamy mounds, which were dotted with a pair of ripe, juicy cherries. I stood in front of him, his face buried between my breasts. My nipples stood pink and proud, both inviting and expectant, waiting to give and receive sensations.

Wang was not chatty during sex, too busy keeping his hands and mouth elsewhere. One of his fleshy hands grabbed my breast and squeezed it like a sponge full of sweet juices ready to burst out. His big, wet mouth found the nipple of my other breast and he started sucking it, making a slurping noise. I was instantly aroused, and found myself getting wet down below. Momentarily, I forgot his ugliness and concentrated on the sensation and electricity my wonderful assets were transmitting to the rest of my sensual body. While enjoying the pleasure he was giving me, I did not forget to encourage him to work harder for me.

"Oh, my God, you are such a good baby; yes, suck me, suck me harder, you know how much Mommy likes to feed you, don't you?" I moaned and urged him on, my body trembling a little, pushing my tits further into his greedy mouth. I closed my eyes, my moaning growing louder and more lewd, like music to his ears.

Despite Wang's pockmarked face, disgusting, fat body, and tiny dick, he gave me one thing I really enjoyed and damn it if I didn't make the best of it. I let him play with my two precious treasures for as long as he liked, feeling an amazing power surging inside me.

Sometimes when I was on my own, I would fondle them myself, tantalising them with pressure and squeezing them hard. The sensation was so strong that I could easily make myself come, releasing the build-up of tension.

Wang did not need my help to keep me satisfied. My nipples were hard, engorged, and erect, even though they were also a bit sore due to his ferocious sucking, which bordered upon biting into my tender flesh. Doesn't pain sometimes equal pleasure? I call my twin peaks my pleasure fountain, and it's true.

I never expected that I could actually enjoy having sex with men until Wang came along. He had no idea that his obsession with my beautiful tits had, in no small way, transformed me. It was then that I knew that I could take pleasure from my body for my own sake, not just for men.

The Chairman must have been mistreated as a child, a fleeting thought shot through me: pure speculation. Over his regular visits in the last couple of months, I had become acquainted with his bedroom antics. When his energy sagged and he wanted his desire fulfilled, I gave it to him. By then he'd had enough of an ego massage that he was now a strong and sexy man who was expert in treating women in bed. At the end of the day, he didn't come here to give me pleasure but to satisfy his own. That much I always kept in mind. I never allowed my self-indulgence to go beyond that knowledge.

I lowered myself, to move my face level with Wang's little brother. Time to indulge him, his small dick sucked and his balls caressed, I did it all expertly, making sure that he enjoyed himself so much that he would want to be back in no time. Leaving just a little room for fantasy required skill. If it took him longer than usual to get hard, I didn't let it on. I just kept my hands and mouth busy, using all I have. I had no place to go, so I had all the time in the world to make him come. I reassured him what a sexy man he was, and how much I loved being fucked by him and him alone.

With the full extensive service of my mouth, my tongue, my hands, and all my other expertise – including my tits to rub him up and down and back and forth – he was guaranteed to climax before he went away, every time. Even if I couldn't fully cure his semi-impotency, I could at least make him feel more than adequate and like a highly desirable man.

Nobody would complain about their ego being boosted, especially someone as important as Chairman Wang.

He loved coming in my mouth, watching me swallow his sperm and lick my mouth, moaning with pleasure while telling him how delicious and full of nourishment it was to my hungry body. He patted my bare arse, his contentment written all over his face.

"You're a terrific fuck, worth every penny," he said.

For that rare compliment, I stood up and shovelled one of my breasts into his saliva-filled, greedy mouth, ready to give him another feed. My two babies were still hungry and pining for more. He pinched one of my nipples, and bit the other one, making me squeal. Then he pointed at his watch and reluctantly let go of his treasure.

Time to get home, wherever that may be.

While Wang got dressed, my mind left him, mentally calculating how many more clients were lined up that day and how quickly I could process them.

At the reception room, the Old Bitch came to say her good-bye. Clients like Chairman Wang did not pay cash for each of their visits. They had it put on a tab, and his minions would come and settle the account once in a while.

I watched the Bitch's humble bowing and nodding to this senior government official and tried not to listen to her flattering, fake hospitality and 'warm' invitations for his future visits. In my mind's eye, my plan was one step closer to its eventual realisation.

Chairman Wang did not know it yet, but in my grand scheme for the future he had a role to play. What role exactly? I had yet to devise it to my full advantage.

One thing was certain: he would be back before the season changed again.

Chapter 27: Pearl's Diary, 15th October, Saturday, Fine

I HAVE NOT written anything since returning from our holiday in Majorca in September. Consequently there is a lot of catching up to do.

It was such a relaxing and enjoyable time that I didn't feel like leaving that beautiful Spanish island in the Mediterranean. Now with England right in the middle of Autumn, and with wintry times approaching with an alarming speed, I decided to have something to look forward to. I just went online and checked Thompson, Expedia, and a couple of other low budget airlines. Woo-hoo, I've found a good deal to Southern Spain during Christmas. I've notified Liyuan and Andrew that it would be my treat, and splashed out for a 5-day trip to Malaga: better than a week, because it's more and more difficult to drag Liyuan away from her computer games and her room, which she has filled with her music stuff, like a mixing deck and a guitar.

Last weekend Andrew took me to London to watch our favourite actor, Kevin Spacey, at close range. The tickets were for Old Vic and the play was The Philadelphia Story, *a love story set in the 1930s America. Spacey was brilliant and I absolutely loved him, even more now than before if that's possible! It was a happy-ending comedy, quite Shakespearian, with witty lines and snappy dialogues. Both Andrew and I enjoyed it, very much!*

By chance, I spotted a fellow interpreter – Andre, who does French and Spanish – with his exotic, South Asian girlfriend, who is a solicitor based in London. They were on the same row, so he came over to us during the interval. Apparently he met his girlfriend in Birmingham Immigration court. Fancy that! Romance is everywhere!

After the theatre, we returned to my friend's house in Uxbridge. Hawar is originally from Iraq, in the Kurdistan area. He was a poet back home and became as a freedom fighter during Saddam Hussein's regime. He came over to the UK at about the same time as I did. After we met in one of several AIT centres we both frequented, we got on like a house on fire and became good pals. Earlier on Saturday afternoon, he had organised a BBQ in his back garden and treated us with his home-made Kurdish style kebabs, minced lamb skewered on shiny, iron bars. Andrew was so impressed that he told Hawar: 'you make the best kebabs I've ever tasted.' I know he truly meant it by the amount he consumed during the feast.

On Sunday we visited Tate Modern, Andrew's favourite hang-out in the British capital. Despite my lack of stamina, and the discomfort on my small feet, I was more than happy to tag along in his artistic pursuits. Andrew has exquisite tastes in art, and I love him for it!

On Monday, Andrew and I went to our local park and picked blackberries. Most of them were on their last legs before all the summer fruit dropped and the leaves fell, stripped for the winter, until next year. I always felt a pang of pity that so few people bothered to pick them whilst they were ripe and juicy, allowing them to rot on the ground instead. This would have never happened in a country like China or India. They would be sold in the market or fed to the children: no such sinful waste of resources and nutritious food.

Anyway, Andrew and I fought through the thorny branches and filled our barrel with blackberries, and our hands with bloody, red stains, not to mention a few scratches on my arms. Still, the sweet smell and lovely sight of the jam we have managed to boil and packaged made it all worthwhile. I went out and bought several jars to contain our efforts, and there is no way that we can consume them all. In fact, I don't much care for jam at all; more a fresh fruit person. I don't care for bread either, especially the English toast-type bread. The solution, like the year before: the jam would go to our friends and neighbours!

I did my duty and called Mum early in the week. Father and she enjoy living in Chengdu, happy to leave Chongqing behind. I know why. Apart from the more mild weather in the Sichuan capital, my mother's relatives are all in Chengdu. She can socialise with them and play her beloved MJ. While Father is still the same: unhealthy and unhappy. His only comfort and blessing is his appetite for good food. For him, death would be a relief, but he has a strong desire to carry on, no matter how sick he has become. I admire him and hope that I have inherited his spirit.

In terms of work, this has been a very busy week, with regular AIT (Asylum & Immigration Tribunal) cases, a crown court case, and a couple of police bookings. Considering that only a few months ago I had only occasional Tribunal work, and one unexpected but regular client in the form of 'Lunatic' Wang, I'm very happy that the courts are requesting my services, as well as the police forces.

Yesterday had been a very stressful day. It started okay, as I did admin work from home, sending out my recent invoices to the Derbyshire Social Service. At around 1:00 p.m., I got a call from Peterborough. The officer asked me to get there as soon as I could and preferably no later than 5:00 p.m. I had plenty of time to get ready, especially now that I had my own Mio Mytec GPS. It seemed to have worked okay since Andrew bought it on eBay a week ago. We made use of it during our trip to London last weekend, as well as earlier this week when I drove to Stoke.

But NO, it refused to work! I tried so many times and eventually became so frustrated that I just screamed in utter despair and anger! I called Andrew. He was at a meeting and had his mobile switched off, so I left a message. I was in tears as frustration got the better of me. It was terrible! What's the matter with me and technology? It didn't help that Andrew was not available when I needed him the most!

He must have heard my thunderous cursing! On finding out the reason for my call and locating where I was, he left work immediately and caught up with me at Sainsbury's car park, just as I was about to join the M6. He could not get the damn GPS to work either, so offered to drive me to Peterborough himself. Bless him; he's a godsend: dear, dear man. By then I was in no state to drive, as a severe headache had started its merciless assault on my senses and my vision had become blurred with sickness.

The defendant at the station was a real *ASS*, no other word for him. According to him, he was a doctor in China. He went to Tesco and picked out about £5 worth of groceries and walked out without paying! He was stopped by security and taken in for questioning by the police, for theft, obviously. He vehemently denied it, his excuse being that he forgot his wife's birthday the day before and had a phone conversation with her that morning, during which she reminded him. They probably had a fight/row about it, so he was preoccupied, hence forgetting to pay on leaving the store. He even blamed the alarm that failed to set off at the exit; it was as if it's the door's fault, not his. What cheek and how ridiculous! It was annoying, with his feeble attempt to claim his innocence, and his irritating manner. Instead of answering questions, he tried to 'interrogate' the police during the interview. "Why did the alarm not work? Did you go and check if it worked?"

That guy was a wanker, with a big chip on his shoulder. I could tell that he was dodgy just by looking at him. He acted as if the whole world owed him something. Despite my growing irritation and impatience, I interpreted what he had to say and assisted the police doing their job.

He was more or less let off and was told to go back one more time after the police investigation. Before he was released, he was offered a 9:00 a.m. appointment on Wednesday but he was not happy with it. "Ten is better for me," he insisted. By then, my tolerance towards this man was really wearing thin and I felt like saying, "Shut the fuck up!" I didn't: of course not. Was it my hormones playing tricks on my mental state? Perhaps just one of those stressful days?

By the time I came out of the police station, the sky had opened its massive mouth, pouring down torrential rain, lightning, and thunder, reflecting my mood. On our 100 miles return journey, Andrew and I witnessed incredible shows of nature – the lightning was like a firework display, only more scary: but awesome.

What a relief that Andrew came with me and I was not the one driving in that condition!

Chapter 28: Ah Fang's Traveling 'Profession'

SPRING FLOWERS, SUMMER breezes, autumn leaves, and winter snow; seasons swap without warning, at their own pace, stopping for no one. Before I know it, I have been in the UK for three years.

During this time, I've met many people, the majority of whom come and go like lanterns, without leaving a dent in my memory. To be honest, I would press the delete button and erase the best part of this period of my life, if our memory was like a well-functioning computer, or if I had absolute control of my mental faculties. Most of the time, I just make myself unfeeling and go about my days without thinking too much. Thinking, after all, is a luxury for the intellectuals and lucky souls.

Still, there are times when my daily musings dance around how I could escape, daydreaming about it and imagining a life other than my own. I keep my eyes open and my ears sharp, trying to figure out a way out of my misery. In my 'profession' it's difficult to make real, trustworthy friends; although it is easy to talk to other working girls or even our uncles and aunties, most of whom are simple beings trying to make a living, just like us.

As I sit on the train from Nottingham to Birmingham, where my next rota is to begin tonight, I allow my thoughts to recall some of the things that have happened to me and how quickly time has flown me by. I have learnt quickly that simply harbouring a desire to escape is not enough. I need to have concrete plans and careful implementation to succeed. Eventually I began the first stage of my exit strategy: not an easy task, but I have made progress. Compared to when I first arrived, my English is so much better. I wish I'd had a chance to go to school, like those lucky students. Since that fortune eludes me, I make the best of what I have. I practice English with clients, when they are in the mood for a little more than just fucking me. I make efforts to chat to other English speaking girls from other countries whenever a chance presents itself.

"Your ticket, please?" The male voice of the conductor call me back from my roaming thoughts, as I withdraw my eyes reluctantly from the window overlooking the beautiful English countryside. I hand my ticket to the fat chap and smile at him, a practiced smile.

"Thank you." With that he hands back my stamped rail ticket and goes his way, unsmiling and hurried. *He's probably having a bad day.* I wonder if he has a family, or if he could be one of the customers who frequent my 'work' places. Maybe it's part of my professional habits, now I have come to distinguish people – men anyway – in broadly two categories: clients or non-clients.

My mobile vibrates with a text message in Chinese.

waiting outside the station

The sender is unknown, but I know it would be my pickup driver. He would deliver me to a location that is to be my home for the next seven days. Although I have frequented Birmingham, I never knew which house I'd be taken to in advance, as these premises seem to be mobile – they could be anywhere in the country, yet identical inside. For a working girl like me, it does not make a damn difference where my next station is, except some locations serve a slightly better class of clients, if I could put it that way.

On exiting the New Street station, it takes me a minute to spot a black BMW parked among a few black cabs. I don't know if it's the Chinese obsession with branded goods or it's because the bosses are showing off that they are making shitloads of money: perhaps both. I have had my fair share of riding in posh, top-range cars. Perhaps one day I'll learn to drive and have a car of my own. Nobody can be forbidden to have dreams, even soiled goods like me. It's quite possible that because we are right at the bottom of the pile, we have a lot more to dream about. From the rock bottom, the only way is up.

With that defiant thought, I lower my head and step into the back seat of the waiting 'taxi'. I've never met the driver before, but no matter; they are all the same to me, minions working for the boss, the Big Brother for whom we are all slaving. They think they are different, superior, because they don't sell their flesh. I beg to differ. At the end of the day, they probably sell more than they'd like to admit to themselves. They sell their souls to the devil, doing dirty work for what? For the money they'll only gamble away in a casino? Even though they are allowed to drive posh cars, in the eyes of the Boss they are 'prostitutes' too. They would never see it this way, and who am I to educate them? I keep my opinions to myself.

Over time, I've learnt my lessons, never enquiring about his name or where we are going. He would only give me a nickname anyway. So I settle myself in the plush leather seats and look out of the tinted window. Even though I don't drive, I possess a good natural sense of orientation. If I paid close enough attention, I could actually recall the routes if I have to. Who knows? One day, such skills could come in handy.

"Where are you from?" I hear the driver addressing me. So he wants a chat: probably a green hand, new recruit.

"Changle. How about you?" I turn away from the window and see the back of his head. He is wearing sunglasses, even though the sun is hiding behind the clouds. Maybe he has ugly eyes and doesn't want people to see them.

"We're *laoxiang*." He chuckles and switches to the dialect with which we are both familiar.

"I only arrived in England a couple of months ago. Because my brother and cousin both work for the Boss, and I can drive, I was given this driving job as a favour."

No wonder he is chatty. Unfortunately, before I can ask him more about the Boss, we have arrived at our destination. A nice-looking, detached house, with a row of identical properties on both sides of the road. I am pleased, if that was the correct way to describe how I feel. Compared to some of the really grotty and rundown council flats I have worked in, this is definitely an upper-scale location. And hopefully that would lead to better clientele too. I make a secret wish.

"Lao Zhang, come and get your supplies," the driver yells, his voice impatient, harsher than the one he has used with me.

A middle-aged man rushes out to the driveway, with his cardigan hanging over his shoulder. A northerner, I gather. They tend to employ northerners as 'housekeepers' and Fujian natives as drivers and more senior managers on the hierarchy. 'Housekeeping' is a tricky job – when the brothels are raided by the police, the uncles and aunties are the ones who get arrested and often put away for months. Really unlucky ones end up being deported after serving their sentence. Because they are the ones who do not belong to the tight-knit criminal gang, only performing temporary work paid on a weekly basis, they cannot reveal significant information to the police even if they want to.

The Big Guys of criminal rings are no fools. They have perfected their art in evading detection most of the time: the higher up, the safer and freer from risk. Their money and their power make sure of that, and people's fear too.

As the two men busy themselves with transporting groceries from the car's boot into the house, I make my way through the door, heading straight upstairs. I have been in the business long enough to know the ins and outs of every 'workstation'. The sizes of brothels may vary: usually two to four bedrooms as our quarters, with two to three of us working on each rota. The earlier arrivals get first pick of the rooms.

The first door on the left side of the stairs is open, so I pop my head in for a quick survey. The curtains are drawn, a dark-red, velvet-type material. There is a medium-sized bed in the middle: not quite a double, but not a single either. No bedcover, but two soft, puffy pillows are propped up at the head. A red table lamp is lit on the bedside table, giving the room a warm and soft glow. Without checking, I know there would be essential supplies in the drawers. On the far side stands a wardrobe for my clothes, and hopefully a duvet or blanket for the nights. Next to the wardrobe is a bin, mainly for disposal of condoms. I guess one can call it fully furnished: fit for purpose.

I dump my little suitcase at the door and decide to have a tour. The room right above the stairs is the washing room. I go in and am pleased to find that they have a bathtub, not just showers. While most of the time I take showers because it's quick and uses less water, I do enjoy a bath from time to time, especially when I feel like a thorough cleansing and a bit of time to shut out unpleasant thoughts, even just for a few minutes.

The door on the other side of the bathroom is closed. I push it open and am greeted by complete darkness. As I adjust my eyes, I see a body curled up on the bed. Someone has obviously got in before me and is taking a nap, probably after a late night. "Sorry" I say, before I quickly and carefully shut the door.

The room in the far corner is ajar and with a light push it flies open. A shaft of daylight is bursting through the open window, as well as cool, fresh air streaming in. I instinctively wrap my hands around my arms, protecting myself from the assault of the autumn chill. It's the smallest room in the house: only a single bed and hardly any furniture. The bed is made. A black rucksack is under the rack of clothes hanging on a simple stand covered in clear polythene. It's obviously the housekeeper's lodging.

The clock on the wall points at 12:00 p.m.: Monday noon. I reckon that I have a little time to myself before the customers arrive. I saunter back to the first room I have surveyed, lift my suitcase, and walk in. I shut the door behind me, pull the curtains, and try to open the window.

It refuses to give. I inspect all around it and cannot find an opening. Looking out, I see the back garden, unattended, unlike the ones on each side of the house, where the grass is cut and plants and flowers in bloom. Rows of houses come into my view farther away.

It's not the first time that I let my imagination run wild about the people in those houses. What do they do on a working day? Do they know that their neighbouring property is a whorehouse? Do their husbands come here? What would they do if the wives ever found out?

Chapter 29: "The Dragon" Ambition

IMPATIENT AND ANNOYED, Ah Long sat in his chauffeur-driven Lamborghini, which was taking him through the busy streets in Hong Kong. He held a cigarette between his yellow fingers in one hand, and a mobile in the other. He had just landed at the Chek Lap Kok Airport, having spent over 15 hours in the air from Los Angeles to Hong Kong. His business on the West Coast of America had flourished so much in recent years that he now had a solid foundation from which he could let his people manage while he sat back and watched his bank accounts balloon. He had so many different accounts in such huge quantities in so many different countries that he had to employ a team of professional accountants to look after his financial affairs.

When he started out in the 1980s, he never anticipated that this trafficking business could be so profitable: a massive cash cow. In a relatively short period of time, it had thrived under his genius management and expanded beyond his wildest dreams. At this point, Ah Long's chain of enterprises could very well get him into the Forbes' Rich list, if only they were all legit and aboveboard. No, his wealth was not for show. Having a luxurious yacht in Monte Carlo and playing golf in Scotland was not the type of a dream lifestyle that propelled him.

Ah Long was a quietly ambitious man, understated: no Murdoch, Gates, or Branson. He was his own man and he knew what made himself tick. What drove him was not simply large sums of money in the bank to spend on beautiful, young models, skiing on Swiss mountains in the winter, and cruising the Mediterranean in the summer. Oh no; Ah Long was a hardworking man, and that work ethic was inbred in his Chinese genes, no matter how much wealth he had been rewarded with. It was never enough. He was like a climber; there is always the next mountain to climb. Life is one steep climb after another until you lose that zest to conquer and achieve, then life ends there.

Now that the American side of business was well under way, the system in place and working nicely, he had set his eyes on Europe, which was, even if not quite virgin territory, certainly new enough to present exciting and fresh challenges, just what Ah Long needed at this time of his life. He was in his prime. The Westerners say that life starts at 40, while the Chinese say 'Men stand at 30', which is more or less the same thing, specifically referring to men like Ah Long. After all, women don't really count, do they? Over the centuries, they have depended on men to provide for them; why should that change, just because some Western liberals, bleeding hearts, and feminists say so? Ah Long was a young-looking 40-something, so no matter how you looked at it, his life was on an upward slope.

As he inhaled one last, greedy suck from his cigarette, and wound down the window to throw out the butt, a quick heat wave attacked him. Even though it was supposed to be autumn, this was Hong Kong: hot, busy, noisy, and buzzing with pulsating energy, a fire dragon that never sleeps.

It was almost midnight; the streets in Central were still heaving with people of all ages, hurrying in different directions. Wafts of cooked food and spices filled the air as their car sped through a row of restaurants on both sides that were still open and entertaining tourists from all corners of the world, all seeking adventure and excitement in this Eastern paradise.

Ah Long pressed the button as the window went up, shutting out the sights and sounds of the steaming streets. His attention shifted back to his mobile and he scrolled down to his favourites, pressing the one that said VP. His driver was taking him to Victoria Peak, where he had recently purchased a new property: an HQ for his business interests in Asia, a remote-control centre reaching the four corners of his empire. It was previously owned by a shipping tycoon, and offered one of the best views on Hong Kong Island. In fact, people who have been there were often left open-mouthed at what they saw, the panoramic views of Central, Victoria Harbour, and Kowloon.

But it wasn't the views that made Ah Long splash out. The views – no matter how stunning and mind-blowing – were no good to him, since he was a globe-trotter, not some kind of retired, stay-at-home old fart. It was the exclusivity of Peak's address that made the decision for Ah Long. Before the Handover, it was the location reserved exclusively for the top brass: white British and Europeans. The area was dotted with top-range shops and fine restaurants, not to mention the gated villas and mansions.

The phone was answered on the second ring: "Wei," responded a woman's voice. For a brief moment, Ah Long was thrown, trying to place where he had heard that voice before. It sounded familiar, yet was not the one he was expecting at the other end of the line.

He wanted Ah Tai, his cousin, who he had sent to Hong Kong a few days before him to oversee his new operation. Ah Tai has been with him for a long time, since his early days in Japan. If there was anyone Ah Long would have trusted his life to, it would be none other than Ah Tai. Ah Tai was his top dog;

even better than a dog, because Ah Tai would do whatever the Dragon ordered him to do.

"Where the hell is Ah Tai?" he demanded on the phone. "He knew that I was coming tonight and I expected to see him at the airport. What the fuck is going on? The driver knew fuck all when I asked him."

"Sorry, Dragon Brother." The female voice was soft and soothing, almost singsong; women often adopted that voice to placate him when he was in one of his moods.

"Ah Tai was going to come and meet you earlier, but something unexpected happened. He had to go and sort it out. Because you were on the plane, he could not reach you. But don't worry, Dragon Brother, Ah Tai told me to wait up for you. He'll explain to you later."

With a girly chuckle, her dialect changed to that of his.

"Don't you remember me, Dragon Brother? I am Ah Mi from your hometown. We met when you came to Fuqing last year. My Second Brother and Third Brother worked for you in Japan."

The woman continued her chattering on the phone, as if Ah Long had all the time in the world to listen to her saga. He interrupted her before she could utter another word.

"Okay, shut the fuck up. I'll be there in a few minutes, and make sure you tell me everything you know about Ah Tai when I get in."

With that, he pressed the end button.

Bloody hell: women. They just talk nonsense all the time, trying all they can to make small talk whether you are in the mood or not. Ah Tai better explain to me what he is up to and how this woman got here without my knowledge. Hang on. Perhaps Ah Tai did mention to me that girls were being brought out from Fuqing. Perhaps he has started the ball rolling after all.

Ah Long sank back into his comfy, leather seat, his shoulders relaxed, his thoughts already drifting ahead to the future he had drawn for himself. Some people came into this world to serve and to be dominated. Not Ah Long. He was a self-made man, and he was Master. He was born to dominate others and change their lives, for better or worse.

To be or not to be, Ah Long had their fate firmly in his clutches.

Chapter 30: 9.11

ON THE MORNING of 11th of September, 2001, Jack woke up early. Years of being in the Army had left him with an inability to enjoy a good, long lie-in, even during his 'off' days.

In his house in a village outside Hereford, which Moira and their two children had called home since relocating to England a few years ago, Jack was on annual leave from duty. He had promised his son Jimmy that he would be home for his birthday this year and planned it accordingly. He knew that his wife, as understanding as any army wife could be, had become increasingly dissatisfied with his long absences, especially on special occasions. His children, although still young, began to miss him too. That was one of the reasons he and Moira had come to an agreement that they would stop having any more children. Catholic or not Catholic, more offspring would be unfair to her.

He turned to his bedside stand and saw the time dimly flashing at him, its green hands pointing at 5:30 a.m. He refrained from jumping out of bed, as he had become accustomed to do. His wife needed that little extra time in bed. She had changed her night shift for a day shift starting at 7:00 a.m. so she could be back in time for the birthday celebration that evening.

He felt a slight move from her body and her sleepy voice came while her eyes were still closed: "What's the time, Jack?"

"Only half past five, luv. You've got a bit of time snoozing, sleepyhead." He leaned over and planted a kiss on her forehead. He had made love to her the night before, which must have tired her out. He smiled as he recalled their intimacies of the night before. *It's a damn good feeling enjoying a woman's flesh without having to fantasize a strange, sexy scenario, or having it off with my hand under the bedcover.*

His wife turned to face him and snuggled up to him. He felt an instant hardness and his breath quickened. He whispered to her as he licked the tip of her ear. "Can we have a quickie, hon? I want you now."

His voice became hoarse and his desire more urgent as he gently maneuvered her soft, warm body onto her side and slid himself inside her from behind. *Oh God, this feels so good.* He let out a soft sigh. He heard Moira gasp the moment he entered her. It drove him wild as his hands cupped her ample breasts and applied pressure to her pleasure points. Moira was fully awake by then. She arched her back and gripped him firmly.

Minutes later, he rolled off her, feeling relief. He watched his wife turning on the light and putting on her nursing outfit. Jack had wondered why some men fantasized about shagging nurses. He had been married to one for as long as he could care to remember. It was her womanly feel and touch his body craved and responded to, not her outfit.

"Remember to take Jimmy and Heather to school, and then collect them at 3:30, okay?"

Sometimes Moira sounded just a tad too much like his own mother when instructing him what to do. Her Glaswegian accent had not lessened, even though she had been living in this part of England for over five years: partly to be closer to Jack's base, as well as to provide a better environment for their children.

Morning passed without anything noteworthy. Jack fixed himself a late lunch in the kitchen and started channel-hopping with his remote TV controller, when suddenly breaking news from BBC flashed on the screen: The Twin Towers of the World Trade Centre in New York had just been hit!

Jack sat at the edge of the sofa chair staring at the images, gobsmacked, not believing his eyes, as the hijackers crashed two airliners into the skyscrapers, one of the world's most-notable landmarks collapsing after the other, killing many working in the buildings as well as those on the planes. Horrified, he saw people jumping out of the buildings, and the skyline of New York turning into smoke and dust, followed by utter destruction and devastation.

His eyes were glued to the screen when his phone rang. It was his Squad Leader at the base: "Jack, you saw what's happening in New York?"

"Yes, sir. I can't believe..." Incredulous, his attention still on the TV.

Before he could finish his sentence, he received his order: "When can you get back to the Base? I know you're on leave, but these are unusual circumstances, to put it mildly. I need your arse back here as soon as possible."

"Yes, sir. I'll get going right away." He took a glance at his watch. "I should be back within the hour."

End of conversation.

He placed a quick call to Moira at her hospital and left a message: *Have to get back to Base; please make alternative arrangements to collect children from school.* No time to speculate about what Moira would have to say to try to explain to wee Jimmy why Daddy was absent again while he opened his birthday gifts and blew out the candles on the cake, which had been chilled in the fridge.

One day Jimmy would understand.

******

Following briefings at Langley, and their own headquarters in England, the British SAS formed part of the Task Force assigned to strike in Afghanistan – the heart of the Taliban and Al-Qaeda – in retaliation and retribution. Their target, as their briefings emphasized time and again, was Osama bin Laden. Together with the Americans – the troopers of Delta – Jack and his teammates flew out in their C-141 Starlifter. Prior to the mission, they had waited in Bahrain for two days as the helo maintenance crews reassembled and prepared the aircraft so their presence would not be easily detected by the enemy.

Armed with the intelligence information the CIA had received from their agents within Afghanistan and the Taliban, with the cooperation of Afghan United Front, as well as intel gathered through satellites and monitoring, the Task Forces were able to organize the invasion effectively. The ground forces were backed with tremendous air support by the USA Air Force. Within weeks, they drove the Taliban out of Kabul, sending the leaders fleeing to Pakistan, although it would take the Americans nearly ten years before they eventually located bin Laden and killed him.

For Jack Gordon, the highlight of his career came with his participation in the war against terror. It was in Afghanistan where he truly witnessed the massive casualties, civil and military, caused by the incessant fighting in one of the toughest terrains. He witnessed firsthand how human beings could be easy prey to man-made destruction.

9.11, a prominent memory chip, more so for Jack than many.

Chapter 31: Good-bye, Ah Ming

TWELVE MONTHS AFTER that first unexpected call from the mental hospital, Wang Ming still occupied a place in Pearl's work diary. She made less-frequent but still regular, visits to his one-bedroom flat. The Social Services had secured an accommodation for him, as well as paying for his continued medication and a weekly maintenance. For a while, they all went through the motions, checking up on him on a monthly basis, asking routine questions while he repeated his assertions. "I can't sleep at night, why? I can't sit down either, why? I have to stand all the time, or walk back and forth. What's wrong with me?"

"Have you been to see your GP?" Peter asked him and Pearl interpreted.

"No." Simple answer.

"Why not?"

"I don't know."

"Can you please go and see your GP? It's only a few streets away from here, and you have the address."

To make sure, they showed him the map on his GP's leaflet, and Pearl circled the address and highlighted the route to get there.

The next time, the conversation started with exactly the same opening line by Ah Ming. Again he was given the same solution to his problem of not being able to sleep. "Have you been to see your doctor?"

Did he ever listen? Pearl could not help wondering. If he did, he never acted upon it. It was like a dance confined on the stage, a play with the same script, a tragic-comic performance repeated each time to the same tune.

"You should just record what he is about to say and play it when you visit him every time," Andrew had suggested, one of their private jokes. It was becoming a drag for her, and for Jane and Peter, the social worker and the mental-health nurse.

Then the routine was to change.

"Pearl, can you come with us to see Mr Wang tomorrow?" It was Jane.

"Sure: the usual time, at 3:00 p.m.?" Pearl quickly double-checked her diary; she was free.

"Yes. We're going to inform him that we can no longer support him. We'll give him one month's notice. Then he'll have to find his own accommodation. We won't be able to give him any living expenses either." Jane emphasised the fact that they now had a case law under which they could show they had no more legal obligations for Wang Ming's care.

"I understand," Pearl assured her, although it troubled her, making her feel apprehensive about Wang's likely reaction to this piece of news. He had become accustomed to the routine. *What will he say or do when I deliver the blow to the safety bubble around him?*

Her job might be straightforward interpreting, an agent to facilitate communication between him and his caretakers, but Wang did not see it that way. He always addressed her directly, making his demands on her, totally oblivious of her role as an intermediary.

The niggling worry stayed with her all the way as she hit the now-familiar road leading north. She was the first to arrive at the terraced house, where Wang's flat was on the first floor. She decided to wait for Jane and Peter outside. The memory of

Wang Ming lashing out at her at the solicitors on the previous occasion was still fresh in her mind, and disturbing.

The official delivery of news happened quickly. After interpreting Jane's announcement word-for-word, Pearl became Wang Ming's mouthpiece. Without being fully aware of it herself, Wang's agitation registered in her voice too: "Why? Why? What am I going to do? Where am I going to go? Where can I go?"

Jane repeated what she was there to say – with Peter emphasising its finality – in as polite a way as possible, as was the typical English way; Wang retaliated with a series of rhetorical questions. The 'dance on the stage' began again, and again, until one party – the English side – decided to withdraw. The all-too-familiar game was played out one more time; Pearl had witnessed it so many times before.

In his insistent but feeble attempt to fight, Wang Ming's facial expression remained unchanged. Only his pacing around the room became more hurried. There was no place for him to escape to. Pearl watched him, almost like a shadow of a ghost floating up in the air, and a sense of unreality stuck her.

Eventually they left, without convincing Wang Ming. He was still repeating his questions as they filed out of his flat, one after another.

Pearl's final contact with him came a month after this visit. An unfamiliar male voice on the phone said that he worked for the agency that held the housing contract where Wang had been staying, paid for by Social Services. He asked Pearl to speak to the tenant and issue the final notice that he had to go.

"I have tried to speak with Mr Wang, and he shouted at me in a language that I do not understand. Was it Mandarin?" he asked Pearl.

It could have been his dialect. If so, I wouldn't have understood him either, Pearl thought, but didn't see the need to elaborate. "It may very well be Mandarin. What do you want me to do?"

"Just tell him that he has no choice but to leave. Here he is." Without further ado, he placed the phone in Wang Ming's reluctant hand.

It was not something Pearl wanted to do, but Wang Ming was already on the line. Pearl could hear him shouting: "What are they doing to me? I have nowhere to go. They can't throw me onto the streets. I have no friends, no family, no English. Do they want to kill me? They want me to die?"

"Wang Ming," Pearl called his name, in her most reasonable and professional tone. "You have to listen to me. You can't stay there any longer. You have to go."

"No, why? Why do I have to go? I don't want to go. I do not want to go." His agitation was streaming through the electronic wire, loud and real, hurting both Pearl's eardrum and her core.

"Wang Ming, please listen. Why don't you look at it this way? At least, they have not deported you. Just leave and do something to help yourself." She did not know whether she sounded like a teacher, or just someone repeating words she did not mean.

Whatever else she had said to him that day escaped her. She felt her mouth moving on its own and delivering the harsh message she was asked to deliver.

His desperation found its way to haunt her. *Poor, poor man. What is he going to do? Where is he going to go?*

Chapter 32: The New Mistress for Madam Lin's Paradise

IN NO TIME at all, Madam Lin's Paradise became one of the hottest places in Fuqing, all thanks to China's further opening up and gigantic, economic boom.

For the rest of the world, it was the massive foreign-currency deposit in the mighty Bank of China and staggering growth rates; to ordinary Chinese people, it was something more practical and simple: more cash than they had ever seen or knew what to do with.

The demand for 'relieving' all that stress for high-powered men and business tycoons helped to expand the once-forbidden sex trade beyond recognition. Who could have predicted that what the Communists had so forcefully banned, and uprooted so effectively for decades, would be back with a vengeance, mushrooming everywhere at an alarming speed?

The staunch founders of new Socialist China must have been turning in their graves, and so would have been Chairman Mao. The right once reserved only to the Emperor himself – his well-kept top secret of holding on to his virility and long life – was now out, easily available to anyone who had money. Young and virgin flesh could be easily bought and sold in the unlimited chain of 'massage parlours' for the public and, in more private dealings, directly between a rich client and whomever they fancied to keep as their mistresses and concubines.

Ah Mi, the sex-slave girl for 'Mama Lin', did not have to wait long to get out of the clutches of that ugly, ignorant, wretched witch and the dirty, old man Papa Lin. With favours from the likes of her influential clientele – such as Chairman Wang – Ah Mi soon shed her first layer of skin: that of the poor little 'rice girl'. Before she turned twenty she got her wish: her own, trendier, and more lavish Madam Lin's Paradise, which soon overtook the original brand. In fact, the new, younger, and prettier Madam Lin – aka former 'Ah Mi', the name nobody dared utter and which quickly disappeared into oblivion – soon 'stole' the majority of the clients from the Old Madam Lin, hugely decreasing her cash flow; it drove the old man to alcoholic heaven and the old woman to near despair.

It was easy to steal the thunder from the old Madam Lin, who had ruled Fuqing's sex trade, and it gave the 'adopted daughter' an unrivaled satisfaction to strip Mama Lin of her title. The new Madam Lin had everything that the old woman didn't possess – youth, intellect, and a scheming nature, plus an uncanny knack to use anyone and everyone to her advantage. Most importantly, she had power over men: powerful men, men in charge of multi-million dollar businesses, men who had a say in who went to prison and how long they would stay there.

"How old are you?" Madam Lin asked the scrawny-looking girl with sinewy arms, her eyes scrutinizing the girl's potential, as if assessing a cow or a horse in a farmer's market.

A bit lacking in the flesh department, but her tits are well-formed with large, pink nipples, inviting to men.

The girl did not know where to put her hands, whether to cover her chest or private parts, feeling unprecedentedly embarrassed; her shy eyes did not know where to look. Madam Lin inspected every part of her body with a severe expression on her face, typical of any boss-man or woman in China, not least a Madam with a fierce reputation. The girl hesitated a moment as to whether to reveal her real age or lie about it.

"17, my 'fake' age." She decided that it was probably best to be upfront with Madam Lin. Everyone in China had a 'fake age', which is calculated with an extra year, counting the time when babies were growing in their mother's wombs.

No sweet sixteen for this girl in front of her; Madam's mouth turned up in a sarcastic curve but her eyes stayed stern. Her hand reached out and squeezed the girl's bare upper arm and traced the muscles downwards. *Strong arms and hands, good. Men would like that,* she concluded. *Definitely a potential cash cow.*

"Now put on your clothes. You can start working today." Madam Lin issued her instructions. "I don't care what your name is back home, but here you're called 'Ah Jiao' from now on."

Madam Lin went over the House rules. She knew how crucial it was to establish the boundaries from the outset, and she always made sure that those under her were fully aware of her authority, and feared her. Fear was healthy and necessary. There was no need to be Boss if your underlings had no fear towards you.

Once on her own, Madam Lin smiled a smile of a victor: younger girls were coming to her, leaving the old Mama Lin in droves. It would only be a matter of time before her 'mama' shut her business down, and there was not a damn thing the old woman could do about it.

******

She sat on the lap of Ah Tai, let him finger her down there, and made tantalizing moans in response. Here in her private quarters she was not Madam Lin, lowering her status only temporarily. She no longer entertained any clients in her 'parlours', but it did not mean that Madam neglected her own needs for sexual gratification.

Unlike with her businesses, she maintained a low profile regarding what she did in private, and kept her fuck-buddies in semi-secrecy. She only allowed men with certain 'merits' to be entertained in her new townhouse, which was a generous allowance from one of them. The qualifying lovers either possessed bottomless pockets, or had power beyond measure.

Ah Tai came highly recommended. He was only in town for a short visit, the purpose of which was known to a limited few: strictly need-to-know basis. Compared to some from the Underworld, who operated just below the surface and whose reputation went ahead of them, Ah Tai was not a bad bet. Apart from the well-known fact that he was the right-hand man to the revered Dark Power "The Dragon", a local legend, Ah Tai was tall, handsome, with almost a Northerner's pale skin, and a young-looking 40 year old.

Ah Tai stood up and put her down upon the soft bed, which was covered with a down-filled blanket imported from Italy. Her stickiness following his expert finger work excited him. "You can't wait to be fucked, can you, you little bitch?" He smiled as he mouthed his endearment. Some men liked to talk dirty, only because lewd and loose women liked to hear it.

"Of course, Ah Tai. Please fuck me, and fuck me hard," she cooed, her voice a sweeter tone than natural. "You are so big and hard, like a high mountain, just like your name." She spread her legs wider, one of her hands massaging her hardened nipple, the other reaching for his penis that was, like an angry general, standing proudly above her painted face.

One of her hands got hold of his dick and placed it gently into her mouth; the other hand caressed his balls. She licked him and sucked him, making soft, satisfying noises at the same time. In and out, she could feel him getting harder and his breathing become heavier: an animal-like grunt just under his breath.

He pulled himself out of her painted mouth and, with one push, turned her body over onto her hands and knees. As he penetrated her, he shouted: "Motherfucker, you are so fucking wet and tight. I'm going to fuck your brains out."

In and out he thrust, then up and down, faster and more urgent with each movement. It was both savage and satisfying; she thrashed and convulsed under his weight, her juices mixing with his semen as he ejaculated into her and collapsed upon her back.

"You're such a fucking whore, but I love doing this to you. You enjoy being fucked hard and senseless, don't you? You cheap whore," Ah Tai jeered at the woman now lying under him. He'd fucked women of different ages. Somehow he liked her. This woman had no qualms about being ravaged. She loved it, as if her whole life depended on it. A rarity, a motherfucking, born whore!

Watching the man lying wasted next to her supple body, she knew she had done well. She began her questions casually: just a post-sex, friendly chat.

"Ah Tai, I heard that you're traveling around the world. How is Hong Kong?"

"Hong Kong is fucking great! I love that former colony of the British Empire. The English people must know something that we Chinese didn't know. Ah Long is planning to do big business over there. It's payback time for the once Great Britain. About time, too, in my opinion. We Chinese people, descendants of the Yellow Earth, should take the lead and invade the rest of the fucking world, for a change." Ah Tai sneered, a satisfied smile extending from his mouth to the rest of his face, red and sweaty from his earlier exertion.

"Really? Is that what Ah Long wants to do? Relocate from Hong Kong to the UK?" Madam Lin's voice was filled with genuine curiosity. Her life in recent years had been interesting enough as her business expanded and became bigger and seedier – making her more money than ever – but she was not a woman who would rest on her laurels, not at her age. She wanted more; precisely what, she was not quite sure yet. Who cared? Perhaps adventure and excitement, to spice up her life.

"Oh no, Hong Kong will always be our base, but Ah Long is ambitious. He has a global view. Now that we're doing so well in America, he is expanding to Europe."

She was smart enough to understand what he was referring to, even though he did not spell it out exactly. She might not have any idea how big and wide-reaching the Dragon's business empire would go, since she was only a very small fish in the big ocean up till now. Yet, her instincts told her that she could play a bigger part. If she played her cards right, she could very well jump out of the small pond of Fuqing, and go swimming in the oceans with whales and sharks. How cool would that be? In her world, there was no bigger shark than Ah Long.

He was called "the Dragon' for a reason.

Part Three: Winter Chills

Chapter 33: Jack in Afghanistan

IT WAS A long, quiet yomp through the desert; but the noise of the chopper still hadn't left my head. Bagram airfield was 600 km and three hours away. The sun was coming up behind me. Already children were up and laughing, dogs barking, motorbikes tearing down the lanes; and the Taliban – we call them Talis – were sleeping off last night's drugs.

Jez was two kilometres to the north and Mike two kilometres to the south. We split up earlier. This was Nad-e-Ali, Helmand Province, Afghanistan. To be precise, this was 31 degrees, 38 minutes north and 64 degrees and 14 minutes east at 794 metres above sea level. The wind was blowing at a steady 10 kilometres per hour from the east.

The Talis were still in charge, no sign of the victory parade into Kabul around here. Women and girls were locked away inside, and the poppies were being harvested. Apart from the tearing sound of the motorbikes, the scene could be something out of the Koran.

We were here to gather intelligence – maybe to eliminate some Taliban leaders – not to be seen, not to be heard, and certainly not to be captured. The briefing at Bagram was just that – brief. The spooks knew that this was a strategic command centre for the Talis with a lot of comms, both satellite and mobile, coming out of the Helmand Valley at this point, close to the highway between Kandahar and Herat. Iran was 150 kilometres to the west and Kandahar, spiritual home to the Talis, was 110 kilometres to the northeast. Other than that, they knew very little. So, not the kind of place for one of Hereford's finest to be found.

This was what I had been training for. My pulse picked up. Through the Schmidt and Bender scope on my L96 sniper rifle, I zoomed in on a group on motorbikes about 200 metres away. They were laughing, and then I saw money changing hands: a lot of money in bundles. I noted the location and time, feeding the grid into my Garmin GPS for the debrief in three days' time.

The temptation to tap one of them had to be put away for now. Being discovered was not what I was here for. I would not break radio silence until sundown, at which point I would have spent the whole day finding out how this village worked. Set in the middle of corn and poppy fields, this was a wealthy suburb of Laskar Gah, a green and fertile ribbon running through the desert along the Helmand River. Laskar Gah was a key strategic point on the road to Kandahar. Kandahar would fight harder than Kabul did.

Hunger made itself known. I munched a mouthful of flapjack, and swallowed a small amount of water. *Need to save that for when the sun really gets up.* This was one bloody dry land, and thirst could kill.

Crack, crack!

The sounds followed two puffs of mud ten metres to my right. *Shit – are they shooting at me?* I brought the L96 sight back to my right eye and scanned the guys at the meeting. They had gone. Silence reigned. No more shots.

Then I saw him, behind one of the mud walls about 100 metres away. The sun glinted off his glasses. A studious Tali, but that glint had given him away. To kill or not to kill? Somehow he had seen me, but did others know?

He lifted a satellite phone to his ear and it looked odd against his flowing robes. That action made up my mind. One in the chamber. Wind behind at 10 kph. His head in the crosshairs, I steadied my breathing and squeezed the trigger.

Bang! The shot rang out and he was gone in an instant, falling behind the wall. I could not see him. *Do I move or stay here? Stay here!* Moving would make it very likely that I would be seen.

The air was cut by the sound of a car engine roaring through the mud-walled alleyways. An old Mercedes 280 rumbled towards the walled compound where my target fell. I withdrew the muzzle from the hole in the wall in front of me, reloading. I placed the L96 carefully on the floor and reached for my pistol. Still staring through the hole, I listened for any sounds around the grain store that had become my base. Nothing. The car engine had stopped. Shouts echoed from the compound, as the body was discovered. I was 90 percent sure that I had killed him, so he had no story to tell. One minute he was on active service, the next he was carrion.

That's life, and death. Three thousand died in the Twin Towers. The balance had been slightly redressed.

The Mercedes sped out of the compound, heading for Laskar Gah. Two motorbikes followed. Then the dogs started barking. The men were harvesting the poppies. Schoolboys were trudging to school. All was back to normal, except the Talis now knew that they had company. At sundown it would be time to move.

Removing the sight from the L96, I polished the front and rear elements with a Calotherm cloth until all the dust was gone, and slipped the caps on. Dust to dust, ashes to ashes. First kill in Afghanistan.

My breathing had nearly returned to normal, but my heart was still going 19 to the dozen. Four thousand miles from home. Moira and the kids were still in bed, in the middle of the Herefordshire countryside. Safe and sound.

From behind the grain store, the sound of clanking bells brought my head snapping around. Then I heard the bleating. I peered through a crack in the mud wall to see a teenage boy driving a herd of goats down the lane, their bells jangling as they went by. An idyllic scene of total innocence, but as he passed I saw the AK47 slung across his back.

He could be my next kill.

Chapter 34: Pearl's Prison Visit

TO KILL TIME and boredom, Pearl listened to her iPod.

Why do people want to kill time? Pearl wondered. She was perfectly happy to sit back and listen to the beloved music that she had spent hours and hours transferring from her CD collection to her iPod library, or burn the CD – again, why use the word 'burn', as if English was not complicated enough, with its changeable tenses and different voices.

The new, pink iPod Nano was her treasured Christmas gift from Andrew, which had been put to good, regular use. Who had said that music was food to the soul? Few things made Pearl happier than when she was immersed in her beloved classical and modern music, like humming to the beat of Latin sounds with J Lo's sweet voice. Following Ricky Martin and Gloria Estefan, Pearl had discovered a whole host of musicians from that part of the world. Top of her favourite picks included songs of Cheikh Lo, a Senegalese musician, a highly usual choice for someone originated from China. Not only did the energetic salsa sound and African beat lift her spirits, they relieved the tedium of long-distance travel, which had become a regular fixture of her work.

Looking out of the window, the green, green pastures sped by: lush fields dotted with cows and sheep grazing lazily under the cool, low rays of the sun. Pearl was enjoying the views of the fabulous English countryside from a fast-moving Virgin train, heading up north, leaving the sunny Midlands behind with each click clank of the train wheels.

As the train slowed down and pulled into the station in Preston, the city where the prison was located, Pearl saw that the sun had indeed been left behind and rain, in the Northwest of England, reigned high and mighty. The sky was different shades of grey, with the constant drizzle further damaging visibility. *Wise of me to have worn a warm, woolen coat and hat, complete with an umbrella pressed into my hand the minute I left the house in the morning.* She smiled at the image of her thoughtful husband as she got off the platform and rushed towards the exit, overtaking older and less-hurried passengers.

It was also Andrew who packed her sandwich bag, containing her usual simple-yet-essential breakfast: a brioche and a banana. During her three-and-a-half-hour long train ride she had consumed them both, together with a coffee ordered from the passing trolley.

As well-travelled within the UK as she had been, it was her first time to Preston. When she was booked by the solicitor a few days before, she was given instructions as to which bus to take. She looked up through the pouring rain and then down at the slippery, wet road, and she was reminded of Andrew's text 'instruction.'

Take a cab. Even if we have to cover it ourselves, it's better to get to the right place on time than be lost or late.

He was always thinking of her welfare and making decisions like this, as if she was incapable of making them herself. Perhaps he just knew her too well.

She did not mind though. She knew that he was doing it for her benefit. He understood her caution. Having been brought up without much money and little material indulgence meant that budgeting was always foremost in her mind. Even if it was someone else's money she was spending; it made no difference to her.

The second she settled herself in the back seat of the black cab, another text message brightened her phone screen with a ding.

Got there OK?

Yes, stalker, ended by a smiley symbol.

Before she could press 'send', she heard the driver's announcement. "Here you are." The cabbie stopped, and repeated the fare that was flashing on his screen. He had a strong accent, and only with the help of the indicator on the dashboard was she able to tell how much he was asking: £4.20.

"Can I have a receipt please? Thanks! And keep the change." Pearl handed the South Asian driver a fiver, more than enough for a short ride from the station.

The raindrops kept falling, faster and more furious than before, as Pearl walked towards the imposing front gate of the prison.

"Hi." The man wearing a turban smiled at her and offered his hand. "I assume that you're Dr Church. I'm Gups Singh. We spoke on the phone."

"Yes, Mr Singh. We did. Nice meeting you." Pearl smiled back as they shook hands briefly. She had come across an overwhelming numbers of South Asian solicitors, as well as taxi drivers, in the UK. Had she been a regular patient in hospitals, she would have seen quite a lot of doctors from the Indian subcontinent too.

Together, they went through the check-in point as the security guard did his job. Pearl handed over all her properties, except her badge and a key to her locker. Even her scarf had to be left behind.

"Guess that could be a dangerous weapon," she joked, although the prospect of going into prison cells on a rainy day was hardly a lighthearted affair.

Mr Singh did not laugh, his tone turning serious. "Do you know anything about the Morecambe Bay tragedy?"

"Not a great deal, just what I've read from the newspaper."

"My client is one of the gang masters they have arrested and detained here. I'm going to take instructions from Mr L, and I need to know if he's going to plead guilty or not at the trial at the Crown Court in a few months' time."

"Okay." Pearl nodded, feeling her responsibility.

So here she was on that wet, windy, winter day – her first visit to prison – assisting a solicitor with his consultations before one of the biggest trials in the UK criminal-justice system involving Chinese illegal immigrants.

The dream-shattering, tragic story began on a bone-chilling, unforgiving February evening in 2004, when a large group of Chinese cockle pickers slaving in Morecambe Bay were swept away – and among them 23 were killed – by the fast-moving, merciless tides. They were all illegal immigrants from Fujian Province employed by Chinese gang masters, who were collaborating with local English businessmen.

Pearl, like many of the TV audiences and newspaper readers across the UK, was horrified by another tragedy which had gripped the Chinese community; following the notorious mass deaths back in 2000, when 58 out of 60 illegals in the back of a lorry were found dead in Dover after they had been smuggled from Belgium to the UK. These poor sods were packed into a sealed container on a steaming summer day, and all but two were suffocated after their only air vent was shut by the Dutch driver, who was later sentenced to 14 years on manslaughter charges.

With the Morecambe Bay Disaster, the tragedy hit headlines and attracted even more media frenzy, because of all the drama and controversy surrounding these deaths. Layer after layer, the story behind was revealed. As the unexpected tides swept the cockle pickers under the rising waters, one of the sinking victims made phone calls to the emergency services, calling for help. Possibly due to his lack of English in communication, there was some confusion as to how real and severe their risk had been.

Another victim was reported speaking to his wife in China, five thousand miles away, clutching a mobile in his hand, as he and others sank and were quickly swept away by the dark, cruel waters on a chilling night. He had been smuggled to the UK, a foreign land, to give his family a better life. As it turned out, he had lost his life, leaving his family in further financial ruin; his untimely death cut off not just the future family support, but the ability to pay back debts that had already been incurred, and were mounting.

Fifteen cockle pickers survived to tell the tale, having witnessed their mates being washed away, and that fateful incident was forever etched in their living memory.

To local fishermen and residents alike, Morecambe Bay was known for its treacherous sands. Even experienced fishermen stayed away on that particular night; one or two kindhearted ones had even tried to warn their Chinese competitors prior to the tragedy, to no avail. Fate had its own course to run, when men were helpless. Those who drowned were mostly young men in their prime, along with two women. In total, 21 bodies were recovered after the rescue mission, and the remains of one of the victims were found as late as 2010.

As the images of these drowning illegal immigrants came alive in her active imagination, Pearl and Mr Singh passed the security check and were ushered into one of the consultation rooms. They took their seats. Mr L, one of the two Chinese gang masters arrested shortly after the incident, came into the room wearing his prison outfit and a yellow apron, to mark him out.

A young man from Fujian himself, Mr L – together with his criminal partners – was charged with manslaughter and a number of other crimes.

"Hello, Mr L." Mr Singh offered his hand, introducing his interpreter for the day.

"This is Dr Church, your Mandarin interpreter."

Chapter 35: All in a Day's Job for Ah Fang

WHEN THE MORNING sun shines through the silver-coloured blinds, I try to keep my eyes closed a little longer, although the clanking sound from the kitchen has already woken me up. Uncle is up and making breakfast.

I do not feel like getting up at all. Tough night, that was.

The last client I had was an ugly beast, a big lump of white flesh, fishy eyes, with disgusting odour from both his breath and under his arms. He had what we Chinese call 'fox-stinking smell', which became much worse with every movement he made. He obviously had a lot to drink before he came; possibly fucking a whore was to make him feel better about his miserable life. I doubted very much that he had a wife or girlfriend, as he was an awful sight to look at every day, even for me; and a prostitute was supposed to be blessed with less-judgemental eyes.

His body was so fat he found it difficult to shift its weight. Below his massive beer belly, his small dick was almost invisible amid layers and layers of fat, puffy flesh rolled down by gravity. He also had fat rolls of cash, however. He paid up front for an hour, but time seemed excruciatingly slow-moving. It took me forever to get him off, and most of the time he pinned me down with his massive weight, puffing while pushing, and nearly squeezing the life out of me, petty and miserable though it may be.

Apart from his disgusting physical traits, he was a nasty piece of shit too, obviously enjoying exerting pain on my tender body. My arse is now probably blue and bruised from his ruthless spanking. My breasts are sore from his pinching and biting, and all the bones in my small body seem to have been rearranged after being crushed, pushed, and shovelled about. At one point, when he hit me hard on the cheek of my bottom, it hurt so much that I could not help from letting out a loud scream. I covered my mouth quickly. There was no point alerting the Uncle downstairs. I knew that there was little he could do to help me, except to get me into trouble with Madam later.

For one thing, Uncle's English was hardly sufficient to argue with the guilao; secondly – and more importantly – the 'white ghost' was twice as big and definitely more intimidating! I could tell from his mean-looking shifty eyes. If the police were called, what would they do? They would take us all in, let the punters go, and then, with the duty solicitor they called on our behalf, pester us girls for a damn statement. Finally they'd release the working girls but charge the Uncle with managing prostitution, just like the time before. What happened next? I lost two days' income and received a severe telling-off by the real 'Manager': the madam. As if that was not punishment enough, I was then dispatched to a rougher location and given a further reduction to my meagre earnings, on top of being subject to more idiotic clients: all means designed to make me repent.

Stop right there, a voice in my head snaps and summons me back to reality. Some things are best left where they belong: *in the past*. If I were granted a superpower, I would have liked to erase some of the nasty experiences from my memory. If I was not careful, they had the most stubborn and powerful audacity to creep up on me and shake me to the core. I did not need it, not now when I was in this semi-hellish existence.

With the resolve to face another day, I snap out of my reverie and open my eyes, ready to get out of bed. In my peculiar 'profession', I spend more working time nude than being covered in clothes. There is only one advantage: I can indulge myself in sexy underwear without having to justify my purchase to anyone, and nobody can tell me off for showing too much of my flesh to men: least of all my judgmental parents. Their whips are now too far to reach and they are, in fact, completely in the dark as to what I have been doing for a living.

As I saunter into the *en suite* bathroom, where there is a full-length mirror, I scrutinise my naked body, checking to see if I have any obvious injuries inflicted by the dirty, fat man, whose face I can now hardly recall: only his disgusting, fleshy weight – still heaving in my mind – and his smell, Still lingering in the airless, stuffy room.

I examine the body in front of me: my breasts are still firm with my youth, but my nipples feel tender and sore, the moon around them is a darker shade of red, having been roughly handled. I reach for my toiletries and take out a soothing cream, which I bought from a Chinese herbal shop in London a while ago. It has peppermint in it and I feel an instant coolness on my skin, as well as a sharp sting on application. I screw up my eyes in discomfort, but I know it will sooth my pain. I do not have the luxury of taking time off.

A few other bruises are on my arms and thighs, so more special balm is applied. I turn around a little and try to identify any unwelcome sights on my butt. Compared to the rest of my body, my butt was a touch too small for my liking, pert as it is. A few punters have told me how much they loved my small, tight arse, because of the kind of pleasure it had provided them. I don't know why these guilaos come to The Oriental Darlings, as one of our brothels is named. Is it because they want exotic, Oriental flesh promising exquisite, sensual pleasure? As far as I know, they have not come to me to discuss Chinese classic literature or how much they admire China's rich, long history and culture heritage.

On finishing off all the 'cosmetic' touches to my visible bruises, I brush my teeth and apply the usual skincare and makeup. I proceed to pick out the only comfy piece of clothing I have in my suitcase, a white, cotton T-shirt I bought from Miss Selfridges, with a printed COOL sign in the front. I do not feel cool at all.

I decide to put on my killer, black shoes instead of the soft slippers. Who knows; although it is only morning, we do get 'Early Birds' once in a while, especially during the weekends, which are the busiest days in my profession, unlike most others. For normal folks, the weekends are for recreation, such as taking their children to the park or enjoying a leisurely walk in the country with their dogs. Some men, somehow, tend to pursue a slightly more expensive and energetic activity, like paying their local brothel a visit to have their dicks sucked by exotic creatures. So for us working girls, weekend means working and slaving away for our keep, keeping both clients and Madam happy.

I raise my voice a little as I walk past Chloe's room. "Ready to have breakfast?" I pop my head in her door and note that she is still in bed, her curtains drawn. *She probably had a rough night too.* She only arrived yesterday so I hardly know her, except her English name.

All of us have adopted English names –I have no idea what they mean or if they mean anything at all – like our Chinese names. My name Fang means fragrant, sweet-smelling – to describe grass or flowers – and it also means virtue, a good name and reputation. *How ironic.* I cannot help but smile, a sarcastic one. *What were my parents thinking when they gave me that nice name? Did they expect me to live a virtuous life without sin and shame?! Virtue my ass! Would anyone ever associate a girl who sells her flesh as virtuous and sweet-smelling?*

I don't remember exactly when my English name Fanny came about, but it was credited to one of my early clients. When I tried to spell Ah Fang for him, he gave me a dirty laugh and then addressed me as Fanny, while he fingered me down there. It was only later when my English got better that I asked one of my more friendly punters, who told me what it meant. By then, the name was stuck, and I had kind of accepted it as my fate: it even seems appropriate to have a name like that. My clients like it; or shall I say that they like my fanny more than they like me as a person. Well, given my job description and the kind of men I come across, who could blame them? If I were in their shoes, I wouldn't like myself either, and I don't.

"Hello, Uncle Ma," I greet our 'housekeeper', or 'nanny' as we call people like him. Nannies are mostly men, because it is not babies they are supposed to be looking after; girls like me need a multipurpose nanny – their job is not written down but strictly imposed by their employer, who also happens to be my employer. My duties are to serve clients' sexual needs and make them happy customers for whatever length of time they spend with me, and to grab as much cash as possible. The cash I make is to keep many more people happy, such as paying for the services of Uncle Ma. During the week when I am working here, he is my cook, my cleaner, my cashier – taking money from the clients – and my protector. As a bodyguard to front the brothels, if something of a terrible nature happens, the Uncle has no other alternative but to use force. I know that there is a long wooden stick hidden behind the front door, and there are plenty of meat cleavers to choose from in the kitchen drawers, if the need to protect arises.

"Eat well,' he replies, businesslike. Protocol forbids him to become too close to us working girls, and we to him. After nearly a week in the same house with him, I have found out a little more about him than most of the other Uncles I have worked with. I have only met one Aunt so far. I guess it is not the most suitable job for a woman, given the 'protector' part.

Uncle Ma originally comes from Shenyang, a city in the Northeast of China. Damn bloody freezing place, I can imagine. He looks tough, and his face is brown and weather-beaten. He has told me that he is 42, but he looks ancient in my eyes: even older than my dad, who would turn 50 this year. The thought of my father still gives my heartstrings a tiny poke, but the pain has eased.

I eventually managed to get in touch with my parents. I had to. I have given them so much worry and heartache, and there is no way I can ever take away the pain I have caused them.

Naturally, I withhold the information that I am a sex slave for the snakeheads.

"I'm working in the UK and making decent money," I said to my mum, trying to comfort her - she was sobbing her heart out. She made me tearful too. "Don't worry about me, Mum. I'll come and see you as soon as I get my legal status in the UK." I always signed off quickly, the minute my mum or dad started asking more probing questions.

They have no idea, and it is better that way.

Just as I am finishing my rice porridge, pickles, and steamed buns – delivered the day before as a special treat from Madam – I hear Chloe sauntering downstairs in her heels. Seconds later, her tall, skinny frame appears at the kitchen door. Through the daylight, I can see her better. She has very pale skin and stands at least half a head taller than me, with big, black eyes standing out on her slim face. Her painted eyebrows, thick eyeliner, and red lipstick highlight her flawless skin. Her clothes look expensive too. She must be a northerner; I immediately make an assumption.

"Morning, Chloe." I smile at her. Before the breakfast is over, this girl will tell me how she has ended up here, and while I bet that the beginning of her story may well be different from mine, the ending, until this moment in time, remains very much the same.

A girl like me has to work for her keep – isn't that written in my stars?!

Chapter 36: East to West - From Beijing to Paris and England

WAKING UP AND shivering from the chill that pierced the night air, her bare arms and upper body uncovered by her duvet, Madam Lin opened her eyes in darkness and waited for her normal, sharp senses to resume. She did not dream often, but once in a while she would wake up screaming, like that winter night in cold, freezing February 2004.

The dream she had just awoken from had taken her to a land that was very faraway, the land she had left, with the intention never to return. However, in her dreams, she did go back, as if a part of her still belonged to that place.

As she lay still, she recalled what had haunted her, depriving her of her sleep. She was on a luxurious cruise, with Ah Tai. The sea was a deep blue, while the sky was light blue. She was sipping a drink, a very sweet drink in a long, elegant-looking glass. Ah Tai was speaking, but she couldn't hear what he was saying, so she shouted for him to speak up. All of a sudden, the cruise turned into a small, old boat, which started to rock violently. She was in it all by herself, drifting away from the shore. She could see her mother, the old Madam Lin, pointing her dirty fingers at her, cursing in her local dialect. She turned away from the old woman and looked at her own hand, which held a drink earlier. The long wine glass was gone; in its place were broken pieces soaked in blood, her blood. She did not just see red, sticky blood dripping from her hands; she saw a big hole in her chest, blood pouring out. There was no heart inside.

"Ah Tai," she shouted, and jerked awake.

Ah Tai was nowhere. She had not seen him for days. "On business" was what he had told her before he went away just over a week ago.

She checked the time on her mobile and it read 3:00 a.m., too early to rise, even for a hardworking young woman like her. Now fully awake, she let her thoughts roam, taking her back in time. She did not know why, but Beijing came to her mind; all the memories associated with that place came rushing back.

The first and only time Madam had been to Beijing was a brief affair a few years before, when she sold her prospering brothel business and paid her own passage fare to Europe. Many unfortunate, poor, young men and women could not come up with the 300,000 RMB to pay Ah Tai and the smugglers, so they saved, borrowed from families and friends or, in desperation, resorted to loan sharks, with a grand promise that once they had arrived in the highly developed Western European countries, they would have jobs waiting for them. If they were lucky and worked hard enough, they could not only pay back all they owed but have all their dreams come true. Did anyone buy that? Yes, by the hundreds and thousands.

Madam was a different type of fish in the sea of immigrants. For starters, she had made enough of a fortune to afford the most expensive and efficient route: a direct flight from Beijing to one of several chosen destinations across Europe, whichever was easier to get in at any given time. Given her sexual liaison with Ah Tai – the feared snakehead with a reputation preceding him – her migration, while still illegal, had been much simpler and smoother. Madam had her pick. Rome? Paris? Prague? Warsaw? Dublin? Even Oslo and Helsinki were alternative landing locations with her South Korean tourist passport. No, it was not just her name on it, but also it had her photo. Besides, the immigration officers in Europe were so dumb that all Orientals, from the very pretty to the extremely plug-ugly, all looked alike to them. No, they could not possibly tell their age either. On looking at these strange names, even their gender confused the poor Western officials!

Paris, she decided.

She chose the French capital without too much deliberation. What was there to ponder? All foreign countries spoke languages she did not understand. At least she had heard of the French capital, which was often compared favourably to other destinations. Even in her undereducated mind, she was well aware of Paris's reputation for culture and cuisine, not to mention the inevitable references to romance – if French men were romantic, they were more likely to go to brothels, wasn't that so? Another plus for Paris was its proximity to the UK, which was the ultimate goal for most Chinese illegals, as it had the reputation 'of respecting human rights' (official line for asylum seekers) and was known in reality for its leniency, or lack of efficiency, in locating and deporting illegal entrants.

As she pulled the bed cover towards her neck to shield herself from the winter chill, she smiled at herself in the utter darkness that enveloped her inside the newly leased property, for which she had signed the rental contract only the day before. *Yes, I am so much smarter and better than those other poor fuckers!*

Madam Lin had every reason to feel pleased with herself. She never thought herself as being luckier or prettier than any other women she had come to meet. Oh no: she was neither shallow nor vain about her appearance. Yes, she had a better start in her journey to the West not because of her looks, but what was behind them, which counted far more than any beauty a woman might possess. She had seen girls with very pretty faces and young, lithe bodies; but even with their angelic looks and to-die-for, virginal bodies, were they blessed with more fortune and happiness? Only in fairy tales – and Madam Lin did not believe in fairy tales - they were for hopeless romantics and wimps. In real life, beautiful people were often too fragile, too arrogant, or too dumb. Nobody had everything or was given a blessed life without a good reason.

Madam did have a shitty beginning in life, but she did not allow herself to constantly complain about her fate nor feel sorry for herself. What use would that be? Instead of self-pity, she worked hard and took control of her life. In time, she bettered herself, more than many girls and young women in her circumstances could manage. At the end of the day she became the boss of innocent, fresh-faced, even educated, middle-class girls, who would sell their flesh to make Madam rich. They may have been born in decent homes and enjoyed a life of ease, but they still ended at the bottom of the human pyramid. So what had luck to do with any of it?

Her bedside clock had night vision, and its green hand pointed at four o'clock: probably the darkest hour in a British winter. Madam Lin was usually fast asleep at this hour, as very few matters disturbed her sleep, much less her conscience. But not tonight. Going back to sleep had eluded her after waking up from the nightmare, another highly unusual occurrence, if at all. It seemed that her life had come to a watershed with the news she had received the day before. She knew she had to lie low for a while, until this crisis blew over.

Her thoughts returned to the phone conversation nearly 12 hours before. Prior to that, she had trouble getting through to Ah Tai, her on and off lover for a few years, largely due to his work schedule and constant need to disappear from time to time. When she had been in Paris, he had helped her set up her back-street massage parlour in District 13. It was by pure chance that they evaded capture by the French police one night, when Ah Tai was in town and took her out for a special treat. It was her birthday that week, and she had asked Ah Tai to take her to *Moulin Rouge*. Her desire to experience it gripped her after she had seen a pirated copy of the film produced by their very own piracy factories, which Ah Tai oversaw as part of The Dragon's profitable businesses.

After viewing the singing and dancing Nicole Kidman and Ewan McGregor, an unusual impulse took hold of her - Madam fancied a bit of Satine for real, and felt that she had earned it. After all, she was making a lot of money for The Dragon Enterprises. *Since Ah Tai seems unlikely to ever propose to marry me, which is not my fault, I have to bleed him a little. He can't possibly begrudge me such a modest request.*

Ah Tai needed a little persuasion, but that was something Madam was good at. After a mindless fuck and sending Ah Tai to blissful heaven a few times that night, he relented and dispatched one of his minions to secure the highly demanded show tickets that weekend.

While her girls and the housekeeper were rounded up, detained, and lined up to be deported back to China by French law enforcement, the Madam and her smuggler lover enjoyed the fabulous Cancan dancers, with their equally fabulous costumes and music, at 82 boulevard de Clichy, inside that world-famous, well-lit, windmill-like show house, with champagne and dinner for two as a part of their treat.

Madam and her smuggler lover were most definitely out of place there, among the well-groomed couples and rich businessmen entertaining their clients, sipping champagne leisurely and at ease. For one thing, Ah Tai hated the Western food, even the most sophisticated French cuisine. In all the time he had spent in the West, he had never acquired any manners. He poured the expensive drink down his throat and devoured the food in front of him in a quick session of guzzles, complaining bitterly how disgusting they were compared to his local Chinese dishes and white spirits.

"Fuck the French for charging ridiculous amount of euros for such disgusting, inedible food. If I wasn't starving, I'd shovel such garbage in the fucking chef's big mouth!"

It was a good thing that he was speaking their dialect, which even fellow Chinese customers could not understand. Better still, and a true blessing that Ah Tai's temporary, culinary suffering had saved them from the police cell in Paris that night, and a fate not worth contemplating.

Every cloud has a silver lining. The bust of her 'massage parlour' turned out to be not just a sensual treat, but a God-sent chance for her. Finally she was able to persuade Ah Tai to arrange for her next leg of journey, a dream destination for many: the Land of Hope, Great Britain. Time for a change indeed.

Here she was, nearly two years later and after many relocations, a fair share of travels in this small island, in relative terms of course. London had been exciting and fun, yet lost its attraction for her due to too much competition, and it was too chaotic to her taste. Madam did enjoy her brief stint in the Southwest of England. Ultimately, she had found the Midlands most appealing: not as hectic as London, more peaceful and quiet, yet still blessed with the urban convenience in transport and more affordable properties.

The phone call from Ah Tai eventually came, after her frantic dialling to all his mobiles and possible contacts unanswered. *Something must be terribly wrong.* She sensed it but did not have the faintest idea as to what exactly, until the news of Morecambe Bay cockling disaster made Breaking News on all TV stations across the UK, and soon all over the world. She was aware of Ah Tai's business involvement up north, although she did not have a comprehensive knowledge of Ah Long's empire. Her instinct told her that the 'Tragedy', as it was called by the media, had intrinsic links to Ah Tai and Ah Long.

The news spread quickly. A few people, who could be the culprits behind the operations employing Chinese illegals for cockle picking, were reported as being arrested. Her concern for Ah Tai escalated as time went by. Her worry was plunged into a deep fear when she failed to reach Ah Tai, but instantly evaporated after hearing his voice on the phone. The screen showed an unknown caller but it was unmistakably his voice, despite being a little faint and hushed.

Before she could ask any questions, Ah Tai spoke first: "I'm not in the UK, so no need to have any concern over my safety. Just so you know; I'm unlikely to return for quite some time."

He continued to make arrangements regarding his unfinished business. He assured her that the money she had deposited on his behalf was sound and safe in their Hong Kong branches.

"I don't think that anyone will come to you and ask about me. You are in no danger; not linked to me in any way." He paused. She could hear faint, unidentifiable noises in the background, guessing that he might be at an airport or just stepping out of a ferry or something, but she knew better than to ask where he was. If he wanted her to know, he would find a way to tell her. She was in the game long enough to abide by the unspoken rules.

"You know what to do with the property you just rented. It's in your name and it's a Chinese herbal shop. You're a Chinese doctor with all the necessary documents I have given you. Just keep an account of the profits and transfer them to the Hong Kong branch once in a while. I'll take care of the rest."

With that, Ah Tai pressed end and was gone. Where, she had no idea. When would he be in touch? She didn't have a clue either. For now, she was on her own.

Sooner or later, someone would come to her. She would never be alone, even though she might appear to be.

Chapter 37: West to East – Pearl's First Trip to Fujian

MINUTES PAST MIDNIGHT on a week day, in the dead silence of a cold night, the ringtone from the landline disturbed the peace, piercing through the darkness.

Pearl had just drifted into sleep when the call came through. Her husband picked it up. "Hello."

"Hang on, Inspector. It's my wife you want to speak to." Andrew spoke into the phone and passed it to Pearl, who by then was awake and alert. She mouthed a 'thanks' to her husband before she spoke into the handset.

"Hello, sir. It's Pearl Church here. How can I help you?"

"Hello, there. It's Inspector Charles Green here. Dr Church, have you got a minute for a chat?" asked a friendly, male voice.

"Sure. What can I do for you, sir?"

She had perked up, even though she'd had some difficulty in falling asleep recently, and had only managed to succeed in a shallow sleep, after reading a book for an hour or so, to exhaust her brain sufficiently. She had been dreaming one of her many bad dreams, fighting demons or saving the world from destruction. Sometimes when she relayed her dreams to her husband on waking up, she would impress him at the kind of action she went through in her subconsciousness. "Sounds a bit like a Bruce Willis film to me," he had commented.

Right now, Pearl was nodding as she listened to the Inspector, who had offered an apology for such a late call. Pearl had responded, "No problem."

Her makeup free face wore a serious expression as she listened quietly for a few more minutes while the Inspector explained the reason for the urgency.

"Sir, are you asking me if I can go to China with you?" She sounded incredulous.

"Yes, that's right. Would you be able to?"

"I think so," she sounded a little uncertain, as she turned to look at her husband, who, by now, was also fully awake. "When?"

"As soon as we can make the arrangement. Likely to be a few weeks from now."

Twenty minutes later, after Pearl replaced the phone to its cradle, Andrew's questions went straight to the point. "Do they want you to go to Fujian with them? Is that to do with what happened at Morecambe Bay? No wonder they could not wait till morning and an Inspector called you, not the usual PC or DC. Am I right?"

"Yes, you're a smart ass, Andrew." She smiled at her husband, whose quick thinking never failed to impress her. She loved him all the more for it.

"Yes, they need to speak with the families of the victims and hopefully get statements from them. Wow, can't believe that they've asked me to go to China with them."

Her excitement at this unexpected news was hard to contain, spilling over.

"I don't think that you'd be able to sleep for quite some time, am I right?"

Her slightly guilty smile confirmed it.

"I'll go downstairs. I need my sleep." he leaned over and kissed her good night, for the second time that night.

******

Pearl's Diary, on a cold winter day in 2004

It has been a week since our arrival in Fuzhou, the capital of Fujian. There are a dozen officers from the Northwestern Police Force, and two teams. The smaller group stayed in Hong Kong, where they are going to trace the money trail. There were large sums of money transferred from the UK to the banks in HK. It could very well be where the Gang Masters operated. They had Mrs Wong, the Cantonese interpreter, with them.

The rest of us, nine officers and myself, continued our journey to Fujian, where almost all the illegals who died in Morecambe Bay nearly a year ago were from. Half of the police officers have already been here before, a few months ago, led by Inspector Green. Apparently after this unprecedented tragedy struck, they liaised with the Chinese police in Fujian and requested cooperation. The Chinese authorities set up a special team, assisting the British police with their investigation. They flew over to the UK and helped with identifying the bodies and providing items for DNA tests.

From the bits and pieces of conversations I overheard en route, the British officers came to Fujian and met with the victims' families. Because a couple of bodies have never been found, and due to uncertainties surrounding some of the identities of the dead, they had to get help from the family members in identifying and supplying further corroborating DNA evidence.

This time we are here to prepare statements for the trials, and so far the progress has not been great. We've already spent half of the estimated time and we still have two thirds of the statements to take. I can tell that Inspector Green is not terribly happy, especially with the constant Chinese feasting and nonstop Ganbei.

Last night we were taken to another top restaurant in Fuzhou, hosted by the Police Headquarters and their Chief Superintendent, minus the mayor and other civil officials who had been present on the first official banquet on our arrival. It was slightly more relaxed and less rigid. Still it was a trial to the British guests.

At around 7:00 p.m., we were collected by three official cars: the top range of black, shining Mercs, plush, leather seats, genuinely imported, probably made to measure. They must be doing very well, *I thought to myself. I wonder if the British were thinking the same? So far, the newcomers to China have been suitably impressed.* "Nothing like what I had in mind," *as DS Steve had commented.*

"Blow me," *I replied when I was asked what I thought.* "The new wealth we see in China is staggering, even for someone born and bred in this country." No kidding. What was China like twenty years ago?

As the dishes were brought in by pretty, young waitresses dressed in Chinese Qipao – red, silk, figure-hugging dresses decorated in yellow flowers – local beer and expensive Chinese spirits were poured. Personally I was more interested in the large variety of fresh seafood, which Fuzhou was famed for. As mouthwatering as were the raw oysters beckoning my attention, I was aware that my job was to make sure that the interactions between the two parties went smoothly. I needed to keep my employer – the British police – happy, as well as not to offend the Chinese hosts. In fact, because I have a Chinese face and I speak their language, they treated me more like their employee than a guest from overseas. To the Chinese officials, I was just a minion. At best, in their eyes, I was an educated Chinese who was working for Capitalist Britain. At worst, I could be seen as a 'traitor' to the Motherland.

"Miss Zhang, translate this for me." *The man shouting at my ear was sitting right next to me, holding a cup of Chinese spirit in his hand. He raised it in front of him, pointing at Inspector Green on my other side. I knew what he wanted. As the chief host, he wanted ganbei – to empty the cup with the chief guest. Once he had started the ball rolling, all the other people under him would do the rounds. Their sole aim: to get their British counterparts merry and drunk! The more drunk the merrier: typical Chinese hospitality.*

"Inspector Green, guess you have no choice but to drink this round." *I smiled at him. Even sitting down, he's a lot taller than the rest of the crew. He nodded politely to the Chinese police chief, a typical Fujianese man in his fifties, a dark-skinned, medium-build man who knew that he possessed power over many. Inspector Green emptied his small cup of pure alcohol; a slight sign of distaste appeared on the corner of his mouth, which only I detected. I already knew what he thought of this peculiar Chinese custom. Even before the feast began, he had been adamant with his instructions to me: "Pearl, I'd like you to* emphasise *strongly to the Chinese that I don't care for drinking, so please ask them not to waste their tongue and time on me." He had seen enough ganbei shit to want to preempt the Chinese's relentless 'assault' on the table.*

After a couple of rounds, Inspector Green firmly and repeatedly refused any more ganbei challenges coming his way. After dogged efforts by a number of the Chinese officers of different ranks, it slowly sank in that they had picked the wrong man. Okay, the Inspector was a hard nut to crack: no matter. There were soft targets elsewhere, especially the fair-skinned, good-looking, blonde Jenny MacKay, the 32-year-old sergeant. It was her first trip to the Far East, and she was super keen to experience a foreign culture at first hand. She was hugely impressed with all the unusual dishes parading in front of her, stuff she had never seen or heard of in all her years of eating Chinese takeaways.

During the previous meals, she had asked me what each dish was called, and tried to remember their names so she could try and order them back in the UK. I did not mince my words: "You won't be able to get such dishes in the UK, definitely not in takeaways." Sure enough, Jenny stopped enquiring about the names and contents of each delicious offering. She just dug in to her heart's content, and then paid compliments to her Chinese neighbours. "Yummy" was a constant on her lips.

Unable to say no to the insistent hosts, Jenny and the other British officers drank whatever their Chinese counterparts persuaded them to pour down their throats without too much protest. Perhaps they felt that a balance was called for so the Chinese would not be put off completely by the Inspector's cool rejections.

Had Jenny sat closer to me, I might have cautioned her to take it easy. Two hours later, when both food and drinks were consumed to the limit and

228

there was no more room for the still half-filled table, the Inspector rose. Enough was enough. He seemed completely fed up, in both senses.

"Time is up, lads and lass," he said as he clapped his hand.

I turned to Chief Lin and gave him the most charming smile I could command: "The British officers are very tired, and they have a lot to do tomorrow. Can they be excused now? They have to liaise with their UK office before it's too late. They are truly grateful for this wonderful feast!"

I felt obliged to explain so as not to offend the Chinese, thereby keeping their 'faces' intact and their generosity acknowledged. Who was footing the large bills? None of the hosts present, I was sure. How much would that cost? Some poor family could live on it for months!

Only Jenny was protesting on leaving the restaurant. "Why are we leaving now? I'm having so much fun! Let's have some more of that delicious drink."

Giggling hard, and totally unsteady on her heels, she needed two of her colleagues to support her as we filed out of the VIP banquet room to our waiting transport.

She was still laughing when she was half pushed, half carried into the back seat, jammed between the Inspector and DS Steve.

"Sergeant MacKay, watch yourself. You're making a fool of yourself!" Inspector's face was stern and there was no hiding the displeasure in his voice.

"Me? Making a fool of myself? Who the fuck are you?" Jenny suddenly stopped laughing and turned to face her boss, waving her arms accusingly.

"Oh yes, you are not fucking Inspector Green. You can't possibly be that arsehole who sat on the interview panel and gave me a hard time? I knew that he did not like me. God, I wish I never applied for that goddamned promotion. So bloody humiliating!"

Before she could continue, the car swerved to avoid a pedestrian. The driver cursed in Chinese and I heard a loud swishing sound coming from behind. I turned from my passenger's seat just in time to see Jenny vomiting the food she had consumed not long ago. The car was instantly filled with a sour, fishy, and disgusting smell. With his 'What the fuck' under his breath, I knew the Inspector had been the unhappy recipient of Jenny's unwanted bile, both verbal and culinary.

What a way to end a fabulous feast!

Chapter 38: Jack in Iraq: Second Battle for Fallujah

THE SUN WAS setting over the Euphrates River. Muezzins called from multiple minarets around the town. Fallujah was the "City of Mosques", with 200 or more for the 300,000 people who once lived here. Most of them had left for Baghdad or beyond, escaping the first battle, which ended in an uneasy truce.

Since then the insurgents had taken control and heavily fortified and booby trapped the maze of streets. Special Boat Squadron had been in there for the past week, backing up US Delta Force in their robes and beards. That night was the night. Even the Black Watch regiment was involved, intercepting those insurgents who sought to escape the kill zone.

The US Marines led the assault from the northeast. I was here as observer to watch how the "cleanup" proceeded. The insurgents were an interesting mix, mostly Sunnis and members of the former ruling class. They had pulled in men from Baghdad, Chechnya, and even the Philippines in anticipation of the big showdown with US forces. Everyone knew it was coming down; it was just a question of when everyone was ready. It turned out to be this evening, November 7th, 2004.

The light showed on my radio and I raised it to my ear. "Iraqi Commando Brigade and Delta are moving in to secure the General Hospital." This was off to my left, at the end of the old metal bridge that led straight into downtown Fallujah.

I put the sniper sight up to my right eye and focused on the main road outside the hospital. Insurgents were guarding it, filled as it was with their mates from the first battle back in April. I could see the Iraqis crawling though shrubbery, and then the insurgents' trucks exploded as they were hit with RPGs. Delta were well back, pulling the strings. For political reasons the Iraqis had to be first in. The evening sky was lit up and the muezzins fell silent, as my ears were filled with the "crack, crack" of small-arms fire.

Way over by the highway to Baghdad, a giant flash lit up the evening sky. The city was plunged into darkness. They must have hit the main electricity station, as planned. I was here to watch and report back to the spooks. London was worried that Fallujah would turn into a PR disaster. They knew that the US Marines were keen to destroy the insurgents, whatever it took. The city still had many noncombatants. Not everyone could afford to leave after the first battle. It was going to be a bloody mess. You could not fight a battle in the streets of a city and avoid heavy casualties on all sides.

Over on the other bank of the river, the streets and houses were lit up by parachute flares, and then I saw the deathly glow of white-phosphorus grenades. Insurgents ran screaming from their houses and trenches, their clothes on fire, and jumped into the river to try in vain to stop their skin from burning off.

Using white phosphorus was not banned by the Geneva Convention, but it was not the prettiest form of warfare.

I got on the satellite phone to HQ in Baghdad. "The attack on the Eastern Bank has begun. Iraqi commandos are storming the general hospital. I can see armoured vehicles crossing the old metal bridge. City is in darkness."

And then I just watched, listened, and waited. The water tower I was lying on top of gave me a great view across the city. On top of a small hill, it was higher than any other building, including the general hospital. I had been here since the day before. There was a small platform inside the top of the tower where I slept the night. The water level was low, probably because the city's water system was wrecked back in April. I kept low, watching things through the sight on my sniper rifle. Same unit I had in Helmand. Tried and tested, bringing death to 112 men so far. My mustard outfit matched the dusty, yellow cement of the tower. The rifle's job was to help me watch while others did the killing. I was out of this battle, just a spectator reporting back to the public schoolboys in the Green Zone so they could send their briefings to Number 10. After the bloody battles of April, they were right to be worried about how this would go down with the Sunnis in Baghdad. The Shia had Basra and the Sunnis had Fallujah.

Several flashes lit up the skies from first the north, and now the south of the city, followed a split second later by the crump of mortars exploding. Over the river a man ran screaming from a building, his right arm missing and blood all over his face. The mortars were finding their mark. The building opposite had been identified as command and control. Ten seconds later, a volley of shells hit the building and it imploded, all three floors crashing to the ground. No one would be getting out of there.

Over to my left, the small-arms fire and RPG rounds burst into life and death as the commandos pressed home their advantage. Surprise had now gone and the insurgents were fighting back with everything they had. A truck with a rear-mounted, fifty-calibre machine gun was reversed at speed to the hospital gates, and its deadly hail began. Two grenades into the truck stopped the assault and a mortar landed right on the cab.

The resulting explosion rocketed the cab five metres into the air. Then all was quiet.

Insurgents started to run across the metal bridge, and they were cut down before they reached halfway. The injured and dying threw themselves over the edge into the river and were swept away to drown in the muddy rapids downstream.

The Iraqi commandos crossed the bridge unopposed, and started to poke around in the remains of the imploded HQ building. As they stopped for a cigarette, a young woman walked over to them and detonated herself. She disappeared and so did five of the men. The remaining two were minus limbs and screaming in agony. One of them lay on the road, twitching, with his guts hanging out. The other had blood spurting in torrents from a thigh injury. They had only seconds, or at most minutes, to live. One hour earlier they were playing cards in the back of a pick-up truck. Now they looked like they had been through a mincer.

One of the Americans appeared on the scene. Delta force by the look of him. He strolled across the bridge, alone. A young girl approached him with her arms outstretched. He spoke into his head mic. She got nearer, and he pulled his pistol and shot her between the eyes. She fell in the dust, arms still out in front of her.

Another girl had followed her out of the house. She was crying, and shaking visibly. The soldier dropped on one knee and leveled his rifle. He was going to shoot her, too. From the profile of the first girl it was obvious that these were not suicide bombers. They were leaving the buildings, and trying to cross the river before the next shells would land. The second girl approached with her arms held out in surrender. At that moment, I could not stand to see her executed too. The impulse to save her was far more pressing than anything else: overwhelming all my other senses.

The Delta force solider was in my crosshairs, and I squeezed the trigger, aiming at his shoulder. I heard him cursing as his body lost balance. He was hit and he went down.

The girl kept walking towards the bridge.

Chapter 39: Ah Fang's Punter

IN A LONG, dark tunnel, my eyes strained to see if there was anything to the front, back, or sideways. Tentatively I stretched my arms forward: nothing. On my right: void. On my left, my fingers touched something slippery and instinctively my arm withdrew. My body gave a small tremor. Moving slightly towards my left, my hand slowly reached out again, with my weight resting on my right leg.

Something smooth and slick made contact with my open palm. In the darkness there was no telling what it was or its colour, but I could smell something faint, like a body odour. I took a deep breath, trying to inhale the scent. All of a sudden heavy breaths bore down on the side of my neck, my hands were gripped, and I was face down on the ground.

Piercing pain shot through my body. I opened my mouth to scream, but no voice came. I tried to break free, but not a muscle stirred. I did not know what had happened or where I was.

An instant later, I was no longer in pitch darkness, but in a blinding, white light. I felt weightless, my body floating in a vast space. I was drifting upwards as if flying. I looked down and could make out tall buildings shooting up. I had a bird's view of a city for which I had no name, but the view was becoming less and less clear as my body continued to move upward. The sky was a fabulous blue with no clouds, and as if being pulled by magnet, I was sucked towards the shiny light, so bright that I had to cover my eyes.

"Ouch!" I cried out when my hand banged on the corner of the bedside table; a shooting pain stabbed through me. *Damn*, I then realised where exactly I was and what I was supposed to do. I must have drifted off after lunch, before my first afternoon client was to show up.

I reached for my mobile to check the time and it said 1350. I had 10 minutes to polish up my makeup and double check that everything was in order. There were plenty of condoms in the drawer, and the lubricant was handy too. Over time, I have learnt to insist on clients using protection. It simply wouldn't do if a working girl became pregnant. I have been made aware that my time would not be up until my debt was paid in full.

As I put the final touch to my eyeliner and reapplied my lip gloss, I heard the door downstairs open and a male voice talking with Auntie Sun. Her English was poor, but she was competent enough to extract the right amount of money from the clients. She had volunteered her saga during our earlier chat over the lunch table. She had two children in China who needed support for their education. Her husband left her and the young children to go to America, having been promised a fortune. Initially he was sending money home on a regular basis. Then it suddenly stopped after a year. No news, no money, nothing. It was as if he has been wiped from the face of the earth. Her story reminded me of what I was told by Aunt Hua, almost identical.

Everyone I met had a sorry tale to tell, some more heart-wrenching than others. Perhaps there too many similar stories; they lost their appeal, good and compassionate as their hearts may once have been, but utterly numbed over time.

How many times had I heard Auntie Sun wail about her pitiful tale? I had lost count and I could recite it by heart after the second time.

"We waited and waited, and we tried to locate him by asking other villagers and their relatives overseas, but nobody had any idea where he was. After two or three years, we eventually decided that we could not wait for his money any more. So we went to everybody we knew and borrowed more money for my fare. If my children could not depend on their father for support, I had to do my duty as their mother." Auntie Sun was not complaining, even though she had every right to. She was simply stating facts of life. Her children were left behind with their elderly relatives, like millions of children of migrant workers in China when their parents went far away to make a living.

Footsteps coming up brought my attention back to the here and now. I rushed out of my door, in case the client went to the wrong room. Although there were only two of us – Lulu and myself – I knew she had her first client and now it's my turn.

At the top of the stairs, I saw the man; or rather, I saw him vaguely in the dimly lit house. Auntie Sun called up to me in Chinese: "One hour, full service."

"Follow me," was all I had to say to the man as I led him into my 'palace' and closed the door.

Unlike some clients, who grabbed me as soon as they entered the room, this man stood by the door and seemed to be in no rush in getting into my knickers. A little surprised, I looked at him.

He was what some Chinese people called 'Ah Cha' – literally meaning inferior – referring to people from India or Pakistan: south Asians of any description. I don't know who first used that term: probably Cantonese people, who seemed to have prejudice against anyone who was not Cantonese. Seriously; those from Hong Kong's main island felt superior to those from the New Territories, only miles away from them. What do I know? I have come across quite a few Asian people – usually males, understandably in my profession – and I have no idea where they came from. They all look similar to me, except some are younger, better looking, and more generous with their tips.

This man appeared familiar, especially when he smiled at me. I have seen him before, but I just could not place him right now.

"Don't you remember me, Miss Li?" He spoke at long last.

It clicked. His voice reminded me where exactly I had seen him before: at Branston Police station a few months ago. He was wearing a smart suit then, and he didn't have a cap on. As instructed by various snakeheads and Madam on numerous occasions prior to the police raid, I was to give false details on arrest, hence Miss Li, one that came to me at the time.

"Oh yes, you are my solicitor." I returned his smile with a nervous giggle, blood rushing to my face and hot with embarrassment. *Damn, am I in trouble again?* I cursed in silence.

Perhaps he read my mind. "Don't worry, young lady. I'm not police, and I'm not here to arrest you." His black eyes were on me steadily, watching my reaction.

Then why are you here? I thought, but didn't say it out loud. Instead I nodded and smiled at him some more. Maybe he was no different from the other men who came here.

"You want massage?" I asked tentatively, unsure if I should approach him like a normal punter, or treat him with extra caution. Despite my limited understanding of the law, I knew that lawyers had magic powers, and they could make me go to prison if I were not careful.

"Is that all you do, massage?" There was a distinctive tease in his voice, and it brought to mind that he had asked me something similar at the police cell last time. He obviously didn't believe me when I confirmed that being a masseuse was what I did for a living.

Shit, I don't remember his name. I racked my brains trying to recall. On my release from police detention, he gave me his business card, reminding me to call him if I was ever in trouble again. "I will," I had promised him earnestly at the time, but the moment I walked out that police station, I tossed away his card. What's the point of carrying it around and risk being found by the police – they would know instantly that I had been arrested before. Worse still, if my managers discovered me keeping details of a solicitor, they would suspect what I was up to and give me serious shit.

With a stroke of luck, his surname returned to me. "Yes, Mr Khan. I told you that I work in massage parlour. I do good massage. I make you relax and happy." I gave him one of my best practised smiles, tilting my head slightly aside, looking innocent. Men loved it.

"Call me Ahmed; I told you, too, at the station."

With that, he stepped forward, his face only inches away. His hand reached to the small of my back, pulling me towards him. My scantily dressed upper body crushed into his firm, tight clutch.

He held me like that for what seemed a long time, but it must have been only seconds, as I felt his breath getting heavy by my ear, his hardness against my belly. He was nearly a head taller than me.

"Ahmed." I murmured his name, raising my eyes to meet his.

"Now be a good girl and do what you do to other men. I promise that you'd never get into trouble again." He spoke quickly and in a hushed voice, his mouth brushing against my earlobe. I knew then exactly what he wanted from me.

Without another word, I stepped away from him, ridding myself of the black-lace, see-through top, and the red, lacy bra and matching thong, in a sequence I've done many times. Like a practised performing artist, in no time at all, I was completely naked, leaving nothing for imagination.

He stood still, his black eyes fixed on me. Lust, all over his face.

Chapter 40: Madam Lin Meets Malcolm

A STRANGE MALE pushed through the door at No 18 High Street, Northgate, a district on the northwest of Birmingham. A mature woman, in her early 30s, was sitting behind the glass cabinet counter in which various items of Chinese medicine were on display. Behind her sat a row of large glass jars containing dried plants and herbs of different shapes and descriptions.

"Can I help you?" Madam Lin looked up from her bookkeeping. She was calculating the profits of the month while serving customers. Mondays were usually quiet, so she had made it a habit to look into her financial affairs on a lean business day.

The man in front of her was panting, short of breath and sweaty despite it being a chilly March day, still British wintertime. On close inspection, the guy was pale-looking and fat, with bad skin full of spots on his face spoiling his otherwise-decent looks. He was at least thirty kilos overweight, making him at least double her slim frame. *He needs more than these slimming pills I sell here,* she noted.

"I hope you can." He paused, perhaps to get his Qi – in Chinese, his energy – back. He went on to explain that he had been coughing forever and he had been to see his GP, who had proved to be 'as useful as a chocolate tea pot', so, as his last resort, he decided to try his luck at the Chinese herbal shop.

Madam Lin didn't fully understand what he was saying, especially with his very broad Brummy accent, but she was smart enough to work out more or less what he was in there for. He wanted some of her mystic Chinese herbs to cure his flu.

That was how Malcolm and Madam Lin's paths came to cross.

******

Not long after their first meeting, Malcolm gave up his unsatisfactory job in a small accounting firm and became Madam Lin's assistant. His assistance, however, was not limited to her financial affairs, but in all aspects of her life; including that of her sexual needs at the times when she allowed him close to her physically. That did not happen very often, but when it did, Malcolm felt that his long suffering had been all worth it.

Look at me, I mean, who would actually look at me, let alone screw me? More often than not, he depressed himself with his low self-esteem, especially on days when he was feeling particularly unworthy and unloved. As a child, he had been bullied at school. Kids were cruel. He had been called all sorts of names – like "Fatty", "Spotty", and "Pig Face" – even by those who were fat themselves. It was not as if he was the only fat kid in the class, and he wasn't even the fattest, but he got picked on time and again and he never quite understood why. Then he stopped caring. *Call me whatever you like and I just pretend that I do not hear.* That motto served him well, and over the years he got by just fine, with a thick skin and desensitised heart.

He had never been lucky with the fairer species, though. What teenage girls in their right minds would want to go out with someone who all the cool kids tried to avoid? As for him, Malcolm knew from their disdainful looks – and perhaps all the gossip bitchy girls enjoyed more than anything else – that he would only humiliate himself further if he tried. In the end, it did not matter. He had glimpse of his old man's dirty magazines to entertain himself when he first started his sexual urges, and then when he started working his way through various part-time jobs, he had money to buy his own.

There was one short spell of luck in his love life when he attended college and studied for an accounting diploma. There was a girl in his class who was also fat and unpopular, a bit of a loner just like him. After some very obvious hints that she was interested in going out with him – and after they both went out to the end-of-term pub crawl in the city centre, during which they both got fairly drunk – he walked her to her house, where she still lived her parents.

It would have been one of the most awkward moments in his life had he actually been sober, but he wasn't. Neither was the girl in question, whose name was Tracy: not that her name really mattered. It was his first time with a woman in real life, and his education about the opposite sex thus far had come from porn magazines. In his household, there wasn't much of a female presence, as his mother was hardly a role model. Apart from competing with her husband in terms of binge drinking both inside and outside the house, she was often blue and black after their post-binge spat at each other. His dad, occasionally working as a handy man when he had to, loved his bitter beer more than anything else in the world.

Malcolm was the older of two boys. His brother Lee was five years his junior. However, unlike Malcolm, Lee seemed to have mysterious, nonhereditary, poor-fattening genes. In fact, Lee was a skinny bastard. Even at a very young age, he had shown contempt towards his elder brother and would rather be dead than be seen hanging out with him. Lee's mates were skinheads, hanging around the shopping malls and outside magistrates' court, and harassing people whose skin colours were anything but white.

Anyway, Malcolm fumbled with Tracy in her bedroom and tried to have sex with her for the very first time. In her small bedroom, with a bed only big enough for her size 20, it was a bit of a struggle to put his overweight body on top of hers. By the time they both managed to get rid of their layers of clothes, and before they could find a position for Malcolm to penetrate Tracy, he came, all over her fat belly, on her rolls of white, flabby flesh. Even though she was only 20 years old, her body told a different story, having indulged herself in junk food and never exercised in her life.

His sexual liaison with Tracy had a shitty start, and it didn't last long enough for him to fall in love with her, nor she with him. They made out a few more times, without a great deal of satisfaction on either of their parts, and soon parted company. End of Malcolm's First Romance.

After Tracy, Malcolm went back to his porn magazines and X-rated videos; then there came internet, even more accessible and more variety. By the time he entered Madam Lin's Chinese Herbal shop, he had no idea that his life was about to change in more ways he could ever imagine.

******

On the day when this fat, white male showed up in front of her, Madam Lin had been contemplating how she could expand her business, as she had been for some time. She was unhappy with the way things stood. After Ah Tai disappeared due to the heat following the Morecambe Bay disaster, he had stayed out of the UK as far as she knew. Madam Lin had kept her side of the bargain, and continued to deposit a slice of her profits to the

HSBC in Hong Kong, although her take in the business had been steadily swelling.

With only one shop, which she had to manage in person, she employed two girls who gave full body and foot massages to customers. It was all legit from the outside, with Madam Lin – as Dr Lin, the local Chinese doctor – to front the shop. In her white coat, and a pair of glasses which were not for the short-sighted, she looked the part. Alternative medicine had been embraced by the British public, especially those in favour of holistic treatment: the hippies and open-minded, middle-class people who prided themselves as being well-travelled and well-informed about other cultures. With many other small, local businesses failing and frequently changing hands, it was easy to find a vacant shop on the High Streets. Consequently the Chinese herbal shops started mushrooming in UK cities and small towns, not to mention a few bigger chains supported by deep-pocketed investors.

Madam's shop was doing okay, enough to support herself with something extra to stash away, as she was charging the customers an average of £80 and paying the masseuse a mere £5 per hour. No, Madam Lin did not feel that she was exploiting them. These girls were mostly illegal immigrants, and they were damn lucky to be given a job at all. This was before the UK Border Agency's new policy to fine employers who were caught employing illegals. Attention: CAUGHT. How many employers were doing this and how many were actually caught? Madam was quite certain that the UKBA would not want anyone to see their statistics. Why? Because they were so dumb that they had absolutely *no idea* how many such businesses were operating under their collective noses. As for their ever-changing immigration policies, they were always a few steps behind from what was happening in reality. By the time it had occurred to them that they had such and such loopholes that people were taking advantage of, the scammers had already come up with new, smarter, different schemes. Just look at the airport security after 9/11; they forbade passengers from bringing liquid on the plane. C'mon, did they seriously believe that the terrorists would use exactly the same method each time?

Meeting Malcolm was good timing for Madam Lin. After treating his flu with her miracle potion of Chinese herbs – the fact that the Madam had limited understanding of Chinese medicine and never been anywhere near a medical school did not matter. All Chinese people knew a thing or two about treating the flu. You just tell people to go home and to drink boiled-ginger soup, take a rest, and sweat it out. By the time Malcolm came to see his 'saviour', his body had been fighting it for days and the virus was already on the wane. Given another day or so, it would have been gone, with or without treatment. Dumb Malcolm did not know that. Of course not; he was a stupid Englishman.

You go to your GP, they ask you: "what can I do for you?" You tell them what's wrong and wait for a prescription. "There is no need for any medicine. If you are in real pain, take a Paracetamol or two. Otherwise, just take a day off work and you'll be as good as new in a few days." With that, your five minutes' consultation is over, and the GP moves on to his next patient, to probably repeat exactly the same conversation.

Even as unqualified as Madam Lin was, she was better than your average British GP. At the very least, she made enquires on his symptoms, her slim, cool hand taking his chubby one and feeling his pulse. Her touch was electric and soothing at the same time. *Even if I do not know what I am doing, at least I should look like I do,* she thought. *Look at him. At least he is tricked to believe that I am an expert.*

After that, it was an easy sell. She dipped her dainty hand in various pots, and filled a brown, paper bag with a number of strange-looking, weird-smelling Chinese items Malcolm had never heard of before nor cared to ask about. He was then given an instruction: "Go home and boil these dried herbs and roots. They have bitter taste. But good for you. Trust me." She had even managed a smile towards her new customer. In her mind's eye, she could see Malcolm's fat fingers holding his big nose, shutting his eyes tight, and drinking the bitter soup in a guzzle. Bravo!

That night, Madam had a dream, where the white, fat male who was at her shop earlier visited the Chinese 'doctor' again. In a dingy bed-sit, the man was boiling the herbs prescribed to him earlier. He poured it in a dirty, large, red mug, with his favourite football team Manchester United logo on, then swallowed it hard; his face, although not distinctive, showed distaste. One of his fat hands moved to his chubby nose and held it before he poured the rest down his throat.

In her dream, she saw the man lying down in his small bed at the corner and discarded his clothes one piece after another. She could almost feel his heavy breath and saw his erection. He began massaging himself frantically. With each stoke, he became more and more sweaty and energised. He shouted: *I'm coming. I'm fucking coming!*

When she woke up the next morning, her body felt heavy and sluggish, as if she had been repeatedly shagged by the man in her dreams. She had an inkling that this man would be back, soon.

Chapter 41: Pearl's First Police Raid

THE CALL CAME early: so early that Pearl was still dreaming. In one of her dreams, she was in her grandma's house in southwestern China. PoPo, Pearl's maternal grandma, who brought her up. PoPo kept many chickens and ducks in the backyard. In one scene, her husband Andrew sat himself down next to the domestic animals, got his iPad out, and started reading as he played his music at the same time.

In the next dream scene, she was driving her car to visit her parents, with PoPo sitting next to her. Somehow she started panicking because she had forgotten to take her TomTom with her. She went back to the house, which was close by. As she went through the front door, she found it unlocked. A few chav teenagers stood by and watched her. She was suddenly gripped by the fear that these tear-aways knew where she lived and would give her trouble. Distracted, she looked around but could not locate her TomTom.

When she woke up to the ringing of her mobile, she was still in a state between sleep and reality, in a haze of dark and melancholy dreams. For a brief microsecond, she was not sure whether the phone was ringing in the other world or this one.

Andrew's voice confirmed that it was this one, the real world. "Pick it up, Zhenzhu; it must be the police."

He was right.

She quickly reached for her clothes, which were lying in a big pile on the sofa chair in her dressing room; the pile was getting higher by the day. She made a mental note that she should do a sort-out soon. Tidying up was not high in her agenda, especially that day, when she had more exciting prospects on the horizon.

Following her brief conversation with the officer on the other end of the line, Pearl got up in record time. "You don't have to get up, Andrew. It's barely six o'clock," she said to her husband without turning her head when she heard a rustling sound behind.

"It's okay. No big deal," he had replied. "You know me. I'm a *Yunque*." Yunque was the Chinese name for lark, one of many nicknames that Andrew had used to describe himself in front of his wife. She was an owl, *Mao Tou Ying*, in his 'Birds' vocabulary.

In the 10 minutes while Pearl brushed her teeth and applied her daily skincare and light makeup, she knew that Andrew would proceed downstairs and lay out her daily intake of multivitamins and iron pills with a small glass of mango juice. He would also pack two brioches (one extra that day) and a banana in a sandwich bag, her choice of breakfast. Simple, quick to eat, and easy to carry, and fuel enough to last her a few hours. Lack of food did not agree with her.

Two hours later, she killed the engine and climbed out of her red Polo. Her faithful TomTom had guided her to a parking lot about 100 metres away from the police station. She grimaced at how she had once screamed into her mobile when Andrew had entered the wrong police station address while she tried rushing to a location in the dark. Unhappy with her outbursts, he had since taken extra caution when updating her maps and entering the details of locations.

"Mandarin interpreter here for DS Graham please." At the front office, she cheerfully notified a grumpy-looking, middle-aged female to her presence. Would a warm smile melt an icy, miserable heart? Not always.

Pearl was not sure whether the people fronting at the receptions were police officers or civil servants working for a security firm. Like many public services, the police had also outsourced part of their services to private firms. Well, there were *officers* who did not wear uniforms, like DS Graham, who greeted her half an hour later.

On the phone earlier, the officer had asked her to come as soon as she could. She had done so, yet they kept her waiting. She knew there was no use to hassle them, as she had worked for them long enough to know that they operated on a different timeframe. Over time, she had learnt that when a police officer said 10 minutes, it was hardly ever the case. It could mean a whole lot longer, and could very well mean hours. Sometimes she thought of taking her time, or at least allowing herself a cup of coffee before setting off – or finishing the one she was drinking – but she never could. She took her job far too seriously. She could not explain why; she simply needed to keep things moving.

The morning went by, with one coffee after another: one of those instant types that Andrew more or less banned from their home. He always used a cafetière to brew his beloved Kenyan. Pearl did not mind the instant, since her coffee drinking came quite late in life and Nescafe seemed adequate to kick off the day, although she did come to appreciate Andrew's efforts toward 'proper' caffeine and energy boost.

Sitting in one of the solicitor consultation rooms, on a hard, barely comfortable seat, Pearl finished her second brioche with her second coffee in a scalding plastic cup, wondering how much longer she had to wait before anything happened. As much as she loved listening to her music and reading the Tess Gerritsen paperback, which she carried in her large, red, leather shoulder bag, any more of the watery, brown instant coffee and she would feel sick and puke.

One officer popped her head through the door and addressed her: "DS Sandra Shaw, from the Vice Team. Sorry to have kept you waiting, Dr Church. The briefing is about to begin."

Action at last! Pearl trailed behind her along the corridors.

"Do you know what's happening today?" Sandra asked.

"Not a clue. I was rather hoping that you would be able to enlighten me on the matter. Is it interviews or taking witness statements? The officer on the phone didn't say." Pearl's mood had greatly improved, now that she no longer had to wait on that hard chair by herself.

"You were not told?" Sandra sounded a little surprised. "We are going for a raid."

"A raid? Of what? Cannabis factory?"

"No, a brothel. I work on the vice team."

"Of course," Pearl nearly kicked herself. "Silly me. You told me earlier."

"No problem. I did not expect you to know." Sandra said. "Is it your first raid?"

"Oh, yes. The very first time." Pearl confirmed, already excited at this turn of events. Her routine-visit job to a police station suddenly added more colour and vibrancy. Her spirits further lifted a few notches.

Sandra showed her into a large office, where Pearl introduced herself to the team and listened intently to the formal briefing that followed.

After a short speech, Sgt Graham scanned around the room and his eyes rested on Pearl.

"Dr Church," he addressed her. "Our interpreter today." He paused to make sure that all his team heard him, before turning his attention to Pearl. "Once the team gains access to the alleged brothel, you will be the liaison between the working girls and the officers, interpreting as needed. Are you comfortable with this assignment?"

"Yes, sir. I'll do my best." She affirmed by nodding at the same time, her tone solemn, and firm.

She scanned around the big office room, noticing some officers wearing body armour and armed with guns of different descriptions. "Would I need to wear the bullet-proof vest?" she enquired, leaning over to Sandra, who had been assigned as her 'chaperone' for the raid.

"Oh no, you don't need that." Sandra smiled, her pretty face creasing and making her looking a little older.

"Okay, everyone?" Sgt Graham addressed the rest of the team. "All clear on what you should do?"

"Yes, sir." Following confirmation from all present, DS Graham concluded his briefing and clapped his hands for dismissal. "Now off you go."

"Pearl," Sandra said. "If you don't mind waiting here a little longer, I'll come back to you when it's time. Okay?"

"Sure. No probs." She watched the female officer leaving the room, following the other officers, almost all males.

Sandra's typical Black Country accent revealed her origin. Pearl was a little surprised by her slim, petite frame, only 5 feet tall, small for an officer. She had a fair complexion and looked to be in her early 30s, but Pearl could not be sure. It was quite possible that she looked older than she really was. Pearl herself had always looked younger than her age. Nobody believed her when she told them that she had a grown-up daughter who had already finished university. "You must have married when you were 12," was one of many comments that appealed to her vanity: a real ego booster, not that she was egotistic in any obvious way. She was brought up to be modest, but with the knowledge that she had inherited great genes.

Left alone in the large meeting room, which seemed to function as a store room also, Pearl spotted a blonde wig on the shelves. *Must be one of many disguises for the police officers.* Pearl put it on and swiped open her iCamera. Click; she saw herself transformed into a blonde. *Damn, I should start wearing blue contact lenses.* She smiled at the thought, certain in the knowledge that she would not change a thing about her appearance. Andrew would never allow that to happen. "You don't need any lipsticks and you look better without any makeup," he had said on more than one occasion, although she tended to disagree with that assessment.

The blonde Pearl smiled back at her dark-haired alter ego from the screen. Not a bad snap; her finger found the send key. One light touch and off it went. Would it give him a pleasant surprise, or would it goad him into losing his cool? It should cheer him up on a grim day; she settled on that positive thought.

Time ticked by, and at three o'clock Sandra interrupted Pearl from her reading. "We're ready to roll. Follow me."

Immediately, all the officers in the team filed out of the station, filling four cars and a van parked in the backyard. Pearl climbed into the white police van after Sandra and took a seat next to her. Twenty minutes later, they arrived at a prearranged location: a churchyard, deserted except for a few parked cars. Not a place even for chavs to hang around; only dead souls floated in the cemetery.

The driver cut the engine and they waited below imposing church spires. All eyes were on the walkie-talkie, waiting for confirmation from the police officers watching the property in question.

The adrenaline in the van was palpable. Pearl looked at her watch, focusing on the second hand as it ticked a full turn and then another, bringing the time to 4:54. Another 30 seconds.

Pearl's shoulders tensed at a bit of static coming from the speaker, but then silence followed.

Tick... tick... tick, and a voice blared. "It's 4:55! At exactly 5:00, you will position a plainclothes officer in front of the house, and follow the two punters onto the premises. Confirm!"

Sirens sliced through the steady hum of the rush-hour traffic as a number of police cars sped towards the location. The unmarked police van was close behind, as pedestrian vehicles manoeuvred towards the pavement to make way for them. A shriek of brakes alerted Pearl to a near collision between a police car and an old woman in a crosswalk, who was pulled back by an alert young man.

"Gosh, that was a close call," the driver announced.

"She was probably deaf," said Sandra. "You would think that the sirens would be loud enough to wake the dead."

A round of tension-relieving laughter echoed in the van, including a nervous chuckle from Pearl. The temporary distraction was interrupted by the sudden stop of the van, throwing Pearl's body forward. They had arrived at the target location.

The brothel looked like an ordinary, terraced house in a residential area. Nothing marked it out except for the multiple police cars parked in front.

"Go, go!" Pearl heard shouts from the armed officers, who had moved quickly to the target. The commotion made her heart pound faster than ever. She felt adrenaline rushing through her bloodstream, as Sandra nudged her out of the van towards the house.

Breathing heavily, she ran past a stone fence, through a front yard lined with hedges, and climbed a steep flight of stairs to the front door.

The next thing she knew, she was inside the house amid frantic noises and a mixture of English and Chinese dialects.

She saw a middle-aged, Chinese male running out to the back garden. One of the officers shouted after him: "Don't run! Come back!"

Seconds later, he was on the ground with two officers, one on each side of him. He was brought back into the sitting room, where he had been watching a Chinese film from a DVD. The voices coming from the screen merged with the cacophony created by the raid. The man shivered and mumbled in a dialect as the officers released their hold on him. He sank onto the sofa, his hands raised in surrender.

Sandra beckoned Pearl to follow her up the stairs. In front of them was an officer holding a gun, aiming straight ahead. The whole incident felt surreal, like a movie scene until then. Following automatically where the gun was pointing, she came back to stark reality.

"Interpreter, come in here. We need you in this room." The voice, demanding her service, lured her back into her comfort zone, and Pearl geared up to do what she did best.

On entering the room, she was greeted with a sight she had never expected to witness in real life: a white, naked male, trying to cover his private parts with a small face towel, standing at the bedside. On the bed sat a petite, Oriental girl, completely naked, using her small hands to protect her modesty; one of her breasts spilled out, leaving no room for imagination what they'd been up to prior to the bust-in. The room was poorly lit; only a red lantern sat at the far corner, lighting the scene like a porn film set.

"Get their information," the young officer barked.

Pearl approached the girl. "It's all right," she said in Mandarin. "No need to worry. They just want to know your name."

The girl complied, her voice small, but with an unlikely hint of pride. "Ah Fang."

Chapter 42: Jack in Green Zone

FOXTROT SQUAD GOT back early this morning. We were knackered. No proper sleep for three weeks and having to watch that hellhole of a battle for Fallujah. Of course, I had added to the US casualties myself; with my own bit of futile "justice". Like all street battles in city streets, the retaking of Fallujah had been merciless and bloody. That was really the sacking of Fallujah by the American and Iraqi armies combined. Nothing had been achieved except the demolition of a large town and thousands of dead, mostly Iraqi "insurgents".

"Insurgents" is a convenient term we use when we want to kill people. Many were Sunnis who had escaped from Baghdad and holed up in Fallujah, and had established command and control there. The town was still home to many thousands of civilians, who didn't have the money or means to get away in time before the Marines "cleaned house". All we three could do was report back to the spooks here at The Green Zone.

Fallujah was a known source of suicide bombers, who were undermining the peace in Baghdad, as they insisted on blowing themselves up in crowded marketplaces, especially those in the volatile Shia areas of the city. Baghdad had rapidly redivided itself along religious lines – Shia/Sunni, both Muslims, but the Middle East equivalent of the Ulster Catholics and Protestants. The Sunnis held most of the positions of power under Saddam, suspicious that every Shia might be an Iranian spy.

So Fallujah had to be cleansed. The amount of ordnance used in that long battle would make the US manufacturers very happy. The Marines were spraying machine-gun fire down streets and alleys for hours every day. It was mayhem.

The little girl I had saved stepped on a landmine before she got to the bridge and bled to death in seconds, so even that was a waste of time. The spooks were unconcerned about what was happening in Fallujah. It had all been cleared in No 10 as part of our special relationship with George W. Bush. This war seemed more about oil and reconstruction contracts as every day passed. "Shock and awe" was completely overdone. Baghdad's water and electricity supplies were ruined, probably for no good reason, and now the city was on its knees. The masses were getting angrier every day. No water, no light, no food, no petrol – George's dream of democracy had a hollow ring to it.

Our compound was pretty cushy though. Bottled water from Buxton, steaks from Herefordshire, lager from Belgium. No expense spared. Down by the river Tigris, we even had our own water purification plant to keep the shits away. A few miles away, down a very heavily guarded main road, Baghdad Airport brought in the goodies and flew out the bodies. It was all working just fine, unless you were an ordinary Iraqi. There were some of these inside the Green Zone. They had fled there after the invasion, seeking somewhere to live during the looting. About 5,000 had stayed. They'd been checked out, and most of them had permission, but they barely hid their loathing for the invaders, and that included me.

I sat playing cards with Jim, from Foxtrot squad. Jim and I had been selected for the Regiment in the same year, and had been pals from the outset. We had seen a lot of shit in Fallujah that we were both trying to forget. Women and children were being slaughtered wholesale, for nothing. He was a Geordie, coming from an academic family. He had taken a step down from Captain in another regiment, and it was his last attempt at getting his purple beret.

Looking at his eyes, I could see that he was burned out. We'd done long tours in Helmand, the preinvasion reconnaissance, and then the Fallujah shit. We both had enough. The Americans thought they were in charge here and strutted around the Green Zone. They were crowing about what were they doing in Fallujah, like it was something heroic, but it was really no different from the Nazis in the Prague ghetto. Shooting fish in a barrel. "Overwhelming numbers" was a phrase you often heard from the Americans, and they certainly had those.

I could not stand them. They loved their technology, and thought it was going to win them the war; but they hated the Iraqi – which they pronounced "Eye-racky" – people. It was obvious that the Iraqis were never going to trust them, and were just waiting for them to leave, so they could start settling old scores.

Delta Force could never understand why we spent time talking to locals, trying to build up rapport and understanding. They thought all meaningful information came from their intelligence briefings, not from the street. They respected what we did; they just didn't like our methods. They thought we were a little too subtle.

As I finished the card game with Jim, and pushed my losses over to his side of the ammo box, the act of pushing took on a strange significance. It was as though I was pushing away my chosen profession, the British Army. For a long time I had become tired of the boredom, punctuated by intense action. I wasn't getting any younger. At 33 the body began to slow down, even with regular training and the extra endurance. Those packs were not getting any lighter, and all the kit we had to wear was a nightmare in 45 Celsius. All the training in Wales and Malaysia, and here I was in the baking desert.

At that moment, it crystallized in my head: *I'm getting out.* Moira would be happy, and it would be great to see more of the kids. There was bound to be some security work knocking about. Jonno had left last year and set up his own consultancy. Maybe I'd join the police, if they still took ex-servicemen.

I said goodnight to Jim and hit the camp bed.

Chapter 43: At a Police Station

"NOW LET'S GET this man booked in, shall we?" the custody sergeant said to Pearl, before he cast a quick glance at the Uncle, who was by now fully clothed and looked no different from many other illegal immigrants the sergeant had booked through the cool, concrete counter that separated him from all the serious, repeat offenders and petty criminals. They might as well be in a totally different world. In an ideal world, yes, they may very well never have to meet, in Sgt White's view.

"What's his name?" He again directed his question to Pearl, his mouthpiece.

"Ah Qing." He replied at exactly the same time as Pearl put it to him in Mandarin, obviously understanding enough English to know that his name was wanted.

Pearl knew that the man would not be revealing his true identity, but went through the motions anyway. She asked the man to write down his full, proper name in Chinese in the little notepad she carried to all her interpreting assignments. Her regular contact with many illegal immigrants over the years had informed her that many of them were barely literate with their Chinese. Even so, they could all write their names; even though some did badly, their writing more like a five year old rather than fifty, as that appeared to be the age of 'Ah Qing'.

Ah Qing's writing was clear and identifiable, showing a certain level of education. "Qing Li, Q, I, N, G, first name, L, I, surname, sir." Pearl spelt out the Chinese pin yin for the sergeant. She followed up with Ah Qing's date of birth, and his current address, where he was arrested a short while ago. Like many illegals, he had no fixed abode, usually staying where his job took him. On this occasion, it was the brothel, his most recent occupation as a Nanny.

Next, Mr Li was given his rights.

"You're allowed to speak to a solicitor, free of charge. Do you have a solicitor, or do you want us to call you a duty solicitor?"

Pearl finished her interpreting; Ah Qing looked confused. "Do you think I should have a solicitor?" He turned to Pearl. "I don't think I have done anything wrong, so perhaps I do not need to have one?"

"I am sorry, but it's not my job to advise you. I am just an interpreter."

She translated what Mr Li said to her back to the sergeant, who explained again that it was totally up to the defendant if he needed a legal representative. "It is your legal right and it is completely free."

Once all Li's details were entered in the computer and his rights given, Sgt White asked one of the officers standing by to do a body search. One of the young, male officers approached Mr Li as Pearl talked him through the procedure. The officer was the one who was at the raid and detained Mr Li as he had made a vain attempt to escape from the backyard.

Mr Li must have realised the seriousness of his situation and eventually requested the service of a duty solicitor.

Pearl had seen enough to know the kind of fate awaiting a brothel manager, or those assisting management of a brothel, a charge Mr Li would inevitably receive at the end of his interview: the one he would doubtlessly deny. She had interpreted during a few trials for the likes of Mr Li. If they were unlucky enough to have a strict judge, they could end up receiving two years or longer. Furthermore, at the end of serving their sentence, they would be deported back to China.

Two punters were detained at the same time: one from Ah Fang's room, caught red-handed and stark naked. It turned out that the girl in the other room was from Thailand, and could not understand when Pearl spoke to her in Mandarin. Sandra had to go ahead and book a Thai-speaking interpreter instead. Since there were not many Thai interpreters around, and it was a rare language, they had to wait for quite a long time before the said interpreter could make it all the way from the south of London to where they were.

It did make Pearl's job at the station easier, as Ah Fang now became her only responsibility. She helped book Mr Li because she happened to be around and Sgt White did not like the 24-hour, telephone-interpreting service, which was 'utter shite' in his words. "You often get someone from another part of the world who has absolutely no idea about our system."

"Now, we're going to call a solicitor for you and you'll wait in your cell," Sgt White mumbled, matter of fact. He then handed the keys of the cells to the officer. "Put him in M5, down there."

Obediently, Ah Qing followed the officer to his accommodation for the night. Earlier, at the body search, he had already been cleared of all the extra items, like the jade Buddha on a red chain (for luck and protection) around his neck, his watch, packets of Chinese cigarettes, his wallet, and his jacket, all of which were secured into a clear, plastic bag and put away in a locker. "You'll get them all back before you are released." Was that a reassurance?

Outside his cell, Mr Li was instructed to take off his shoes and leave them by the heavy, metal door. Nobody had ever explained the reasons behind such protocol to Pearl, but she had arrived at an understanding anyway. The police would not want the detainees to have anything that could arm them, either to hurt the officers or themselves. They did have security cameras in each cell as surveillance, but once in a while they would have criminals who chose to misbehave. Like the one they took in as Pearl accompanied the officer and Ah Qing to his temporary cell.

The lad being booked was wearing a full chav outfit, a shining, shell suit with white Adidas trainers. Pearl had no idea what he was in for: something unsavoury no doubt, a robbery or assault. She had seen quite a lot of them when she had been called at the middle of the night to stations, taking statements from victims of such mindless crimes. Instead of being at school or making good use of their youth, these thugs joined gangs, did drugs, and roamed the streets burgling homes and preying on innocent people.

"Hey Sarge; it's you again." He was loud, addressing the custody sergeant as if this was his front lounge.

When the sergeant ignored his quip and ordered the body search, he started bouncing about, his arms moving aggressively, his mouth shooting off one swear word after another. Two big officers had to restrain him by getting hold of his hands and arms, and putting him down on the floor. The shell-suited chav struggled violently and howled out more F words toward the officers.

Guess the brothel raid has not been enough drama for me today. Pearl grimaced as she spotted Sandra, who approached and escorted Pearl away from the scene to give her an update.

"We'd like to talk to the girl and see if we can find out more information about who is behind the brothels. She has agreed to give us a video interview, but will only do so in front of her solicitor. We have called Mr Khan and he is on his way."

Pearl was ushered into an empty interview room, waiting for the solicitor to arrive as she had done numerous times in the past. She glanced at her watch and it pointed at 7:00 p.m. It was a good thing that Sandra had offered to buy her a sandwich prior to the raid earlier. Pearl detected a little noise from her belly again, so she asked Sandra for a cup of hot chocolate. Then she settled down in the chair, taking out her iPod. *It's going to be an exceedingly long day.* She heard an inner sigh.

Waiting for the solicitor. P xx

Midnight job then. A xx

I should think so. Will update you later. P xx

Sure. Have you had any food?

No, I don't feel like going out at this hour, and I think I can survive for a few more hours :)

In that case, drink plenty of fluid and stay calm. A xx

Good man, Pearl smiled at the thought of her husband. *He knows how the lack of food would do to my mood and nerves.* Precisely for that reason, he had delivered food for her on a previous occasion, when she was working on a job which lasted much longer than she had anticipated.

Where are you?

Finished work and cycled home. A xx

Got a Police call. At Q station in Aston Minor. P xx

Had dinner?

No time. Another statement to take, then two translations to do.

I'll bring you some food. Won't be long. A xx

Thirty minutes later he made a delivery to the station: rice with stir-fried chicken and mixed peppers. The kind Pearl did on a regular basis. Simple and easy to do. Andrew had his own version but just as tasty, especially when hunger was assaulting her sense of balance. The receptionist made an exception for Pearl, allowing her to eat the food her husband delivered. It was much better than the microwave-ready meals that Pearl was sometimes offered. Many Chinese detainees would rather starve themselves than subject themselves to that inedible, prisoner shit.

At 8:30 p.m., Mr Khan made an appearance at last. Then it was a long consultation between him, Ah Fang, and Pearl. Eventually the interview proceeded and the video recording started rolling.

By the time the interview was over, it was 1:30 in the morning. Pearl was so whacked that she wanted her bed there and then. It had been a real trial, mentally, physically, and emotionally.

Now, I need to stay awake and get home as soon as I can. At least at this time the motorway should be smooth sailing. She consoled herself with the anticipation of getting to her warm, cosy bed before dawn.

She had been away from Andrew, and from her home, for over 20 hours.

Chapter 44: Worlds Apart

FOLLOWING THAT VERY first visit to Madam Lin's herbal shop, Malcolm's life had taken a dramatic turn; and it was the beginning of Malcolm's unrelenting downfall.

After the highly distasteful, yet effective, medicine he poured down his throat, he had sweated like a pig that night, fantasising about this petite Chinese woman he had only met during the day. He had wondered what it would be like to be making love to that exotic beauty. The thought of shagging her brought him an instant erection like he had never experienced before. No plastic-tits models or olive-skinned, fake beauty on the magazine this time. This woman was real and she had touched him, without him even begging to be touched. He had let his fantasies take over, trying his hardest to picture her naked body, at the same time masturbating as he whispered her name: *Lynne, my beautiful Lynne, I want to fuck you so much. Oh God, I am coming, I am fucking coming! I'm coming all over your face and your tits!*

He wanted her bad, and he needed a way to get close to her. He went back the very next day.

As the weeks become months, Malcolm left his humble upbringing in the rough, violent part of Birmingham, and moved to another part of the city: only 20 miles away, still rough but not as violent, or as racist. His quick, overwhelming obsession with a Chinese woman ten years his senior with less than half his body weight did not go well with his own family, or their 'friendly' environment.

At the height of their romance, if it could be called that, Malcolm took his girlfriend 'Lynne' home to meet the parents. He had never brought a woman home before, so he felt the need to do this at least once in his lifetime: bring a girl home and show that he was not a complete loser. His own brother, who even at the tender age of 18 had paraded off his 'trophy' shags one after another, had called him that.

Malcolm's first and only attempt to prove himself did not go according to plan. In fact, it was a fucking disaster from the moment he and his 'arm candy' showed up at his parents' door. No, actually, before that.

A few days before, he had called his home: "Mum, I'd like you to meet someone." Better on the phone than face to face.

"Okay," was the old woman's response. End of conversation. She didn't sound thrilled or enthusiastic; not even curious, these feelings had left her body long ago, if she had ever possessed any. Not that Malcolm could imagine it ever present, but she was young once, so maybe there was something in her he could no longer see. Whether she had informed his old man or not had been unclear; Malcolm did not see any point in taking the trouble himself.

Saturday morning would be, in his view, early enough for his parents to be still sober. If his mum understood just how special it was for him to bring a date home, maybe she would even get her fat ass off the sofa and make an edible English lunch for them. If so, he could at least get Lynne to stop her nagging.

Ever since his very first sexual encounter with her, she had bombarded him with questions about his family and queried him about his intentions. For a Chinese person, even someone of Madam Lin's dodgy background, being taken to her man's home was a must: a mark of respect towards her as a woman. Given her particular background, it became even more significant that he took her seriously. As to how she treated him in return, that would be a completely different matter. Double standards? Of course.

Early in the week, Malcolm gabbled that his parents would love to meet his girlfriend - which was not precisely true, hence he rushed it out without further elaboration. Madam Lin did not let him get away with that too easily.

"What exactly do they say? Do you tell them that I come from China and what I do? As a Chinese doctor and businesswoman, right? They excited about meeting your girlfriend? You tell me you never have one before, yes?" Her questions and comments came out one after another, allowing him no time to reply.

Her English had been improving steadily, since Malcolm spent all his spare time with her, following her around like a lapdog as if nothing else mattered. She still had problems with her tenses, and limited-to-basic vocabulary. She spoke with a terrible accent and a high-pitched voice, which some people found to be very annoying. It became even more intolerable when she became angry and lost her temper, which happened an awful lot. Malcolm didn't mind; he was even attached to it, in a weird way. Compared to what he was getting before then, she treated him better, and once in a while – when she was in the mood – she would allow him to satisfy his fantasies. God, how he loved her body and her small, tight hole. It was the blissful moment when he was inside her – she moaning with pleasure – that he had sworn his undying loyalty. *I would do anything for this woman, as long as she let me fuck her.*

He would get hard sometimes just fantasising about her small, naked butt, and her small tits with their large pair of dark-red nipples. To top it all, when Madam was really in that rare, fabulous mood, or wanted something from him, she would suck him off. She gave the best blow job he had ever known. That would be what Malcolm construed as heaven on earth.

That was exactly what he was hoping for the day he told her about their home visit. In his head, he had already played out the scene time and again, tirelessly: she would jump with joy and take his clothes off there and then, in the massage room where the girls worked, which was usually off limits to him. He had imagined that his precious Lynne would apply massage oils on his body, then massage his balls and rock-hard dick until they were ready to burst, finally shooting his load down her deep throat. Then she would cool him down by stopping what she was doing expertly and demanding his undivided attention to her needs, which he would be too happy to grudge.

In his mind's eye, he pictured her purring like a cat and begging him to suck her swelling tits. He knew she loved his lavish attention upon her tantalising peaks, where her nipples turned large and hard at his touch. She even encouraged him being a little rough with her soft mounds. She would order him with her high-pitched voice: *SUCK my tits. I know you like my tits. Come to Mommy. Make it hard. YES, YES! Suck me, suck me, you dirty, English, naughty boy!*

"Hey, you listen to me? I talking to you, you not listen. Where the fuck you are?" Madam Lin's thunderous yelling brought him back from his erotic, daydreaming fantasy. Lynne was not lying below his body begging to be sucked and fucked; she was, in fact, very annoyed with him at that moment in time. Her face turned darker and her small mouth opened wide as if she was going to spit on him. She was a time bomb, on the verge of exploding.

"Sorry, luv. I was listening to you." He mumbled an apology automatically, as he had done a thousand times without ever realising it. What Malcolm could not understand was how neither his apologies nor his endearments ever worked on his petite, Chinese doll. To his constant surprise, they seemed to have an adverse effect; Lynne only got madder with each of his attempts to pacify her. All he could do was to scratch his head, where his blond hair was thinning fast with each helpless scratch.

"Sorry, sorry; that's all you say! Always sorry, always sorry. You stupid, English people. All you know is sorry this sorry that. You don't know shit." A barrage of abuse poured out of her mouth, as her voice rose, higher and higher pitched in both tone and volume, until mounting to a squeal, like scraping ice from a car window on a winter day.

Before Malcolm could open his mouth to utter another sorry, while approaching her to try to give her a calming hug, she had violently thrown both her arms forward and pushed him away. For someone with her height and weight, she was a force to be reckoned with. He almost doubled over but managed to steady himself, still holding his hand out to her, which she brushed away with disgust.

"Go away, you stupid, English pig. Leave me alone, before I fucking kill you." She made more outbursts before she slammed the door and stormed out of the back room they were in.

On the day of the visit, Malcolm rose at dawn. British winter nights were long and dark, so it was not quite daylight yet when he had his first morning tea.

En route to Lynne's shop, he popped into the ALDI supermarket and bought a bunch of flowers. He had only purchased flowers once before, when he spent a long time trying to decide which type of flowers would appeal to Lynne. It was the day after their first liaison when she had allowed him to get intimate with her in her flat above the shop. He wanted to surprise her with a romantic gesture. Never before had he courted a woman, so he was as lost in a flower shop as he was around women.

Sensing his indecision, the shop assistant approached him with a warm smile: "Can I help you, sir? What kind of flowers are you looking for? What's the occasion?"

"Errr... I am not sure. Well, guess I am buying it for a girlfriend." He muttered an admission awkwardly, not knowing where to put his hands.

Twenty minutes later, he left the shop with a colourful bunch filled with red roses, pink carnations, and yellow chrysanthemums, expertly wrapped up into a bouquet with a purple bow, spending more than he had intended. Yet he was almost giddy with certainty that Lynne would be overwhelmed by his generosity.

Like everything else in life, he got it wrong, so wrong that he had no idea how and why. Lynne did not squeal with delight when he showed up at her door with the huge bunch of flowers. The first question she had shot at him was: "How much?"

Taken aback, he did not respond until she repeated, louder this time. "You hear me? How much?"

"Ten pounds. £9.99, to be exact," he muttered in a thin voice, hardly audible.

"Ten pounds?" Her voice was in huge contrast to his. "Aiya. So stupid. English people. You can buy a big bag of rice which last me more than a month. Why buy flowers? So stupid." She went on and on, listing a few more practical items he could have bought for her instead, highlighting what an imbecile he had proven himself to be. "Even a three-year old know this. How can a grown man so dumb?"

In time, Malcolm would come to accept that every time she made a complaint about him being dumb and useless, she would associate it with him being English, so it was not his fault alone. He should really blame his race and unfortunate origin for his unforgivable stupidity.

Learning from his past experience, Malcolm had made a decision this time: spend less money and pick his own flowers. Truth be told, he never had much money himself, so he had found Lynne's frugality rather endearing.

Half an hour later, he pressed the buzzer at Lynne's shop plus lodging.

On climbing a flight of stairs to reach her living quarters, he was greeted by her stern, darkened face. Did she get out of the wrong side of the bed again?

"Who dead? You don't know white flowers for dead people?" she yelled, her pitch rising with each word. "I don't want your dead-people flower."

In poor Malcolm's hands, he held a bunch of pale-yellow carnations, which were not quite white, strictly speaking; but if Madam decided that they were white, then they surely were no other colour but white, colour of death.

"Sorry, I didn't know." A muffled apology, a guilty tone.

"You don't know? You stupid, English people. You don't know what flowers to give a girl?" Her voice had soared to a new height, her temper bursting, like a volcano, or Icelandic ash cloud.

Malcolm was struck by a sinking feeling then that the day would not be progressing as well as he had hoped.

His premonition was proved correct.

When she eventually calmed down enough to get into his car, she was still angry at his stupidity, although by then it was for a different matter.

"I was going to give your parents nice Chinese tea, but you say they don't drink Chinese tea. Why not? Chinese tea good for you. Of course, English people too stupid to understand. Why you put milk and sugar in your tea? That's why you so fat. Your parents fat too?"

Indeed, Malcolm had persuaded her not to bring the packet of jasmine tea that she had intended as a meeting gift to his parents. Knowing them, his parents would most definitely not appreciate that ethnic shit, and refuse it on the spot just to make a point.

"Let's give the flowers to them," Madam Lin suggested. Why not? If the English people were too stupid to observe the thousand-year-long Chinese superstition, it was a good thing on this occasion. Even thick Malcolm could see what prompted her sudden burst of generosity: she hated wasting, so this way not only she could save her jasmine tea for another occasion, she could also get rid of the damned, unlucky flowers the stupid son had bought for her. If they brought bad luck to his parents, then it was totally their fault. It would mean that they had done something bad in their previous life. Even fat Malcolm could not debate with that theory, which had stood the test of time for thousands of years.

Their visit, as if to confirm Madam Lin's firm belief that English people were a bloody stupid bunch with no redeeming merits, was doomed from beginning to the end.

Minutes after they had showed up, and before Malcolm had time to introduce his girl properly, his father had shown his full 'glory' of drunken, racist behaviour. Typical English civilised etiquette did not seem to have a place in this part of town, especially in Malcolm's family.

"What did you see in this fucking chink? I always knew that you were a good-for-nothing son of a bitch!" For an old man who was hardly steady on his feet at noon, it was surprising that he had uttered 'son of a bitch' without his usual slurring.

The old drunk must have harboured enough hatred towards both his son and his own wife that such poisonous venom just poured out of his mouth without a second thought to either. Perhaps he was just too drunk to care.

Utterly humiliated and fuming, Malcolm stormed out of his family home, dragging Madam Lin behind him, with his two fingers towards his old man.

"You're a fucking racist pig, I tell ya."

Chapter 45: "It's the Police for you, Pearl"

THE FIRST SNOW of that winter fell the night before, making the streets clean, white, and light.

Pearl woke up early, earlier than she wanted. Andrew had been up already, of course, pottering about somewhere in the house no doubt, leaving Pearl to her dream world a little longer.

It was a crisp Saturday morning. Soon, Pearl would smell the fresh-brewed coffee wafting through the morning air and have her breakfast in bed, as she had done for as long as she could remember. Until then, Pearl stretched her tired limbs on her bed, savouring the end of the week that had just finished.

It had been an exceedingly busy week, something she had never anticipated when she first started as an interpreter. Back in the first year or so, she was lucky to have one or two jobs a week. This week, she had worked nonstop, finding barely enough time to sleep before she got called out again. She even had to cancel a prebooked job from Immigration and Asylum because her attendance at a police station seemed more important.

In the span of a week, she had assisted the police twice – in two different locations –interviewing Chinese illegals who were caught selling counterfeit DVDs. She was in court for the first hearing of the case following the late-night interview with one of the counterfeit sellers. Depending on which magistrates' court they appeared in, where in the country it was, and who the lay judges were, the defendant could end up treated very differently. The solicitor the defendant received, and his abilities, also would make a difference.

"Your worships, this defendant came from China and paid the agent a massive amount of money for his passage to Europe. He has two children and a wife, and his elderly parents are also in China. He's not allowed to work legally here because he has no legal status in the country. So the agent, the gang master, forced him to go out to pubs and shops and sell fake DVDs because he owes them money. He was doing this under duress. He has been kept in custody since Friday night, so he has already paid a heavy price for his actions."

That was Monday morning. The defendant was released immediately without even a fine. How could the court fine him? He had no income and was not receiving any state benefit. Would the court levy a penalty on him to force him into more illegal activities? That made no sense.

The guy on Friday was not that lucky. His solicitor obviously went through the motions, but did not really care what would happen to his client. In fact, the longer the detainee in question was held by the police and the prison services, the longer they were at the mercy of their legal representative to get them out. This time around, the defendant was charged on several counts of fraud by deception, causing big film companies like Warner Bros, Walter Disney, and 20th Century Fox & Co. hundreds of thousands of pounds loss of revenue. The defendant was refused bail, because he had no fixed abode, no community ties, and therefore he was likely to abscond, reoffend, and fail to appear in court for his next hearing. No bail and back to detention.

Pearl left court at noon, hoping to get home for a bit of rest after a ten-day marathon. She had worked through the previous weekend too, and she desperately needed a break. She had spent more time outside her house than in it. When she was at home – only briefly at nights – Andrew was already in bed. They had not made love for at least six weeks, and she didn't even have time to think about it.

Did Andrew miss it? She didn't know, nor did she ask. He was an understanding soul; she took comfort in that fleeting thought. *I must make an effort tonight. I'll take a nap when I get home and then, perhaps by nighttime, I won't be too tired.*

Her thoughts were cruelly interrupted, by both the ringing of her phone and the deep, male, Australian voice on her TomTom instructing her to turn off M6 and take the second turn on the left.

On the phone was the police from a station in Worcestershire. They had just raided another brothel and they needed her service as soon as she could get there. *Damn, I just drove past it 45 minutes ago. Now no break, more work, and I have to turn around and drive another 40 miles! Why didn't they call me an hour ago?*

******

Andrew came out of his two-hour-long meeting feeling stressed out and weary. The damn boss complained about everything, from the lack of government funding to the huge loss of revenue from the School of Marketing and Communications. More staff would have to be laid off, and Andrew would end up doing the firing and being the bearer of bad news.

He switched his mobile on and new messages popped up on the screen. He read the latest first and saw that his plan to take his wife out for dinner would be derailed, again. She sent the message just before she went into the interview: *Do not wait, another late-night job.*

Bloody hell, woman. The police are going to work you to death and I will be the one to bury you!

His stress level shot up as he headed to where his bicycle was parked. He did not bother reading any more messages; his mood had already been irretrievably damaged. *At least I'm getting out of here and not coming back till next Monday. Fuck the work!*

His usually 15 minutes' ride turned out to be longer as he weaved and negotiated his way around the heavy, Friday afternoon traffic. *Great, just as I am leaving, the population of Indonesia decides to come out to play. Of course, the kids nowadays have to be picked up from school, because they cannot walk anywhere. That's why they are so fat, and so many of them obese.*

"Fucking hell! Watch where you are going, will you? You psychotic bastard!" Andrew shouted, as the car with a South Asian driver on the phone almost ran him over, nearly pushing him off his bike.

"Fuck off, you bloody cyclist!" The driver wound down his window and hurled the usual abuse at Andrew, who had made him swerve and his new tyres screech. Perhaps he was annoyed because he had to cut short his chat with his girlfriend on the other end of the line. God, it was obvious he hated cyclists and it could not have been the first time he had a run-in with a cyclist. To Andrew, the feeling was very much mutual.

Neither was it the first time that Andrew had had a heated exchange with a careless driver. He had once been rammed off his bicycle, forced a summersault and landed metres away, badly bruising his arm, legs, and back, hitting the tarmac with force. The car was driven by an elderly, Pakistani gentleman who was probably half blind. They stopped, and the father and son came out of the car, not to check if Andrew was okay or needed any medical attention. "You were riding too close to my father's car. It's your bloody fault." The son had no hesitation in pointing the finger of blame towards the cyclist. Talk about perspective.

"It's fucking unbelievable how unobservant some people are behind the wheel. They don't seem to realise that they are driving a lethal weapon." Andrew was still in a state when he relayed the incident to his wife half an hour later. The aggressive attitude of the driver's son had left him fuming, more than his injuries. Pearl, on the other hand, became even more concerned about his cycling. In her mind, Andrew had become too obsessed with his cycling and was ignoring the risk that he had put himself under, and the worry that his passion for cycling and better environment imposed on her. But she did not tell him that.

Andrew let himself into the house through the garage, where he parked all three of his bikes: one racing bike, one he used to cycle to work, and another one he could fold up. He had initially bought the folding bike for Pearl, when she expressed a desire to cycle with him at the weekend, but after the bike was purchased, she never used it, not once. Even if she still wanted to, she was so tired after she came home from her interpreting jobs that sometimes she just collapsed. She used to exercise regularly, now she had no time: not even occasional, after-dinner walks with him in the evenings.

I need to have a chat with her, perhaps this weekend. Things cannot carry on like this. She can't just work, work, and more work, Andrew decided, as he opened the cupboard and took out a can of baked beans. He was especially fond of beans on toast – 'pebbles on a raft' as his granddad used to say – something Pearl would never eat unless she was stranded on a desert island with nothing else on offer.

God, he missed his wife's home cooking on a day like this. Those damn, tasty Chinese dumplings! Knowing how much he enjoyed them, she used to make them two or three times a week. When did she last make them?

He couldn't remember; it must have been a while.

Chapter Forty-Five

This weekend, the words played in Andrew's mind.

Chapter 46: Ah Fang's Interviews

WHEN OUR MASSAGE parlour was busted last time, I had very long conversations first with Ahmed, and then the police officers.

Nobody knew of my sexual dalliance with Mr Khan. "You know I love you, but you can't tell anyone about our relationship, unless you want to get me sacked and ruin my career." He was not smiling when he said this, even though we had both been naked and he was caressing me. He repeated this caution again at the police station.

"Of course not! I am not stupid," I had replied. Although I did not fully understand the English system, my instinct told me that it probably had more to do with his marital status than his work ethic. I promised him, though. Who am I to disagree with him?

With the police interviews, I had to dig deep into my past and relive many of the horrors throughout my journey, from how I was kidnapped by the gang, raped, and then trafficked across the borders. Yes, the police used the word 'trafficking'.

To me, however, I was just 'transported' to another part of the world; it was simply the revenge of the gods for my bad and nonfilial behaviour back home. No other explanation or consolation. As children, we had been reminded time and again that, if we didn't behave, we'd be punished by the gods whom we Chinese people had worshipped for thousands of years. I didn't believe my mother when she nagged me, reminding me that our gods were stern and vengeful. Now I know she was right. I would never have ended up like this had I listened to my parents.

After my two-hour consultation with Ahmed, I was eventually ushered into the interview room, where five chairs were arranged to accommodate me, my solicitor, an interpreter, and two officers. They were not wearing uniforms: one female, one male. They identified themselves, then followed with the full process of introduction about each present.

"We have charged Mr Li, the Uncle in your words, with assisting management of brothels. It is a crime in this country. He will go to prison," the male officer informed me, scrutinising me, probably trying to gauge my response.

Challenging him and returning his look, I asked, "Are you going to send me to prison too?"

"Oh no, we are not charging you. You're a victim; a woman trafficked for sexual exploitation. You are someone we want to protect," was his response, with a smile.

How interesting! Where I came from, being a prostitute had different definitions. I would never be considered a victim. I would be just a piece of meat for the men to enjoy.

In China, prostitutes – or 'chickens' – are the lowest of the low in the social pecking order. What decent human beings would want to live a life by destroying one of the most precious possessions they have: a woman's virtue? Whores in China are not victims. They are bitches to be spit upon by normal, decent folks. They are simply flesh to be exploited and playthings for the superior beings: men with money and power. Whores are downtrodden, treated as the scum of the earth and shit eaters.

If I still lived in China, I would never have imagined a life as a whore, not in my wildest dreams. My hardworking parents would never allow that shame to be attached to their only daughter. Where would be their 'face'? That would probably kill my father, a proud man, an educated man of good background. He would have preferred me dead than working as a sex slave. It would be highly probable that he would kill me first with his bare hands rather than allow the hands and dicks of nasty men on me or inside me.

When the police asked me about my family, I was too ashamed. I did not reveal that my father was a teacher turned successful businessman, and my mother a stay-at-home housewife whose only worry was me. Neither did I tell them that I ran away from home.

"Now, Fang… can I call you Fang?" Another officer in the room, the female, began her questioning.

I nodded. *Call me whatever you like.*

"Where are you from?"

"China," I said.

"Yes, we can see that. Can you please be a bit more specific? Which part of China?"

"Why do you want to know that?" I sounded defensive. I heard stories that they learned your real name and address, and then they deported you. I wasn't going to fall into that trap. The snakehead would destroy me and my family if my debt was not paid in full.

Through the interpreter, they explained to me that they wanted to know more about me; they were not judging me. Oh yeah, I may be young and naïve, but it would take more than that empty promise to win my trust. With their constant reassurance though, I eventually relented: There was no hardship in sharing a little bit of my life: information like the area where I came from, and why I ended up where they had arrested me earlier. The officers appeared friendly and nice, and I couldn't possibly give them the silent treatment, as I used to with my own mother.

Hours passed, and I was still being interviewed, although they did stop for a convenience break and offered me drinks. They did that in between changing their audio tapes.

"So let me quickly recap what you have just told us, Fang." The female officer looked at me, hoping to catch my eyes, but I did not let her. I focussed my attention on the interpreter instead.

"You were an orphan in China, then one day you met someone on the street whom you called 'Uncle' but he was not really your uncle. He offered you a chance to go overseas. So you did. He got a passport for you which had your name and photo on it. You spent six months on your journey, passing through countries and places you did not know, except Moscow, which you think is in Russia. During all that time you were detained by the snakehead and his men, with other girls like you. You were forced to have sex with the men and were not allowed to go anywhere outside. Is that right?"

You got that part right. I nodded; unwanted, horrifying images threatened to overwhelm my mind, images which I had tried so hard to forget. I blinked, fighting back emotions, refusing to let them erupt.

They asked for more details, trying to trace the routes I was taken through. I had already gone through that once before, with the Immigration on my arrival at the Heathrow airport, and now I had to do it all over again. Only this time, they used a more soothing tone and seemed to treat me with more sympathy. In return I could not help cooperating: out with the stories about being raped by different men and how I was forced into prostitution. Damn it, not only did I have to live through this living hell, but now I also had to vocalise it, as if it happened to someone else. How I wished against wish that it *had* happened to someone else, not me.

In follow-up questions and answers I broke down a few times, and each time they took a break and offered me something to drink. I glanced at Ahmed occasionally, gauging his reaction. He was informed of some of the horrible stories during our consultation, as well as after our lovemaking.

"There is no harm talking to the police. They will be sympathetic." He had been encouraging for me to open up.

"If you cooperate with the police and tell them who is behind this, they may offer you protection, so you don't have to live like that anymore," he had advised me.

Following that first, harrowing interview – when I let my guard down and showed my vulnerability– I was called back to the police station a few more times. Each time, I slowly but surely cracked open more cans of worms, containing damaging evidence against both the snakeheads and the brothel's Madam.

In the beginning I had different interpreters every time, but then I made it clear that I preferred the elegant, good-looking woman whom they called Dr Church.

There was something special about her. She exuded warmth and compassion that I did not find in the others. Even with my limited English and education, I could tell that her English was excellent and fluent. She was always jolly and friendly towards the police officers and solicitors, as well as towards me: a whore. She always had a lovely, genuine smile on her face. During my interviews, I could see that she had tears in her eyes when I broke down. She handed tissues to me and laid her hand on my shoulder, rubbing it ever so gently, when it became too much for me to bear. She had a good heart; I could feel it with my own heart.

One month or so after that raid, detention, and follow-up interviews, the police came to me with a proposal.

"Would you be willing to act as our key witness when we prosecute the brothel managers and smugglers? We would be very grateful if you would consider it. We know that these 'Uncles' or 'Aunts' are just small fish. We want the big, bad wolves, the traffickers, and we would like your help. Would you help us?" asked one kind-looking officer.

I could see his point. The Uncle who was arrested at the same time as me wasn't even a small fish, more like a tiny shrimp in the big, wide ocean. He was a nobody: just a hired hand trying to pay back his debts to the snakeheads. He received a measly payment for cooking, cleaning, and guarding the girls. Like us, he was provided with free accommodation and food and little else. The only difference: I sell my body to earn my keep and he sells something else. Maybe his time, his soul? I do not know nor care.

I did not know what to say. How could a helpless girl like me help them?

"Would I be safe?" I asked instead.

"Yes, you would. Obviously, you have to change your identity, and you can't keep in touch with anyone you knew before – anyone you have known until this point in your life – who might endanger you," said the officer, looking at me intently.

"This is a decision you will have to make, and make it soon. However, we shall have someone you trust who you can communicate with. This person would be Dr Church. We shall arrange a secure place for you to live and you will be safe." Everything was relayed to me by Dr Church, who, like the officers with her, did not smile and sounded serious and grave.

I took my time to mull it over, my mind taking turns in accepting and rejecting this scenario. In the end, Ahmed helped me to decide once and for all. "Do you want to change your life? To turn it around?" he had asked me. I nodded, and it was then that I realised that this was my opportunity, the only chance I might have. How long had I been dreaming about being set free? This was it. I had to grab it with both my hands.

Of course, nobody knew or suspected that Mr Khan had an intimate relationship with me. He was just my legal representative.

"Let us be clear where we stand," he said to me after one lovemaking session. "I am not going to leave my wife and kids for you. They are young and they depend on me."

"You mean you are going to continue seeing me, and cheating on your wife."

"My dear Fanny, that's where you're wrong." He had laughed at my naïveté, his fingers tapping my head jokingly.

"I am not cheating on my wife." He was not joking anymore. "As a Muslim, I am allowed to have more than one wife, so in theory, you can consider yourself my wife too.

"Of course, due to your dubious status, we can't make it public, can we? Not even to my wife."

Especially your wife, I thought to myself. Whatever he said had to be right, since he was a lawyer. If he instructed me to stay away from other men, I accepted it with gratitude.

"How about the madam, and those behind her? They would kill me if they found out that I was the one grassed on them." That was my fear.

"You will be safe. The police will protect you; the law will protect you."

Who am I to argue with a lawyer?

He also offered to give me basic maintenance support if necessary. As it turned out, Ahmed didn't have to support me financially. The police made it amply clear that if I helped them with their case, the British government would look after my welfare. As soon as I gave consent to be their witness, they went ahead and made arrangements: first in nice hotels, then a house in the countryside.

"You would be completely safe and the Chinese snakeheads would not be able to find you," interpreted Dr Church.

At least, that was what they all believed, including me.

Chapter 47: Pearl's Diary, Sunday 12th, February

MY DAD PASSED away at 12:40 p.m. last Saturday, 4th of February, 2006.

This shocking news came unexpectedly and hit me really hard. Having spent another busy weekend when I worked nonstop for the police. I remember that I woke up on Monday morning, feeling exhausted even before I got out of bed. I don't know why, but some mornings, my body just refuses to cooperate when my mind issues the order to get up and get going. Perhaps I should start listening to my body more.

When I eventually roused myself out of a sweet slumber and dragged my unwilling feet downstairs to the kitchen for my morning coffee, Andrew had already left for work. I did not see much of him even during the weekend. On Saturday he had suggested that we go to cinema following a meal in our favourite restaurant. Our 'date' collapsed the moment the police called my mobile.

I must make up to him this weekend. *I made a mental promise to my husband in my head as I made my way back up to my office/guest room with the much-needed coffee in my hand. Maybe I would be blessed with a free day, provided that I did not get any more last-minute police calls.*

On clicking open my inbox, I saw my brother Bing's name in Chinese characters. He almost never e-mailed me unless it was my birthday (if he remembered) or on the Chinese New Year, which had just passed a week before. His message was brief: Call me ASAP.

A terrible fear gripped me instantly as I dialled his mobile number, dreadful thoughts already preying on my mind. He answered on the second ring, no annoying Chinese pop song playing this time.

"What's wrong? Is it Dad?" I asked before any formal 'wei' or hello.

"Dad is in hospital. He could not stop bleeding." No pleasantries on his side either.

"Oh God." I burst into tears, blurring my vision. "That's awful." My emotions reigned and took away my voice momentarily.

In the next hour or so, my family and relatives took turns talking to me. They were all gathered at the hospital, and waited anxiously but patiently. Aunty Yan, the fast-talker, informed me that the hospital had asked for an astronomical amount of money up front before they took my dad in, then refused my family's request to see him. "The doctors do not know what's wrong with him, but they suspect that it could be bowel cancer," said Aunty Yan, in her usual bullet-like, quick pattern of speech.

"The nurse just came to tell us that your dad kept calling your name. Of course, she didn't know it was your name in the beginning and asked him. His mind was still working and he told her that you were his daughter in England."

On hearing that, I broke down completely, tears washing down my cheeks. I felt dizzy with grief and my heart started to ache. The sobbing made me breathless; I gasped for air. I must have cried a long time, until I ran out of energy. Even though I did not look at myself in the mirror, I could feel that my eyes and nose were swollen, and my face stung with the river of salty tears.

When I eventually calmed down, I placed a call to Andrew. He came home straightaway. I shed more tears in his arms, soaking his shirt. He held me for the longest time, only letting go to fetch water for me, and patting my back gently when the strenuous howling made me cough, struggle for breath.

"I'll drive you down to London and we'll try and get you a visa for China."

My experience with the Chinese Embassy has been frustrating and unpleasant, to say the least. They have never been helpful, and have caused me endless hassles on a number of occasions. Ten years before, they had given me a great deal of trouble when I needed a new passport from them. Then they refused to give me a business visa after I obtained my British passport.

I sat in the passenger's seat as Andrew drove us down to the Capital; ever so briefly, the episode with Dick Appleton and my last, formal, full-time employer came to mind. Would they give me the same shit again this time?

The next couple of days went like a blur as I trailed behind Andrew like a robot. We checked into a hotel on Monday night somewhere in London, not far from the Great Portland where the Chinese Embassy was located. I cried to sleep after calling my family again.

The visa officer was a stern-looking woman in her 40s. You would have expected that someone who shared your origin would understand your feelings, but apparently not so if you are a Chinese official and have power over others. It seems that once you have become an official – no matter how junior or senior – you are superior and you are devoid of normal, human emotions. It was a good thing that Andrew did not understand everything I said to her and how hard I tried pleading with her to give me a visa there and then.

"Come back tomorrow," was her final verdict. With that, she shut the window in my face while I was still pleading with her. I knew it was no use hanging around. I had abandoned my usual pride, completely uncaring how undignified I looked with tears streaking down my cheeks, and others present witnessing it. They were all used to such embarrassing scenes in their lives. Similar and worse scenarios were playing out everywhere in China, on a daily basis.

Whilst in London, Andrew had gone online and made reservations for the first flight available to China. "Provided that your visa is granted, your flight is KLM this Friday, flying to Beijing then to Chengdu. You should be able to see your dad on Saturday afternoon, Beijing time."

"What if I don't get my visa?" I moaned, a torturous fear brewing in me. Past memories and an inability to shake off my low expectations of the Chinese officials erased my usual, optimistic outlook.

"We'll cross the bridge when we come to it," said Andrew, in the most soothing tone he was capable of. "We'll just have to pay the cancellation fee. No big deal, my dear. Don't worry; I'm sure you'll get your visa." He was playing the positive role this time, unlike his usual 'expecting the worst' attitude. It was a good thing that we could swap roles sometimes.

Thank God that when we went back first thing the next morning, I got my visa. My dread was gone in an instant; I would have hugged even the severe woman behind the counter had she been next to me. Instead, she just waved me away as I repeated my thanks.

On Thursday, I packed and called my family a number of times, checking on my dad's condition. Bing sounded unhappy when he informed me: "We're taking Dad out of hospital and will send him off at home. The bloody hospital..."

"Don't worry about the expenses," I broke in. "Get whatever medicine necessary to relieve his pain and suffering. I'll pay for his treatment," I offered. I had already withdrawn the best part of my savings.

Bing replied, his agitation obvious in his tone: "It was not just money. There is no point in keeping him in hospital where none of us can see him. The hospital can do nothing to save him except extracting more money from us. The Chinese hospitals nowadays are just greedy bastards who suck patients and their families dry. No professional morals anymore."

I let him vent, my anger and upset rising at the same time.

On Thursday evening, Dad was home and seemed better, surrounded by family and relatives, with me, his daughter, the only one missing. I talked to a lot of my relatives, who had travelled from other parts of Sichuan to be with him in my brother's flat. We used Skype. Unfortunately, they did not have a webcam, so I could not see any of them. We did exchange a few photos while online.

I informed them that I was flying back on Friday, having already cancelled all my work engagements. Despite Mum's view that it was not necessary for me to go back as, "even the doctor could do nothing," I had made up my mind; I wanted to see Dad one last time. He seemed to understand when the news was relayed to him.

On Friday, Andrew woke me up at 5:00 a.m. and drove me to our local airport. I changed planes at Amsterdam, and then Beijing, eight hours ahead of GMT.

As I was flying over Chengdu plain on the way to Beijing, my dad drew his last breath on earth. I was to find out soon enough that he passed away at 12:40 p.m., a peaceful smile on his face when he left this world to the next.

I was full of regret. Had I been allowed to keep my Chinese passport and citizenship, and had there been no bloody requirement for a tourist visa to visit my 'Motherland', I would have been able to see my dad on his deathbed. Had there been a direct flight to Chengdu from the UK, I would have just made it in time to bid good-bye.

Life, and death play tricks on us, but in the end, all the "what ifs" no longer matter. My tears are blurring my view and dripping onto this page of my diary.

Words dissolve and are lost forever, just like my father. Only my memories of him live on.

Chapter 48: "Good-bye, Zhenzhu!"

NOT LONG AFTER I married my wife – who I still called Zhenzhu, her Chinese name – she had to leave the job she had fought so fiercely to secure.

At the time it seemed that she had committed career suicide in a job market that was at the best of times competitive, and at worst stale with nil prospect for someone as qualified as she was. After two years of constant knock-backs and soul-destroying attempts to get employment, I was rather pleased when I spotted that advert seeking interpreters for Immigration and Tribunal services. I was even more elated when she passed the subsequent assessments and started getting calls for assignments.

To both my own and Zhenzhu's bitter experience, I learnt something that was to stay with me: how unemployment could damage our morale and sanity. It was hell, being damned for eternity when you were in your prime without a regular job. It may not define us as human beings, but it seemed to validate our existence to a much greater significance than perhaps most of us realised or gave it credit for.

In my 30-odd year professional career, I had been suddenly without work twice. The first time happened during the economic downturn in 1991. I was made redundant after only three weeks in a marketing job because the big boss's nephew had been lined up for the post. Horror of horrors, I landed it, with my newly acquired MBA from a top UK institution.

Internal politics. The boss's rival insisted on offering it to me only to spite his opponent and then, in a twist of fate, he himself got transferred two weeks later. The consequence? They got rid of me at the first opportunity.

The second time round hit me harder, and it took me a lot longer to get back onto my feet.

Just weeks after Zhenzhu quit her job, following her Employment Tribunal against that evil dickhead Dick Appleton, I was 'let go' by a law firm I was working for. I knew it was a mistake when I took that job – they offered a ridiculous amount of money for a post which was impossible to fill. In their complex politics within the firm – oh yes, again: 'internal politics' – they created my post so they could get rid of their long-serving but miserable clerk. They did succeed in their scheme after a few months, but she made sure that she took me down with her. Talking about scapegoats.

Toughest times we ever had to endure. Zhenzhu's professional prospect was so dire that all her applications and interviews came to nothing: only constant discouragement and occasional despair. I was faring slightly better. I was at least getting a higher percentage of interviews, but hell; they also came to nil, nada.

Then there was Liyuan, Zhenzhu's daughter, still new in England, struggling with the English language and her new, foreign environment. While her mother was being bullied at work, she was bullied in her predominantly white school. When Zhenzhu's bullying was stopped, so did her income, as well as the pride that came with doing a good job.

It was a godsend of an opportunity when I was eventually offered a post in one of the universities in the Midlands. The salary was not as good, but it was more secure and doing something I had done before, in charge of International Marketing in a large faculty. Familiar ground and nothing too challenging, like a fish in the water. Our life started an upward climb from the soul-destroying rock bottom.

Over a period of time, I knew all the ins and outs; it got boring and I became restless. Having been dealt with the blow of unemployment, and suffering the dire straits of utter financial disaster, I had become a little more reluctant to let go. It was in my bones to seek change and novelty, but this time I stayed far longer than I was happy with. For a while, I channelled some of my energies into helping Zhenzhu with her work and relieving her stress, such as by finding obscure police stations I had never heard of till then.

In the early days, I printed out maps with detailed instructions as to which roads she needed to turn onto, and where the nearest car park was. Then came my early version sat-nav gadget, followed by more modern and better TomToms. I was the one who updated her maps, speed limits, and so on and so forth. Electronic items and Zhenzhu were not friends. Once in a while, I would take a day off just to be her driver, when it was foul weather or late at night. The police didn't know, but when they called my wife to do whatever she was supposed to do inside those cold, concrete cells, I was waiting outside in the car, reading a book or doing my crosswords.

Life was going well for us for a few years when Zhenzhu's job assignments became more regular, and her income meant that we could afford more holidays to places she pined to visit. One of her real passions was travelling; she was born with a pair of itchy feet and an unrelenting desire to explore unknown territories.

After a few years of adjusting and adapting, Liyuan's English got better, and so did her attitude. Her bitter resentment towards her mother had lessened, at least superficially; she decided that she wanted to go to university after all. What a relief that had been for her mother and me. Off to Scotland

Liyuan went, and out of our hands, except the usual, student financial support, which her mother was happy to provide.

Out of the blue, Zhenzhu got frantically busy with the police and court jobs; her expertise was so sought after that she was travelling far and wide, anywhere but home.

Off to South Wales now.

One text burst onto my mobile screen.

Can you book me a hotel in Belfast tonight? Due to snow my flight was cancelled.

Another text was blinking at me. Once she jetted off to Paris for a job, and she had to turn down another offer in Germany because we were on holiday in Majorca.

Perhaps it was in her hardworking, Chinese genes, or perhaps the innate fear of not being able to get another job, Zhenzhu was never able to say 'no', despite my constant dripping of advice.

"You have to slow down, my love," I would say. "We don't need the money." Another reminder.

If she had heard me, she did not take it to heart, and I knew her well enough not to confuse money with what really drove her. She was a first-rate interpreter, and she had the genuine desire to help those in need. She took her duties seriously, although her heart was a bit too much on the soft side.

"Do you have to push yourself so hard, Zhenzhu? There are other interpreters around. They can't slave drive you like this. This is just a damn job, not your responsibility to help everyone who needs help." There was more than a hint of displeasure in my tone, even anger.

"I know. I am not helping everyone; in fact, many people I work with are beyond my help." Her frustration filled her voice; her agitation led her to challenge me: "Does it ever occur to you that I *really, really* love my job?" Her reply contained an obvious sting, pissed off at my lack of understanding and 'interference', despite it being purely out of my concern for her welfare.

"Yes, as a matter of fact. I *do* know how you feel about your job. Still, I feel that you get yourself too deep sometimes. How often do you come home, tearful and distressed? Then you can't sleep at night and have constant nightmares when you do. That is not healthy, is it?"

No reply.

There came a point when she was working nonstop, including weekends and many late nights; her much-needed sleep was deprived, not eating properly or at regular times, and she felt tired all the time. Yet, as soon as she got a call, off she went, no matter how exhausted she had already been feeling.

Nights when she came home at 3:00 a.m. and crept up to our marital bed were becoming a norm, hardly to my thrill. For my own sanity – yet to my utter displeasure – I became a regular in our guest room, a routine 'storm' one floor down at 2:00 a.m. Agitation and resentment started to build up, expanding, invisible yet distinctive.

Another late job for Zhenzhu and again I was going to bed on my own. *Time to have a serious chat with her.*

For a while now I had been increasingly dissatisfied with my work and my life in general. Perhaps a change of scene would do wonders. In the darkness that enveloped me in our double bed, lying on my back, I closed my eyes and recalled, fondly, my time when I saved every penny from work and went to America in the summer: climbing, hiking, and cycling. Before I was too old, I wanted to have another go at it. I could take a sabbatical, perhaps even look for a post across the Pond. Given her love for travels, Zhenzhu would jump at this opportunity, or so I assumed.

It appeared that I was wrong in my assumption in this case.

When I did see her, ever so briefly, I broached the subject.

"What do you think of me taking time off and we try our luck in America?" I said, trying not to sound too formal, or final. She was powdering her face, getting ready for another outing to a police station somewhere, to which her TomTom would guide her.

"You're kidding me, right?" she had replied, not looking at me, concentrating on her task at hand, finishing up her primping for the day ahead.

"You know how hard it has been and how long it has taken me to find my footing. Would it be wise to uproot ourselves now when things are going so well?"

Yes, going well for you: not so well for me.

That was it, and I never thought I'd see it coming: she had become so obsessed with her duties to others that she did not even think that I was being serious. There were times I started wondering if she actually listened to what I had to say, not obsessing about her job and how she could 'change the world for the better'.

Time kept drifting away from us, and in a similar fashion we were drifting away from each other.

Early one morning, at around 7:00 a.m., I did my usual ninja routine; she needed rest. *It must have been a serious case for her to be kept that late in getting home.* I crept downstairs to the kitchen.

"Morning." I gave a start when I heard her sleepy voice greeting me. I was about to make my first brew of the day.

"Oh you're up," I said with my voice full of surprise, and then leaned over to kiss her.

"Thought you'd still be in bed. I hardly saw you in recent days." I knew I was implying more than a hint of accusation in my tone, but I just could not help it. I missed seeing my wife, holding her in my arms. I missed the times when I came home after my stressful day at work and she had dinner ready and a big smile on her face.

"I know, I know. I'm so fucking tired." She wrapped her arms around her red bathrobe, which I had bought her two years ago for Christmas. I could see 'boxes under her eyes', an expression she used to describe those unwanted, sleep-deprived dark circles under her eyes. She looked whacked.

"Last night, as I drove along Chesterfield Road, a stupid, white van appeared from nowhere, and he nearly rammed into me; if I did not swing to the other side of the road in time... Fortunately there was no other car coming my way."

"What the fuck!" I burst out. Foul language seemed to feature prominently in our conversation. It was a good thing that we did not have young children around us.

I could just picture these van-driving morons cutting in front of other cars without a care in the world, because they have a van and probably a small dick to match. God, I hate these white-van drivers! *Another reason to leave this fucked-up country*, I reminded myself.

Still fuming at the unknown, nameless driver, I stared at my wife – she could have been killed, a thought I dared not contemplate any further.

"Zhenzhu, you know that this has to stop, don't you?" I paused for effect, before I continued. "You've got to say *no* sometimes. You can't carry on like this..."

Before I could say more, her mobile burst into a cheery melody. She raised her left hand over her mouth, hushing me as she pressed the answer button with her other hand.

"Pearl Church here. How can I help you today?"

Another bloody duty call; I couldn't fucking believe it!

Instant, overwhelming anger rose inside from the pit of my stomach, spilling outside like a tide flooding over me. I reacted the only way I knew how.

I stormed off, slamming the kitchen door behind me.

******

I knew Andrew was pissed off with me, big time, and it was not the first time. He hated it when I overstretched myself, yet, he was an understanding soul; he would come around, given time to cool down.

The phone call came from Ah Fang. Since she was placed under police protection, I was the only external access she was allowed to use. Needless to say, she called me regularly: very frequently in fact.

Putting myself in her shoes, I appreciated how she must feel: alone, probably scared, with no family and friends in this country, being kept away from what she had known and the community she was familiar with. Loneliness and isolation were her only constant company, not to mention the shadows of her past. With her damning evidence against the gangsters who had brought her over and exploited her sexually and morally, what would be the repercussions? I shuddered at the thought.

My sympathy towards her went deeper, from the usual dose of compassion to admiration for her courage to fight back and to take control of her life. She deserved better than the cards she had been dealt with so far.

Coming from a different world, Andrew did not share my insight and kindred feelings towards immigrants, and I didn't blame him. He had discouraged me from accepting the proposal from the police that I become the sole contact for a witness they were protecting.

"She would be calling you day and night," said my husband wearily. "You would have no peace. You should turn it down. They can't do this to you, or to *us*. They can't force you to do this. You're not a police officer." His voice was climbing higher with each sentence, his temper simmering, barely under his conscious control.

"But I can't refuse. She has nobody in this country, and the police want me to help. I cannot let them down."

"Why are you so stubborn, Zhenzhu? You used to listen to my advice. What's got into you now?"

Indeed. I had no idea what had happened with me. Had I heeded anyone's advice over the years, it was Andrew's. Not just because of his sharp wisdom, but also my firm belief that he always had my best interests at heart. He was a protective sort.

"Why don't you listen to me, for a change? This girl needs protection, and I want to help." I could not let him weaken my resolve.

"You can't help everyone, Zhenzhu. She is not your responsibility. If anyone needs protection, it's you, from yourself!" He had yelled at me, and deep down I knew he was right.

Sometimes I asked myself: *What is driving me toward doing things that are obviously stressful for me, both physically and mentally?*

No answer could be found. I tried telling myself that the next time I was asked to provide a service that was detrimental to my health I would be firm and refuse. Then the rehearsed 'No' never had a chance to leave my lips because, as soon as I heard a voice which spoke to my other side – the side that was soft and forever trying to please – I agreed, whether the caller deserved it or not.

As Ah Fang was speaking on the phone, asking me questions for which I had no answers, I heard a beep that indicated another caller was trying to get through.

"Hold on, Ah Fang. I've got another call."

That call was the police, just as I had suspected.

"We'd like you to come to St Paul's Police station as soon as possible."

I entered the location details in my TomTom and saw that it was two hours away by car. A quick scan around the kitchen, where I had sat for the past hour: my coffee unfinished and cold; I was still in my pyjamas and bathrobe, no makeup, my hair messy as hell.

Andrew was nowhere to be seen.

"Shit, shit," I muttered under my breath. Like a soldier ready to go into battle, I sped into action, rushing upstairs to the top floor, two steps at a time. In the quickest changing routine, I put on my work outfit hanging outside my wardrobe. Same clothes as the day before but who cared? Within 10 minutes, I was ready to roll.

Andrew's darkened face appeared in my mind, ever so briefly, as I locked up the front door and coded the alarm on. Normally he would be helping: entering the location in my TomTom, mounting the device up on my window screen, making sure the Bluetooth was switched on, and that the water supply and other essential supplies in the car were within my reach. By the time I came downstairs, everything was working in perfect order.

Not today.

Not long after I arrived at my destination, I made a horrible discovery: Wang Ming was dead.

Ah Ming, the 'Lunatic Wang' with whom I had spent numerous hours in a mental hospital a few years before, was among the dead in a cannabis-factory fire.

The police were alerted that a residential home had been used as a cannabis factory by the landlord. It was a semidetached house at the end of a quiet street. As usual, the police took their time to complete the investigation, which confirmed that it was indeed a place where cannabis was grown.

The night before their planned raid, it was set fire by an electric fault. Like many similar cannabis factories all over the UK, this property had extra electrical wires set up to illegally bypass the electric meter. It was designed to help the plants grow under artificial lighting. Perhaps someone had acted stupidly, untrained and without caution, hence accidentally setting fire to the house in the middle of the night. Nobody knew for certain how the fire was started.

From the ruins and forensic investigation that followed, the police found the remains of hundreds of mature cannabis plants, worth thousands of pounds.

To my utter shock and horror, the police papers showed that one of the two dead men in the fire was Wang Ming, from Fujian Province. Not believing my eyes, I checked again. Yes, it was his photo that was attached to the file, and his date of birth, which I vaguely remembered, the same month as my date of birth.

He was staring at me with his vacant, expressionless eyes. It was the "Lunatic Wang", I was certain.

Poor man; so he got his wish in the end – not through suicide, but burned to death in a house fire – a horrendous and abrupt end to a miserable life. Did he suffer? Did he pray before he departed from this world?

I said a silent prayer for him: *May you now find peace in heaven, Ah Ming.*

At the scene, the police arrested a Chinese male who was spotted driving around in a car near the property. He was subsequently detained and brought in to the custody. During the interview, the police showed him photos of Wang Ming and another man. "Do you know these two men?"

"No." He shook his head vehemently.

Unsurprisingly, the detainee denied any knowledge of the dead men or the property in question. After the police exhausted their questions, without any proof, their investigation did not get much further.

For me, it had been another long and exhausting day. On finishing the interview that night, I was utterly distraught, drained, and dog-tired.

When I arrived home at around 4:00 a.m., the alarm was still on, which surprised me. There was a written message on the Post-It near the alarm: *We need to talk. I'll call you at noon. Andrew.*

Is he leaving me? A fleeting thought flashed across my mind, but I was too tired for it to register.

I needed my sleep, desperately. I stumbled upstairs and fell onto my bed, fully clothed.

Part Four: Spring Hope

Chapter 49: Business Boom for Madam Lin

YEARS HAVE PASSED; they have left their mark upon my face. It was obvious when I stared at myself in the mirror that spring morning. It had been more than a month after the Chinese New Year – which we Chinese call the Spring Festival, the first day of the new, yearly cycle – yet in England, everything has her own rhythm and timing. So the spring takes forever to drive away the harsh, winter blues.

Where I come from, the weather would by now have been warm and people would have been hurrying from one place to another in a rush to make money. Here in the UK, everything is slow: much too slow for my liking.

Fat Malcolm has never understood why he pisses me off all the time and I just cannot get it through his thick skull, as he will never understand our complicated Chinese psyche.

I may not have gone to university and be blessed with years of fine education and qualifications to my name, but I have been through the harsh training of the School of Hard Knocks, and to me life teaches us more than anything. From what I can see, schools and universities do not teach you shit. From what I hear, English university students drink themselves to oblivion or shag whoever they can get. Yes, my girls have entertained a few of them, those who either spend their grants or their daddy's money. Where they get their cash is not my concern, as long as they use the service which I have kindly provided for them.

Everyone is welcome. I do not discriminate against them because they are black, brown, white, or any colour or shade in between. I do not discriminate against them whether they are old, young, fat, ugly, or whatever, as long as they show me their money. Who in their right mind would say no to the magnificent English pound? The value may change from time to time depending on the fluctuating exchange rate, but it is always better than the Chinese currency, or the dollars, or even the Euro. So for me, the more pounds I make, the better I feel about myself. Money, symbol of success!

If there is any season to pick as my favourite, it would be spring, because there is always something to look forward to in the brand-new year. No matter what has happened in the previous year, I can always start anew, kicking off new business ventures and making fresh plans.

Looking back, I am far from content with what I have achieved in the UK since my arrival. It's coming up to eight years now, and I do not have much to show for myself. When I was in China, in a much shorter period I had established myself as a successful businesswoman from very humble beginnings. Madam Lin, back where I came from, had quite a reputation.

Here in the UK, it has not been as easy, especially after Ah Tai buggered off to God knows where exactly; I had little choice but to take on that stupid Englishman.

Apart from getting fatter with each passing day, and his increasing ability to pour down more alcohol, Malcolm has little merit in my highly critical eyes. Still, I need him. At least with his legitimate citizenship and his ability to speak English better than me (not too difficult since he was born and bred English), he still has his uses.

In the two years since I set up my first herbal shop – from which I ran my first behind-the curtains brothel – I have successfully rented three more properties, all with the help of fat-pig Malcolm. With the sizable profits from these 'massage parlours', I have been able to invest in the property business.

The housing market has been going through a big boom, so with the large amount of cash flowing in my pockets and through my hands, I have bought several run-down houses which I rented to students and other Chinese tenants, many of them illegals in this country.

As a first-rate businesswoman, I divide my businesses efficiently and to my best interest. The properties I own, I came by legally, and they have my name on them. As for the ones we rented for other purposes, like Oriental Darlings or Night Angels, we use a number of aliases. You can never be too careful. What if the police started poking around?

Priding myself as being resourceful and smart, I sent the students and tenants in my care with their temporary IDs, or fake ones, to conduct my business affairs (and some would say 'committing crimes' in the case of credit-card fraud). All I needed to do was to pay for them, be it for driver's licenses or passports of certain nationalities. After all, many Chinese illegals sneak into the country with fake passports and visas. They are everywhere, and they need cash for survival.

Far too smart to trap myself in any rental contract, I instead 'employ' those under me, creating jobs and paying them petty cash. Most landlords I have had dealings with are South Asians, whose mentality is not so different from us Chinese. If I offered to pay them cash and a big advance, they were only too happy to let me use their properties and then leave me to my own devices.

The tenants who rent my properties are easy prey – I tell them that there is money to be made for doing virtually nothing, like running errands for me, which they would probably do for free anyway if I ask them nicely. My only condition is that they keep their noses out of my business and not ask questions about matters which do not concern them.

For a very small fee – or sometimes an exchange of favours where money never changes hands – I have my constant supply of cheap labour. That's Chinese for you. Talking about money is uncouth, if you know what I mean.

Exchanging favours is good, sound Chinese philosophy. Over time, I have managed to lure quite a number of students to work for me under different guises, now that my enterprises are expanding into doing things I have never anticipated before. Like Pinko and Chloe, two Chinese girls whose families are middle class in Jiangshu province. Their parents have poured out all their savings to send their only daughters to study. The girls rented a property from me and, instead of working hard on their studies they indulged themselves by buying branded shoes and handbags from Selfridges, spending beyond their means.

Being a businesswoman, I spotted my chance and took advantage of that. *You girls like your Chanel bags and DKNY clothes: no problem. Here are some credit cards to indulge in your shopping habits.* The next thing they knew, I had them in my clutches.

"That Donna Karen dress cost £2000. You can't pay? No problem. I have work for you."

I am a problem solver, and in the end, who is to blame? I am not their mother, so they can't possibly expect me to provide them with the luxury of carrying expensive, designer bags and wearing fancy clothes without paying me back, right? It all worked out nicely for all.

Then, there is money to be made in selling sex, even a dumbo knows that. My 'massage parlours' have been generating a healthy income for me steadily, increasing by the day.

Huge profits in buying and selling properties has become common knowledge, as the boom continues. I have given Malcolm this task as his main priority. He is as happy as an Easter bunny, as he has never seen so much cash flowing through his own hands and it makes him giddy with pleasure.

The credit-card fraud involved higher risk, and I only ventured into it after some persuasion by Ah Tai's friends. "All you have to do is to recruit willing business partners, like students, or those who have finished their studies and do not want to go back to China."

It sounds as easy as piece of pie. My recruits are supplied with the fake bank cards, which have been posted from different overseas addresses – usually from Hong Kong – then Mr or Miss Student advertises a money-making scam on the internet and seduces many young and naïve people, most of them inexperienced and spoilt single children from China, all brought in with just a little bait, sometimes just sweet talk and empty promises, whatever methods work.

Slightly smarter and luckier ones get away with hundreds and thousands of pounds' worth of electronic goods and trendy items from unsuspecting retailers; while once in a while, a stupid one gets caught and jailed. Well, like every venture, there are risks. In the end, there is not much the police could do, as these who get caught know the drill – explaining, "My friend gave me a card to use and I did not know it was fake," or, "I picked up the card I found on the toilet floor and used it."

Even if the police try their best to probe, the trail is unlikely to lead to me. My student network has been extensive and smart, growing like tree branches, not unlike franchises; those on the 'shop floor' generally have no idea whom their ultimate boss is, or even if they did, they know it is far safer to lie to the police than to face the violent retributions from their Chinese superiors. Our four-thousand-year history has taught them that.

One extra score for me with my fellow Chinese people, which I exploit fully to my advantage: their sense of guilt when doing something illegal or bad. They would blame themselves if they get caught. They would curse their own bad luck, or blame it on some sin committed in their previous lives. Other people in the same shoes are sound and safe, making their families giddy with pleasure and their casinos happy. Tough luck has been the explanation for the failure of many mortals for centuries, and that line of thinking will carry on for centuries to come.

My risk has been kept very small; I am able to share in the profits, receiving well over 70 percent as the larger stakeholder. After all, I am the one with the connections to the source. I am their job-creation scheme.

Ah Tai has expected my regular contributions to the Dragon's pockets, but his pockets are so deep; would he really miss what I once in a while choose to put away in my little piggy bank?

My business interests in recent months have become increasingly more exciting, and profits are going through the roof as all my massage parlours have been doing splendidly. The British curiosity about Oriental beauties has been a surprise even for me, although that surprise disappears almost as quickly as it comes, replaced by delight and determination to make my bank managers even happier.

My wisdom in pursuing this line of business has been confirmed, despite the high stakes. As far as I know, there is no real law against prostitution in this country, and that is good enough for me and my girls.

Last night, I had a dream. I dreamt that I was being chased by a monster, which looked a lot like the one from *Alien*. I saw that film only recently, picked from among the many counterfeit DVDs my tenants have left behind.

I was once approached to join in the fun of the DVD copying racket, which was all the rage for a while, employing hundreds of illegal immigrants all over the country, selling from their shoulder bags at every pub and street corner in UK cities and towns. Yes, I saw good money there, but in my opinion it was not worth the risk on balance. Far too many DVD sellers were caught by the patrolling police officers and had their accommodation searched. I had no intention ever to come to the attention of the police, so I stayed away from the counterfeit side of business. Enough small fishes in that pond already; I preferred my own bigger share of market elsewhere.

Back to the dream; the Alien look-alike creature chased after me, and all of sudden I found myself in a cell, a dark room only big enough for me. My hands reached out and were bounced back by the cold, grimy walls. There was no window, no door: only pitch darkness. I screamed at the top of my voice and woke up.

Is that a bad omen? I look at myself again in the mirror and see the dark circles, unwanted bags under my eyes, more prominent than before.

Some of those antiwrinkle eye creams my girls 'bought' from the cosmetic counter in the Selfridges would help. I allow myself a rare smile.

Chapter 50: Trip To Scotland

"DID I EVER tell you how much I loved Glasgow? So many memories up there."

Her head was resting comfortably on Jack's hairy, muscular chest as he caressed her shiny, silky hair – back and forth – in an intimate and soothing way.

They had just made love in her flat, and she was in a reflective mood, remembering her youthful days up in the 'wild west': the west coast of Scotland. A name suddenly returned to her: Harry, the man who had wanted to marry her, and she nearly let him. What a disaster that would have been. She tried to recall Harry's face, but it had faded to just some rough sketches.

Jack had been in her life for over eight months, since they first locked eyes in the police station the previous summer, although they did not see that much of each other, only irregular, brief 'stolen moments', snatched from his busy schedule and other commitments. She could count their encounters with her fingers.

"How about I take you there for your birthday? Would you like that, hen?" Jack stopped his hand movement, raising his upper body, his hand supporting her head so he could look into her eyes.

Her head jerked up, perhaps surprised at his suggestion of a holiday, her thoughts returning to the here and now.

"Seriously? You're not pulling my leg, are you?" Her eyes sparkled, with a wee smile spreading out from inside her irises to the rest of her face, her cheeks faintly rosy from their earlier, energetic lovemaking.

Jacked moved down quickly to the edge of the double bed and gave her leg a tug.

"You mean this, pulling your sexy leg?" He chuckled, his hands lingering on the smooth skin just above her calf, a teasing tickle following the slight pull and squeeze.

She threw back her head and giggled. Then she sat up, looking at her lover, happiness all over her glowing face.

"No kidding. You mean you can get away? You know my birthday is only two weeks away." She had not had a proper break for God-only-knows how long, ever since her last trip with Andrew six months before he had buggered off to America. The thought of her husband cast a shadow on her postcoital bliss.

"Sure, I'd like to try. I'm owed a holiday or two, at least. If nothing serious comes up, I can book a week off." It sounded as though he was only testing the idea that was already formed inside his head.

"You know, dove, I'd love to spend more time with you and to get to know you properly."

Perhaps he needs to know whether his feelings are simply a phase of lust, or more, Pearl gathered. *What better ways to test our feelings than spending a little quality time with each other in an idyllic place, without interruptions and the constant call of duty?*

"That would be really cool." Pearl smiled, her voice betraying more than a hint of glee at the prospect.

"Well then. That's a date." The man uttered the final word on the matter.

As soon as Jack left that day, Pearl's brain began formulating a plan for her Highland Fling, ticking off items on the to-do list.

The very next day, she rushed to her favourite shops. She did not have in mind exactly what she was looking for, but she knew that if something caught her eye and the price was right, she'd know straightaway it was for her.

Years of shopping by herself had made her a very gifted consumer – an intrinsic and reliable fashion sense so that no matter what she wore, it would effortlessly bring out the best in her. She did not need expensive clothes; just her first-rate judgement as to what suited her body shape and style. Her colour coordination was such an innate gift that, no matter what she put together as an outfit, she always managed to shine. Andrew, with his impeccable sense of style, had never been grudging in his compliments where her choice of clothes was concerned.

She picked her way through the jammed clothes rails in TK Maxx, and her hand paused at a wool dress; it was in her current preferred colour too: a dark pink. It felt warm and soft to the touch. She checked the size and brand: medium, and made in China by Calvin Klein. She checked the price and it was good: not the full price as it would have been in shops like Selfridges. She had acquired a pair of CK jeans during her one and only visit to the USA and found them to be a perfect fit. Her old friend Xiaozhu had driven Andrew and Pearl to their top, tax-free shopping mall in Oregon, full of designer outlets, and insisted upon dressing her in a pair of expensive jeans, and a fabulous silk top from another American brand. Funny that a simple act of shopping can bring back wonderful, faraway memories.

Half an hour later, she had about five items in her basket, and she went into the fitting room to try them on. There was a time when all the items she picked would have fitted and she would have left the shop satisfied and giddy with pleasure, retail therapy.

Sadly, those days were gone. Firstly, she had gained a bit of weight in places she would rather not; and secondly, the quality of the items for sale had dropped massively, making it ever more difficult to find a true bargain. Besides, her enthusiasm for shopping had been on the wane, as every time she went to her wardrobe, it was too packed to find what she was looking for. In fact, she no longer cared much about what she wore since Andrew was gone.

Still, once in a while, the shopaholic buried inside her poked at her and nudged her ever so gently. Besides, a girl has got to treat herself once in a while. Perhaps Jack could take the blame for the shopping spree that day. He had unwittingly given her the motivation.

By the end of that successful visit, she went home with a few fine pieces: the new, CK, wool dress, a silk top with rose print in the front, a pair of lacy knickers, a black bra with a red trim, and matching underpants. She was never into those dreadful thongs, being far too wise and confident to go for something just for fashion. Traces of Andrew's influence were evident. He always discouraged her going for anything less than comfortable. "Don't ever buy anything which you're never going to wear," was his motto. Classy and kind to her skin had been her choice for so long that it was not about to change anytime soon, surely not just because her man and confidante had left her.

Two days before her birthday, Jack picked her up as they had agreed on the phone. He had left his work on a night shift and came straight to her flat. He had already made a booking at a hotel near the Lake District, not quite halfway to Glasgow, but en route. "I thought it would be nice to break up the journey and enjoy a meal at a country inn in the Lakes," he had suggested, after confirming that Pearl had visited the English Lakes before and had some knowledge about the area already.

Pearl was pleased that Jack had been true to his word. Not only had he taken time off as promised; he'd proven far more spontaneous than she had expected. She had been spontaneous once, and deep down she knew that she was still ready for anything at a moment's notice, taking risks just for the thrill of it; but ten years with Andrew 'The Plank' had made her less flexible and more organized and better at planning. That was the way her husband had been. "Failing to plan is planning to fail," had been another one of his mottos. Over time, she had learnt to adapt to his way of thinking and acting. Opposites attract, or so it seemed in the beginning.

Perhaps Jack was more like her in terms of temperament. She sensed the importance of this trip, make or break? What would it be like going on holiday with someone she knew little about? Would it work or would it prove to be a total disaster? She wondered, as she eased herself on the passenger's seat in Jack's car: a silver BMW. Who could tell the exact series or the engine size? Her knowledge of cars had always been sketchy, limited to the colour and the make and little more.

******

On the cool morning of April Fools' Day, in a hotel just outside Glasgow, Pearl woke up to the sound of a text message from her husband.

Have a fabulous birthday, love xx.

In the ten years plus they had been together, Andrew had never failed to make her birthday special, one way or another. If they were not at an exotic location, as they often were, he would book a Michelin starred restaurant, not to mention providing perfectly arranged bouquets of flowers and carefully chosen gifts.

"My special treat for you, my dear, now wait for it..." Jack trailed off as he began kissing her sensitive parts, his hot mouth on the back of her ear, traveling down to her neck, to her soft mounds, tastefully decorated with a pair of hard peaks.

Jack spent the next half hour trying his hardest to get her body excited. Her body did respond partially to his ardent lovemaking, but her mind wandered. Thoughts of her faraway husband were distracting her from the task in hand.

"What's the matter, my dove?" asked Jack eventually, stopping his fondling and caressing.

Instead of replying, she asked him a question, which had been pestering her, disturbing her peace of mind: "What did you say to your wife?" She turned around to face Jack. "Does she know that you're having a holiday with me?"

She had been careful not to broach this sensitive subject. Now that caution seemed silly, lying here with him, knowing that he was still very much married, and so was she. Although her current state of affairs seemed more or less a sin as bad as his, still two 'sins' didn't make it right.

"Does it matter what I said to my wife? I am here with you and I *want* to be here with you." Taken aback, it took him a brief moment of pause before his reply. He spoke slowly to put extra emphasis on his statement.

He leveled his head with hers to kiss her. She did not kiss him back, her thoughts still far away, and she could not seem able to pull herself away from those distractions.

The silence fell, hung heavily in the small space between them. As if by instinct, she pulled the sheets tighter to cover her nakedness. Her sudden distance seemed to put him on his guard too, unsure of himself or what to say next. He reached for his clothes by the bedside and started getting dressed.

"Perhaps we should go somewhere for brunch. I don't know about you, but I am famished." He made an effort at lightening things up, and not so subtly steering away from the uncomfortable subject.

Twenty minutes later, Jack drove them to the pub restaurant near Loch Lomond and they sat down to order. He went for the house special – steak and kidney pie – with a pint of McEwan's on the side. "Got to drink to your special day, right?" He gave her a contrived smile, still a bit uncertain after their exchange at the hotel moments before.

A grey cloud was gathering above their heads, and neither had expected it, unsure how to dispel the doom and gloom on such a day when they should be happy. Pearl avoided looking at Jack, while he searched for signs in vain. They both remained silent, willing the food to arrive.

"Fish and chips, please." A dish she almost never ordered, except once when she was in Plockton – an exceedingly pretty and peaceful port in the Scottish Highlands – with Andrew during one of their most memorable holidays.

Perhaps it is a mistake to come to Scotland with Jack.

Damn you, Andrew, she thought. *Why can't you just leave me alone for once?!*

Jack and Pearl had excellent sex, and she liked the way she felt when she was with her recently acquired "Sean Connery". He adored her body; that much was certain. *Apart from that, what else do we have in common?* Andrew was always there at the back of her mind, taunting her. Sex with her husband was pretty good; he made her laugh and gave her confidence when it was lacking. On top of that, Andrew had been with her through thick and thin, standing by her when she hit her rock bottom, going through her worst nightmare. He genuinely understood the way she thought.

Jack doesn't really understand me the same way.

She knew then, at that moment, that she and Jack were going nowhere outside of the bedroom.

Chapter 51: Shopping Trips to British Isles

CLICKING OPEN HER Hotmail account via iPhone, Pearl saw a message addressed to her business but which had gone to the junk-mail folder. It was by sheer chance that she found it, but not too surprising, given that the sender had been an unknown, not among her usual clients.

Dear Dr. Church,

We found your contact details from the Institute of Translation and Interpreting, and we are wondering if you are available between April the 16th and the 19th. We have a group of Chinese visitors to our manufacturing base in Worcestershire and we need a Mandarin interpreter who can help us with the high-level business negotiation meeting with our Chief Executive, our Communications Officer, and the Chinese partners. We may further require your assistance to accompany our VIP visitors to leisure pursuits they may have during their trip. We are, however, still waiting for their confirmation.
Can you please advise us as to your availability and the rates?

I look forward to hearing from you soon,
Mr Geoffrey Isaac
Head of International Business Development
Morriston Motors

Wow, the famed Morriston Motors. Pearl's pulse raced a little faster, as her eyes rested on the crest of one of the most coveted British super brands. If she remembered correctly, it became a household name, and coveted by those with money, largely due to it being one of James Bond's favoured transport choices.

The Chinese economy was doing amazingly, with an annual growth rate of 9 percent, in sharp contrast to the zero to negative growth which was spinning out of control in the western countries. The banks kept making enormous mistakes and ordinary people were suffering, seeing their debts pile up and having their houses taken away from them due to mortgage default.

Pearl's mind flashed back and forth – from China to the UK – as she switched her iMac on and settled herself down in her office chair to tap out a businesslike reply.

Business interpreting was not something she did regularly, but she was aware what it would involve. The negotiation would be the easy part, working for the British personnel, who would be professional and do things by the book. She was not too keen, however, on being the personal shopping assistant to the Chinese officials and businessmen. She had a fairly good idea as to what that would entail, and her head shook slowly without realizing she was doing it.

Ha, after 20 odd years in the UK and a decade with an English man, my Britishness is taking over from my Chinese roots, she mused.

Her lack of enthusiasm towards the leisure pursuits of the Chinese visitors did not hamper her intention to work for Morriston Motors. The swift and massive decrease in public-service interpreting jobs had only one implication: they would soon dry up completely due to the government's budget cuts, on top of aggressive market domination by exploitive, greedy agencies. The consequence? Her choice of employment was limited and shrinking fast. If business interpreting was what lay ahead, and she had to deal with hard-to-please, demanding, Chinese bosses, so be it. They would just have to keep their hands to themselves.

Unpredictable as her job usually was, she had been sitting at home for seemingly days on end, waiting for calls that never came: a much more regular occurrence, and far more frequent than she liked. Yet, she had an inkling that on the day of her job at MM – as Morriston Motors was known – something else would turn up, just to make her work day a little more stressful. More bad luck.

Spot on. The afternoon before, she got a last-minute request to go to Stoke on Trent for a bail case the next morning. "Turn it down," Andrew would have instructed her. Well, he wasn't around anymore, and she said yes. Who was to blame? Herself or the career she had chosen? Two hundred miles driving and two jobs to do.

The bail case was via a video link. The woman inside the screen, sitting miles away in an immigration detention centre, was to be deported back to China. She was caught working illegally in a Chinese takeaway in the middle of nowhere after an UK Border Agency raid.

"Her removal is not imminent," her representative argued, "hence she should not be detained. She was supposed to have two friends as sureties, but they didn't show up."

"In this case, I am not satisfied that, given bail, the appellant would obey the conditions imposed. Therefore, bail is refused." As the judge announced his decision, the woman in the video-link room lost control, crying and howling, banging her head against the table.

"Please let me out. I can't stand it any longer. I'd rather die than going back...," she screamed, her tears mixed with snot and saliva, her voice that of frustration and despair.

Pearl watched the scene: not a film, not even reality TV, just reality pure and simple. She felt helpless, trying her best to transmit calmness and consolation through her voice via the small microphone in front of her. There was nothing she could do.

As soon as she was released, she hurried towards her car, her heart heavy with sorrow towards a wretched woman she had not met in person; yet somehow their paths had crossed, ever so briefly. Her desperate howling lingered in Pearl's mind; she could almost feel a bump on her forehead, hurting and not letting go. Pain and despair could be infectious too, transmitting through the air we breathe in.

Two hours later – after racing down the M6 toll road, only stopping to throw coins into the machine – she made it to the headquarters of Morriston Motors just in time. No time for lunch, and too much of a rush getting from one place to another: part and parcel of her routine for a number of years now. No wonder Andrew got fed up with her. "Why do you have to punish yourself in this way? One day, you'd regret that you did not look after your health whilst you could; mark my words, Zhenzhu," he had warned her, his tone stern, his eyes sharp.

The thought of her husband had taken more frequent residence since her one and only trip with Jack to Scotland, especially after she was greeted with a huge bouquet of pink lilies – one of her all-time favourite flowers – on return from her holiday. Andrew had made good use of Interflora's online booking, even while on another continent.

"We have been enjoying them since they were delivered last week." Her apartment concierge smiled at her, jokingly asking if she could keep them. The flowers were in full bloom, and the scent was heady.

Her affair with Jack had been put on a back burner, as a new uneasiness spread like a shadow between them. He had tried to talk with her, even hinted that he would leave his wife if that was what Pearl wanted.

What do I want? Pearl's own confusion as to what she really wanted made it impossible for her to articulate her feelings. Was she still in love with Andrew? If so, where did Jack fit in? Would her heart be big enough to love two men at the same time?

With effort, she pushed away her internal turmoil as she steered into a narrow, country road, following a sign to the Morriston Motors manufacturing site. She followed the directions given by her TomTom, still the Australian, male voice Andrew had set up for her. She found her way to the front of Reception and reversed her car into a parking space for visitors.

Approaching the entrance, her eyes were greeted by a single, eye-catching, new Morriston Motors model; a red, open-topped coupe outside its massive showroom, a much-coveted, curvaceous style that marked Morriston Motors as being amongst the top of the luxury car makers.

The night before, she had done a little research and scanned through the Morriston Motors website – *Morriston Motors: Sensational Design, Exquisite Craftsmanship, and Phenomenal Performance for Genuine Sports-car Lovers.* She replayed those words in Chinese.

The Chinese businessmen, whoever they may be, would have a much better knowledge of the functions of Morriston Motors' range, I am sure, she contemplated. *What they do not know as much, perhaps, would be English, and how best to communicate with their hosts.*

On signing in, Pearl was subsequently introduced to the "MM" CEO and Chairman. "Thanks for coming, Dr Church." They shook hands.

In their large, bright, and airy conference room, the Chinese delegates were seated on the plush, leather sofa settees, with coffee, tea and biscuits. The most senior man, Mr Zhang, was probably in his late fifties. He was short with a wiry body, and clad in an ill-fitting, dark suit – a typical southerner's appearance – with rough, wrinkly skin, bad teeth and breath with many years of cigarette staining, and a rough, peasant's palm and fingers when she shook hands with him. It transpired later that he was one of the richest men in Southern China, with his sugar-making empire, his importing and exporting businesses – ranging from textiles to toys – and his new business interest: luxury sports cars.

"The reason I want to represent MM in China is because of my son. He loves MM cars," he had claimed, proudly.

His son, a young man at about 22, was wearing a shining, silk-wool blend, grey-silver suit: a Western designer no doubt, and a much better fit than his old man's.

Junior Zhang, with a young friend-*cum*-interpreter of his own, was busy with the top designer of MM, discussing the specifications for his two personal MM orders. He would be adding them to his collection, which already contained Ferraris, Mercs, Maseratis, and quite a few other top-range cars. He had even had a special house built to keep his collection, with spotlights and air conditioning to prevent any rust. However, his latest obsession was the exclusive design of MM, which in China, was still quite rare, hence having one would set him apart from the other youthful, princeling members of the billionaires' motorist club. When all others were driving a brand-new Ferrari, what could you do to make yourself distinctive? In Junior's case, he got his old man to sign a contract to represent the unique, highly desirable British brand MM, and get himself two prestigious models for free, with all the exclusive trimmings and more.

The negotiations dragged on. Mr Zhang's sidekick – a friend of his who spoke his dialect as well as some English –

continually interrupted Pearl's interpreting to emphasise a point his boss was making; namely, demanding that MM give them exclusive rights to represent them in all of China.

"Mr Zhang wants MM to get rid of your other agents in Beijing, Shanghai, and Guangzhou." The statement was repeated time and again, tirelessly.

To prove his point, Mr Zhang went to extraordinary lengths to discredit other agents by means of a dossier, in Chinese, which he presented to MM's CEO, who graciously accepted. Between the CEO and Chairman, the British car maker did its best to be civil, but remained firm in maintaining their existing contracts with other representatives.

"We know what you are saying, Mr Zhang, but..."

That 'but' was lost, not in the translation, but chosen to be ignored by the recipient. So the round of tennis-ball games continued.

During her break between the negotiation and dinner in honour of the Chinese VIP guests, Pearl received a text from Jack.

Love to C U this w/e. We'll have a good chat when I come up.

She texted back.

Sorry, Jack. Fully engaged this w/e. Got to do shopping with Chinese visitors.

Paid job :) Damn, another time then. Miss you. J x

Damn right. *What shall I say to "miss u"?* She hesitated. Then she typed a reply.

Got to go. Bye.

Earlier, the Chinese party had confirmed that they needed Pearl to accompany a "Mrs Zhang" to the Bicester Retail Village in Oxfordshire, which specialized in branded, luxury goods. "She does not speak any English. My son and I are going to a football match," the father said. Yes, as part of the treat from their gracious host, MM had booked an executive box for their Chinese visitors, watching Man United play Arsenal at Old Trafford.

It was going to be stress, stress, and more stress. Pearl felt apprehensive about the prospect; but the money was good, and she needed it.

Chapter 52: Pearl Meeting Madam Lin

THE NEW WEEK came knocking and Pearl was not ready for it. She was knackered, stressed out, and utterly lacking in motivation.

Just as she had expected, the weekend had proved to be mentally and physically exhausting.

Not only did she have to drive long distances, which was tiring in itself, but she also had to act as 'Mrs Zhang's' personal shopping assistant plus interpreter, driver, and dinner companion all rolled into one, which was no fun at all.

They said 'Mrs Zhang' was indeed not the original wife, and quite likely a few places further down the long line of wives or mistresses. No more than 30 years old, she could not have been the mother of Zhang Junior. From her pretty, heavily made-up face and skinny figure, she probably had not even bore a child, yet was full of airs and graces – that of the typical Chinese brand of super-rich and powerful – issuing instructions without thinking twice how that fell on someone used to Western democracy and social equality between individuals.

While keeping up with the enthusiastic yet fussy shopper from one branded shop to another, Pearl made a mental instruction to herself: *Don't ever again accept such work, even if I do need the money. I should do better than this.* With that bitter thought, she felt almost angry with both herself and Andrew.

If he had been around, he would definitely have told me to refuse it, knowing how much I've hated working for these little-princess types.

Now, without much pause nor rest, Monday morning came knocking in the most annoying form of an alarm clock; Pearl had an assignment in a women's prison.

Still in a somewhat dreamy state, she roused herself out of her bed and picked up her favourite pair of jeans, lying on top of her chair, piled high with various items of clothing. Halfway through pulling up her faded, CK blue jeans, she had a change of mind.

It's my first visit to accompany Mr Khan to see his client; perhaps something more formal and businesslike.

She quickly changed into a two-piece, black, wool and silk blend outfit, with a dark-pink, striped sweater underneath, and a matching silk scarf to add a splash of colour to counter whatever the day ahead would bring.

Negotiating her way out of the city centre had never been straightforward, but given the early start, she made it to the motorway in good time. From there it was an hour and half down M6 and then M5, smooth sailing all the way.

On getting out of her seat at the prison car park, she spotted Mr Khan parking his car in the far corner. She had met him a couple of times before in court, and he had asked for her business card, hence the booking from him that day.

Carrying his typical solicitor's heavy, black briefcase, Mr Khan walked side by side with her towards the prison gatehouse, located a few hundred metres away.

"This case has been to court a few times already." Without stopping, Mr Khan briefed his interpreter.

"Because Ms Lin has not pleaded guilty to any the charges, it's been committed to a Crown Court trial, which is to take place in a couple of months' time. I have already made an initial statement from her, but she is not happy with previous interpreter, so here we are again. Let's hope that she takes a liking to you."

"I hope so. What is she charged with?" she enquired, with a confident smile.

"Quite a long list of charges, actually. From memory: brothel management in several locations, money laundering, fraud, etc. I'll show you the charge sheet later."

They stopped their exchange on reaching the front gate, where they showed their identity cards before they were let through the solid, iron gate – the first checkpoint – followed by a more thorough body search, and finally a going over by a sniffer dog.

Finally, with a few other businesslike men and women – all legal representatives – they were ushered through to the see-through cubical where they were to have consultations with their clients.

A few more minutes later, a Chinese woman in her late thirties, accompanied by one of the prison guards, entered their room. She was shorter than Pearl, slimmer too, with long, straight, black hair, which had a touch of trendy reddish highlights, growing out now she was away from the salon. Her expression was serious, features sharp and hard, her lips thin and mean looking. *Not someone to mess with,* Pearl's instinct told her.

"Hello, Miss Lin." Mr Khan rose and offered his hand as she came in and the door was shut behind her. "Good to see you again. How are you?"

"I'm okay, but they keep me waiting for long time to see you," she answered in English.

Before she could carry on, probably a long line of complaints against the prison personnel, Mr Khan introduced her new interpreter, "This is Dr Church."

"*Ni Hao,*" said Pearl, holding out her hands. She greeted the woman in Mandarin, which meant, "How do you do!"

"*Ni Hao*," Madam replied, giving the new interpreter a quick up and down scrutinization, withdrawing her small, cool hand. Pearl felt a little uneasy under Madam Lin's steely gaze, so she squeezed out a smile to calm her nerves. No smile in return, but at least Madam shifted her attention.

"I have received your letter regarding the court hearing, and some other paperwork." Madam watched Mr Khan, her gaze intense and probing, as he took the seat opposite her, taking out a big file from his briefcase. Pearl sat next to him, ready for the challenge of the day.

"Good, good. We have a lot to discuss today, but first of all, let's go over the statement which we started last time. There are a number of places which need fleshing out."

Mr Khan had his pen and A4 notepad ready, as Pearl proceeded with her interpreting.

Chapter 53: "We Have Your Son. We Want Money"

"WEI, SON." CEO Huang answered his mobile with a cheery greeting, a little surprised that his son in England would call him at this time.

His wife was already asleep beside him. He was exhausted but still wide-awake, having just returned from a function his company had organized, entertaining some business partners from another province. Before he pressed the answer button on his mobile, which was placed on a cradle next to his bed, he had checked the screen, which flashed 'SON' in Chinese.

"Is it CEO Huang?" The voice on the end of the line came from a stranger, with an accent he could not place.

Everyone called him CEO, as was the tradition in China these days. Everyone who owned a company or were in charge of one, big or small, were honoured by the title of CEO. In the case of Mr Huang Dongjin, he was a self-made, successful, *nouveau riche* man. Taking advantage of China's gigantic, economic growth, he had made millions in a short few years. Across China, there were millions of people like him. Cash flowed in and all he had to do was to milk it.

"Who are you? Why are you calling from Huang Qing's phone?" he asked, raising his voice. The suspicion that something bad had happened crept in, as his eyes rested on the clock, whose red numerals blinked 1:30 a.m.

Before he could say more, he heard jumbled voices from the other end, but no one answered him. Seconds later, he heard a familiar yet scared voice: "Daddy, is that you? I need money. Please give them what they want. Otherwise..." The phone seemed to have been snatched off him before he could finish his sentence.

The rest of the day appeared surreal to Senior Huang and his wife. Subsequent phone calls set the ransom money at 500,000 RMB, the equivalent of fifty thousand pounds. A bank account in the Cayman Islands was given: not a personal account, but the account of a company. The kidnappers knew that it would be impossible for the Chinese police to trace the trail.

"If you or anyone in your family or your friends dare to contact the police, either in China or in the UK, your son is *dead*."

The male voice on the phone was cold and cruel, and deadly serious. The parents could not see their son's kidnappers, yet the tone of the faceless gangsters sent a chill down their spines. They knew the score, and the kidnappers did, too: the family would do anything and everything to pay the ransom rather than risk their only child's life.

On the internet, and elsewhere in the media, there were stories that rich Chinese students had been taken in Australia and New Zealand, as well as America; huge ransoms were demanded by local Chinese gangs. In most cases, the victims were let go after receiving the money, but there were a couple of tragic incidents in which only bodies were recovered after the families had handed over everything they had owned back home. But that was happening to other people, faraway in other countries. CEO Huang never expected that such misfortune would come upon his own son, in a country to which most parents sent their only child, because UK was supposed to be safe, with low crime rates.

Perhaps, he was wrong. Perhaps gun-governed America would have been a safer choice?

******

Two days before, over the Easter holiday, his girlfriend Joan Zhang had gone back to see her parents in China. Huang Qing, who preferred to use his English name Jim while studying in a university in England, decided to stay. They had signed a contract to rent a new flat in the city centre, moving away from a shared house in a rough area with a staggering crime rate, highly populated with drug users turned robbers.

Two weeks before, while walking home from university one early evening, Joan had been mugged, losing her expensive Chanel bag, as well as her new iPhone, bank cards, and other items in her prized, designer handbag. Totally oblivious, she was on her brand-new iPhone talking to Jim when two youths cornered her. Within seconds, one youth grabbed her handbag while the other snatched the phone from her ear; both made off through an underpass, leaving Joan on the ground with a sprained ankle. Later, she gave a statement at a police station and confessed to the officer, "I think my high heels had hindered me from giving chase to the robbers." In total, over £5,000 of goods were taken from her.

"No, I won't be able to identify the robbers," she had admitted, without a hint of shame or embarrassment. "They were just black ghosts and they all look alike," she had said to the interpreter who took her statement.

"Would I get my stuff back?" she had asked the police officer, likely to be her only concern for the matter.

"I'd say unlikely." The officer was frank. Such roadside robberies happened in that part of Birmingham on an almost daily basis. It was not the answer a robbery victim wanted to hear. In her subsequent conversation with the interpreter, he confirmed that he had taken many similar statements and it was unlikely for her to recover her property, Chanel bag or not.

On returning to her shared house that night, Joan made a decision and told Jim: "We need to move to a better area, even though it means paying a higher rent." After all, he was the one paying. Besides, she could not contemplate the prospect of replacing her designer bag, only to be filled with a constant fear of it being stolen again.

They checked a couple of Chinese online forums and found a two-bedroom apartment in the city centre with a parking permit: an essential criterion. They arranged a viewing, haggled with the landlord, and paid a cash deposit there and then. They were due to move in when the current tenants finished their contract 10 days later. Joan could not wait; she had family to visit and duty-free shopping to do. After all, what was a boyfriend for if he was not responsible for such minor but inconvenient issues like moving house?

On the day of the move, Jim got up early. Not many Chinese students chose to use removal companies; not simply because of the costs, but also the whole inconvenience of finding a company and negotiating a fee and other related hassles, all of which required a good command of English. The Chinese have been known for their self-reliance; far easier to find a Chinese student who had a car and needed a little extra cash to help out. However, Jim already had a car and, being the holiday time, there was no one to help but himself. Besides, most of his extra cash has gone to Joan, to feed her insatiable desire for luxury, branded goods, and her need to see her family regularly, despite being oceans apart. Who was to blame for being the only child in the family?

In the underground park below the new flat, Jim was busy shifting the last few boxes, all full of Joan's branded shoes and designer clothes. Never observant, to the extent of almost tunnel vision, he did not notice a few Chinese guys walking towards him. Even if he did, it would not have been surprising. The new apartment blocks were right next to China Town, usually full of Chinese students and immigrants from China. It had been a popular choice for the students for precisely that reason. No mixing with the white ghosts, and plenty of food choices, vital for the Chinese stomach.

At 6:00 p.m. on an Easter Sunday, the car park was nearly empty. The voice behind him startled Jim.

"Moving in? Let us help." The speaker was of medium build, with a shaved head and a prominent scar on his ugly face, giving Jim a sneer and a dirty look. He looked like someone straight out of a gangster movie, one of those nasty pieces of work who would not bat an eyelid over killing, and was willing to cause hurt without a care in the world.

Before Jim could utter a word, he felt his arm being held forcefully by two other men, who seemed to have showed up from nowhere. He found himself pushed and shoved into the back seat, secured between the two guys squeezing him. The scar-faced man went to the front passenger's seat, and another man took the wheel. Jim had left the key in the ignition.

When he eventually found his voice, he asked, in a quivering tone, almost inaudible: "Where are you taking me?"

"Shut the fuck up." The scar-faced one spat the words out without turning around, as the two men on each of his side tightened their grip. The one on the right stomped on his foot, which made Jim cry out in pain, and the other slapped his face twice just to make a point.

The driver floored it, and the tyres squealed as Jim's one-year-old BMW M3 sports saloon, bought with Daddy's cash, made a hasty exit, heading to an unknown destination.

Chapter Fifty-Three

Who the hell are these people and where are they taking me? What do they want?

Jim knew that he was in deep shit, sick with fear, but unable to say anything more, dreading what was to befall him.

Chapter 54: Another Prison Visit

PEARL WAS SICK.

On Sunday night she felt a chill, even though the temperature in her flat had been kept at 24 centigrade at all times. An unexplained tightness got hold of her throat, and she started coughing and spitting, her mouth dry, and her throat itchy. From there it went downhill quickly, and by Monday night she had become so unwell that her nose was constantly blocked one side or the other, and she was unable to fall asleep: not a wink. In her bid to fight the unknown virus and get some rest, she helped herself to various pills that she had found in her medicine cabinet – both Chinese and Western – praying that they would help ease her discomfort. They did not.

I should really cancel the appointment, her thought played on her mind, without conviction. Had it been a booking from a different source, she would have. The courts or the police could easily find another interpreter to replace her. Not this one. This was the difficult, demanding Madam Lin, who had made it abundantly clear that she wanted only Pearl as her interpreter, not anyone else. To make matters worse, prison visits needed careful planning and advance booking, and this last-minute cancellation would not be helpful. "Be sure to be there," Mr Khan had instructed her. "I have finalised it with the barrister who is to represent Madam Lin in the forthcoming Crown Court trial. Mr Jones' diary is extremely full and I was very lucky to get a slot in with him."

As sluggish and reluctant as she had felt upon dragging her aching body out of her bed, she exerted her mental will over her physical movements and put on her work outfit. She popped another couple of Paracetamol – together with her multivitamin pills – downing a small glass of water in one big gulp. Thoughts of Andrew burst into her mind; *he would have insisted that I cancel the job, or at least, had I persisted, he would have taken time off to drive me down. Now I have no choice but to fight my own way through the morning traffic and the two-hour, tedious drive down the motorway.*

At 9:15 a.m., Pearl pulled into the small car park outside the prison. It was full, so she reversed a few hundred yards to park on the wet, muddy side road. To add to her misery, the rain had been pouring all the way, and showed no inclination to stop or even slow down as dark clouds hung low on the sky, thunder in the distance. She reached into the back, behind her seat, searching for her umbrella. *They will not allow me to bring in anything of the sort, but perhaps they would not confiscate the tissues in my pocket? Surely they would allow me to blow my nose in my condition?*

At 9:30 a.m., she spotted a portly man climbing out of his Aston Martin. *He's got to be the barrister, Mr Jones,* she surmised. With the kind of fees the barristers charged for their services, he could probably afford top-range sports cars. Yet the public service was under instructions to cut interpreting fees. Compared to the hourly fee of an average barrister or solicitor, her rate was ten times less; yet she was considered expensive, often losing out on jobs to cheaper and less-qualified student interpreters: or non-interpreters, as some colleagues called them.

With the short, fat, pot-bellied Mr Jones and slim, tall Mr Khan, Pearl made her way through the checkpoints, having her bags secured in a locker and her body first frisked by a guard and finally sniffed by the dog. They were then allowed through to the consultation area.

Pleasantries were exchanged between the barrister, the solicitor, and their client. Mr Jones shook hands with Madam Lin, her hand – small, slim, olive-skinned – disappearing in his big, fleshy, white hand. He gave her a broad smile, the kind some men reserved only for the fairer species: "I have been to Hong Kong and China; I love Chinese food, and adore the women there."

With a flirty wink at Madam Lin, he took his seat, which was a bit tight, so had to be shifted slightly. *He loves his food, no doubt; perhaps enjoys his drink a bit too much, too.* Pearl watched him. So far, her interpreting had not been required.

"Okey-dokey, let's get started, shall we?" Mr Jones turned to Pearl at long last. "Please tell Miss Lin that I shall do everything in my power as her barrister. Her trial dates have been set and it will be in the Central Crown Court in two weeks' time."

"I know," Madam Lin broke in before Pearl could finish her translation. "I got letter from court." Without stopping, she switched to Chinese, directed at Pearl; her gaze never left Mr Jones, the man whose courtroom craft would play a crucial role in her fate, significant enough in determining how much time she would be spending in a UK prison.

"How long do you think that they would sentence me for?" Her tone was hard, as well as her gaze. Like all Chinese prisoners, she was not interested in their legal niceties and drawn-out processes; she wanted results. Simply: how long?

"I can't tell you precisely how long, Miss Lin," Mr Jones replied, a well-practised answer he must have given hundreds – if not thousands – of times in his long career as a criminal barrister.

"What I can tell you is that, no matter how many years you eventually receive, you only have to serve half of the time; for example, if you receive six years – I am not saying that it is what you're going to receive – you will serve half of that, which would be three years..."

"I know that already," Madam Lin cut in, impatience in her voice. *Why do they always repeat the same bullshit?* She must be fuming inside, agitation written all over her face. "Just tell me, from your experience, how long my sentence is likely to be. It's been four months in this shit-hole and nothing happens."

For the next two hours, they went through the statement given by Malcolm, who had been arrested at the same time as his boss-plus-lover Madam Lin.

"Your boyfriend... he was your boyfriend, right?" Mr Jones asked. With a noncommittal expression on Madam's face, but no denial forthcoming either, the barrister continued, "That boyfriend of yours, he has categorically denied having any involvement with the brothel management or the money-laundering business for which *you* are the prime suspect and he an accomplice. His denial will not help you at all, do you understand me?"

"Yes, I do." Her voice betrayed a degree of annoyance.

"Don't you think that we should challenge his statement?" He tried again.

"No, I don't think so." Madam Lin was firm in her response. "Neither of us is guilty of anything! I am not pleading guilty, you know that."

Pearl watched Madam Lin's mouth moving – automatically interpreting what was being said – her nose still blocked, her mouth dry, and her mind in a different place. It was hard to breathe properly. *I just want to get home and go back to bed.* Her sickness was making her sleepy, on top of having been deprived of her sleep the night before.

"If you really want to reduce the possible sentence, which you'll inevitably receive if these charges stick..." Mr Jones paused for effect, first looking at Pearl, then Madam Lin. "If you do," he repeated with emphasis, "it would be helpful if you're willing to implicate someone further up your chain of command, so to speak. If there was anyone you can name, it would help your case." He stopped with a steady gaze, searching for an answer in her eyes. Madam was not an easy book to read, Pearl had already noted.

Madam shook her head. "What possible good would it do to me if I coughed up something which the police do not know already? I am not that stupid." Facedown in the canal was no way to go, even a fool knew that.

"Sorry," Pearl managed to say, after a spate of continuous, strenuous coughing and sneezing, loud enough to disturb the people next door. Eventually they reached the end of the consultation.

"Madam Interpreter," Mr Jones addressed Pearl, as if in court. "I have a remedy for your cough. When you get home, drink plenty of whisky; mix it with cloves and honey. You'll be as good as new tomorrow morning."

"Really?" Pearl raised her eyebrow. She could not help sounding dubious with his 'secret weapon' against her type of flu.

"It can't be much worse, can it?" he commented.

"Guess not." She smiled in reply.

They got up to leave.

"Wait," Madam Lin commanded, her hand reaching to a carrier bag she had with her. As if by magic, she fished out two sets of woven-paper swans and vases, and put them on the table between Pearl and her.

"I made for you," she said, in a slightly softened voice than the one she usually adopted, addressing Pearl first, her gaze steady.

"Wow, they are so pretty," Pearl gushed, taken aback that she was presented with such an unusual, exquisite gift, especially from a prisoner she had only met a few times. She looked at Mr Khan and Mr Jones, wondering if they were supposed to accept gifts under the circumstances.

Madam turned to her two legal representatives in turn, her voice businesslike. "I attend art class and I made these origami figures to give you, too."

To Mr Jones, Madam handed a blue and purple swan, and to Mr Khan, a vase in the same colours.

Finally, Madam Lin picked up a pink and green swan and a matching paper vase before she placed them with care in Pearl's opened palms. Looking Pearl in the eyes, giving her a long, lingering, and meaningful look, she commented in Chinese, "Be very careful with them. They are very delicate," emphasizing each word.

Pearl repeated her thanks, holding her first-ever origami set in her hand, taking care that they didn't fall or blow away in the gathering squall on the trudge back to her car.

What an interesting and strange end to a prison visit.

Chapter 55: Jack Gordon's Visit to Hong Kong

ON COMING OUT of Hong Kong's shiny, fairly new, modern Chek Lap Kok Airport, they were greeted with an unrelenting heat wave, and the sounds and sights of the former British colony: now just another extension of Mainland China.

After just over 12 hours of continuous flight over Siberia and Mongolia with Virgin Atlantic, Jack Gordon had just landed in the buzzing hub of East Asia. His travel companion was Mrs Candy Wong, his Cantonese interpreter and guide. The journey had been tedious; Jack was not a big fan of long-haul travel. Yet compared to what he'd had to go through in his Army days in those noisy Hercules turboprops, this was luxury. On the flip side, despite the budget cuts that financial year, he had managed to get them upgraded to Premier Economy, although Business Class was out of the question due to the massive fuel price increase and budget tightening.

He had harboured a secret wish that his interpreter would be his beloved Pearl, but it was out of the question. It was mostly Cantonese spoken in Hong Kong, not Mandarin, so Mrs Wong would have to do. *I have not seen her since our brief holiday in Scotland, and damn it, how I've missed her.*

"Jack," Candy addressed him, calling him back from his reverie. They had established their familiarity on a first-name basis on the plane. Candy, about 10 years older than Pearl, was already a grandma three times over. She had come highly recommended to Jack from his fellow officers in the Met Police. A Hong Kong native, Candy came to the UK when she was barely a teenager. She had worked as a police interpreter for the better part of her adult life, which was almost as long as Jack's time in this world. Quite a record.

"We'll go to our hotel first," Candy's voice was authoritative. She was on home ground after all.

Before he could reply, Candy had waved over a taxi and started shooting out a series of Cantonese orders to the driver. Living up to the former colony's reputation for efficiency, while the verbal exchanges were still going on the taxi driver had woven his way out into the line of cars heading towards Central. *Even to my untrained ear, I much prefer the sound of Mandarin.* Jack allowed his thoughts to roam as he sank into the back seat.

"Have you ever been to Hong Kong before?" Candy had enquired. She was a chatty woman.

"Oh yes," Jack replied. "Only once, though, and a very long time ago."

Yes, it seemed like a lifetime ago. His one-time visit to Hong Kong had been when he was still in the SAS, and his memory was suddenly refreshed, flooding back. Kai Tak was the main airport back then, and he vaguely remembered that he stayed in Kowloon, across the Victoria Harbour, in the northern part of Hong Kong Island. He'd actually had his dragon tattoo done there, in one of the several tattoo parlours. He was with a mate of his, Jimmy, after they had completed one of their covert missions in the Indonesian jungle and were given two days leave afterwards.

"What the heck?" Jimmy smiled broadly, showing his crooked teeth. "What better memento can you get than having dragons inked on us permanently in a place which called 'Nine Dragons', by a man who has done thousands of them, and probably had Bruce Lee as a customer?" he had joked, pointing at Bruce Lee's film poster for *Enter the Dragon*, which featured prominently on the tattoo artist's shop.

This time around was much less intimidating than landing at Kai Tak, which was rated by pilots as the second-most dangerous airport in the world to approach. As the planes landed, passengers could see people having their dinner on the nearby balconies of flats built right next to the airport. Passing over Hong Kong Mountain, the plane would suddenly drop like a stone and make a sudden turn to the left to line up for the runway. Chek Lap Kok was tame in comparison.

I wonder if that tattoo parlour is still around, Jack mused, calculating how long ago that had been. His reminiscences were interrupted on arriving at their hotel, the Renaissance Harbour View Hotel.

"The hotel is perfect in terms of location," Mrs Wong had said earlier, as if reciting from a tourist brochure. "The hotel is overlooking the harbour and has a lovely view of Tsim Shat Siu. The Metro station is only five minutes' walk away, and so is the tram. The hotel is handy for the Star Ferry across to Kowloon side. Very good suits over there." She sounded enthusiastic, full of advice, perfectly suited for her part as an elder, wiser local guide.

Are you getting a commission by any chance, Mrs?

"Sounds perfect." Jack had nodded his approval. So far, so good; Mrs Wong seemed competent and keenly helpful, although a bit on the controlling side. Probably a given due to her age and expertise, and Jack was happy to play along. *She is no Pearl; get over it*, he reminded himself. *We are here to work.*

He raised his hand and the time on his watch read 1800 hours. It had taken them exactly 45 minutes from the airport to the hotel. For a three nights' stay, he had to negotiate with his boss: "Sir, I am happy to take Premier Economy flight, but I would be very grateful if I do not have to compromise on the lodging. After twelve hours of transcontinental torture in the big, tin bird, a decent place to relax would be more than welcome." And deserved, which he did not add vocally but just under his lips. He needed space to recover from the claustrophobia.

"Of course, Jack. Get me some results." The chief went ahead and cleared it with the head of the financial department.

Chasing money trails in London was complicated enough, even with well-trained accountants by your side and no language barrier. This was going to be a testing three days, and he needed to sleep well when he was not working. The jetlag was already starting to kick in, so he took his shoes off in the bathroom and stuck his feet into the comforting, cold water jet of the pristine bidet.

The Chinese were going to be obstructive and secretive, as they could see no advantage in cooperating with the guilao police officer. *I hope Mrs Wong is up to the job of persuading the Chinese bankers in their cloud-scraping buildings to provide the necessary evidence so we can nail the snakeheads back in the UK.*

As if on cue, he heard Candy addressing him: "We'll meet up for dinner in an hour's time."

They were at the hotel reception, and Candy had made the necessary arrangements, including instructions for dinner. And food was something he was looking forward to, remembering the lively Hong Kong nightlife.

"We are going to take the Star Ferry across to the Mainland." Another friendly order was issued by his interpreter; she shouted after him as he made his way to his room, away from the busy lobby.

"Yes, ma'am."

He waved his hand, followed by a fake salute towards the bossy Mrs Wong.

Chapter 56: "Officer, I Was Kidnapped"

DESPITE HIS FEAR for his life, he had noticed the directions they took; it was towards London and the south. The sun was on the right side of the car all the way.

Jim Huang could not recall how long they had been on the road. They stopped in one of the motorway service stations to refuel when he had begged them to let him go to the toilet. He had already pissed in his pants earlier when it hit him what kind of situation he was in. The smell of sweat and piss had not just disgusted him, but pissed off his captors, who had punished him in return with more punches and kicks.

Unsure whether these people were after his daddy's money, or revenge of sorts, his mind had been busy speculating as to why they had picked him up from the moment he was forced into the back of his car and squeezed between two gangsters. His simple logic did not help make sense of the situation. What was it that these men wanted from him, a normal Chinese student in a UK university, like hundreds and thousands of others? There were fellow students far richer and flasher than him.

By the time they arrived in a secluded location, it was completely dark. As he was dragged and pushed out of his car in his piss-smelling, fear-infected state, he was led through a series of doors and into a dimly lit room: a bedroom no bigger than the one he had shared with his girlfriend back in Birmingham.

From there onwards, it was a long, torturous wait; the gang members took turns to guard him, while they went about their business, whatever that might be. In all the time during his kidnap, Jim was allowed only a very brief conversation with his father in China, who had been instructed to transfer money into the gangsters' account. Obviously how much and to where he was not consulted. They did not torture him, as he had dreaded. They even gave him a sandwich once, but he was too shit-scared to eat.

Eventually word must have come that it was no longer necessary to detain him any longer. Since all the communications between the gangsters were conducted in their dialect, Jim did not understand what was said, except when they did it with their body language, or using Mandarin for his sake. Again they dragged and shoved him into a car: this time with a black cloth over his eyes. They drove some distance, took off his blindfold, and pushed him out of the car.

"Go fuck yourself, you rich, little prick," one of the man had shouted, while the others laughed, jeering and whistling, one giving him two fingers. Jim watched the car speeding away, blowing dust all over his face. Disoriented but hugely relieved that they had let him go, he strained his eyes, trying to read the number plate and the make. Except that it was not his BMW, and it was black, he was no wiser as the car disappeared into the distance.

He looked around: a dirt track somewhere in the country. Where, he had no idea. Apart from his clothes, he had been stripped of all his belongings: no mobile, no wallet, and nothing he could use to call help.

Automatically, he started walking, not knowing where it would take him or how he could get back to Birmingham. *I need to find out where I am, and perhaps I can get a lift from a kind driver on a main road,* Jim decided, and kept walking.

Not a single soul was around; only herds of sheep and cows in the fields, making noises of their kind. Darkness was approaching, as well as imminent rain. Just then, Jim spotted a man with a dog walking towards him.

It was the man with the dog who told him where he was. It was also the man with the dog who took Jim in his car and drove him to the nearest train station, covering the train fare. The good Samaritan had offered to call the police on his behalf, but Jim had declined.

On returning to Birmingham, he got the concierge on duty to call his landlord out in the middle of the night. "I lost my keys," he had said to his grumpy landlord.

"I would have to charge you for that, you know," said the landlord. For once, Jim did not have any energy or inclination to argue; he simply nodded. *If only you knew what I had just gone through.*

Utterly shattered by his ordeal, he crashed to his bed and fell asleep instantly. He did not wake up until 12 hours later.

In his conversations with his father, he had been informed how much his father had to pay. "Do not mention this to anyone, son, especially the police. The money is gone, but you're safe." His father went on to say how much it had worried him, and Jim's mother. "Come back to China as soon as you can. UK is no good."

When he spoke to his girlfriend, Joan thought differently. "You have to go and report what has happened." she instructed him, pissed off at the same time. "Maybe the police will find them and return your money," was her valid reasoning. "If you don't file a report, maybe they would come back to ask for more." Her voice was a shrill, her fury spilling out over the long distance call; Jim could picture her angry face even at such a distance, as if she was right in front of him.

Some 36 hours later, Jim was sitting in an interview room at a police station not far from China Town. After some waiting, two uniformed officers came and ushered him into an interview room.

"So young man, what is it that you want to report?" enquired Officer A.

"I have been kidnapped, by a gang," he blurted it straight out.

"Do you know their names?" Officer B asked, raising one of his eyebrows. Even as a long-serving police officer, it's not every day that someone came in and said he had been kidnapped. This was England after all, and not like some South American countries.

"No, I never met them before, and I don't understand their dialect. They must from Fujian, because I heard from friends that there are Fujianese gangs in Birmingham, London, and Manchester."

"Would you be able to identify them if you ever saw them again?" Officer B continued the questioning, after exchanging a curious glance at his colleague.

"Sorry, please repeat." Jim looked genuinely puzzled; he obviously did not understand the word "identify".

"When you see the people who took you, would you be able to recognize them?" Officer A asked again.

"Maybe no; maybe one, he has scar on his face," Jim replied, trying to form a mental picture of the scar-face.

Hindered by "Jim" Huang's limited English vocabulary, near incomprehensible accent and lack of accuracy in describing the necessary details, the officers called an interpreter.

"A Mandarin interpreter is on the way. Once she gets here, we'll take a full statement from you," Officer A informed him.

"Is there anything I can get for you? A coffee, tea, or hot chocolate?"

"A water, please," he replied, and waited while jumbled images of the gang returned to haunt him.

******

It had been a rough night.

At around 8:00 p.m., Pearl was called to a police station some 80 miles away to attend an interview with a detainee, a young, fresh-faced Chinese student who had arrived in the UK barely a month before. By the time Pearl saw Mr Yang with his solicitor, the young man of 21 no longer appeared fresh-faced. He looked like hell, pale, his face covered with a few fresh, bloody scratches, his eyes bloodshot.

Earlier, at around 12:00 noon, he had picked up two of his mates to go shopping in Manchester's Trafford Centre. His friend, Li, had just finished his studies and would be returning home the following day. Mr Li's girlfriend, Mei, decided to join them on their shopping expedition at the last minute, despite a looming assignment to be handed in the following day. So off they went, in spite of the fact that Mr Yang had neither UK licence nor insurance. He had only bought the brand-new Toyota over the weekend, eager to try it on the road and show his friends what his car could do.

Predictably, the two friends, one sat on the passenger seat and the other in the back, did not wear any safety belts. *We do that all the time in China; what is so different in England?*

"The law, unfortunately, Mr Yang. This is England." The lawyer stated the obvious, which, apparently, not so obvious for Mr Yang and his friends.

Mr Yang, laughing and joking with his friends, was traveling at a speed of 90 mph, on a rainy day, with poor visibility.

"Mr Yang, you were driving way too fast on roads that were wet and slippery. An experienced driver would have slowed down, especially when they were passing a junction where a lot of cars joined the motorway," the interviewing officer stated.

"What is a junction?" Mr Yang asked, looking slightly confused, after Pearl had translated it for him. Subsequent questioning transpired that it did not even occur to him that he should have read the Highway Code and passed the relevant road tests first. "I didn't know," had been the answer to many questions regarding road safety. "Now I know," he had said once or twice.

Now it was way too late.

Hitting standing water, he skidded into the overtaking lane, so he pulled the wheel hard left to avoid hitting the barrier. BANG; he crashed into the back of a car traveling in the inside lane and his car swerved and spun several times, leaving the road and hitting the trees at the top of a steep bank.

The driver had escaped with a few scratches to his arm and shoulders, while his friend Li was thrown out of the car, landing thirty metres away in a farmer's field, dead on impact. Li's girlfriend Mei had been taken to hospital and was still in critical condition. The doctors were not optimistic: if she lived, she would be either a vegetable or, at best, severely disabled for life.

After a very long and draining interview, together with the solicitor's consultations, it was well past midnight by the time it ended. Before she left the police cells, Pearl had overheard Mr Yang speaking to his family in China. He was sobbing as he relayed to his father what had happened.

Tired and sad, Pearl's heart was numb: *After just one month in the UK, this young man managed to kill one of his friends and critically injured another through reckless driving. He would no doubt serve a prison sentence for dangerous driving, his solicitor had warned him. But what about the dead young man, Mr Li: the only child who was never to return to his parents? How would they cope when they landed at Heathrow Airport tomorrow to be greeted with the news of their son's death?*

With a heavy heart and a fried brain, she asked to be buzzed out of the cells and got into her car outside the station. She sat for a moment, without turning on the ignition, and summoned her will to drive. The knowledge that there were people like Mr Yang on the road made her fear for her own safety; you could be killed or injured, no matter how safe and cautious a driver you might be. Unwanted images of upside-down cars and what was said in the interview were played out in her mind, time and again, all the way home.

By the time she got home at 3:00 a.m., and lay her physically shattered body down on her bed, she knew that her sleep would be irretrievably disturbed. Dead and badly damaged bodies would visit her dreams and turn into nightmares. She was cursed that way.

At around 8:00 a.m., when she had only drifted back into semi unconsciousness, she got another call. This time it was at least local.

"Dr Church, we would like you to come to the station as soon as possible," said the officer. "We have a young man here telling us that he was kidnapped. His English is not very good, so we do not know exactly what happened or how it happened. We need to take a full statement from him, so be prepared that you may be here for quite some time."

It was Detective Constable Pierce. Pearl had worked with him before on a different case.

Chapter 57: Hide and Seek

TRY AS HARD as she could, Ah Fang never anticipated just how hard it would be to change her fate.

For three months now, she had been under the protection of the police, under the strict instruction not to contact anyone from her previous life: her life as a working girl. Packed away in a secluded location somewhere in mid-Wales, she had only occasional visits from the police. The only other outside contacts had been Pearl, and her lover and legal adviser Ahmed Khan.

With her interpreter, it was sustained via regular mobile telephone conversations. Pearl had no idea where Ah Fang was staying, except that it was somewhere safe and secure. Every time Ah Fang called to ask how long she would be hiding from the rest of the world, Pearl had repeated the same official line: "Until the police investigation is over and the perpetrators are behind bars." Truth be told, Pearl was just a transmitter, with no knowledge of the full extent of the investigation or what the police were up to.

Mr Khan, her lover in secret, had been representing one of the several defendants in Ah Fang's case. Despite that privilege, he too had no comprehensive knowledge of how significant Ah Fang's testimony would be. Since it had become clear that his firm – Raja & Khan's Solicitors – was to act for Madam Lin, the main defendant in this big-scale criminal case ranging from brothel management to kidnapping and money laundering, he had to hand over the legal duties for Ah Fang to another firm. Conflict of interest. His behind-the-scenes and entirely unprofessional liaison with one of the key witnesses was kept well under wraps.

"You don't want to ruin my career do you, my sweet flower?" he whispered into Ah Fang's ear, half joking, half serious, moving on to lick her earlobes and collarbone, lying stark naked on her bed, wrapping his hairy, dark arm around her pale, soft flesh. It was no secret that their physical differences excited him.

Ah Fang turned her small, makeup-free face to her South Asian lover and gave him a coy smile, astutely aware how much Ahmed loved her free spirit and her sexy, young body – especially the latter. Feeling lonely and isolated in a place where she had no one to talk to, she pined for his occasional visits, willing to do anything to keep him happy. It was such a contrast from the life she had led since arriving in the UK, surrendering her virtue and flesh to unwanted men and being exploited mercilessly by nasty gang masters.

"No Pain, No Gain." She understood this perfectly; having to subject herself to this temporary suffering of isolation for her long-term freedom, a shiny light which she could almost see at the end of the long, dark tunnel. *I have come too far to go back.*

Yet, once in a while the rising temptation to reach out, almost too strong to resist, came to her in a weak, dark moment: just a call, someone from her previous life – someone like Chloe or Pinko – working girls like her. Ah Fang felt a little like a fish out of water, not that she missed the pond she was in.

Ah Fang checked the time on her mobile and it was five o'clock in the afternoon. A pang of hunger struck her all of a sudden. She reached for her clothes on the floor.

"Can you stay for dinner?" She looked at Ahmed, expectantly. *Please say yes,* her eyes and voice seemed to plead. It was boring and uninspiring cooking and eating by herself, day in and day out. Her days had been so routine and tedious that she felt that her sanity would be gone by the time the trial started. Trying times indeed.

"Sorry, luv," He did not sound very sorry at all. Getting hold of her arms, ridding her of her T-shirt, he pulled her towards him, his voice a hoarse command. "I am hungry only for you. I want to eat you."

She felt his hot breath traveling down her neck and becoming more laboured: his rough, hairy body against her soft curves. Ah Fang giggled as Ahmed's head went down to her most private parts. He was serious in saying that he wanted to eat her.

In their short verbal exchange earlier, he had blamed his workload, on call for days before he had managed to find a few hours free. She understood: why waste precious time on food when his physical desire for her was far more urgent, definitely a priority to be satisfied? The truth could be that his wife would have food ready when he got home, even if her plump flesh no longer held his attention.

As Ah Fang's brain was busy speculating on her lover's domestic situation, her body responded enthusiastically to Ahmed's fervent touching and probing, sucking and fondling, ready to explode with a mounting climax.

Just then, her mobile flashed and burst into her favourite tune at the same time. The Chinese folk song as a ringtone had been downloaded and assigned to Pearl, her official link to the outside world.

"*Wei, Ah Yi, Ni Hao.*" She picked it up and answered in Chinese cheerfully, shifting her upper body away from the sweaty, hairy torso attached to her like glue seconds before.

Ahmed's expression showed annoyance and displeasure, not at simply being unable to understand her chatter, but a more serious offence: his interrupted passion.

Turning her head away from the bed and her sour-looking lover, Ah Fang's attention had shifted. She had been calling Pearl *Ah Yi*, aka Aunt, showing respect. Although Pearl was by no means looking her age – the same as her own mother – there was no way that she would call Pearl by her first name. Not according to the Chinese rule book.

After a brief chitchat, Pearl got down to business. "A police officer will come and collect you on Friday. They have arrested some more suspects in your case and need you to come in for a video identification. I shall be there, of course."

Ah Fang nodded vigorously, even though the caller could not see her, as she noted the time of collection and what would be required during the ID parade.

"I'm going to call the officer now and inform him that the arrangement has been made. Bye-bye, Ah Fang. I'll see you soon."

"88," Ah Fang replied cheerfully, signing off with her Chinese 'good-bye', smiling into the phone as if the caller could see her.

******

The sun was shining beautifully outside, almost tropical for a spring day, with the temperature reaching above 20 degrees in the sun. The air was clean and crisp, a clear, blue sky with no clouds anywhere. Even the mountains miles away could be easily seen. It was one of those rare, fine days that subconsciously lifted your spirits, and it was enticing people of all sorts out and about. The real sun lovers let it all hang out, lying lazily on the grass in the park or their back gardens.

Ah Fang had gone out shopping. With a generous allowance for living expenses, the State had provided her with vouchers for designated shops where she could obtain her daily essentials. With just herself to feed, and unlimited time with little to do, shopping had been her major pastime. Unless she had official business with the police, or consultation meetings with her legal representatives – which had decreased dramatically over time – she had more time on her hands than she knew what to do with. She had requested to attend English classes, but the police had made it clear that she needed to wait. Exposing herself to the public would not do any good for now.

In the Tesco Super store, only 10 minutes' walk from her secure lodging, she had taken her time wandering from aisle to aisle selecting the fresh fruit and vegetables she loved. She nearly squealed with delight when she spotted lychees, similar to Longan – 'Dragon Eyes' as it were called in Chinese – a local speciality from her hometown. She craned her head to check the price tag: £2 for a small packet with around 10 lychees. A bit pricey; she hesitated before she decided to treat herself that day. She was feeling almost happy, with the prospect of seeing Pearl the following day, and the possibility of pacing more quickly towards the future. Unknown to her, her happiness was transparent through her smile.

As her hand reached high up to the top shelf and touched the spiky fruit through its thin plastic packaging, she instinctively felt someone watching her. Her head jerked slightly and she glanced around. There he was, a tall, thin man standing at the far corner; he did not carry any basket or trolley and his eyes were fixed on her, but turned away quickly as soon as her eyes turned his way.

Her heart missed a beat, and then started beating faster. *Is he following me? The gang has found me?* The thought put such a sudden fright in her that she did not dare contemplate any more. Seized by panic, she dropped the lychees; her interest in shopping had instantly vanished.

They can't possibly find me. How can they? Nobody knows that I am here, except the police, and Ahmed, not even Dr Church. There is no way that they would tell the snakeheads my hiding place. No way. Wait, does anyone else know? Have I told anyone else? Oh dear, I spoke to Chloe last week. She promised that she wouldn't tell a soul. I didn't even tell her where I was, even though she had asked me. Oh shit, shit. Maybe they've bought Chloe or maybe they've tortured her to confess. Oh God. What have I done? What am I going to do?

Various speculations and scenarios played out in Ah Fang's head, making her frantic; she almost forgot what she was there for and made a dash to the exit. Only when she spotted a security guard did she realise that she had not paid for what she had in her basket and went to the checkout point.

Calm down, she reminded herself and quickly scanned around her, trying to see if the man was still watching her. She could no longer see him, but she spotted a couple of other Chinese faces and her suspicions intensified. One second she dreaded that she was going to be caught and God-only-knows what they would do to her; the next second she tried desperately to push away her fears and console herself that she was just being paranoid. *I am perfectly safe here in the middle of nowhere, and nobody can harm me. The police have assured me. Nothing bad will happen to me.*

It was with that positive note that she paid for her food and hurried out of the store.

I am only 10 minutes away from home. I'll lock myself in and call the police, if I have to. She quickened her usually brisk walk to a near run, the imminent danger and deep fear still in her gut making her tense; her bladder was pining for a pee.

Trying her best not to look over her shoulders, she turned the final corner, minutes away from her house on a quiet, residential street. She heard hurried steps behind her, making crunching noises, which eerily echoed her ever-quickening heartbeats. Without turning around, she broke out in a run.

Then she heard a deadly calm voice behind her. "Stop, bitch. You have nowhere to run to."

Ah Fang stopped in her tracks. She knew then that it was no use to hide anymore. All of a sudden, an unknown kind of calm descended on her. Her body turned around, as if pulled by a magic, invisible string.

Inches away from her stood a scar-faced, malicious-looking Chinese male, bolstered by his two beefy sidekicks, one on each side, ready to jump on her in a flash. They did not look friendly.

A black car made a screeching sound as it pulled up the pavement and stopped just behind the men.

The sun, at that very moment, had mysteriously disappeared; low, dark clouds were closing in.

Chapter 58: Body in the Lake

APRIL SHOWERS INDEED. It seemed to have rained far more than it had been dry in the past months, and the temperature simply refused to pick up. The only difference seemed to be whether there would be fine drizzle, fast showers, or furious torrents.

On Friday morning, Pearl woke up to the pattering sounds of showers against her bedroom window. *Damn, another miserable and wet day,* she muttered to herself.

She had spent the morning engaging in her typical routine: checking up on her Facebook friends and Twitter followers, which had been steadily increasing. Over 2000 followers in a short space of one year was no mean feat, especially when she was hardly a nerd and very much an amateur in the vast virtual world. She shared some of her holiday snaps and made various comments on friends' posts. Before she knew it, midday had arrived, and she had an appointment to attend to.

Reluctantly signing off from cyberspace, she raided her refrigerator and took out a packet of frozen buns, which she had bought from the Chinese supermarket, and microwaved a couple of them. Within minutes, her simple lunch was in her stomach and she was ready to brave the real world. *Not enough nutrition,* she noted. *I'll have to make it up by preparing a decent dinner later.* Her near-future food planning nearly made her forget her task on hand and taking an umbrella occurred to her just as she was locking up.

Carefully reversing her car out of its space below her apartment, she negotiated her way around the busy city centre and drove to the Central Police Station on London Road. No more visitors' parking permit issued by Reception - withdrawal of another service; she had to drive around to find a space at a NPS car park some ten minutes away.

The earlier drizzle had become more intense and dense as she made her way to her appointment. *Good thing that I remembered the umbrella.* It would not be fun to be soaked, even though the wind was steadily pelting raindrops on her clothes and her shoes already were damp from the potholes filled with water. The rain did not appear to be in a hurry to stop anytime soon.

Shaking the rain off her brolly outside the station, she then approached the front desk and signed herself in. She gave the name of the officer who had booked her, and settled herself on one of the unyielding, plastic chairs in the waiting area. It was a busy station and people came and went: some to report crimes, and others were the petty criminals and lowlifes who regularly hung around waiting for their friends to be bailed out. She heard one or two cursing the poor weather.

Half an hour passed; Pearl's patience was wearing a little thin, despite her iPod playing her favourite band Coldplay. It was one of those days when her mental state was not in top form, restless and lacking in concentration. Something was working against her usual sense of ease.

Minutes ticked by. She got up and went to the counter, addressing the front-office receptionist. "Can you please ask for DS Stanley for me again?"

It took the officer another 20 minutes before he showed his face.

"Come with me, Dr Church." The good-looking, middle-aged officer had Pearl follow him down the narrow corridors and through a couple of doors with security codes, leading her into a small interview room.

"One of our officers went to collect Miss Li at the time she agreed to, but she did not answer her door or her mobile. At this moment in time, we do not know where she is. Perhaps you can help us and find out." He handed over his phone to Pearl to dial Ah Fang's number.

No answer. Two minutes later, still no joy.

For the next hour or so, Pearl kept trying Ah Fang's mobile. Always the same outcome; it went straight to the voice mail, not even the owner's voice, but a machine-coded, male voice speaking standard, perfectly pitched English.

Eventually, DS Stanley said to Pearl, "Perhaps she's gone to see someone or misplaced her mobile or something. Let's hope that she'll get in touch with you or us soon."

Pearl was not convinced. "But I spoke to her only yesterday and I reminded her. She sounded quite pleased that the case was moving forward."

"Maybe something unexpected came up." DS Stanley cut in. He had other duties to attend to. "Whatever that may be, we just don't know." He reaffirmed his belief. "There is nothing we can do if she does not answer her phone, is there? I cannot spare an officer right now to go and look for her."

Of course not, you have forms to fill, Pearl thought, without being judgmental or cynical, just acknowledging a simple, well-known fact.

As he accompanied Pearl through the security doors on the way out, after signing off her claim form, he promised her, "We will keep trying her phone, and as soon as we are able to, I'll send our officers to the safe house to check on her. In the meantime, if you hear anything from her, do call us with her whereabouts."

"Of course." She nodded with emphasis.

"We'll have to arrange another time for the identification," DS Stanley offered, as he shook Pearl's hand and waved her off at the front of the station.

Outside, the rain had not stopped. In fact, it was getting faster and more furious. An ominous gloom descended on her.

A week later, Pearl received a call from DS Stanley. "Dr Church, I have very bad news."

Oh shit. Pearl nearly swore, but managed to stop herself; her grip on her mobile tightened, her palm suddenly sweaty.

"I'm afraid, regarding Miss Li," DS Stanley's voice was grave. "A body was discovered floating in Gravelly Moor Lake."

"Oh my God."

"You know: the one under the A38 flyover?" DS Stanley paused; Pearl worked her brain to locate the spot, but her mind was blankly full of dread, waiting with bated breath for the sergeant to continue.

"We think it is Miss Li, although I'm waiting for the final DNA confirmation from the postmortem result."

"Oh no." Hand over her mouth, Pearl was too shocked to continue. She was standing at her kitchen sink when the call came through. The dreadful news hit her like a hammer between the eyes; her heart started to pump like a steam engine. This was the last thing she had expected.

Ah Fang, the strange girl she had become very fond of in their recent dealings, had seemed so full of life at their last meeting. That young, pretty girl had her whole life ahead of her, but now it had been cut short, cruelly and abruptly.

"What happened to her?" Pearl croaked; her throat tightened, emotions arising from somewhere in the pit of her stomach traveling up to her brain and making her eyes misty instantly, with tears sure to follow.

"We don't know for sure, because her body had been in the lake for several days and a lot of the evidence we would want to gather would have been destroyed during that time. Let's wait and see what the PM tells us."

With that, he ended the call. He had already told her more than she should know. They both knew that.

Slowly, Pearl moved away from the sink and pulled out a chair by the dining table. She sat down; her mind full of images of Ah Fang, her smiles, her phone calls, her tales about her family and wild days in China, all crashing to the front of Pearl's consciousness. She felt afloat in a place defined by an unknown, but with a clear sense of grief, something she had never imagined possible towards a near stranger. As tears flooded down her cheeks, a dam exploded, and Pearl felt a deep gloom tearing her from every direction. She had no one to comfort her. The thought that she was utterly alone only added to her distress.

What a waste, she cried out in silence, reaching for a box of tissues, wiping tears away from her eyes. She focused on the photo of Andrew, which she had just hung on the opposite wall that morning.

After what seemed like a long time, the thought of her estranged husband propelled her to get up and climb upstairs to her office. She clicked on her iMac and the screen lit up, the colours bursting into a life of their own. She opened her Hotmail account and checked her inbox.

There he was; Andrew's name popped up in her incoming mails. She clicked it open.

Going away for a short break over the weekend, cycling a bit, climbing a little, outdoor stuff.

Simple, informative, and to the point: typical of Andrew.

She scrolled down her contact list; there was no one else she could possibly confide in about matters relating to Ah Fang. The naked truth stared back at her: *I miss my husband!*

That night, Pearl tossed and turned for the longest time, unable to fall asleep. When she finally drifted into a shallow sleep, Ah Fang's indistinct face appeared, both her hands reaching out from the bottom of a lake, which quickly turned into a deep ocean with giant waves, crushing and washing away the helpless, Chinese girl.

"I'm coming to get you," she shouted but no voice came out. She jumped into the rising waters, her arms and feet kicked hard, trying desperately to swim forward, fighting against the powerful, unrelenting waves, towards the small shadow that was swiftly being devoured by the massive, deadly darkness. She heard Ah Fang's muffled voice: "I am going home." Then the young girl disappeared, without a trace.

"No, Ah Fang!" Pearl cried out, a long, chilling howl in the depth of night. With that, she jolted awake, her nightie soaked in sweat, her eyes filled with salty tears.

Chapter 59: Pearl's Second Visit to Fujian

THE MAY HOLIDAY in China had been hectic, buzzing and steaming hot. All transport systems were stretched to their limit and used to their full capacities during the three-day, national holiday. The most populated country had seen an amazing economic boom, but it had its drawbacks.

The traffic was busier than usual, even after the long weekend. In a big city like Fuzhou, that kind of busy is on a different scale. Fuzhou Changle International Airport was jammed, heaving with human rivers of passengers, coming and going via both domestic and international flights.

Pearl – together with DI Jack Gordon and DS Sharon Sweeney – had just landed there after two legs: the first a 12-hour BA flight from London Heathrow to Hong Kong, followed by a two-hour transfer via China Eastern to Fuzhou. Altogether they had been traveling for nearly 24 hours when their plane touched down outside Fujian's provincial capital.

It was a very hurried and hushed affair. Only a week before, Jack had alerted Pearl that the National Serious Crime Squad investigation of the Herefordshire fire had resulted in some significant progress. Ah Lan, one of the initial survivors who subsequently died in hospital, had given the police a couple of crucial names of the gang masters, who operated in the UK but had strong connections to Fujian, where they had originated.

Combined with leads from a number of other organized-crime investigations, which also pointed to the same people, the NSCS had decided to send Jack and one of his detective sergeants to China. Tracing the source could very well help them to follow the trail of the 'snakeheads' and track them down.

This time, Jack made sure that Pearl came along as their interpreter. His boss did not need any persuasion, as Pearl's impeccable records spoke for themselves. Even if nothing else, the fact that she had already been to Fujian following the Morecambe Bay cockle-pickers drowning tragedy a few years before was qualification enough for this mission. Twenty-one illegal workers had been swept away by the tide while harvesting seafood. They all came from Fujian province, as did their gang masters. Nearly a decade later, the British police were still on the money trail, unable to trace the majority of the profits that the gang masters had obtained and laundered.

Jack had no trouble persuading Pearl, either. She had her own reasons for revisiting Fujian.

There they were, outside the airport with their luggage, on the 7th of May 2012, a Bank Holiday in the UK: just another normal day in Fuzhou. They were cordially greeted by the local police in the persons of Assistant Chief Song and his driver. It was a Mercedes 600 series in black, spacious enough for five passengers, and cool enough to protect them from the soaring heat, which had already climbed to 30 degrees, and was still rising. Back in the UK it had been 10 degrees and raining before they boarded the plane the previous afternoon.

From there onwards, it was business Chinese style. They were dropped off at their hotel, the centrally located 5-star Shangri-La recommended by their Chinese hosts. "It's only 45 minutes from the International Airport. Your hotel location is ideal for your business needs, close to the police headquarters, and handy for shopping and leisure pursuits," Chief Song stated and Pearl translated faithfully.

"We really appreciate the help the Chinese police are giving us, for booking our hotel and everything else. No doubt, we will need more help in the coming days," Jack had replied.

Prior to their trip, without her one-time 'secretary', Andrew, Pearl had actually gone to the Trip Advisor website and checked it out herself – it was the only luxurious hotel in Fuzhou. *Guess being a police interpreter has its advantages.*

Now the tedious long haul was at last over, and they checked in without delay. "Thank God!" Pearl let out a sigh of relief. *Let's forget about my duty, for a while anyway.*

With a tired smile on her face, she kicked off her shoes, drew back her curtains, and was instantly wowed with an amazing view of the rapidly expanding city sprawl. She had requested a room high up, so hers was on the 20th floor of this 26-floor skyscraper, one of the tallest in the city. There were builders' cranes as far as the eyes could see, and more tall buildings rising rapidly. It was 21st century China, after all.

The hand on her wristwatch pointed at six in the early evening, and the city was beginning to light up. She had one hour to herself before the local police chief's welcoming banquet, scheduled for seven that evening: in an exclusive venue no doubt. Not enough time for a nap, which she desperately needed but had to forego until much later.

Here in China, the control she once enjoyed in England had to be given up. Experience had taught her to get her mind right from the outset, to avoid the major stress and frustration that would inevitably follow. She knew few people could fight the Chinese hospitality, least of all her, not without damaging the mission. "We need the local police on our side." Jack had said: orders from above no doubt, and common sense too.

A nice, long bath would do, for now. A foamy soak in steaming water would do wonders for a tired body and mind, especially after that torturous, long-haul trip. The hotel offered sauna and a steam room, and even a Thai style masseur only a phone call away. Pearl picked up the little card advertising the services but put it down as just quickly. There was no time for that indulgence.

Listening to the relaxing sound of the running water, she stripped, shedding each piece of her clothing onto the marbled floor, her mind already drifting.

******

She was woken up at dawn by people arguing noisily outside in the corridor.

Jetlag was never fun, making her already irregular sleeping pattern further disturbed, like a pack of shuffled Mahjong pieces, scattered and chaotic, unable to make sense to a new player. It seemed to take her longer and longer to get over it each time she headed East.

In her heightened state of mind, she recalled her first return visit to China 18 years before, after six, long years away from her home city of Chongqing. She was so excited to be reunited with her daughter Liyuan, nothing else seemed to matter. She did not remember any jetlag whatsoever, just the joy and elation of seeing her family again.

Her thoughts shifted to the present time frame: Liyuan was all grown up and living a life of her own in Scotland, and her husband was somewhere in the USA, free as a bird, doing things he had done as a young man, reliving his dreams of being outdoors in the expansive space he craved.

What am I doing here? she asked herself, almost sounding like an accusation. The question flashed through her mind briefly, but long enough for a defensive answer to register: *I am living the life I want and that it has a purpose. I damn sure know exactly what has brought me to Fujian.* The surfacing of that knowledge to her consciousness propelled her to haul herself out of her comfy bed and get dressed in quick session.

The last few days had been hectic and flew by like a blurred chain reaction, one act after another, like she was a puppet. Jack, Sharon, and their faithful interpreter had been chauffeured to various meetings with the local police, who were hospitable and in control, making sure that their visitors' every need outside work had been met. The police chief had assigned them exclusive use of a transport, at their beck and call; everywhere they went, they had company.

The British team was entertained every night, at different posh eateries in the city, a constant flow of officials joining them for continuous Ganbei, the Chinese style drinking marathon. They were treated to the best food money could buy: a variety and type of food they had never heard of in all their combined culinary adventures all over the world.

Remembering her previous visit to Fujian, and how the officers responded to the typical Fujian hospitality, Pearl had warned Jack and Sharon what was to be expected. Fortunately for her, both Jack and Sharon could hold their drink and remain physically and mentally on top form.

Proving himself to be a jolly fellow who enjoyed his Chinese spirits and beers, come what may, however, when it was time to stop, he would show a different side. In firm but friendly fashion, he would hold up his hands and smile graciously, "Thank you so much, from the bottom of my heart." He looked around and held the Chinese chief's gaze. "Honestly, I have never eaten such beautiful food in all my years on earth. What can you say? We Brits are not exactly known for our culinary sophistication, are we? As Pearl, our wonderful Chinese expert would tell you, in Scotland, we eat that black, shit-like stuff we call haggis."

Raucous laughter all around, following Pearl's translation. One or two even applauded.

Further joking and jabbing at the British/Scottish cuisine made the Chinese companions giddy, on top of that wonder stuff in glasses which were filled up before they were empty. Most Chinese people were so obsessed with their own type of food – and food in general – that compliments made them giddy and proud beyond what was necessary. Given the Chinese chief prided himself as some kind of expert in Chinese spirits and condemned scotch and all related whiskey produced in Jack's motherland to be somewhat inferior, Jack went along and nodded his agreement. He did wink at Pearl once or twice, in mock horror. His good sense of humour shone through all that noise and excessive consumption of divine food, making Pearl's work easier and more tolerable, even fun.

As a credit to Jack, he had become quite good at picking up on Pearl's signals when talking to the Chinese, and where possible he always consulted her before and after their meetings with their Chinese counterparts to find out the real meaning and message behind what they were saying and doing.

"That was really cool what you did just now." Pearl, in turn, encouraged him with a genuine smile. "Nothing pleases the Chinese hosts more than showering praises to their food and drinks."

He had held her counsel and acted accordingly. From her time with Andrew, she had picked up a few tricks in dealing with men. No harm in giving men compliments when they're due; ego boosters were good tonics and could sometimes lead to unexpected returns. She could see a little of Andrew in Jack, but their differences were far too prominent to ignore.

As friendly as they presented themselves, when it came to the inner workings of the snakeheads operating in Fujian, the Chinese police seemed evasive and less than forthcoming, in complete contrast to the warm reception at their dining table. It was a lot of hot air and not much substance. Pearl could sense Jack's frustration at the lack of progress; she so wanted to help, but it was out of her hands. To the Chinese, she was nobody at best and 'an imperialist running dog' at worst.

Three days after their arrival, the information on Ah Long and his gangs in Fujian was limited to little more than what they had started with. The Chinese police had initially denied any knowledge of who "The Dragon" might be. "So many people either name or call themselves dragons, big or small, because it is an auspicious sign," had been their response.

However, to give the British police their 'face', the Chinese made a promise: "We shall look into our files for various leads on gangs operating in our vicinity. Please be patient with us."

Patient? Three days already gone and they were no closer to the truth about the gang. The question on the Brits' minds: how hard would the Chinese look?

Absentminded, and letting her thoughts roam, Pearl went through her morning routine: brushing her teeth, followed by a quick skin-care/makeup session. Pearl slipped into her cool, summer outfit – an orange, cotton vest under a short-sleeved blouse and a pair of white, linen shorts, her must-have, white-orange summer hat, and finally her sandals – and was raring to go.

The move had been forming in her head ever since she'd had confirmation of her visit to Fujian. She just needed a few hours to get this over and done with. Then she would feel better and carry less weight on her conscience.

Ah Fang's smiley, young face came to her mind's eye. Before her disappearance – with her body later found in the lake, and the possibility that she was murdered – Ah Fang had confided in her interpreter during their various meetings.

"My father's business was doing well and they wanted me to go to university and make myself useful." Ah Fang's face had appeared to hold a soft glow.

"Naturally. All parents want their children to do well. What's your father's business?"

"It's not a big business, but he does export and import different things between Fujian and other provinces. It's a silly name really. He calls his company Lin Fang Import and Export Company, naming it after me. Not creative at all. I sneered at him when he told me."

"I'm sure he did not mind; he would have forgiven you, anyway. No parent would hold such a minor disagreement against his only daughter."

"Maybe you're right. I was young and foolish, and I did not appreciate my parents. One day I'm going to return to China and be a good daughter to them. Yes, I'm going to make up to them."

"Of course, you will, Ah Fang," Pearl had replied, feeling sorry for the young woman in front of her, sad and tearful, also dreamy and determined. She embraced Ah Fang, patting her shoulder in an attempt to comfort her. Emotions gripped her, making her eyes water and her glasses misty. *I am really a softie at heart.*

"C'mon. Don't be sad. Let's hope that you will see your parents soon and make them proud one day." Pearl believed what she had said.

Weeks after that conversation, Ah Fang was gone, for good. Poor girl, her dream of a family reunion was forever crushed.

Being an illegal, with no official status in the UK, Ah Fang's death made no impact. Pearl had checked the news media after learning of Ah Fang's death, and all she could find was a short piece in the local *Post*.

A young woman's body was discovered earlier this week by the fishermen in Gravelly Moor Lake. The identity of the body is unknown and the cause of death has not been established. A postmortem will be carried out later this week, Heartlands Police have confirmed.

Did Ah Fang's parents know of her tragic passing? Pearl doubted it. Even if they did, there was not a thing they could do, except to mourn her. They could not possibly go to the Chinese government and ask them to put pressure on the British Police to solve a crime – *a Chinese illegal immigrant working as a sex slave in the UK was murdered and dumped in a lake.* Who murdered her? Who cared to find out? She had no diplomatic value. She was a nonentity when she was alive, and after death she no longer existed.

It would have made sensational headlines if she had been a British citizen, like that British woman in Bristol who was killed by a Dutchman and her body found after Christmas. The story had dominated headlines for months. Why would the law enforcement in the UK release information on a fish-ravaged and almost unidentifiable body in a lake; especially when the police had no leads on who had killed her, nor resources to investigate an illegal's sad demise? There were far more serious crimes to solve, like the man who had shot at a police officer, and the riots that caused the death of many good and law-abiding UK citizens. Moreover, the best part of the police time in the UK seemed to be spent on filling out forms and doing paperwork. Even the police themselves were complaining about it!

Pearl had done her homework. On arriving in Fujian, she had contacted her brother in Chongqing, who had called his contact in Fuzhou, who had made use of his various local guanxi, and in turn tracked down an address, now in Pearl's possession. Before leaving this world to the next, and without knowledge on either part, Ah Fang had assisted Pearl by providing her with a vital piece of information: her father's company name.

In the place where Ah Fang was born and raised, armed with a note safely secured in her handbag, Pearl walked briskly through the hotel lobby and out into the Fuzhou morning heat, set to rise as the day progressed.

Perhaps wisely, she did not call the 24-hour ride provided by the local police, nor did she request that the hotel book a taxi for her. She needed to do this on her own, and she did not want anyone to know that she had a private agenda in coming to Fujian.

No one. Not even Jack Gordon.

Outside on the pavement, Pearl did one last thing to complete her attire that day; she swapped her normal glasses for her new Vuarnet sunglasses.

It was still early. She had a few hours to herself before her meeting with Jack and Sharon at noon. They had requested a morning off: free from their Chinese minders, and from one another. It was a Sunday, after all, and even an interpreter needed a break.

She waved down a taxi and read out the address she had to the driver.

"It's in Changle City and it will take 45 minutes to an hour to get there," the driver said, in his heavily accented Mandarin.

"Fine. I'll pay you 100 yuan and book you for the whole morning. How does that sound?" She was quite confident that he would jump at this offer.

"That's too cheap. I'll do you a good deal. 200 yuan." A good haggler, he was.

"Well, okay then." Not too pleased with the price, but she needed to get back to the hotel in time for lunch.

"Hop in, then," shouted the driver, pleased with his scoop of a customer for the day.

Pearl climbed in, completely unaware that the occupants of a black BMW were just around the corner, watching her every move.

Chapter 60: Jack's First Visit to Fujian

ON SEEING PEARL at the Heathrow check-in point, Jack's heart leapt to his throat, catching his voice. Had it just been him and her, he would have scooped her up in his arms and given her body a tight squeeze, and her cheek a loving peck, banishing the tiny, weeny awkward moment that had descended in the distance between them.

Oh Darling Pearl, how I missed you!

Jack could see from Pearl's flushed face that she felt the unease too. The moment was framed in time, from which they both quickly recovered, as Jack went over to take her suitcase from her. There was no need to betray his feelings in front of his subordinate, even though Sharon had been working with him for a number of years and they knew each other well.

"Have you met Dr Church, Sharon?" He looked at his two travel companions of the fairer sex, and they smiled at each other politely.

"Call me Pearl, please." All professional with her usual, friendly smile, Pearl offered her hand to the female officer.

During the long flight between London and Hong Kong, Sharon sat between Jack and Pearl. The two ladies spent most of the time chatting to each other, while Jack was left to his own devices. He entertained himself with watching a film to kill the tedium. He did not find the latest Ben Stiller flick funny at all. With effort, he tried to sleep when the lights went out, as the 'chatty hunters' took a break from their chitchat.

No harm for them to establish a rapport, since they will be working together for the next few days, Jack thought, summoning his understanding side, *but I'd rather be sitting next to Pearl and feeling her nearness. Oh God, I miss her touch. I wish I could go back in time when we shared that lovely intimacy. I do not like the invisible wall which is now standing between us.*

Determined to get some rest by closing his eyes, he found that his mind was not cooperating fully with his command. Instead, his rambling thoughts centred on how he could get Pearl to himself and talk about things that had been left unsaid after their last and only holiday together.

I need to sort out my domestic life, the logic of it was loud and clear in his head, *if I truly want to make any progress in my romance with Pearl.* It had become amply clear to Jack – the moment he saw Pearl at the airport – that he was ready to make a break with his past. *I would not be the first man to leave my childhood sweetheart for another woman, nor the last.*

There was only one consolation, or perhaps compensation: what would set him apart from those middle-aged, hormone-charged men would be the woman he was after. Pearl was not some bimbo secretary two decades younger. For goodness sake, she was his interpreter, nearly a decade older and from a different cultural and racial background! People would talk. *But what the hell. Let people judge. I am damned anyway. I don't care. I only have this one life and I don't want to be sixty and look back with regret.*

In his mind's eye, he pictured what some of his more bigoted colleagues would say behind his back, but he had reached his own conclusion. *I am over 40 years old, and I should know what I really want by now. As for Moira, she can keep the house if she wants, and take anything else from our marriage. The kids are grown up and they, at least, should understand my actions.*

It was with thoughts for the future that Jack Gordon fell asleep, fitfully, to be woken up at regular intervals by sundry noises, or the food trolley smashing into his shoulder. Another feeding time! That's what long-haul flights were about: eating, drinking, watching movies on a tiny screen, and trying one's best to sleep in the tight seats where passengers were packed like sardines. *How do those jet-setters and frequent fliers deal with a lifestyle like this?* Jack shook his head in disgust.

"Thank God this is over." He heaved a huge sigh of relief when their journey was at last over.

"Yes, here we are at last!" Pearl cheered. Even the usually serious Sharon showed her white teeth with a tired smile.

On checking in, Pearl handed their passports to the counter and dealt with all the necessary officialdom.

"You are in room 1818. Wow, 18 is a very lucky number for the Chinese people," commented Pearl, as she handed the room keys to Jack.

"I wouldn't mind a swap, if you like," half-joked Jack. He saw her face turning a lovely pink, her eyes avoiding his.

What he had really wanted to say was, "I'd feel really lucky if you would share my bed with me."

With a bit of effort, and Sharon's presence, he managed to keep that thought to himself. It did give him an instant hard-on, as he played out the scenario in his head, and again later, especially after a luxurious, bubbly bath in his suite. He found himself in a massive room with the biggest bed he had ever seen, covered in pure, white cotton and a tasteful bed cover. Quality seemed the hallmark.

Unlike most hotels he had stayed in, this one looked unique; his room had two full-size windows on the side and in front of the massive, king-sized bed; there was also an adjoining office and reception room. *Guess there are some perks to traveling overseas to places like China. They do treat us with the best living quarters. Wonder how much time I can actually stay in that bed, and whether or not Pearl will feel like joining me?*

As if on cue, there was a knock on his hotel room door: a soft tap, one, two and then the knock became a little louder. *My darling Pearl.* Jack's heart thumped, feeling his spirit lifting quite a few notches, despite the jetlag.

He was behind the door in a flash and pulled it wide open, his facial muscles flexed, with a beam of welcome ready to transmit, only to be greeted by Sharon's smiling and heavily made-up face. Her room was only a few doors away on the same floor.

On seeing the bathrobe-clad Jack, Sharon blurted out a quick apology: "Oh, sorry, Boss. I did not expect to catch you semi-naked."

Sorry my ass, Jack mused. He could tell that Sharon was not truly sorry in the least. Recently split from her long-term boyfriend, it had been obvious from the very beginning that Sharon had the hots for Jack. Somehow her fantasy never made it past a bit of simple, harmless flirting. It was common knowledge that Jack was married and faithful, hence widely respected for that, especially among the female officers who were rare species in the Force. During the occasional nights out with fellow officers, Sharon had let rip that her own boyfriend had refused to commit after eight long years with her, and in between he had cheated on her numerous times. Each time she had taken him back, until this last time, when he had slept with a friend of hers. That was it; the end of both her relationship with the cheater, and her friendship with the girlfriend. Jack was not completely oblivious to Sharon's affection towards him.

"No problem, Sergeant. Come on in. You can take a seat in my *posh office* and I'll go get dressed. Be with you in a mo," offered Jack, and with an exaggerated hand gesture, he let her in and headed towards the inner room, where his evening attire was laid out neatly on the bed.

No police outfit at all for this trip, and he even had to leave behind his gun in the UK, where he did not normally carry weapons around anyway, a nice change from his army days when he had to carry a heavy load most of the time. However, his job with serious crimes sometimes required the use of a gun. Here in China, the last thing he wanted was to get into trouble with Customs on entering this once mysterious, highly controlling country. Just in case, he did take his army knife, which he always carried in his suitcase. In any event, he did not expect that he would need to use force anywhere in China.

No diplomatic incidents would be tolerated: that much he was prepared for.

******

China was booming and I could see why. The West was going into a downhill spiral, its economy utterly and completely stuffed by greedy bankers and incompetent politicians, while the Chinese people were keeping themselves busy, and their banks were rolling in RMBs as well as American dollars. Their newly found wealth was truly staggering and an eye-opener for me.

Ever since we arrived in Fujian, our schedule has been full. Our Chinese hosts seemed to have decided that our every waking moment should be occupied; whether usefully or not, I reserve these observations.

The welcoming banquet lasted four hours, with us chomping and slurping our way through at least twenty different dishes, and almost all of them looked or tasted nothing like the Chinese food I've had back in England, despite being a regular in Leicester Square and having sampled the many restaurants in London's China Town.

Pearl did her best to explain to me and Sharon what these were, and to be fair to her, I think she looked a bit confused herself when trying to identify these local delicacies as they were presented one after another by pretty, young waitresses in their fine dresses and big smiles.

"I think this one is a kind of prawn." She pointed at one, which happened to be passing in front of me on that spinning table in the middle.

"Bloody hell. They look huge. King prawn, tiger prawn?" A little bit of a show off of my knowledge of Chinese cuisine, but really I had no idea: simply guessing.

I saw her chatting to the Chinese police chief, probably trying to confirm the exact type, and the chief seemed to be giving her a lecture. By the time she turned to me again, I had already consumed a couple of them and they were delicious, although they tasted nothing like what I had before.

"Mr Song said that there are many different types of prawns and they all have different names. He also said that you don't have this type in the UK, and in fact nowhere else in China. It's a speciality of Fujian." Pearl relayed what she was told.

Before she carried on passing the full, detailed lesson on prawns which the Chinese chief obviously enjoyed doing, I said to her: "Don't worry your pretty head, Pearl. I've come to the point that I don't really care what they are. So far so good. I'm just going to eat whatever they serve and see what is the worst they can do to a Scot's untrained stomach."

"Fair enough, sir," came a giggle and a radiant smile, spreading quickly from her eyes to her whole face, making me want to hold her and kiss her there and then. Clever lady, she really was. She knew that I was trying to make life easier for her.

"Actually," I was enjoying myself so much that I wanted to tease her, holding her attention on me a little longer, "I do not think that it's fair that you continuously interrogate our host about the contents of each dish, then pass on all that information as to which type of seafood it is, and what kind of medical and nutritional elements they offer to our bodies, on top of treating our taste buds."

She blushed deeper; her face glowed even more with embarrassment. I knew she'd fall for it, so I winked, which made her relax a little, followed with an appreciative smile. Her sensual mouth looked so kissable that I could not help from leaning over and, with my head almost touching hers, put one of my arms on the back of her chair.

Even in our exclusive VIP room, it was way too noisy for me, as all the stiff-lipped Chinese officials seemed to have loosened up and were talking and joking at the top of their voices, in total contrast to a typical English meal in a British restaurant. I had to move closer to her to be able to hear what she was saying. If high tolerance of human noise was what was required to get up close and personal to my darling Pearl, then so be it.

To be honest, to a guy from the rough part of Glasgow, having spent years in the Army and SAS, do I really care what kind of shit I eat? Food is fuel. Surviving was important, and so was staying a step ahead of the enemy, not what I put in my mouth only to be crapped out a few hours later. I did not tell her that, of course. I knew she enjoyed the finer things in life, unlike my humble, slightly uncouth, Scottish self.

Naïvely, I had expected that the welcome feast was a one off, and the rest of our stay would have gone easier and with more time to ourselves. No such luck!

The next morning, we were whisked off as soon as breakfast was over. Following an extensive tour of Police Headquarters and introduction to a number of personnel who dealt with organized crimes and snakeheads, it was my turn; a presentation of what the British police had discovered in a number of our investigations, and how some of the connections led us all the way to Fujian. Everything took longer, because we needed to wait for Pearl's translation, as efficient as she has always been.

The Chinese assigned a team to work with us: a driver, a police inspector from their headquarters, a sergeant, and a constable. Well, they used different titles, but Pearl made life simpler for me by assigning them each a British equivalent. These people shadowed us everywhere we went. I have lost count how many new faces we have been introduced to in the course of three days, and I don't remember their names either. I try my best to remember their surname, and got by through calling them Mr Zhang, Mr Chen, or Mrs Wang. As for their first names, they are simply beyond my limited linguistic capabilities.

"You know that in the Mainland China we write in simple forms, while in Taiwan and Hong Kong, it's different. They use more traditional characters, hence labelled complicated forms." Pearl took it as her duty to educate us culturally and linguistically, but to a language-blind, uncultured policeman like me, I have come to see what they use in China as anything but simple.

What would it be like without our competent interpreter? Pearl had proved time and again what an invaluable asset she was. She made it her business to address them all according to their titles, another cultural eye-opening for me. Life was certainly simpler back home, at least in the case of addressing your colleagues and superiors. Calling your boss 'sir' or 'ma'am' was all that was needed, in the police force anyway.

Yesterday morning, like a set alarm, our limo came and collected us for a ride. Changle city was our morning tour, beginning with a talk by the local police about the background of the immigration history of the city.

Apart from our usual police-officer companions – our minders – we were joined by another car full of strange faces, our day escorts. One of them – Mr Zheng, according to Pearl – was our tour guide. He was chatty and provided us with some very interesting statistics.

"The majority of young people in many of our villages went overseas, to give their families a better life," he informed us, while pointing out one of the villages to us as we drove by.

"Is it possible for us to talk to some villagers?" I asked, thinking it might shed some light into what we are investigating.

"You will not find many villagers, except for older people and children." He spoke through Pearl.

"I take it as a no then," I shrugged my shoulders, not forgetting to give my interpreter a wee, understanding smile.

"That's right." Pearl confirmed it, wryly smiling back.

From the various conversations she was having with the officer in our car, and the guide – who had no authority except to share some of his local knowledge – I could tell from their body language that not too many questions were to be asked by us. Okay, set on the receiving mode.

Looking out of our car window, in place of crops in the former farmers' green fields I was greeted with many grand, detached four- or five-storey homes, built with the money from the sweat and blood from those immigrants slaving away in Chinese takeaways overseas. The mansions were built in Western styles, grand and luxurious, waiting for the return of their masters.

To me, these massive mansions cast a poignant and sad shadow on a fine, sunny day. I saw the beauty of the architecture against the green, lush mountains stretching to the clouds high above; I simply could not understand why anyone would leave their homes in such a heavenly place and seek their fortune across the oceans. If it was a shit-hole like the Gorbals, I could at least appreciate the motivation.

By the look of Pearl, I could see that she shared my feeling, and in fact, she more or less expressed it for us all: "It's so sad to see such beautiful homes empty, and a peaceful and serene village in such a state of affairs."

I could feel her raw emotions as her voice broke, with her eyes misty. I so wanted to hold her hand and give her a hug. This woman brought out the protective urges in me.

Before lunch, we were driven to a lush valley where they had built a Buddhist temple, Taoist Holy shrines, and Christian churches, all constructed though generous donations from overseas Chinese according to our guide. He proudly informed us: "They were especially built for the elderly parents and young children to go and pray for their safe journey to the West, and their prosperous homecoming one day."

We were allowed to get out, and enjoyed the peace and quiet; there was not a single soul there but our entourage. Pearl eagerly took out her camera and shot some snaps.

"C'mon, Jack. Smile. Pose for the ladies." She was in high spirits. Never a keen participant where photography was concerned, I did not mind her shooting pictures, as long as she showed that brilliant smile of hers. I was game.

In the afternoon, our tour continued to a different destination: Fuqing, another of the satellite cities ringing Fuzhou.

Again a lengthy, formal talk was followed by a more leisurely tour. Pearl did most of the talking with our Chinese hosts, but gave us enough to know what we were supposed to see. She was kept on her toes, and it was good to see that she seemed to enjoy it.

"Fuqing was much smaller a decade ago." Pearl pointed at the many tall buildings being erected as our car drove along the newly built boulevard, lined with trees of Chinese origin on both sides.

"There were green fields here only a few years ago; now posh apartments and high-rise office buildings have been constructed. Fuqing is now a sizable city with a huge property boom, and the majority of investments came from those who had gone abroad and made it."

You don't say. Fuqing was another hotbed of mass emigration. I knew that people from this area were known by the Met police; because our law-abiding London Chinese community feared them and would do everything to avoid them: Fuqing Gangs. I would not be surprised if we bump into people who were being paid by Ah Long; after all, this was one of his bases, the reason why we were here in the first place.

Our last stop was a mausoleum. One of the richest Fuqing natives had built it as a resting place for his parents. The money he had poured into this monument was staggering, millions of US dollars. Reportedly he had bought the whole village where he was born and raised, and then turned it into a philanthropical project, including a cemetery, primary and secondary schools, old people's homes, and a park free for all visitors. Other building projects were lined up.

A very interesting day indeed, yet what had we got to show my boss back home?

Never mind. Here I was on our third day in this foreign yet exciting land; my jetlag had more or less gone, and I felt I deserved a bit of indulgence for myself. Time to call Pearl and have that chat with her about our future. I reached for the phone on my desk and dialled her room number.

No answer, and it kept ringing.

Chapter 61: Where is Pearl?

FOR A FEW seconds, Pearl was totally disorientated, unsure where she was, or what time of the day it was.

Surrounded by pitch darkness, she initially thought that it must have been one of her usual nightmares from which she was waking up. She was so often haunted by them that it was sometimes difficult to tell whether she was still dreaming or not.

No, I am not dreaming, it hit her quickly, as stabs of pain assaulted her, like shafts of fire, burning her head, her throat, her chest, her bottom, and every part of her body. Her mouth felt dry, her tongue had a bitter taste, and her whole body was screaming of hurt and pain.

Commanding her willpower, she tried opening her eyes, but they were throbbing, and something sticky was making her attempt futile. Habitually, she moved her right hand, fumbling for her iPad, which had become the first thing she did on waking up in recent months. It was handy to keep it close by, hence the new nightly ritual of laying it on her side of the bed before she finally went to sleep. No iPad or iPhone was there. She was not in her hotel bed either.

She stopped moving and thought hard. *Where am I? What has happened?*

Her headache increased as she tried to remember what had happened to her and why she was not in her comfy hotel bed. She could not call to her fuzzy mind what had brought her to this alien place, but instinct screamed in her head that whatever this place was, she should not be there.

Slowly, her eyes began adjusting to the darkness, somehow getting a feel of her surroundings.

Tentatively, she raised her hand and touched her forehead. Ouch! A bump the size of an egg and hurting like hell. Gently and with caution, she traced the contours of her face, swollen and burning hot, assaulting her with an excruciating pain when applying a tiny, little pressure. At the corner of her mouth, she felt a sticky patch, which was beginning to dry.

It could be blood. I must have fallen, or did I get beaten up by someone? The thought formed and brought a glimmer of distant memory. *Yes, I was definitely hit by some thugs before I passed out.*

The pain became sharper as she tried to think back. The strain of remembering was causing more stress to her already-sore head and eyes. She closed her eyes, directing her energy to figuring out why someone would hit her and throw her on the hard floor of a deserted room.

How long have I been in this godforsaken place? Who brought me here?

Slowly, her memory began to return. Then all of a sudden, like a thunderstorm, the portals of memory opened, allowing everything to enter; one puzzle piece after another, she started piecing together what had happened in the few hours since leaving her hotel that morning, assuming that it was that morning and not a day or some days ago.

With the dam of memory threatening to overwhelm her whole being, the feeling of danger gripped her throat tightly and nearly choked her. All her senses were suddenly on high alert.

✳✳✳✳✳✳

Upon entering the taxi outside the Shangri-La, she had settled in the back seat, her mind fully occupied, yet drifting, uncertain.

What shall I say to Ah Fang's parents? Shall I tell them that their only daughter died a horrendous death in a foreign country, where she was cruelly murdered by nobody-knows-who, and nobody would care enough to investigate? Or should I spare their pain by pretending that I know nothing about how she died, and that her body was not discovered for a week and she was no longer identifiable because her face was eaten by fish?

Before leaving the UK, Pearl had learned a little more surrounding the discovery of Ah Fang's body from a familiar source. Mrs Wong had called her about a case she was involved with during one of their conversations.

"I was assisting the police with a case of a missing person of Cantonese origin," Mrs Wong had said to Pearl, in confidence. "A restaurateur's wife disappeared not long after she had given birth to their first child. The doctors knew that she was suffering postnatal depression and had given her some pills to take. But because she didn't speak English, and her husband was too busy with his work to care for his wife's condition, she was not receiving the treatment that she needed."

"How awful," Pearl had murmured her sympathy. She had come across similar stories, and every time it tugged at her heartstrings. She listened to Candy as the seasoned colleague continued:

"A couple of weeks ago, when he returned home from work after midnight, his wife had gone, leaving their six-month-old baby crying herself to sleep.

"When the mysterious female body was reported, the police immediately associated it with Mrs Ng, who was reported missing. They called Mr Ng and, of course, me. We both went to identify the body."

"That must be terrible," Pearl interjected.

"Oh Pearl." Mrs Wong sounded pleased to have found a sympathetic ear to which she could release some of her steam.

"I don't think that I am going to sleep tonight, and if I do, I'll be having nightmares!"

"Sorry to hear about that," Pearl had replied, but it was more than her sympathy that Mrs Wong wanted. She had a horrid story to share, and there was more.

"The body was so damaged that there was hardly any face left. I can't even describe what it smelt like and what an awful sight that had been. No words for it. The pathologist told me that the body was already messed up badly before it was dumped into the water. There were many internal injuries. The poor woman, whoever she might be, was tortured before she was killed. I had to go in with the man and translate what was said. It was horrendous! Considering what I have seen in my interpreting career, this must have been one of the most distressing experiences."

I bet. Thank God that it was you rather than me. The thought flashed across her mind, but didn't need to be said out loud. Without horrific scenes like identifying dead bodies, Pearl had enough nightmares springing from her normal life.

The worst part for Mr Ng and Mrs Wong? Having been put through that heart-wrenching identification process, the salvaged, naked body turned out not to be his wife's. At least, Mr Ng still had hopes to find his wife alive, which was no longer the case for Ah Fang, whose body was eventually identified. She was forever gone, vanished into darkness, swallowed up by ghosts, end of her story, done with this world, and nothing more. She didn't even have a loved one to identify her remains.

"Motherfucker!"

The taxi driver shouted at a cyclist and honked just for emphasis. An elderly man had come from behind him and cycled across in front of him, causing him to do an emergecy brake, nearly catching the back of the bike.

It jolted Pearl back to the here and now. She had been completely oblivious to what was happening on the road, and was startled by the driver's outbursts.

Under normal circumstances, she would be curious enough to enquire what had happened and have a chat with the driver. In her traveling experiences far and wide, talking to taxi drivers had proved one of the best ways to find out local information, and to familiarize herself with the strange environment. Not today. The middle-aged man on the driving seat had made several attempts to talk to his seemingly interesting yet aloof passenger; she, however, remained resolute. She had far more pressing matters on her mind.

Should I really go and see the parents? What if I bring unnecessary heartaches to them? What if they decide to take this up with the British authorities and get me into trouble?

Coming to this part of her reasoning, as she had done numerous times before, she became doubtful about her decision to proceed. *Perhaps I should just turn back before the deed? It is not my job as an interpreter to get involved in such matters. What would Jack say if he found out? What would Andrew say to me if he knew what I was up to?*

The images of the two men in her life troubled her. She knew what Andrew would say; the man was forever ready to pass on advice, solicited or otherwise. *Pearl, you can't take on such responsibilities. They are not yours to take. You can't right all the wrongs in the world. Stop it right now!*

But I've got to try to do what I feel is right. I have a conscience and I am a parent too. How awful it must have been to lose an only child in another country, and they don't even know how she died. Pearl argued her case with her imaginary Andrew in her head.

As for Jack, she simply did not know him well enough to speculate how he would respond to her visit to a victim's family on her own initiative. Surely that could not have been in the rules' book of the British Police, nor that of professional interpreters.

Conflicting thoughts fought their way through her mind all the way from Fuzhou centre to her destination in Changle.

"Here we are," the driver announced, calling Pearl back from her reverie. He had stopped outside a gate in front of a number of tall, concrete, residential buildings, all identical to one another.

"I won't be able to drive in, because I do not have a permit," said the man, matter of fact. "Don't worry, I'll wait for you here when you finish. Give me a call when it's time to pick you up." He handed Pearl his card with his mobile number on it, as Pearl paid him the agreed fare.

On approaching the security guards, typical of many residential homes in Chinese cities, she reported to the elderly gentleman who looked like the man in charge of people going in and out.

"I'm here to visit Mr Sun Lin." Instead of reading out the address, which was a long number on the 8th floor of Building Number 5, she showed the man the address on her piece of paper.

The man waved her in without further ado, not even bothering to point out where the building was located. She was going to ask, but stopped herself at the last minute. She did not want to appear too foreign, a total stranger to the neighbourhood. Better to remain inconspicuous.

She spent the next 90 minutes in Ah Fang's family home, where her tears mixed with those of Ah Fang's mother, who had held onto Pearl's body, completely lost in her grief at losing her 'fragrant flower', regretting bitterly the fights they had traded with each other. The father stayed silent most of the time, as they sat listening to the mother's tearful reminiscences in between her heart-wrenching sobs and howling.

When she finally got up to leave, she felt an utter exhaustion, as sadness and depression tore at her insides, The grim-looking father stood up at the same time. He held out a piece of paper, which he then pressed into her hand.

"It may be too late for any kind of justice for my daughter," His voice was shaken with grief, as if something was caught in his throat which made him croak; "But this is surely one of the men responsible. We know there is no point in going to any police in this country. They are corrupt crooks. But you may be able to do something with it back in England."

Despite their persistent offer to see her off, Pearl insisted that she make her own way out.

"I have a taxi waiting for me just at the gate," she had repeated.

She hugged the crying mother one more time at their door, between the normal, inner, wooden door and the iron barred security outside. Reluctantly, the grieving woman eventually released their faraway visitor from her own private hell.

They stood at the door, the man's arm around his wife's, supporting her. They watched Pearl leave.

While walking down the seven flights of stairs in the residential building, she stopped once to get her breath back, and let out a huge sigh of relief. Despite the tears and raging emotions, she felt better having done it, a weight lifting from her stressed shoulders. Did it give the parents some kind of closure? Probably not. A little consolation? Maybe.

At the landing, she smoothed open the crumbled piece of paper Ah Fang's father had just handed to her. All she saw was a name and an address in Fujian. She put it into her inside pocket in her handbag and continued her descent downstairs.

Turning the next corner, just one flight above the street level, she saw two men walking towards her. Before she could say, "Hi," and move away from them, they approached her and grabbed her arms tightly, one on each side. One of them said, in a hushed voice, "Don't utter a sound, unless you don't want to live."

Without another word, she was dragged down the last few steps and bundled into a black car parked just outside the exit of the building.

They had been waiting for her.

Chapter 62: "Pearl, I Want You Back"

TYPICAL OF HIM, Andrew made a snap decision.

Totally unaware of Pearl's whereabouts and the situation she had suddenly found herself in, Andrew had been away for a long weekend, in Estes Park, where he cycled up steep hills in the Rockies.

On return to his faculty on a Monday, he sat in front of his PC, sorting out the hundreds of work e-mails accumulated during his absence. Time sped by as he did his usual, efficient weeding out of junk and answering the ones of some significance. The ones that did not need immediate attention he left for another time.

During his weekend in the Rockies, while he cycled during the day and camped at night under the starry nightscape of Colorado, he recalled his last camping trip with his wife in the Highlands of Scotland, where it did not just rain, it poured, with strong gales from the North Sea.

Now on his own, he had ample time to reflect on his life: over half a century had gone and how many more years were to come? He wondered. He recalled all his relationships, ones that had stood the test of time and lasted. Apart from his family, from whom no matter how distant and unconnected he might feel, he would always know that they were family and that was that.

But Pearl, oh Pearl. She had been in his life the longest — longer than any other women in his life — and the only one to whom he had ever proposed to marry.

Why did I leave her to fend for herself? Didn't I promise to love her and protect her from harm? What am I doing thousands of miles away on another continent, while she is left to deal with the pain of separation all on her own? When did I become the type of selfish bastard that I despise? Damn fool!

He made up his mind then: *I am going to clear my diary as soon as I get back to work, and book the first flight to the UK. I'll persuade Pearl to come to America. My life is meaningless without her, and if she refuses to join me here, I'll go back to her.*

The lunch break came, but for once, his stomach took second place. He went online and checked on all possible flights back to England. *I have been in America long enough to figure out what I really want.*

More than anything, he wanted to get his wife back; life without her was not worth living.

******

After they climbed out of their car, Jack and Sharon headed hurriedly towards the front gate of the police headquarters. Jack's gait was fast and furious, his shoulders rigid and tense, reflecting what was going on inside his head. Pearl had been missing for a whole damn day. Jack had been frantically trying her mobile, again and again, unable to locate her whereabouts.

"When did you realize that she was missing?" One of the senior Chinese police officers sat them down and asked Jack. Sergeant Deng was the one who had the best spoken English, hence the designated one to take an official statement from the British visitors.

"Early yesterday morning," Jack answered, his voice grim and his facial expression even more so.

"How do you know for sure that she is missing? She could be visiting her friends and have forgotten to inform you." The officer looked Jack square in the eye.

"No, I don't think so," Jack replied, a tad on the sharp side. "I know her. She would never do such a thing. As far as I know, she has no friends in Fuzhou. Her family is in Sichuan Province. If she had friends here and she wanted to visit them, she would have told me, and I would have been happy for her to visit."

"Now tell me everything you know, from beginning." Sgt Deng demanded, taking out his notebook from a drawer in front of him. He did not even offer the British Officers chairs, or tea, as they had done in the previous days.

Jack didn't care. All he wanted was for them to find Pearl, not spend time sitting in their offices, enjoying their elaborated tea ceremony and polite bullshit with no substance.

The Chinese authorities hadn't acted quickly to search for her, certainly not as soon as he had notified them the day before. He had asked the manager of his hotel who could speak English to call the police on duty for him. He had been advised to wait. Granted, it was a Sunday, and he, an experienced officer, had hoped and prayed that Pearl would turn up before too long.

Perhaps she went shopping and switched off her phone?

His concern and worry intensified when she was not at their lunch as agreed. In all the time he had known her, she had never missed an appointment, never been late, not even once. Unless she'd had a personality transplant, it would be totally unlike her to pull off a disappearing stunt like that. Something bad must have happened to her. Jack became more and more certain of this as time slipped away.

Even if Pearl did not want to have anything more to do with me romantically, I would not wish to see her in harm's way. My fondness for her came from the bottom of my heart, and I care for her deeply.

He found himself thinking more of her than anyone else in his life, although he had only known her for a few months. If Jack had gone to a therapist, as the Americans tended to do on a regular basis, he would have been told that he was in love. Even without the help of all that psychobabble, Jack realized that what he was feeling was precious; only the lucky ones on earth were blessed with such life-affirming emotions.

"Now, tell me, Detective Inspector Gordon," Sergeant Deng checked his notes so far, his small eyes fixed on the British Officer in front of him, his voice formal and without emotions. "How much does Ms Zhang know about the gangs you are investigating? Do you have any idea if she had any involvement with any of your victims of the gangs, or the gangs themselves when she was in the UK? Maybe..."

Before Deng continued his questioning, Jack stopped him. "Hang on a minute here, Sgt Deng. What are you suggesting? Do you mean that the gangs we are investigating may have something to do with her disappearance? Do you...?"

"No, that is not what I am getting at, DI Gordon." Deng interrupted Jack in mid-sentence in return.

Jack could tell that the Chinese man in front of him had become impatient – perhaps towards the British 'interference', a phrase the Chinese media was very fond of using. Pearl had warned him and Sharon about the Chinese sensitivity in such matters. "The Chinese official stand has always been that foreigners have no right to poke into the internal affairs of China." But Pearl, as far as Jack was concerned, did not fit into China's 'internal' affairs. To him, this was personal.

Even without Chinese genes, Jack Gordon could see right through people like Deng, a traditionally brought up and hard-nosed chauvinist. *Women, in your narrow minds, are not equal beings. Does someone as highly educated as Pearl Zhang rattle you, making you feel inadequate, Mister?*

Jack kept that thought to himself, but could not help feeling an increasing disdain towards the arrogant, macho Chinese officer.

"There is nothing you can do," he told Jack, his voice firm and crude, as if he was a teacher or a parent addressing a naughty child. "Go back to your hotel and wait."

With that, Jack saw Sgt Deng closing his notebook and barking out an order in Chinese. Their driver appeared through the door.

"He will take you back to your hotel," Deng said.

"When would I be notified about your search?" Jack made another attempt, his temper simmering just under the surface.

"No need to concern yourself. We will tell you in time. Make yourself comfortable. You are our faraway guests."

There was an evident emphasis on the word 'guests'.

Chapter 63: Mission Impossible?

AFTER BEING DROPPED off in front of their hotel, Jack let himself out, moody and belligerent, without saying thank-you to the driver, or paying attention to whether Sharon had got out okay or not. He heard Sharon quickening her steps to catch up with him with a question, a little breathlessly. "What are we going to do, Boss?"

"We should probably think what we *can* do first, before considering what we *are* going to do," he answered, his voice tense and his frustration evident, ready for an outburst at any provocation.

Whether his anger was directed towards the Chinese or himself was not important. All the way back to the hotel, Jack did not utter a sound. His once calm and collected exterior had now been replaced by his indignation towards everyone and everything, a state of mind which was a bit alien even to himself. He did not like what he was feeling.

"Sorry, Sharon. I don't mean to take it out on you." He realized that he was reacting just a little too harshly to an innocent question.

Sharon nodded, replying in an even softer voice. "No problem, boss. I understand. I'm also worried and concerned about Dr Church."

Even in his state, Jacked noted that she had put an emphasis on Pearl's professional title. "I'm just not sure if there is anything we can do. After all, we are on Chinese soil and we don't have jurisdiction here," she continued, searching for his eyes.

"You're right. Of course." It was his turn to nod his agreement, vainly attempting a contrived smile, which didn't have a chance to register before it was gone.

From the earlier conversation with Sgt Deng, it was as clear as day to Jack that the Chinese did not give a damn about their missing interpreter – had she been a Chinese national, the British involvement would have been nonexistent. She would have just disappeared from the face of the earth without any explanation whatsoever.

Didn't that kind of thing happen in China all the time? In such a massive country, there must be millions of crimes for the police to solve on a daily basis; finding missing persons was not exactly high on anyone's agenda, unless this missing person happened to be someone with important guanxi and unlimited cash to bribe the poorly paid officials. Jack knew it, despite his limited knowledge about China, whose mystery and enigma had not lessened a great deal with his experience, which after all was only a three-day, scratch-the-surface kind of experience.

The British had no idea; the police in China in general, and Fujian in particular, were notorious for being corrupt. How else did the snakeheads operate so efficiently there? How did hundreds of thousands of people escape overseas each year, given the tight control of the Chinese borders? If the local police were not in it, with their hands deep in the pie, how could the snakeheads thrive and their criminal activities achieve such a far-reaching scale?

Everybody knew that it was good for business; snakeheads supported the local economy, not to mention the unlimited supply of foreign currencies pouring in from all directions into the Chinese banks, including the many underground banks, the loan sharks – where did their cash come from?

The sad truth: 'The Dragon', and his smuggler underlings, had bought many in the police force, as well as any politician or official of any significance.

Because Jack had no idea, he was driven by his blinding fury and unrelenting desire to find Pearl.

"I just wish that we knew where Pearl is and that she is safe. She is my responsibility," Jack murmured.

No response came from Sharon, except nodding her agreement.

They collected their keys from Reception and got into their lift. Facing Sharon, Jack, with measured words and a calmer voice, addressed his subordinate.

"You're absolutely right, Sharon. This is China, and what do we know?" He gave her a wry smile, with the intention to soften his serious expression.

Back home, Jack the Scot was well known for his Sean Connery type good looks, and quite a few of his female colleagues had the hots for him. What made him even more attractive was that he seemed completely oblivious to his own superior, physical attributes. But Jack had more than just good looks. He knew when he should lead, and how. Overreacting now would achieve nothing.

"The only thing we can do is to let the Chinese do their job, and hopefully they will find Pearl safe and sound."

He paused before going on, "After all, without our interpreter, we are not going to be able to communicate effectively with the Chinese anyway. Time for you to take time off. Go shopping or do a bit of sightseeing or something. You've worked hard and earned your break."

"How about you?" She looked at him quizzically.

"Shopping? *Moi?*" He pulled an exaggerated face. "Don't worry about me. Go and enjoy yourself. I could do with some R&R, perhaps catching up with some e- mails."

"Okey-dokey, you're the boss man," Sharon conceded.

They bid good-bye outside the lift and headed to their own rooms: she to the right and he to the left.

******

The morning broke; through a small window high above on the far corner, the sun streamed into her room. Pearl woke up from her fitful sleep during the darkest night of her life. This time, it was not her nightmares that jerked her awake; the reality was far worse than any of the bad dreams she had ever had.

Her head still hurt, and every inch of her body screamed in pain, given any tiny movement from her. Her memory, however, had returned with a vengeance, alerting her to the clear and present danger that had befallen her, all too suddenly and totally unexpectedly.

After she was bundled into a black car with tinted windows, she was forced into the back seat between two mean-looking Chinese men. By the look of them, they were local Fujian Chinese. Neither spoke a word, except occasionally using their body language when Pearl tried shifting her body or posture. They tightened their grip on her at the slightest provocation, inflicting immediate, physical hurt to whatever tender, female part they came in contact with, using their iron fists and heavy trainers. It was obvious that they were the hired muscle for whoever had decided to kidnap her.

There was an iron barrier erected between the back seats and the front; Pearl could not see the driver or the man on the passenger seat. But instinct told her that the man in the front was the man in charge of the thugs. Summoning all the calm and courage she could muster under the circumstances, she shot her questions at him: "Hey, who are you? Where are you taking me?"

Chapter Sixty-Three

No reply.

All she could hear was her questions hovering and echoing in the narrow space she was confined to.

Okay, he is trying my patience and testing me. She raised her voice, repeating her questions the second time, hissing: "Who the hell are you people? Where are you taking me?"

Still no answer was forthcoming. This time, the iron grip on her arms tightened more and the man on her right gave her a look that was both a warning and a threat.

"Ouch," she cried out involuntarily. "Why do you have to be so nasty?"

Her body twisted, in her effort to throw her weight towards the hard man next to her. The man on the other side pulled her back hard, making her face turn towards him. Before she could see what was coming, vicious smacks rained on her, making her eyes see stars and her ears ring. She felt a sharp, burning pain on her cheeks, which quickly spread across her whole face, and she tasted blood.

"Fuck off, you bastard," she spit at her assailant, before he punched her. A cracking sound followed. *Did these fuckers just break my nose? Or was it just my glasses?*

"Stop hurting me, you crazy..." She screamed, as shooting pains began to overwhelm her senses. Her vision blurred, making her unable to continue cursing.

Calm down, she applied her willpower. *Concentrate and think.* She stopped struggling and closed her eyes. *I am really in deep shit. These people are not taking me for a picnic, that's for damn sure. They want something from me, but what?*

For what seemed a long time, Pearl sat rigidly, wedged tightly between her captors and waiting for the pain to subside. The car shook and bumped along an uneven, dirty country lane; each jerk and movement reminded her that she was in the custody of unknown men, who would continue to inflict vicious injuries on her person if she didn't comply. *Why?*

The car screeched to stop.

The thug on her right side got out first, and pulled her as the other thug pushed her out from the back seat. They kept their grip on her arms as they wrestled her through a courtyard. By then, her face was so swollen that one of her eyes was forced shut while the other eye was hardly good enough to see what was in front of her. She did not recall exactly when she and her glasses had parted company: perhaps when she was punched.

Despite the cool reasoning in her head, which instructed her to cooperate with her kidnappers, the fire in the pit of her stomach was unwilling to comply. She tried resisting as she was pushed and shoved by the two men. One of them spoke at last, only to shout at her in a voice that was both cruel and chilling to the bone: "Move your motherfucking ass and don't you dare utter another word, you fucking, English dick-sucking whore. We'll kill you if you even think about escaping. You hear me, bitch?"

Once they were inside what seemed to be a deserted house, with one final, powerful push, she flew across the room and landed hard on the floor, her head hitting the concrete wall with a thud.

She passed out instantly. She did not hear the door banging shut and being locked behind her.

Chapter 64: The Rescue

THE TASTE OF blood lingered in her mouth, metallic and unsavoury. One eye still refused to open, and her head was throbbing. *What the hell are they doing to me?*

She was alone and strapped with gaffer tape to a plastic chair, but she could hear voices from down a corridor and behind the reinforced door. There was nothing else in the room, so she looked down at her feet. A small pool of blood had formed there and was turning brown. There was blood on her knees too. She quickly realised that this had come from her head. Slowly, she began to remember the beating, and the repeated questions about "the numbers" and "the names". She must have passed out, and had little memory of the pain.

Probably due to her tough upbringing and strong genes from her parents, her threshold of pain tolerance was fairly high. Her will to fight, and survive whatever ordeal she had to go through, helped her to hold on. *Clench your fists, grit your teeth and face the enemy with dignity*, she kept repeating to herself.

Footsteps down the hall focussed her mind and one good eye on the door handle. The door lock clicked and the handle went down. Pearl realised that more pain was coming, fast and furious.

Her torturer materialised in the form of a semi-naked man with only short pants on. His upper body was tanned, hairless, and full of tattoos around his biceps. He had awful breath when he bent down to shout in her face. "Bitch, if you don't give us the fucking numbers we are going to take your life instead."

Her head still fuzzy and throbbing with pain, she managed to mumble through her swollen lips, "What numbers? I have no bloody idea what you are talking about."

Her outbursts were followed quickly by another massive blow to her already swollen, bloody head.

As her battered head hung down, and a mixture of blood and saliva spilled from her mouth onto her torn blouse and vest, she heard the door lock click again.

His patent leather shoes were polished enough to see her face in, had she been that close. *Who is this – someone new? Maybe he would let me go? It's obvious to any fool that I know nothing of any value. Who are these people?*

A new voice said: "Get the battery and cables, she's a tough little bitch."

Footsteps went down the hall and came back after a few minutes, struggling under the weight of a truck battery. The battery was placed at her feet and cables with crocodile clips attached to the terminals. In her mind's eye, Pearl recalled a scene from a spy film where this treatment had been used.

It's time to try to save myself from more torture. What can I do? They want numbers, so I'd better give them numbers.

"The numbers you want are 34-26-34. Will you let me go now?" she pleaded through her snot and tears. Hard against hard had not worked. She needed to change her tactics.

"No, you stupid bitch, it's a PIN number we need. Four digits not six. We know you are lying. Now it's time for a little shock."

One man ripped her blouse and bra right off and the other clamped a metal crocodile clip on each exposed nipple. Pearl screamed out. "How about 5-6-7-1?" she guessed in desperation.

"Wrong again!" said the man in the shiny shoes.

The pain was heart-stopping in intensity. Pearl passed out immediately.

******

Andrew had been on the go nonstop ever since he got back to the UK two days before.

Pearl would get the surprise of her life if I showed up at her door without prior notice. How would she react to my sudden appearance? Would she take me back? Can I persuade her to leave everything behind and start afresh across the Pond? All kinds of questions traveled through his mind, but none would deter him from the sole aim of his trip: to get her back, no matter what.

Where the hell is she? All his attempts to contact her – texts, phone calls, e-mails, and Facebook messages – all went unanswered: unlike her at all.

After he had 'stormed off' all the way to America, they had been both hurt and disappointed. For the first six weeks, they had let their emotions take over their rational thinking; their pride stopped one from speaking to the other.

It had been hard, perhaps more so for his wife, until one night when she was overcome with sadness and loneliness. It was Pearl who took the initiative and sent an e-mail. She asked how he was and what Colorado was like. Writing had always been her preferred means of communication. No angry, accusing tones; each word chosen to express certain feelings and no room allowed for misunderstanding.

Slowly, and over time, they reestablished e-mail contact. Interestingly that had been the channel of communication in the early days of their courtship, when she was in Leeds while he lived in Sheffield, she pursuing her studies while he working in a university where they met. Now, a dozen years later, their only connection was through the e-mail again.

The most recent e-mail Andrew received was two weeks earlier, when Pearl mentioned how little work she was getting because of the general economic downturn, agency exploitation, and fierce competition from fellow interpreters on the scene.

"She's been called away on a last-minute police job," had been Andrew's first thought.

He booked himself into the Ibis hotel in China Town, due to its prime location, two minutes' walk to Pearl's new apartment. He opened his suitcase and fished out his old UK phone, which he had kept during all his time in the USA; although he only used it sporadically to call his family. He knew that was the number that Pearl knew by heart, and if she ever felt like it, she could reach him.

The moment he had plugged the phone in the socket and the charging started, he heard a loud beep. A message was shining on his phone screen.

In Danger. SOS! P

The number was unknown but looked to be a Chinese mobile number starting with the international code 0086.

What the hell does that mean? Pearl in China? Why is she there? She can't possibly be visiting her folks in Sichuan.

He had been to China with Pearl not long before he left for America. Pearl had been so stressed out by the whole family business that she had sworn that she would not go back unless she was forced to, or drugged.

Has her mother died all of a sudden? But why use words like In Danger and SOS if she is only with her family?

Too many questions hit Andrew all at once, with only one conclusion: Pearl was not in the UK. Both her home number and mobile were unanswered, except her usual, cheery greetings on her voice mail. It at least answered the question as to why her Facebook instant messages went unanswered – China blocked many social-media forums like Facebook.

Action man that he had always been, Andrew started making calls and searching on the web for any information he thought might help him in finding out what Pearl was up to. From her brother Bing in China, Andrew established the precise location: his wife, in the past week, had been in Fuzhou.

"I only spoke with her a few days ago when she asked for help with an address," Bing informed his English brother-in-law, sounding surprised that Andrew was calling him and not his wife.

Andrew had no time to go into any details. His contact with Pearl's family had been kept minimal and always had Pearl as an intermediary. Using simple English and clearly spoken, he instructed Bing to get in touch with his contacts in Fuzhou.

"Please e-mail me whatever information you have on your contacts in Fuzhou."

Andrew got off the phone and closed his eyes for a briefest moment: *Thank God Bing speaks and writes English.*

The fact that Pearl was in China with the police had also been confirmed by her brother. Andrew needed to find out which police force.

After the Midlands Police denied any knowledge of her visit to China, Andrew tried the Metropolitan Police in London. He recalled that in one of her earlier messages Pearl had mentioned working with officers on the fire disaster in Herefordshire, which had been all over the news for weeks.

Perhaps, like Morecambe Bay, they needed to go to Fujian to identify bodies and take statements. Andrew's fine intuition and logical thinking never failed to point him in the right direction.

Eventually, he was put in touch with DI Jack Gordon in China, after being passed around, tossed from one contact to another, and finally to the man who mattered.

Jack Gordon also confirmed Andrew's worst fear: his wife had been missing in China for two days, and they had absolutely no idea where she was or what had happened to her.

The two men in Pearl's life exchanged all the information they had gathered until then, and each had an action plan. Jack noted down Pearl's text message to Andrew, and the phone number from which it was sent. He immediately got in touch with his old contacts in the British Intelligence, both in the UK and then in China. At the same time, he would put extra pressure on the local police. He had been extremely unsatisfied and annoyed about their dragging their feet, although he did not let on over the phone with Pearl's husband. Andrew could tell, nonetheless.

As soon as he ended his conversation with the Detective Inspector, he packed his small, cabin suitcase with a few essential items and grabbed his passport and money. No time for waiting for luggage, and maximum efficiency was required from then on. Minutes later, rushing out of his hotel, he broke into a run towards the New Street station just around the corner. He jumped onto the next train to Heathrow, then hopped on the first flight to Hong Kong and then Fuzhou.

En Route at Hong Kong's Chek Lap Kok Airport, Andrew Church tapped in a text to Jack Gordon.

Boarding in HK. C U in 2 HRS.

His plane touched down at Fuzhou Changle International airport at 1830. With only his cabin luggage, he was out at the taxi ranks minutes later. With his perfectly pitched Mandarin, the driver shouted, "Okay," and set off towards the bustling Fuzhou centre in the rush hour.

Here he was; exactly 24 hours after he had landed in the UK, he had subjected himself to another long-haul horror, which he abhorred yet found absolutely necessary.

In the southern city of Fuzhou, he had only one mission in mind: find Pearl!

******

A splash of cold water jolted Pearl back to consciousness, soaking her already-wet clothes and making her shiver, despite the heat both outside and inside her battered body.

Making an effort to open her swollen eyes, she sagged from the excruciating pain on every inch of her bruised and beaten body – her nipples, her stomach, her arms, legs, her head. She could not tell which part of her hurt more.

She heard the voices of her torturers. One man was laughing, obviously enjoying the sight of a battered woman, or whatever entertained his petty, screwed-up dick-head.

Pleasure is such a strange concept. Her mind was still working; her highly developed intellect never deserted her, despite her state. *Some people find others' misfortune a source of satisfaction and delight.* Even in her utter isolation and desolation, she was able to see the motivation of the enemies who were terrorizing her body and soul.

"Are you ready to talk now? English whore? Why the fuck did you have the name and address of Ah Tai? Where did you get it? SPEAK!" The interrogator raised the bamboo stick in his hand and smashed it down on her nearly naked body, already badly bruised. Her clothes had been torn to pieces, her flesh was bloody. He obviously wanted to mess her up some more, inflict more damage.

Who is Ah Tai? She directed all her remaining energy to the name and frantically sought through her mental files. It hit her this time, just as the thrashing came raining down on her. *Ah Tai's name and address?* She remembered it then.

In her still-foggy mind, a scene played: of Ah Fang's father pressing a piece of paper in her hand, like a black and white film she had watched a long time ago. She could not recall what Ah Fang's old man looked like or why he had handed her something like that. Nor could she remember exactly what she had done with it.

One thing was crystal-clear: these men, whoever they were, must have found it in her possession. What's more, they wanted to know how she got it and what she was going to do with it. Ah Tai, a totally alien name to her, must be someone important, a crucial, missing link to why she was in this goddamn place and being subjected to such cruel treatment.

"Stop hitting me, you sick bastards," she shouted at the top of her voice – or what was left of it – the words coming out hoarse and croaky, unlike her own.

"If you want to know something from me, you need to be nice to me. Didn't your mother teach you that, you stupid fuck?"

She continued to curse and spit blood until the man stopped hitting her.

I can't be weak. I have to fight them, until I draw my last breath. She repeated that in her head, making it stick.

"Tell me now, bitch, before I beat you to death. Where did you get the name and address? Where is the PIN code? We know that you know it." The man with the stick yelled louder and became more hysterical with each shout. Perhaps he was under pressure to get results.

"I don't know what the fuck you are talking about, you evil bastard," she shouted back with equal ferocity. "Are you an imbecile or plain crazy? How many times do I have to tell you? I don't know any fucking PIN number. But you don't believe me." She spat; this time only blood came out of her mouth, mixed with hot tears streaming down her cheeks.

The man stepped back, raising his weapon; the bamboo stick had already turned red with her blood. She felt her body tense up before the thrashings landed on her bare, tattered skin. Dried blood mixed with the fresh, gushing flow of new injuries.

"Stop hurting me, you sick fuck." She struggled to free herself from bondage, unsuccessfully; the chair rocked slightly as she continued her verbal counterattack. "You'll be haunted for the rest of your life. I'll come back and haunt you after death."

Then she stopped shouting, adopting a calmer voice and steady tone. She had reconciled to the belief that these people would not stop torturing her until they got what they wanted from her. She needed to give them something, anything.

"I can tell you where I got the name and address, if you stop hitting me." She was in no shape to make demands, she knew that, but it did not stop her trying.

"Just spit it out, bitch!" The man raised his bamboo stick high up, but this time it did not fall.

"Someone gave it to me," she muttered, defiance still in her voice.

"Who gave it to you?"

"I don't know the man. I do not know his name."

How can I get out of this trap without giving up Ah Fang's father? They would be merciless towards the Lin family, just as they have been towards me now.

She was frantic with her thoughts. By now she was sure that Ah Fang was murdered by these people.

They would kill me too, as soon as they have tricked me into giving them the information they wanted. But why the hell have they been asking me for the PIN code? For the love of Jesus Christ, I have no fucking clue.

She asked herself again, *Why? Obviously they were not asking for my own PIN code to my bank accounts. My savings would hardly be the money these gangsters were after. Who else? Madam Lin?*

Like a thunder in the dark night, it was Madam Lin who came into her mind when she felt the cruel thrashing landing on her already smashed body.

Damn!

Then she heard someone calling her.

"Pearl, Pearl. Where are you?"

No mistake. It was Andrew's distinctive, booming voice. *He has received my Mayday call for help and he has come to rescue me: my knight in shining armour.*

Before she could answer, the man hitting her had thrown away his bamboo stick and put his coarse, large hands over her mouth. Another man ran towards them, shouting: "Kill her, kill her now."

She felt the man's hands leaving her mouth, moving to her neck, trying to choke the life out of her.

"Andrew...," she called out, with slowing and laboured breath.

Struggling to free herself, she twisted her body and shook her head vigorously, trying to bite the hands just below her chin.

Her hands had been bound, and she had little strength left. Yet her will to live was strong and unyielding, more so now she knew that rescue was so near.

Using all the energy she had, she threw her weight towards the man in front of her. Their bodies tangled and they both fell, but her assailant fell harder upon his back, breaking Pearl's fall. The chair she was tied to fell on top of her, knocking her out.

Shortly before she lost consciousness, she heard shouting in both Chinese and English, footsteps running, cracking and banging noises, bodies wrestling, and gunshots.

Seconds later, perhaps longer than seconds, Pearl vaguely felt someone taking hold of her: a familiar embrace, both firm and gentle. Her body was lifted.

A lightness of being enveloped her, so soothing that all pain abandoned her, carrying her upwards to the blue sky.

Epilogue

FOUR WEEKS LATER.

"Jack and I," Pearl began, searching for Andrew's eyes, the colour of the blue sky outside the plane window, through her tear-blurred vision. Her emotions were tearing her up.

"Sssh..." His fingers reached out, brushing her lips gently, his other hand handing her a tissue.

"You don't have to tell me anything, love." His voice even gentler, understanding, consoling and firm.

"Jack was a brave man, an outstanding officer, and remember: he died for *us*."

Andrew emphasized *us*; his emotions, which he had successfully kept under control, were spilling over. He stopped himself in time, before his own guilt overwhelmed him.

It was true. It was Jack Gordon, the courageous Scot, who had survived the Troubles of Northern Ireland and the wars against terror in Afghanistan and Iraq, who gave his life to save Pearl from her torture and imminent death, allowing her and Andrew to escape.

The drama in Fuzhou returned to Andrew, flashing by, one scene after another, like a slide show on his iPad.

First scene: Andrew sat in a taxi on his way to the Shangri-La; Jack received a tip about Pearl's location, although her fate was unclear. British Intelligence worked with the Chinese Secret Police in Beijing and pinpointed the exact coordinates of Pearl's cell phone. It was in a deserted, old farmhouse within the borders of Fuqing, which the gangs had used as one of their many holding places, used as a place to torture and to kill. It was known to the local police, but their hands were tied, as those in the know had long been bought and their souls sold to the devil.

Second Scene: Jack's tall frame in front of the hotel. He jumped in the moment Andrew's taxi pulled up outside the entrance.

Third Scene: They redirected the taxi, offering the driver double pay if he could get them there as soon as possible. En route, Jack had instructed Andrew: "Follow my orders, and do what I say. Our strategy? To take the gang by surprise, locate Pearl and extract her within the shortest possible time frame." Andrew nodded solemnly.

Fourth Scene: On reaching the farmhouse, it was dark, an advantage for a former SAS member who had special training to work in darkness. "The gangs will not expect that the British would come to Pearl's rescue, a mere interpreter," Andrew had reasoned.

Fifth Scene: Quickly and silently, Jack entered the farmhouse first, Andrew two steps behind. Both of them were armed with Swiss army knives, the only weapon they had. Andrew could hear his own heartbeat.

Sixth Scene: One of the guards sitting behind the door was nodding off, probably drunk. Jack knocked him out with one massive punch, without the guard uttering a sound; just a thud from his falling on the ground.

Seventh Scene: The other guard spotted them and started shouting in Chinese, while reaching for his gun.

Eighth Scene: Jack stabbed him in the voice box before he could raise his hand to shoot. Efficient and super-fast, Jack twisted the man's arm and turned the gun toward the guard. Bang!

Ninth Scene: "Take Pearl and run, Andrew. I'll cover you." Jack's last words, an order full of authority and no fear.

Final Scene: Andrew picked up her limp, bloody body and, carrying his wife, made the run of his life towards the entrance, where their taxi had been waiting. Behind him, he heard more rounds of gunshots, and he never saw Jack again.

There is no need for Pearl to know that now, Andrew decided, his expression resolute.

In time, we'll have to talk about what had happened. The Chinese will probably send a report to the British explaining the death of a British officer in China, but I know the Chinese officials better. They would no doubt blame the British for their "Imperialist" interference in China's 'internal affairs', rather than admitting any fault of their own. Had the local Fujian Police not been so corrupt, Jack Gordon would still be alive.

But that was China, and there was nothing Andrew, or anyone, could do about it.

What he could do, Andrew mused, was to take his wife away from the dangers that she had involuntarily exposed herself to. It was supposed to be freelance work, and she was simply a police interpreter. Neither of them knew just how much peril that proved to be or how close to death she would come.

By her hospital bed in Birmingham, Andrew said to his wife: "You're coming with me to Colorado."

He had already started making all necessary arrangements for them to leave as soon as the doctors gave her permission to travel.

She nodded: no resistance at all, just a tired and resigned smile. Andrew was now back in her life. Nothing else mattered.

How should someone feel after a near brush with death?

Different people may have different reactions, and many may start reevaluating their lives. During her hospitalization, she had plenty of time to reflect on what she had been put through. Her recent trials had only reaffirmed her faith in living her life to the fullest, and loving the man she was destined to love for the rest of her life. That had been true from the day they had met nearly 13 years ago.

It was also in her hospital bed when she was informed of Jack Gordon's sacrifice.

The man who had soothed her loneliness, and adored her, had paid the ultimate price for the woman he had fallen in love with. He had laid down his life to save hers, and that of her husband. There was no greater love on earth than his selfless and heroic act.

On arriving at the hotel in Fuzhou, Andrew had collected Pearl's passport from the hotel safe, a die-hard habit which he had insisted on during all their travels together, and one eventually adopted by Pearl. He had refused the local police's offer of hospital treatment for his wife. He wanted to get Pearl away from the Chinese soil as quickly as he could. His mind would not rest until they were back to the UK, as far away from danger and death as humanly possible.

Back home, Pearl's injuries had been too great. She needed a number of surgeries and time to recover. Doctors had insisted on her complete bed rest, and refused her request to attend Jack's funeral.

Andrew went on her behalf, and talked to Jack's widow and her two children. Moira had no idea that her husband had cheated on her with his interpreter. As it turned out, she would never know, now that her husband had taken that secret to his grave. The widow would mourn him as a hero who had died in the line of duty; so would his children, and those who had known him and loved him. His memory would live on.

When she was eventually released from hospital, and all arrangements had been made for their US emigration, Andrew promised her doctor that Pearl would continue her medication as well as receive counseling in America – they were, after all, going to the home of therapy.

As weak as she was, she helped Andrew to pack. They had already donated the majority of their belongings to the nearest Oxfam charity shop, and some to her friends and Andrew's family. Knowing her, Andrew had given her 'permission' to keep items of sentimental value. "Best not to exceed the limited luggage allowances with the airline," had always been his practice.

The day before their cross-Atlantic flight, Pearl scanned around her more or less empty apartment. A little distracted, she picked up the paper swan and vase set Madam Lin had presented to her during one of her prison visits, as if from another lifetime. She knew that Madam was to appear in Crown Court that day for sentencing. The court had called for her services a couple of days before, and she had turned them down.

Funny how things change in a short space of time. Before her China trip, she would never have refused a court booking, let alone the sentencing of one of her regular clients.

She tried calling to mind what Madam looked like, but that memory had already faded: vague, distant, and impossible to recall.

The colours of the origami objects had also faded, the swan and vase gathering dust during her absence; absentmindedly, she brushed the dust away by blowing air into it with her mouth. First the swan's head fell off, then the body opened up.

Inside the pink and green swan there were numbers – in Chinese characters, not Arabic – a four-digit number looking suspiciously like a PIN.

The mystery became as clear as a bright, summer day – *these are the numbers the gangsters were trying to beat out of me. What is it?*

Madam Lin's fortune stashed away from the gangs? How did they know that I had them? More crucially: why was I given the numbers?

For the life of her, Pearl could not work out why. *Why me? A mere interpreter?*

Questions hovered above and inside her already-tired head, still slowly recovering from her recent ordeal.

What did Madam Lin say to me when she gave me the gifts? Was it something like: be careful, they are delicate? What did that mean?

The huge question marks remain, persistently troubling my peace of mind, yet no answers come. What happened to Madam during the trial? How many years would she receive?

In her distant memory, she recalled that, on being pressed during their last consultation, Mr Jones had anticipated that Madam Lin would probably receive six to eight years' prison sentence. "On serving half of your time in jail, you would be released to serve the rest of your sentence in the community. Because of your naturalization and British citizenship, it would not be possible for them to deport you back to China, although I'm sure that's what the Brits would want to do," Mr Jones had said with a wink, trying to make a joke of a serious matter, not atypical of British humour.

Would she be reformed in prison, or would she continue her criminal career on parole? Pearl could not help wondering about Madam's future. *Only time can tell. It's not a question I can answer nor concern myself with. I have enough questions of my own to contend with.*

Her mind drifted back to that question again: Why?

Andrew had questions of his own. Many of them could wait, except one.

"How did you manage to send me that text?" he asked his wife at last, as he held her hand and squeezed it gently.

"One of the guards came to give me water, in between their torturing sessions," replied Pearl, as the horrendous memory of what she had to go through came rushing back.

"He was probably drunk. Anyway, his mobile fell out on the floor and he didn't notice it at the time. My hands were not tied up at the time. As soon as he had left the room, I keyed in your number, the only number that had been etched on my memory."

She smiled, training her thoughts on the positive. Her words melted his heart. One of his arms reached for her shoulder, pulling her slightly towards him, giving her a gentle kiss on her soft, silky hair. He did not want to interrupt her.

"I did not know, of course, when and if you would see it, and how you would react on seeing it," she continued, her eyes momentarily moving away from her husband, turning again to the blue sky above the clouds just outside the small window on her left.

"Someone up there," she murmured, dreamingly, "was looking out for me that day. Perhaps, my time has not come yet." She looked at Andrew, her eyes full of love.

Then her lids closed and she rested her head on his shoulder, a broad, strong, climber's shoulder. *My rock.*

Pearl Zhang lives to tell the tales: not just her own, but those of many who have left their homeland, full of dreams and grand ambitions, to seek a better life across the oceans. Ah Fang, Ah Ming, and hundreds and thousands of others; have they found the life that they sought so desperately, and have they changed their fate?

The answer, as always, is not hers to find.

Each human being follows his or her own path, but hope is eternal.

It is hope that has been living inside Pearl all these years. Sometimes she feels its weight, a responsibility. Granted or not, she is carrying the hope of many – all those living or dead – on her two shoulders.

The flight attendants come with their next round of food and drinks. Pearl looks out of the aircraft window, as the Land of Hope slowly disappears from her view.

Below is the cold, grey Atlantic, and at the other end, the American Dream is waiting.

The End

If you have enjoyed this book, please leave your comments where you purchased this book. All reviews and feedbacks are much appreciated.

Thank you for following Pearl Zhang and her dramatic journey from the East to the West. You will learn more about her life from The Same Moon and Trials of Life, the first and second of her "Journey to the West" trilogy. Please visit the author's blog for more updates about her books and current projects at http://www.junyingkirk.com.

Printed in Great Britain
by Amazon